The Returned

Amanda Cassidy is a freelance journalist, commissioning editor and former Sky News reporter. Shortlisted for the Irish Journalist of the Year Awards, and more recently the Headline Media writing awards, her features have been read by over seven million people and she has several thousand followers on Twitter (@amandacassidy). She's a frequent contributor to national radio, print and television and holds a BA in French and Italian from Trinity College Dublin. When she's not on a plane, you'll find her in her cottage in Dublin where she lives with her husband and three young children.

Also by Amanda Cassidy

Breaking
The Returned

THE RETURNED

AMANDA CASSIDY

CANELOCRIME

First published in the United Kingdom in 2023 by

Canelo
Unit 9, 5th Floor
Cargo Works, 1–2 Hatfields
London SE1 9PG
United Kingdom

A CIP catalogue record for this book is available from the British Library.

Ebook ISBN 978 1 80436 009 5
Hardback ISBN 978 1 80436 520 5
Export Trade Paperback ISBN 978 1 80436 521 2

This book is a work of fiction. Names, characters, businesses, organizations, places and events are either the product of the author's imagination or are used fictitiously. Any resemblance to actual persons, living or dead, events or locales is entirely coincidental.

Cover design by Blacksheep

Cover images © Depositphotos, Shutterstock

Look for more great books at www.canelo.co

Printed and bound in Great Britain by Clays Ltd, Elcograf S.p.A.

1

For Bobby, one of my most beautiful chapters

One

The week before Christmas

Every Sunday evening, May pours herself a drink. Nothing fancy, mind. A dash of gin, a jiggle of ice. Always just the one. Anything more makes her groggy, especially at her age. But it's almost Christmas. She's helping with the young lads and Nancy's been pouring wine. May babysits when she can, to make things a little easier on poor Nancy when it's busy at work. It's the neighbourly thing to do – even though their houses are almost five miles apart. Say what you like, and the villagers did gossip, but Nancy Wills wasn't a bad sort.

Considering.

May watches the young mother stoop down by the fireplace and throw a jagged log deep into the hottest part of the fire. The weight of it sparks hundreds of tiny embers which scatter like fireflies, dancing bright against dark soot. Hugh had been here too, until an hour ago when he'd left for his work night out, waving to five-year-old Joey on the trampoline outside. While May had changed the baby's nappy upstairs, she'd overheard both Nancy and Hugh arguing. It ended, as the couple's fights usually do, with the angry slam of a door. After a grim-faced Nancy leaves the house, May takes another sip of red and enjoys the release. But the peace is short-lived. Vee, Nancy's sister, drops in with gifts for the kids. A peace offering, she says, whatever that means.

When the house has finally settled, May smooths her patterned skirt and hooshes her behind a little deeper into the cushions on the armchair closest to the fire. She refills her glass from the wine bottle next to her on the sideboard and watches the hypnotic shards glow spectacularly against the hearth.

She dozes off.

Jolting awake, she's suddenly aware of a smoke alarm beeping urgently. Nancy is standing in front of her, screaming. The room is engulfed in thick, black smoke. It's far too hot.

That's when May thinks of the little ones upstairs.

Both women stare at each other in horror, paralysed by the realisation. Then Nancy pushes past her and, tucking her face into the bend of her elbow, begins to make her way upstairs. May watches the young mother disappear into the haze like a ghost into a cloud, one arm extended ahead of her. Reaching out.

Nancy feels her way upstairs, disorientated and desperate. She knows this house by heart – every landing creak, every scuff of carpet. At the top, gripping the wooden banister, she makes a sickening, split-second choice. Eyes streaming, she bursts into Joey's bedroom, calling her five-year-old son's name, praying he isn't too scared to move. He does that sometimes – hides if he's frightened. She's tried giving him coping mechanisms for his anxiety. Hugh thinks she's reading too much into it, but all she knows is that Joey's behaviour isn't like her friends' children and that worries her sometimes.

'Joey,' she screams, thick smoke catching in the back of her throat. She tries to force her streaming eyes to make out the familiar sprout of his curls.

'Joey,' Nancy croaks again. She makes it to his bed and roots around the soft fold of the sheets with her palms.

Empty.

She tries to scream his name again, but her roar is punctuated with violent coughing. Dread frays the corners of her mind. Her breath is sticky and her lungs painfully tight. The next bedroom, her and Hugh's, faces onto the back garden. Nancy's legs give way and, blinded by black plumes, she crawls the last few metres towards the door, pushing desperately against it, clawing her way towards the baby – towards her younger son. The blast of heat is cruel against her skin. She cries out as the smoke clings to her, seeping into every pore.

What she sees in that moment will haunt her for the rest of her life.

Flames arch high around the window of the bedroom, licking at the walls and ceiling viciously, leaving black claw marks. Her drapes sway

grotesquely with the force of the fire. She'll never forget that sound
– the whoosh and crackle that pulled everything towards it. When she
re-lives this night, over and over, Nancy will wonder if she'd just gone
upstairs a few minutes earlier, what might have been. Or if she hadn't
forgotten her phone and returned to the house. She'll go over every
smoke-filled second wondering if she could have saved him, had she
made a different choice. Acrid smoke chokes as she drags herself around
the side of the double bed.

Everything is black or blackening.

Reaching what she thinks is the chest of drawers, she hauls herself
upright, and with the last of her energy hooks both arms heavily into
the tiny cot that sits next to the bed. The flames have reached the
other side now. Her bedclothes flare brilliantly, momentarily lighting
up the swirls of fog. She wants to lie down, to float away into this great
mesmerising heat. Her hand loses its grip on the edge of the cot. But
it's the feel of those tiny spindles that spur her on – the memory of
the last few weeks spent poking her hand in through that narrow gap
between them, to stroke his warm, velvety palm.

With one final push, she leans low into the cot, searches the bedding
with both hands, carefully. Then frantically.

How could she even consider life without him?

There's nothing. She feels nothing at all. Just the cruel curl of empty
blanket, the crisp sheets she tucked in so neatly just hours ago.

Her lungs are screaming. The flames are at her feet. She understands
that this is all her fault. She thinks of Joey and how she finds him in her
room sometimes, watching his baby brother sleeping. She tries to call
both her sons' names again and again but there is no more left of her
voice.

Nancy traces the small rectangle of the cot again with both hands.
She fills in the spaces where the baby should have been with flattened
palms, tapping and fanning. She uses the bony part of her shoulder
to stem her streaming eyes. Head bent low, she can just about see the
outline of it.

There's no doubt in her mind. The cot is empty. The baby is gone.

Then the baby blanket goes up in flames and her sleeves are on fire.
She opens her mouth to scream but her body is ablaze. She stumbles

backward, intense pain ripping through her. Everything is lost. The light fades, turns inside out. Then suddenly there's nothing left at all.

–

The Christmas air stings Nancy's cheeks as the fireman holds her back from her burning house, both his hands wrapped around her waist as she tries to run back inside. Eight-foot flames lick maliciously from its roof. They'd only just got to her in time. Emergency sounds rise and fall around her.

'It's okay,' he's saying gently. 'It's okay. It's going to be okay.' But she cannot imagine anything worse than this moment. The trauma unfolding beneath that dancing orange finale – and she, watching it happen, a helpless spectator. Nancy strains against his grip, a guttural sound ringing in her ears between coughs. She claws at his arms. Then she feels the pain – the scorching sting of the skin, the fire in her fingers. Blue lights melt into vivid reds, twisted shadows distort. Someone says her name. Hugh stands helplessly as the angry amber flashes against night sky. They should have been out looking for Santa among the stars.

'The baby's gone,' Nancy cries over and over. 'I can't find Liam or Joey,' she repeats frantically. 'They're gone.' Someone is screaming too close to her. Her eyes roll with the violence of the pain, and she folds back into it. Only then the wailing stops.

At the hospital Nancy is sedated. Wrapped tight. There are confusing beeps and agonising bandage changes. Nancy wonders why nobody can answer her questions until she realises that she isn't awake at all. Strangers' faces float above her, whispering, hurting her kindly. She senses a window to her left where daylight stings. The smell of one of the nurses becomes familiar; oaky – like leather and a tree she can't remember the name of. She tries to respond to the gentle sentences that go up at the end, but her body is dragging her back down into the silent pit where she knows she's safe from reality, from the truth of why this is happening to her.

Eventually Nancy becomes aware of her sister's presence. Vee, born Vera, is older but smaller than Nancy, with soft brown eyes and graceful movements. Right now, she's pressing her fingers to her temples, breathing wet, fretful sighs. Nancy's movement jars her, and she lifts her head. Vee's fingers are long and thin, spiderlike.

'Oh God, Nance,' she sobs, and she reaches out, rests her hand protectively on her sister's shoulder. Nancy hasn't seen her in weeks. Not since that final argument. But now the world is too bright and Nancy flickers on the edge.

As she descends back down, one word catches her, forces her eyes open.

'And Joey has been asking...' her sister is saying. 'But I'm not sure you should...'

Nancy turns her head towards her, wincing at the stiff material compressing her face. She tries to speak, closes her eyes with the effort of it for a moment and then tries again.

'Joey?' she manages to croak. Nancy's hands are bandaged too – but she lifts her arm, tries to reach out, as if for him.

'Joey is with Hugh,' Vee says, her eyes brimming with tears. 'He's safe with his dad.' She takes her sister's arm and rests it back down on the bed gently. 'He's okay, Nance, he's not hurt.'

Nancy cries silently.

'The baby?' she mouths, her words slightly garbled. 'Baby Liam?' But Vee seems to understand. She squeezes her lips together.

'We won't talk about that now,' she says delicately. 'We need to get you better. Rest now, Nancy girl.'

Though too weak to allow herself to explore the meaning wedged between her sister's whispered words, Nancy knows that Vee's presence here means something terrible has happened. Because Vee had vowed never to see or speak to her again.

'I'm so sorry.'

One sister looks at the other, who shakes her head and closes her eyes.

Despite her agony, Nancy knows that the bitterness remains between them, jagged and cold. Things between them would never be the same after what they had decided to do.

She wants to ask if Gerald has come to see her. But even in the haze of pain and grief, she knows she absolutely can't.

Two

Detective Sergeant Ally Fields

Six years later

I pretend to be asleep as Frank gets ready for work. I slow my breathing, mouth slightly open just for effect. The bedroom door creaks, and the light from the hallway bathes everything lemon yellow for a moment, before darkness swings back. I hear the flush of a toilet, taps cranking on, and a few minutes later, the shuffle of shoes. The front door of the apartment closes, echoing slightly, then the entire place is dawn silent.

I flop onto my back, starfish across the double bed.

The familiar heaviness creeps around me, pressing against my skin, pushing me back down.

What the hell am I doing?

Even for me, this whole thing with Frank is pretty messed up. Squinting at the time on my phone, I relish the unadulterated stillness of the pale six a.m. light to simply think. I've always found it easier to process life in the mornings – to sort and file all the flittery moments of the previous days or weeks. Brain admin, I call it.

Frank calls it lazy.

The baby pedals sharply against what feels like my kidney and I'm forced out from under the duvet to the chilly bathroom. I shower quickly, wincing at the sting of the hot water against stretched skin, and try to shake the gnawing anxiety that starts to grip. I know I've been putting off the decision for far too long.

The jacket buttons of my suit won't do up any more, but I shouldn't complain. I think of my little sister, Sammy, and how happy she seemed when I told her about this baby – delighted her big sister was finally going to experience the joys of motherhood. I smile when I imagine her finally being an auntie. But down at the station, I've spent the past few months trying to conceal my budding bump – mortified at the *obviousness* of my biology among a sea of dudes. As I waddle around the squad room, it is as if my giant belly is screaming, *Hey look lads, Ally Fields had sexual intercourse.*

In fairness, the crew at the precinct are as stereotypically male as you can imagine. Major Crime Unit is even more laddish. Not that anyone would dare say anything about Detective Sergeant Ally Fields, now I'm at this level. Well, not to my face, anyway.

Another jab. This time to the bladder. I gulp my prenatal vitamins with full-fat milk straight from the carton, scramble some eggs and eat them standing up. Then, predictably late, I rush-plait my hair in the lift. Frank scolds me for barely making time to eat from one day to the next, and yet since I've been pregnant, I've been meticulous about my diet, even stopped smoking. Maybe subconsciously I'm making up for the failures in circumstance that gave way to this baby's fledging life. Sometimes I have to remind myself to be grateful. Because pregnancy had never been on my radar – but despite everything, it is beginning to feel surprisingly right.

But there is no glow. Not yet anyway.

The mirror in the elevator is nobody's friend, but I look particularly washed out this morning as the lift lurches down into the basement car park of my apartment block. Pulling faces, I fluff my dark, straggly fringe a little, to distract from the bags under my eyes. A slather of burgundy lip gloss disappoints. Nobody warns you that being pregnant at forty-two drains the life from you. The glow people talk about is reserved for twenty-six-year-olds with perky tits and their mothers on speed-dial, devoted partners, and time to shop for Transformer-esque buggies. Not a single book describes bulging veins *down there*, or the fear of wiping every single time you use the bathroom. Or spotting – godawful word. Everyone keeps telling me how lucky I am that this finally happened. Especially at my age, they always add, like I'm some kind of medical miracle.

I am grateful, of course I am. The problem is that this isn't how I imagined it would be. It wasn't supposed to be this... complicated.

The car park is grey-quiet as I walk slowly towards my old black Discovery, my flats slip-slapping the concrete, the pressure of a migraine threatening behind my eyes. The space where Frank usually parks is empty and will remain empty for the next three days, giving me time to think about what I really want. If I can somehow define what exactly it is that we have between us, it might help me come to terms with this new chapter in my life. Besides, it's my turn to think.

He's the type to always get exactly what he wants. Admittedly, it's what drew me to him in the first place. He said he fell for my pale complexion and inky black hair. I got that from my Cork-born dad. My mother was once a cool ice blonde. But what few know is that personality-wise, I'm all County Kerry. In fact, I got my temper from my grandmother I'd been told – a Currolough girl through and through. My own mother's face flashes into my mind, and I blink her away. She haunts me in a way I find hard to explain.

Weaving through the empty roads, not yet rammed with morning traffic, I concentrate on controlling the nausea. But I'm still not sure if it's the baby or the decision I realise I'm probably going to have to make.

I think of Frank's face – the confidence, the swagger, the unobtainability of a guy like him. Six foot two, surprisingly blond, elegant – poised, as if ready to pounce. All part of the attraction, no doubt. Plus, his hands on my lower back were burning hot, even through the pink velvet ballgown the night we met. Later, after that first flash of lust, I realised it was perhaps the complications that saw me coming back to Frank time and time again. That familiarity of chaos, the whisper of mayhem that I always seem to run towards.

But is that a world where I want to raise my baby?

I dismiss the creeping dread. I can't think about that right now.

The migraine descends as it usually does – not pain, as such, but a texture against the back of my eyes like the relentless crashing of waves. I pull on my sunglasses despite the dullness of the early morning light. The radio news buzzes, but I deliberately don't tune in. My day will be peppered with other people's bad news. It is my job to sort it and break it to the wide-eyed, trying to correct the wrong by making the outcome as right as I possibly can.

But these mornings, they are just for me.

I switch to Sunshine FM. Dua Lipa serenades. Dublin city yawns awake too. The morning air is laced with the usual city scents: fast-food, smog, early morning tide. I take the coast road, overtaking the rattling bin trucks and admiring the dazzle of Howth in the distance, a sliver of land wrapped around Dublin Bay like a Christmas bow. Twin shadows of the red-and-white-striped Poolbeg stacks shimmer against the water's reflection. Early morning dog walkers silhouette against a silver horizon. I breathe it all in, every quiver and stir. Sammy thinks I love this part of Dublin because it reminds me of home. But the truth is that the loud vibrancy of this city is everything the house we grew up in wasn't.

The baby kicks hello as I arrive at my building – a six-storey buttermilk monstrosity, all concrete and too-small PVC windows. This is Precinct 12, the docks of Dublin city, where the Garda Major Crime Unit and drug squad live. Upgrade imminent, they'd promised, every year since 2011, but nobody was holding their breath. Major Crime took over the entire sixth floor. The penthouse, we joked, but smoke breaks on the fire escape overlooking Dublin city weren't half as bad as we made out. Better than traffic guys stuck in the basement breathing in fumes from the arterial road that ran past the River Liffey, through the heart of the city.

I root in my handbag for my key fob and the barrier to the adjacent car park creaks upwards slowly. There are only three other cars here, of which I recognise two.

Wincing from the tiny baby gymnastics low in my belly, I leave my usual offering by the sad humps of the doorway sleepers each side of the precinct steps and zap myself into the building.

In just three weeks, I'll be out of here.

Maternity leave is an alien concept to me. All that time staring at a tiny human. In truth, the idea of not having work as a distraction makes me uncomfortable. 'Having a baby is life-changing, Ally,' my sister reminds me at least once a day, but the reality is that I never expected it to be this confronting.

Predictably, Clarke Casey is in already. I see the skim of his dark brown hair behind his computer in the desk space next to mine.

'Morning, DS Fields.'

Clarke, my anxious-to-please newbie, jumps up to make me coffee as I walk past his extremely neat desk towards my own scattered mess. Not a bad cop, I've told the boss – but needs to toughen up if he's to handle bigger cases, lose the Daddy's-boy expression, quit smiling so damn much. Not that we'd be getting anything too big for a bit, unfortunately. HR had been in touch – 'a winding down period' they called it. They'd probably never know I'd tweaked my dates slightly to make sure I wasn't sitting at home with too much time to think before the baby came.

Boss doesn't know that either. But he's promised not to let me wither out here in the few weeks before I'm chained to a baby.

Half an hour later, the boss – Inspector Nolan – spots me and gestures me into his glass-fronted office at the other end of the open-plan room. I heave myself out of my seat, swigging my decaf Americano, and hoping for something good this week.

The migraine pulses painfully as I edge open the stiff glass door with my hip. Nolan glances up. He's sitting behind his desk, leaning his elbows on the table, sandy hair across cool blue eyes.

He motions to close the door.

'I've something for you, Fields,' he says, using one hand to brush back his too-long fringe, and I try to blame the knots in my stomach on the baby.

I nod, avoiding those eyes, and shut the door tightly behind me, manoeuvring my unfamiliar bulk. I can feel Garda Detective Clarke Casey watching from the other end of the open-plan office. Nobody misses a thing around here.

Nolan hands me the case file that's come in overnight, which I quickly scan. Apartment fire, suspected arson. But it's the location of the incident that makes me hesitate. I focus on not letting my hands shake in front of him as I read on, my mouth suddenly dry.

'Fields?' He leans back in his chair and trains his eyes on me. 'Tell me if you'd prefer something else – I can give it to Cummins.'

No way I'm letting Cummins have this one, even if I have to go back to Curro-bloody-lough, County Kerry.

'Fatalities?'

'One dead and a twelve-year-old kid in hospital.'

'Can't local cops deal with it?' I try to adjust my voice, not to sound shrill and defensive. We are only ever called in if there is something specific, something unusual that stands out. Otherwise, we risk looking like we are stepping on the toes of the local police. Nolan gets up and walks to the window, everything about him constantly in motion.

'There's talk that one of the local cops is involved.' He stares across the city, and I stare at his back, trying to keep my tone steady.

'They suspect a local Garda might have started the fire?'

'Localish. Currolough serves a much wider area now after the other station closures. It's a cop from one of the towns an hour away who used to work out of there.'

I think of County Kerry – its vast wild coastline, small, scattered villages between valleys, all those tiny police stations shuttered and streamlined to one central policing hub in the biggest town in the area.

'Several witnesses saw him at the scene, moments before the fire,' Nolan explains. 'Say he was acting suspiciously. It's a matter of ruling it in or out, finding our guy, keeping it on the down low if it is a cop.'

He turns and stares at me. The pain is building behind my eyes. Spirals of static dance at the corners of my vision.

'Mightn't it complicate things to have a Dublin cop head down to a country station?' My voice is smaller suddenly because honestly, I don't know if I can go back there. I'm picturing a little cottage reflected against a silver-grey lake, three bikes thrown haphazardly in the front driveway. I'm picturing BallinÓg – just ten minutes from Currolough, the place that haunts me.

'You're from around there, aren't you?'

But I don't trust myself to answer.

'Fields? I hope all this pregnancy stuff isn't getting to you.'

Nolan gives an almost involuntary flick of a hand, as if the tiny life inside me is something that could be swatted away.

I shake my head, the swish of my long plait against my back comforting.

'It's fine. I'll be fine.'

'I need you to keep this low-key, Fields,' he says, eyes narrow. 'I need this wrapped up quickly and quietly. You'll be briefed by Inspector Ken Mulligan down there. He's the one who called it in. Good guy, I've known him since forever. I've told him you're coming. Bring Casey.'

The coffee on the table in front of him hasn't been touched. A pale, milky crescent puckers on its surface. Files are piled in mismatched stacks across his desk. A crumpled bag, stained buttery dark, balances on top of one paper tower. For someone so sure of himself – so stern and well-presented – Nolan's messy office always surprises me.

'It's all there on the call sheet.'

I mumble something in the affirmative and turn. I'm addled, and I don't want to lose my cool here in front of him.

'DS Fields,' he says, sharply.

I freeze, my back to him. Inspector Frank Nolan drops his voice.

'You were asleep when I left, Ally. I didn't want to wake you.'

I turn slowly but cover my mouth with the coffee cup so he can't see my expression. I feel eyes from the open-plan desks on me. On us both.

A few minutes later, I make my way straight to the ladies' bathroom, lock the thin cubicle door and drop my head into my hands. In the distance, male voices echo in the corridor – loud and confident. There's the usual crackle of a police radio. A lift door cranks shut somewhere in the bowels of the building. I massage my ribs, just below the elasticated band of my maternity pants where it's most tender from what happened last summer.

You see, this baby, this pregnancy – it wasn't supposed to be with my boss.

And it certainly wasn't supposed to be with someone else's husband.

Three

Clarke Casey is already up, bouncing beside me when I eventually return to my desk, his face hopping with anticipation. That's the thing with newbies, they always seem so full of expectation, of unbridled optimism about the job at hand – even this overgrown one. They haven't yet learnt how it feels to be kicked in the shins by life in this job. They don't yet know the bleakness that always surrounds. Or maybe it's just Clarke's private school upbringing that grates. This guy was all pure joy and bubbles under his Hugo Boss shirt.

'Let's go.'

This is what Frank does to me; uses me for jobs like these that he's not bothered with but knows I'll see through. He'd never have sent my colleague Detective Sergeant Pete Cummins. Because Cummins wouldn't report back every tiny detail like I would. I know Frank's using me to be his eyes and ears. He knows I'll do anything to please him, to help get his lousy promotion, and that makes me angry and sad in equal measures. Why am I so tough in every part of my life except around him? When did I let him get such a hold over me?

It's laughable how little we know about each other. I'm growing his child, yet he doesn't even know about the biggest tragedy of my life – the one that shaped everything. Yes, I am from County Kerry, but my memories of Currolough and its surrounds leave me dazed, like a place from a dream, just noise and light. I guess that's trauma for you – colour without shape, featureless monsters that roam by night. Faces in the reflections of buildings that make you start as you walk past.

'We're heading out.' I've barely got the words out and Casey's at me again.

'What's going on, DS Fields?'

Ambition is one thing, but this guy Casey is obsessed with saving the world. Someone said he'd left his job as a solicitor after five years to retrain as a Garda. I don't mind passion, but it's too early for this excited Labrador. I try to tune him out as we jog down the steps towards the gated car park next door. The little bag of pastries has disappeared from where I'd placed it on the pavement earlier.

It's a typically dull January day, the sky a moody grey. I wouldn't take the patrol car. The last time I'd taken it to a suspicious death, I had rocks hurled at the windshield by furious locals. Fucking pigs, they'd spat. That's another thing, shedding the uniform. I'd been so proud to don it at first, straight out of Garda training, but now that I'm out of traffic duty and domestic fuckups, I couldn't be happier to pull on my navy Marks and Spencer's suit every morning.

In the end, I opt for my own car. Easier if I have to throw up too, I figure. I pull my supermarket sunglasses down from the crown of my head. The world darkens a fraction.

'Jump in.'

Casey is almost fit to burst. No playing it cool with his boss here. Not at all.

I stick the destination into my GPS: *Currolough*. It has been a long time since I've been there, despite Aunt Roe's insistence I come visit her in nearby BallinÓg.

I loosen the seatbelt over my bump and try to ignore the exhaustion lapping at the corners of my mind. It's only ten a.m. I consider swallowing some painkillers but think of the delicate thing suspended in my belly and choose the pain instead.

'What's going on?'

He's practically vibrating.

'Potentially an arson case.'

I glance in my rear-view as I reverse, turning the wheel sharply as I manoeuvre the Discovery out of the car park, which is almost full now.

Clarke Casey is only four years younger than me but looks about twenty-five. Maybe it's on account of his frame. He's all angles and knees. He's tall too – has that stretched out appearance of a teenager. Short brown hair, brushed neatly to the side, impeccable manners, dead posh. I glance at him as he reaches for his own seatbelt. He's quite sallow-skinned for an Irish man – but the tiny freckles I see scattered over his lower arm as his shirt sleeve rises give it away.

I notice that he's brought his overnight – a bag perpetually packed for situations just like this – and realise that I don't even have mine. I think of Peterson's tiny petrol station on the outskirts of Currolough that sells just about everything under the sun. Mum used to send us up there on our bikes for bread and milk – and cola-flavoured lollipops for our trouble. But a lot has probably changed in the decades since I'd set foot in there. Peterson's might not even be standing any more.

–

We hit M50 traffic immediately – long ribbons of taillights swirling red in the January haze. We won't get close to Kerry until after lunchtime, and it gets dark soon after that. Once stalled in traffic, I consider telling my sister Sammy where I'm headed, imagining her in a floral dress, feeding a wet-nosed toddler, always time for my frantic emergencies. But I can't even contemplate talking to her with Casey stuck here beside me, fiddling with his phone, his thumbs annoying me. I imagine her face as I tell her I'm on my way back to Currolough and ease my foot off the accelerator despite the pick-up in traffic. Suddenly I'm in no rush to get there. Maybe I shouldn't tell her I'm going back at all.

Casey glances at the map on my GPS.

'Currolough,' I say. 'Ever been?'

He shakes his head. He probably holidays in more exotic places than the rainy armpit of Ireland. No banana-and-sand sandwiches among the dunes for the Casey family each summer, I bet.

'Ever attended the scene of a fire?' I ask Casey, massaging my temple with one hand, eyes always on the road. He's only been with us six weeks, greener than green. The other lads call him Saint Clarke, but it's only because he gets me my coffee order first each morning. I know he's only trying to impress, but the sooner he learns how things really go around here, the better. Mean works in this world. No room for warm wishes and high hopes. Surely he's learnt that after five years in and out of the court system?

He shrugs. 'Never. But I've done a lot of traffic stuff, domestics, you know, horrible things...'

I glance at my phone, wondering if I should tell Sammy I am going home or not. The truth is that I have no idea how she might react.

'The majority of what you've seen is mostly bad luck,' I tell him instead. 'But until you've seen the effects of violence with intent, you haven't seen anything.' I look over at him for emphasis and then back at the road.

'I've seen it all. I've seen too much of what people can do to hurt one another. Remember that case Cummins had before Christmas where the father pushed a pillow over his kid's face so hard, she pulled her own hair out in the struggle. Remember that? That's horrible. Or the woman I found with so many stab wounds I couldn't even begin to count them. That's the kind of stuff we are dealing with, Clarke. The rest is just called fucking life.'

I draw a shaky breath.

Jesus Christ, heading back to Kerry must be hitting me harder than I thought. The muscles in my arms are taut from my grip on the steering wheel. I try to relax my shoulders by rotating my neck in slow circles until I hear a tiny crack. I toss my sunglasses into the central cupholder. Outside the window, the blur of buildings has given way to dark green fields and smudges of hedgerow.

'So, it's a murder. Is it a kid?' Clarke Casey eventually asks quietly, rubbing his palms on his chinos. I realise I am making him extremely nervous.

'A child is in the hospital. One adult fatality, most likely the father. The mother wasn't in the apartment when the fire started. It's a second-floor apartment just outside Currolough.'

'How old is the kid?'

I glance sideways at Clarke. It's not his fault I'm in shit form. My sister says I'm scary when I get like this. What's the word she uses? Intimidating. I prefer to think of myself as direct, no-nonsense. Except when I'm with Frank. He likes to be the only one in charge.

'The girl is twelve. No update on her condition yet. Have a look.'

I hand him the information, and as he reads, we leave the motorway behind.

'So why have we been put on this?' Clarke says, looking up after a few minutes.

'There's a few witnesses claiming a Garda from one of the local stations is involved,' I tell Clarke. 'When there's suspicion on one of our own, our merry band of detectives get the call. Press will be all over it of course.'

The roads grow narrow. Boughs heavy with leaves lean across the rougher tarmac, casting jagged shadows that seem to reach for us. Birds scatter across patchwork fields alongside groups of cattle. I crack the window a little and let the wind buffet my hair, whipping my fringe across my face. It helps ease the headache slightly. Casey reads quietly next to me, his face screwed up in concentration. He reminds me of a choirboy – clean-cut, wholesome – and totally out of his depth. Neither of us say anything for a while. Farmland gives way to the odd cluster of houses. We cross a humpback bridge. I start to smell sea in the air. I decide, as we navigate through another small town, not to tell Sammy that I'm returning. The truth is that I'm not ready for this and I'm not sure she is either.

Clarke and I listen to the radio for a while, the drone and jingle of late morning talk shows. There's no mention of the fire yet but knowing the news cycle it's likely to make the main one p.m. radio bulletin. Probably lead story.

In Sailfin, we take a bathroom break and I refuel the car. Clarke brings me a green juice I didn't ask for and reads the paper as I continue through the river town of Ha'penny and a long bottleneck through Cairncantor. The news of the fire breaks online first. Clarke's monitoring Twitter. He reads out some of the comments as I try to make up time on the Ballyfergus motorway. There are a few pictures online of emergency vehicles and crowds outside the Bayview apartment block where the fire started and some confusion over the death toll. The trending hashtag is CurroloughBlaze, which we will wade through later as part of our evidence collating. It wouldn't be the first time that amateur photographers turning up outside a crime scene captured something that changed the course of the entire case.

Then there's a sign announcing the turn-off for Currolough. A slower speed limit changes the tempo of the car. Houses are closer together now with schoolchildren in groups, heads together, bags weighing them down as they make their way home along the narrow footpaths. To the right is a line of shops and an unfamiliar hotel.

I used to know Currolough like the back of my hand. Back when I was a kid with scuffed knees and hair down to my waist. Sammy,

Brendan and I grew up the next town over, BallinÓg, an even smaller village with a scattering of homes sheltered from the wind by the surrounding valley. Three villages shared the local school at the top of the hill – a small, draughty schoolhouse where Brendan would play pranks on our teacher, Mr Reynolds. We'd shared bunks, in our cottage between the woods and the lake, whispering secrets at night. The low murmur of our parents chatting downstairs at night was our lullaby. It was a happy enough childhood. For a while at least.

Once I have the Discovery off the main road, we take the left in the fork, past fields with low stone walls, the lake hunkered down, a vast green-grey slick glinting in the afternoon light. White birds skim and soar. I watch them for a moment, admiring their grace, until the sting of a memory flits and catches somewhere too deep. I blink it away. Past the next small bridge, the true beauty of Lake Lagan dazzles. Even Clarke Casey whistles his appreciation.

'Spectacularly savage,' he says reverently, voice low, his eyes ahead.

'Wait until you see the show-stopping beaches,' I tease, but the swell of something resembling pride creeps in, like someone's placed a warm shawl around my shoulders. This was my home, and its beauty is undeniable. I have to remind myself that it's possible to be both nostalgic and deathly frightened of having returned. My aunt still lives here, you see, next to Lake Lagan, and it has been too long since I've seen her. Baby chooses that moment to remind me it's almost time to eat again. The slightly dented service-station apple and green juice has left me even hungrier.

By the time we drive through the town centre, it's after two p.m. Its transformation is incredible. The main street is a hive of activity, even for an off-season January. Pretty flower boxes, painstakingly kept, line the bottom of the shop windows, giving a quaint village feel I never remembered. Pastel-painted picnic benches dot the outside section of each of the two pubs that bookend the town. Signs promising live music, trad sessions and whale-watching trips are propped by the door-ways. There's a fish and chip shop where the post office used to be and an unidentifiable bronze structure that looks halfway between a dolphin mid-leap or the branches of a tree, taking pride of place in the village square. People, tourists I imagine, sit at its base, wrapped in mostly navy puffer jackets, eating lunch from brown paper bags. Their faces twitch skywards as they chat, as if wishful thinking alone could make the sunshine burst through those low-misty clouds. I hadn't expected it to feel so… welcoming. It throws me a little. I picture Mother's face again, her hair wet from the lake after a swim, speeding around Lake Lagan from BallinÓg into Currolough in her old lime-green Mini to buy my school shoes. And me, clutching her hand so tightly, so hopeful that things were finally improving. It was as if I could squeeze all my love into her flesh, to warm the chill of her increasingly empty eyes. I can almost see our ghosts on the path of the main street now, my long plait hanging down my back, her blonde bob pulled back into a damp ponytail, our fingers entangled, glancing in shop windows every now and then. The bitterness of the memory comes at me violently. I shake away the sound of crashing water that suddenly fills my head. As we cut through the heart of Currolough and out through the other side, the smell of black smoke permeates the car. We follow its sad, thin plume towards the Bayview apartments.

Four

'Not exactly like the sales brochure described, I imagine,' Garda Detective Clarke Casey mutters as we turn in through the black apartment gates. The drab blocks loom ahead of us, the grey exterior broken up only by cheap white balconies that give it a prison-like feel. We'd agreed en route that it was important not to make our interest in the police officer too obvious at first, given the sensitivity of the matter and the possibility other Gardaí may also be involved. We'd also have to look at the mother, Audrey Jones, especially as we learnt from the call sheet that she'd been the only one to escape unharmed.

'Maybe it was something straightforward, like an electrical fault,' Clarke says diplomatically, as I manoeuvre into a gap behind three squad cars that are pulled up alongside the entrance door shrubbery to one of the blocks. The Garda Tech Bureau van has already arrived too. A few reporters click half-heartedly as we arrive, but are herded back by one of the uniforms, his arms spread wide. A suspicious death makes a change from covering the annual horse fair, I imagine. But I know that they're waiting for their money shot – the removal of the body on the stretcher. The black-sheathed tangibility of tragedy that will make front pages in all the evening papers.

'I guess we'll find out. But when you have seen as much tragedy as I have, you'll probably be less likely to think things just happen,' I tell him. 'People are capable of all kinds of bad behaviour, Casey. Remember, some just hide it better than others.'

Without thinking, I massage the soft tissue between my ribs with my thumb, specifically the one broken with one swift shove last summer. I quickly let my hand fall when I realise what I'm doing. The pregnancy has made the injury flare up once again.

Clarke Casey shoots me a look.

I press the buckle and the seatbelt retracts. Easing myself slowly out of the car, I join Clarke around the front of it.

We both look up surveying the building.

Bayview, a four-block structure, is a relatively new residence, just five minutes out of town, but the wooden cladding around the communal entrance hallway is stained dark by damp and the aluminium-framed windows seem to sag slightly. A quick Google search earlier told me that it's mainly accommodation for employees of the nearby Elan electronics company which subsidises the rent. In a place as beautiful as Currolough, it's hard to fathom why anyone would choose to live here, beside one of the area's busiest roads, with views across to an industrial park. As a company, Elan is known for wooing staff with pool tables, bean bags and junk food on tap. Maybe they never have to be at this place much at all, but I pity the family members trying to make this grim section of the world seem like home.

I start my investigation the way I've been taught – trying to patch together the circumstances that led to this tragedy. Absorbing it. Was it deliberate? Violent? What traces of evidence remain? I know it's my job to find those clues, but I also feel a certain responsibility on a personal level to find out the truth of what happened to those who probably never saw it coming.

A Garda walks towards me. Tall, mid-thirties, I guess. When he speaks, his voice is thick with the same Currolough accent I'd deliberately shaken off years ago.

'Detective Sergeant Fields?'

When I nod, he introduces himself as one of the officers on duty and Clarke steps forward to pump his hand enthusiastically.

'Inspector Mulligan is upstairs,' he tells us, and leads us towards grey double doors to the side of the building with an exit sign above, explaining that the lift of this particular block hasn't yet been cleared safe for use. Four fire trucks are wedged close together at angles, with thick snakes of black rubber hosing coiled around their base. The air is still dense with smoke.

I make sure to trot up the steep stairs ahead of the men. Halfway up, my legs are screaming, and I discreetly support my bump through my jacket to lighten the load. I curse the need to pee again.

As we step through a door leading from the concrete stairwell onto the second-floor units, a few uniformed officers and scene-of-crime specialists mill around outside the smashed apartment door marked 2D. The first thing the team from the Garda Tech Bureau does is to photograph the place. I'll liaise with them throughout the investigation.

I pause at the door to slow my breathing.

The fire had been brought under control early this morning, the officer tells us. The other twenty-four residents from this particular block have been evacuated.

The smell of acrid smoke is inescapable. The forensic team have their work cut out for them. Both Clarke and I step into our paper suits.

'Through here,' the officer says, gesturing as we zip. Holding onto the landing wall for support, I pull on the matching white shoe covers, refusing Clarke's outstretched hand. The material of the suit stretches tight over my swollen belly. I snap on my gloves. Then the officer leads us into apartment 2D, and, as we duck past the police tape, I catch my own reflection in the hall mirror. The silver glass in it is cracked, most likely from the urgency of the fire fighters dragging in equipment to quell the blaze. I stare back at myself, dead-eyed and bare-faced under the hooded suit but for my stain of lipstick. Clarke loiters behind me as we move deeper into the blackened remains of the family home. The smell of some kind of fuel, like petrol overwhelms. It's usually the first sign a fire has been deliberate.

There are photos on the walls – the standard portrait shots, styled in black and white, of a family of three. There's another one of a couple sitting on a beach, but as I bend to look at it, footsteps approach. A man strides towards us, his chestnut hair and elongated face giving him startlingly equine features. Inspector Ken Mulligan, I presume, the one who called the control centre overnight. A woman appears behind him, also wearing protective clothing. A strand of fair hair falls across her forehead and she flashes a tight smile in greeting.

'DS Fields?' Mulligan reaches for my hand, and I introduce Clarke.

'I understand you are giving us a dig out with all of this?' Though his tone is convivial, Mulligan's words come out serrated. It wouldn't be unusual to feel like we're stepping on his turf. But they'd requested assistance from Dublin. That's what Frank had implied anyway. There are tiny smudges of white at the corners of his mouth when he speaks. I try to ignore them as he introduces us to the others in the room.

'This is Dr Greta Muldoon, pathologist for the Southern district,' he explains. I know Greta, a sweet woman with sad eyes. She steers us towards another smoke-choked room – the open-plan living area. The body is slumped across the sofa, one leg dangling off. There are no signs of any outward burns or injuries, but I know from experience that in cases like this, it's usually the smoke that gets you first.

'Victim is Eddie Jones, electrician, aged thirty-four,' she tells us.

I feel Clarke's shoulders stiffen beside me. It's the first time he's seen a body. Out with me, anyway. I've seen too many to count, but you never get used to the brutality of death, the transformation of all that vitality into an empty shell. Probing slightly as she speaks, Dr Greta Muldoon tells us that on initial presentation, Mr Jones likely died as a result of smoke inhalation and that the angle of his body suggests he was sleeping at the time. I notice the number of empty wine bottles on the table next to the couch and littering the floor. This looked a lot more than a casual evening nap. But rule one of an initial scene scan is never to be presumptuous. This could have been set up on purpose to look like something else.

'What time did it start?'

Dr Muldoon defers to Mulligan, who straightens up.

'Neighbours rang it in about ten p.m. and the fire department were here by ten past.' He pauses, as if awaiting praise.

'Smoke alarm was working. We think Jones must have been passed out, or even been unconscious when the fire first started.'

I nod, looking up at the small white box on the ceiling and then back at the vic's legs. He hadn't heard a thing by the looks of it.

'No obvious sign of trauma to the body,' Dr Muldoon observes, moving a gloved finger along the man's torso, exposing dull flesh. 'But we'll see what the PM throws up.'

'And the kid?' Clarke speaks for the first time, shuffling forward in his shoe protectors, clearing his throat self-consciously. 'How is the little girl doing?'

'She's in hospital. Still in surgery,' Mulligan says. 'She broke both legs dropping from the balcony. The bushes took the brunt of her fall, otherwise it might have been a different story entirely.'

I wince involuntarily, thinking of the height. Poor kid. I shut my eyes. The nausea has returned – a seasickness that churns.

Glancing at me quickly, Clarke continues with the questioning, and I'm grateful to him for the moment it takes to steady myself.

'What about the mother?' he asks.

'Audrey Jones was out jogging at the time the fire started. She's currently at the hospital with her daughter. Ms Jones normally works at the post office in the town centre. Her husband, Mr Jones here, was an employee at Elan.'

The ambulance crew interrupts us as they pile into the small apartment with a gurney, and Dr Muldoon crosses over to speak with them. The forensic team continue to chart anything that could be construed as evidence, despite the thin film of soot across most available surfaces.

I walk across to the remains of the kitchen units. One of the Garda Tech Bureau, a guy called Jake I've worked with before, crouches with a clipboard over a section of the laminate flooring that's been melted in parts. He's poking through the charred rubble but glances over his shoulder at me.

'Most likely started here,' Jake says gesturing towards the door, which is much blacker and more blistered than any of the others. 'Blocked the hallway exit. Burnt both rooms pretty good, but the flames themselves didn't reach as far as the living room.'

The countertops are blackened out hulls. I step over shards of smashed white dinner plates on the ground and wonder if they had also been broken by the fire crew during the emergency. The rest of the kitchen looks neat and tidy except for the fire debris. There's a shopping list stuck to the fridge, a still intact photo of Audrey and her daughter. They look alike – both slight and dark-haired, the same closed-lip smile to camera.

'See that?'

I examine where Jake is pointing. A melted red mess close to the chalky remains of whatever's been burnt. I also spot the corner of what looks like a white and blue checked tea towel.

'Fuel canister?' I guess and he nods. I ease myself lower, towards where he's indicating, and try not to wince at the effort. It's one of those small containers that most people use for storing fuel for lawnmowers. The smell of it thickens the air. 'And look over here.' Jake uses a small metal rod to move a heap of material that's burnt through. Ashy pieces collapse in on themselves, disintegrating as he nudges them.

'Some kind of material. Most likely soaked in the accelerant. They're placed so they caught the curtains, and it took off from there.'

I imagine the whoosh as the fibres took light, the speed of the spread, a child's legs dangling in mid-air, a man oblivious on the couch.

Who would do something like this?

Why?

Out through the open door of the balcony, I spot Mulligan on his phone and follow him out. The sky remains overcast, flat and suffocating. Snapping off my gloves, I take a lungful of cold air. It's only when you are free from something that you realise how overpowering it has been all along.

By the looks of it, the fire was concentrated towards the front of the apartment – the exit. Out here on the balcony, it's as if there was no fire at all. There are a couple of plant pots with startled dead branches and a faded children's sandbox leeched of its original colour. A cheap-looking barbecue sits under a torn canvas cover. Dead leaves gather in one slimy pile angled up against the balcony wall. This doesn't feel like a happy home. As Mulligan finishes his conversation, I lean against the barrier to cough my lungs clean and close my eyes as I imagine little limbs hitting tarmac. Clarke joins us outside and I watch him gaze over towards the next-door balcony. It has a perfect line of sight into the living room of Apartment 2D. 'I want you to speak to whoever lives in that unit,' I say quickly. I'd learnt in other cases not to handhold. Not Clarke and not Mulligan. We'll have to do a little investigating of our own without necessarily involving local law enforcement, especially if one of them is a suspect. Never underestimate the curiosity most have into other people's lives.

Clarke nods and makes a note in his notepad.

'Now...'

He looks slightly alarmed by my tone, but turns and leaves. I push down the nagging voice of my conscience telling me to ease up on my rookie, and instead turn to Mulligan, who's finished his call.

'What can you tell me about this Garda whose name keeps being mentioned?'

He frowns, and glances over his shoulder.

'Everyone knows everyone around here,' he says, by way of explanation. 'It's a somewhat delicate matter, as I'm sure you can appreciate.'

He seems nervous, but I'm not entirely sure he's being straight with us. Small-town officers are tight. I remember that from my early days up at the station in Galway – the huddling of those who'd been in kindergarten with each other's cousins. Or in some cases, those who'd been in the same classes together since they'd been young kids.

'According to the mother, Audrey Jones, a Garda had been harassing them for weeks. He'd been calling on their buzzer repeatedly, even following her a couple of times, she said. A neighbour corroborated the story. She said the same man returned to the block again at the time of the fire last night, but without his uniform. She let him through the glass community doors. The same cop was also first on the scene of the crime, just ahead of the fire brigade. He was the one who broke down the door.'

'So this cop was first on the scene too?' None of this looks good for him.

Mulligan shifts uncomfortably, like he doesn't want to admit what's coming next.

'One other thing.' He lowers his voice. 'The Garda wasn't supposed to be on duty last night. He took a leave of absence last week.'

'Would there be any reason for this Garda... Barrows to have contact with the Jones family in any other capacity?'

He shrugs. 'There's nothing on the system. The family are relatively new to town. They moved from Dublin for the husband's work. The kid is in her last year at St Killian's Primary over the road. No immediate red flags.'

Not yet, I think. Not yet.

'Was the place insured?'

Mulligan shakes his head.

'Well... yes, but not by them. It was a rental. Most of these apartments are owned by Elan.'

I picture the high-walled electronics factory in the retail park across from where we're standing. Everyone in the town knew someone who worked at Elan, the uniform had told us earlier as we climbed the stairs. It had brought a lot of employment to the town – better infrastructure and community amenities. But it had also brought a lot of outsiders to the area, he'd said, lowering his voice. Something many die-hard locals didn't love I gathered, reading between the lines.

'Has Audrey Jones given a statement?'

'She's at the hospital, but we've asked her to come to the station at six this evening for a more in-depth interview, once everything goes okay with the kid's operation.'

We'll have to speak to the kid too, I think, as the baby thumps me from the inside out. Maybe I shouldn't have deliberately fluffed my due date to the station's HR. Maybe I should be feet up on the couch, eating Pringles and shortlisting baby names like other mothers-to-be.

'Any other witnesses?'

He shakes his head slowly.

'We're gathering them currently. Garda Press have issued a statement appealing for information. So far, nothing useful. It made the one o'clock news so hopefully we'll have more of a picture in the coming hours. CCTV in the area is being called in as we speak. I'm sure those vultures will uncover something too.' He jerks his head towards the ever-increasing huddle of reporters gathering in the car park.

I watch Clarke below us, striding across the tarmac past the fire trucks, all business. He seems to say something to the officer supervising the press scrum. He's looking for information about the neighbour, like I told him. As the Garda points towards another block, the group of journos shout something to Clarke, and he turns and has a conversation with them, his willowy frame bent slightly towards one particular journalist. I sigh, resisting the urge to shout down at him to never talk to the press. He *knows* this. I feel the agitation build. What the hell is he playing at? But when I squint, I see that Clarke isn't speaking, he's listening to something the long-haired female journalist is saying and writing it carefully down. His brown head bobs as he nods along encouragingly. Then, after a few moments, he turns and disappears back into the chaos of the emergency services.

Mulligan and I step back inside the apartment, pulling on fresh gloves from a box just inside the door. The air turns heavier once more and I try not to inhale the sharp sour petrol smell. I pause for a moment to absorb my surroundings. Despite the smashed photo frames on the ground and partly charred interior, it seems like a typical family home set-up. There's an exercise bike tucked up to one side of the living room, an office area with an old desktop computer in the other. I pick up a few papers scattered on the desk – electricity bills, school notices, a few supermarket leaflets advertising this week's grocery offers. The bedrooms I walk through don't jar either; Harry Styles poster-strewn walls in the little girl's room, books by the bed next to the locker in the other, an electric toothbrush left casually on the side of the sink, Nike trainers kicked under a small white bench I recognise from IKEA that I'd considered getting myself. Why would someone deliberately start a fire here?

Why would someone want to harm this family?

I have to find everything about who the Jones family were, what they had, what they did, who they socialised with, what their friends or work colleagues said about them. It's always a very long and drawn-out process of elimination, but I just need something that will lead us towards the first stepping stone that I need to figure out what happened here.

At the front door, Mulligan and I remove our protective suits. Mine crumples to the floor and I kick it off, stepping on the material of one side to free the other foot, unwilling to bend low again. I do the same with my shoe covers.

'There's something else you should probably know,' Mulligan tells me as he shimmies one arm out of his suit awkwardly. I resist the urge to help him struggle out of it. I doubt he'd thank me for highlighting his difficulties. Men are like that sometimes.

He lowers his voice. The arm pulls free with a jerking motion.

'It might be nothing,' he adds, as if debating whether or not to tell me something. 'But a few years back, the same cop, Garda Gerald Barrows, was involved in something… similar.'

I glance at him sharply from the other side of the hallway, my hackles immediately raised. This is how it always starts: a missing piece that might just fit.

'What do you mean similar?' I say, and I notice that beneath his protective gear, Mulligan's shirt is immaculate, unrumpled despite the urgency of today's case. He fusses with straightening his jacket shoulders.

'Six years ago, Gerald Barrows was first on the scene of another house fire nearby – one down by the lake. It was the home of a family called the Wills. The mother, Nancy Wills, was badly injured in the… eh… incident, but it's been the source of some conspiracy theories for the last few years.'

'What do you mean conspiracy theories? What happened?'

'The mother Nancy Wills – she lost her baby in that fire,' he answers. 'But for some reason, she's always claimed her son wasn't in the cot when she ran back into the burning house to grab him.' Mulligan looks distraught as he explains. Such big tragedies in such small places can traumatise entire communities, and I've seen that haunted look in the eyes of people I know. I know it far too well. But the idea of a mother running back into a burning building to find no trace of her child terrifies even those of us who've been around the horrible things block a few too many times. I tuck my arm across my bump protectively, trying to shake some of that horror away.

'Jesus Christ. Was it arson?'

'Actually, that fire was ruled accidental. It's believed the baby perished in the incident.'

'Believed?'

'His remains were never found.'

He hesitates. Out of respect perhaps? But I get the sense he's trying to keep his tone neutral.

'Nancy's five-year-old son, her other child, escaped unharmed,' Mulligan continues. 'But the baby…' He gazes past me into the distance, obviously upset by the recollection.

'The thing is, Barrows was a good friend of the Wills family…'

To me, it seems that linking this Barrows cop to both fires was a huge leap. But maybe there is something I'm missing.

'Barrows was presumably the local Garda, so wouldn't it have been perfectly reasonable that he'd be the one first on the scene back then?' I ask, studying his face.

Mulligan shrugs.

'That was the thinking for a long time – that the mother was grief-stricken and prone to denial, but earlier this week something else happened that now casts doubt on everything we knew about that fire. There are too many coincidences and they all involved Barrows.'

The hallway is growing busier as officers gather in the doorway of the apartment. I shift on my feet, trying to ignore the urge to use the bathroom.

Clarke is back. He strides towards us, his fingers busy on the screen of his phone. When he looks at me, it's clear there's something he wants to tell me, it's written all over his face, but I don't want Mulligan to lose his stride either. I picture the blackened skeleton of a roof behind trees Clarke and I had noticed as we drove close to Lake Lagan on our way here and wonder if that's the house Mulligan is talking about. If so, it isn't far from where Aunt Roe lives. I shiver, despite the uncomfortable warmth of the hallway.

Mulligan closes his folder, but he still seems distracted.

'I'll never forget that fire,' he says, a haunted look on his face. He lets his words hang in the air a minute, not needing to emphasise the trauma of what he's remembering. But it's obvious that he's back there. Reliving it. I've many questions for him because I don't believe in coincidences either.

'It was the week before Christmas,' he says quietly, and in the light of the hallway, his face takes on new shadows. He looks greyer somehow, more haggard. 'Six years ago… the night that poor baby died.'

Five

When Nancy left the hospital a few weeks after the fire, the world looked too bright somehow. It jarred with the empty darkness that consumed Nancy now. Neighbours waited on the road by Peterson's convenience store to salute her sister Vee's Nissan as they passed by, despite the rain. A shared mourning, Vee explained to Nancy – the acknowledgement that she wasn't alone in all of this. Or more likely, for a glimpse of the monster, Nancy thought unkindly, wondering about the ratio of concern to curiosity that drove people to stand out waving in the rain after the local priest announced at mass when she'd be leaving the hospital.

Her skin had calloused over the last few weeks, but so too had Nancy's heart. Scar tissue puckered and dragged one side of her face downwards. The hurt of what happened that night was now stamped on her skin, forever. Her twisted fingers were another unavoidable reminder of her sins. The fire had scorched her in ways nobody could ever understand.

'Don't look,' Vee said, as the Eastbourne Road shifted lakeside. The only route to Hugh's mother's house, where the family would stay temporarily, was past Nancy's blackened hull. But she couldn't help looking. Her head bumped softly against the glass of the passenger window as Vee navigated the grassy verge of that lonely Kerry road. A brand-new phone sat in her lap; the challenge of using it hadn't crossed anybody's mind. The streaming rain matched Nancy's quiet tears, which she wiped on the sleeve of the loose shirt she had to wear over the bandages. She looked at the pitiful remains of their home, the guilt gnawing relentlessly. The worst part was that she knew she had set this chain of horror in motion because of the decisions she'd made. She knew this was a punishment. The pain of her burns nothing compared to the ache she'd now have to live with every single day for the rest of her life.

Investigators had told her and Hugh that the intensity of the fire had destroyed everything upstairs and half the downstairs. Her house was now a devastating monument to darkness that had sucked everything in – every photo, every item of clothing, every teddy bear.

Everything good.

–

Later that evening, after the bandage changes and an hour of excruciating physio she had to do, Nancy watched Hugh tuck Joey into the spare bed of his mother's pristine house. They were only a fifteen-minute drive away from the ruins of their own home, but it felt like another world entirely, with his mother's formal cups of tea and shallow digs about responsibility and working mothers. She'd always been like that, making Nancy feel like she was never good enough. A half-thing. Well, at least now she'd been proven right, in a way. She was neither herself nor the person she'd dreamt of becoming someday – she was trapped forever under this grotesque mask. With one child, without the other, somewhere that felt like halfway between life and death – a dream and a nightmare. A smoky, twilight existence. From the doorway, Nancy blew her son a kiss. 'I love you, my prince,' she whispered hoarsely, praying it wouldn't always be like this, praying that her eldest son would stop being afraid of her. If only Joey would stop screaming in terror whenever she came near him. Not that she blamed him. He was just five years old. Nancy had thirty years on him, and she still couldn't look in the mirror without overwhelming panic. This was trauma on top of trauma for Joey. How would he ever get over this after all the progress they'd made on his behaviour before this tragedy? She watched Hugh hush their son gently, stroking his hair. And at that moment she felt a disassociation that made her legs almost buckle beneath her. She was the common denominator for every bad thing. Perhaps they'd be better off without her?

The fire had taken part of her face and her fingers as well as her baby son. Well, that's what the authorities thought anyway. Two weeks after the fire, a tall man with dark curls protruding from beneath a flat cap had come to the hospital with his report to tell Nancy that an electrical fault caused the oil heater in their bedroom to go up. And that it had probably been the cause of the fire. Jim Aylesbury, the man said his name was. Hugh had admitted that he'd left the radiator plugged in, thought the socket was smoking the few days before. But she knew differently. She didn't remember any smoking sockets or faulty heaters. Why hadn't anyone warned her about such things?

'It simmered, possibly for an hour or two, before finally going up,' Jim Aylesbury read from his report, his face passive, not ever meeting her eyes. 'Then it took off fast.'

If she was looking for compassion, this wasn't her guy.

She remembered buying the heater, knowing it was going to be a particularly cold December. She'd suggested it – trying to keep her baby warm and safe in their bedroom, the only room without double glazing. It had been that precaution that could have killed them all. In her worst moments, Nancy wished it had.

'You were lucky it wasn't in the middle of the night,' he said, and she glared at him in disbelief – her brown eyes hard and unchanged, despite the distorted flesh around them.

Lucky?

She took a deep breath, pushed down her anger and tried to form the words she'd been repeating to Vee, to Hugh, to the nurses and to herself since the fire. 'But the baby wasn't in the cot,' she had said, trying to grasp at the elbow of the man's grainy jacket. Aylesbury moved an inch – the polite way of shaking her off.

'That cot was empty. I know it was. You have to find Liam,' she'd begged.

'The emergency crews said you thought your five-year-old son's room was empty too, but he was okay in the end, isn't that right?' Jim's eyes were deep-set, his face expressionless. She wondered for a moment if that was something people like him practised for situations like this.

It was so hard to piece that night together, her memories of it clashing and skidding, like a car gliding across ice, but Nancy was beginning to rake the reality from her torrid visions of that night. Someone had appeared outside the house carrying Joey, wrapped in a crinkly silver blanket, as she was being wheeled into the ambulance. She pictured her boy's face, his hair dishevelled, cheeks wet with tears, the whites of his eyes showing. She remembered Hugh stepping into the ambulance, pulling her close, his fingernails devil black. God, she didn't deserve him – her ever-patient Hugh. That stab of guilt again. She'd put him through so much over the years.

She remembered that Vee had arrived hysterical into the roadside commotion at some point too. Nancy pictured her elderly neighbour May standing close to the house that night, looking bewildered. She'd seen May once again, in the hospital, standing at the door of her ward, staring in at Nancy. But maybe it wasn't May after all – because May would have come in and talked to her, wouldn't she?

Someone else was there by the ambulance that night too. Gerald Barrows maybe? Her memories folded inwards again and disappeared. She tried to grasp at them and failed.

–

'What's lucky is that Joey was out on the trampoline looking for Santa,' she'd explained, that day in the hospital when he came with the report. 'And thank God for that, but my baby wasn't in the cot. I'm telling you, he was taken. The police know this already. I've told Inspector Mulligan. I've told them all.'

'Is that what you *think* happened?' The question had been posed in a neutral way, but it pushed her over the edge she'd been barely hanging onto.

'I know it was,' she'd shouted – a raw primal reaction, her heart pounding in terror as she thought of the baby out there somewhere without her.

'I understand you are upset...' Aylesbury had started to say, but she'd cut him off, screaming loud enough to bring a few nurses to her doorway.

'You cannot understand this. You can't possibly know what this is like.' Nancy flailed, sickened.

Then, exhausted by the flood of emotions, she'd lain back on the pillow, paralysed by her helplessness.

'Did you find him?' Nancy had eventually asked, quieter now. 'Tell me that. You must have found evidence he was there?'

She'd met his gaze, challenging him.

'In the room? That night.' The mother tried to steady her breathing. 'Did you find my baby – my Liam – in that house at all?' she'd demanded.

Aylesbury had cleared his throat, glancing at the folder he'd removed from his bag and placed in front of Nancy on the hospital tray between them.

They both stared at it.

'Actually, in cases like this when the fire burns at such an intensity as the blaze at your house did, Mrs Wills, and for so long, little evidence is found when it comes to organic materials. The mainstay of the fire centred around the master bed, and he was so... small.'

She'd looked up at him sharply while he'd continued talking, but more quietly this time.

'To be honest, we wouldn't expect to find much in terms of... remains.'

A wave of nausea hit Nancy and the room spun.

She tried to force the oxygen into her lungs.

'We...' The man had stopped and wiped his hand quickly across his face. He looked at her helplessly. 'I'm sorry. Do you need...'

But Nancy had interrupted him.

'No,' she hissed. 'My baby son was taken. There's no other explanation. He wasn't there. You even said it yourself. There was nothing found. And it wasn't the fucking heater,' she'd spat. 'Surely you have to find DNA to declare someone dead? There has to be some evidence for you to say he's... gone.'

'While that's a matter for police, I will say that as far as I know forensics is usually only carried out in cases where foul play is suspected.'

As in, not this one.

Nancy knew what she saw. But more than that, was the unshakable feeling that if her baby had died, she'd know. She'd *feel* it.

Wouldn't she?

–

As the weeks went on, the more she insisted that the baby was alive somewhere, the more pitiful the faces of those around her became. The Gardaí came and took her statement, but she could feel their reluctance. They hadn't even sent a forensics team, she'd shouted at Hugh, begging him to fight their corner while she was so weak. But then weeks passed and it was too late. The only energy her grieving husband could muster was focused on Joey. Where she expected urgency, she got silence and sad, tilted heads. A terrible tragedy, they called it.

This was her baby. Her tiny son with his tiny perfect fingers.

'Liam,' she'd whisper into the air when there was nobody around, unsure if she was calling him or reminding herself that he'd existed at all.

As the pitying looks gradually changed to concern, they began appearing on her husband's face too. It was then she realised she was completely alone in her insistence that her baby was still out there somewhere.

Nancy knew, when they buried that little box of burnt debris on the hillside graveyard near Lake Lagan, that it wasn't her baby son. Not even close.

Hugh remained quiet, distant. In fact, he hadn't said much at all to her, not since that night, overcome perhaps with the fact that he hadn't been able to protect them all. And because Joey still found it so hard to be around her, she was bereft of him too. She missed her family. She tried so hard not to miss Gerald Barrows too – but he was nowhere to be found.

Standing at the graveside service, Nancy was barely aware of her surroundings, but she could sense mourners recoiling from her misshapen face. Her long dark hair was now shorn short on one side, completely absent on the other. Perhaps, she should have worn a hat. Her scars throbbed painfully. She looked around at the villagers with suspicion and mistrust. Why are they crying? They'd never even known him. 'Which one of you took him?' she also wanted to scream. But in a way, she understood this punishment. It was her own fault she was standing there that day.

On the tiny gravestone, engraved in delicate gold swirls, was the caption she'd chosen.

'So small, so sweet, so soon. Baby Liam Wills. Taken from us.'

Nancy didn't shed a single tear. She tried to catch Hugh's eye as they gently lowered the coffin into the ground, but his face remained turned away from her, hollow and pale. How would their fragile marriage ever survive this?

All she knew was that her baby son was out there somewhere, and that she needed to find him. As they placed the too-light box into the earth, Nancy Wills saw someone in the distance. She'd recognise his Garda uniform anywhere.

Gerald.

Gerald Barrows.

But then the sunlight shifted, the branches arched in the breeze, and she realised it was just a shadow.

It was just a trick

of

the

light.

Six

A full-chested woman in a dirty apron takes our sandwich order at the small cafe in Currolough, a few minutes' walk from the police station. I take off my blazer jacket and massage the soft flesh between my ribs as Clarke pours us both a glass of water from the jug on the table. He takes care not to let the ice plop too heavily into the small glasses. I tap my phone to check the time – we have less than an hour until the scheduled interview with Audrey Jones at Currolough station. The reporter we've arranged to meet is already running a few minutes late.

The smell of toast makes my stomach growl. Self-care isn't something I'm used to. In fact, I'd spent the last decade stuffing garage-bought bread rolls and full-fat Coke into my mouth between callouts. I'm not programmed to take the time to nourish myself. Until that line turned up on the pregnancy test, I'd always treated meals as just another inconvenience.

'Okay, tell me again exactly what she said,' I say, pulling out my laptop. I'd been slightly irritated that Clarke had agreed to meet the reporter he'd spoken to outside the Bayview apartments. For all I knew she'd given Clarke her number for something other than police information. Entirely possible given that he was an attractive enough guy – if you liked that tall, geeky look, I suppose.

But when we phoned her from the Discovery on our way back to Currolough from Bayview apartments, her urgency to meet seemed genuine. She had information she needed to relay. Over the phone, the journalist, Cynthia Shields, told us she was adamant that we focus on Garda Gerald Barrows – specifically his involvement in the missing baby from the fire six years ago. She is convinced it's all linked. But something happened this week that she says needs to come to light.

43

Her hands are tied because it hasn't been released to the public. She's powerless to do much about it without our help. She'd be here any minute.

'Don't forget, we don't know that the baby *actually* went missing,' I point out to Clarke, knowing what grief can do to a person – how it can distort reality sometimes. Clear heads are needed.

'Didn't they find the baby's body?'

'Apparently the fire burnt too intensely. Nothing left at all. Mulligan said.'

Clarke exhales.

The sandwiches we ordered arrive, neatly triangled with crinkle-cut crisps heaped onto the side of the plate. I take a bite of smoked chicken and tomato with one hand and run my hand over the control pad of my MacBook Air with the other.

I google Cynthia Shields. She's my age, with various writing awards for human interest stories, mainly Irish but some in the UK. Her profile picture shows a self-conscious smile, a spray of faded freckles and wavy, red hair. She's mostly Galway-based and from the quality of her features and the publications she writes for, she seems very credible.

I still hate that we have to approach things from this angle, though. The police down here should be across this. They should be leading the charge. Journalists shouldn't have to call on the cops to rake back over closed cases – especially those that involve grieving mothers and suspicious links to local cops.

Cynthia's latest article was updated a few days ago – some exposé on a land development deal in the Midlands. She had forced an inquiry. I was quietly impressed. When we google Nancy Wills, there are pages in the search engine of various different articles that include her name, mostly about her claim that her son didn't die at all in that house fire. That he was taken.

I finish chewing and take a slug of my water.

'So, let's get this straight,' I tell Clarke. 'Nancy Wills reported her baby missing every few months for the past six years,' I read aloud, but low enough so only Clarke can hear. The cafe itself is busy with tourists and a few builders in high-vis jackets nursing mugs between cupped hands.

'And nobody bothered to properly investigate. Gardaí didn't send forensics, just the fire inspector,' he says. 'But, in fairness, they probably thought she'd gone a little mad with grief.'

I look directly at him. Clarke tries to stifle a yawn, giving me a glimpse of his orthodontist-perfect teeth. His eyes are slightly hooded and creased at the sides, as if never far from a grin.

'You will make a great detective someday, Casey. I mean it,' I tell him. 'But there is no excusing those types of presumptions. I hope you would take ideas like that right out of your head before you arrive on a scene or to a witness. The problem is that jumping to conclusions like those colours your perspective immediately. You'll start seeing things that aren't there – making the story fit the way you want it to fit – if you already think you know what happened before you even get there. Do you know how many actual crimes are dismissed because a woman is accused of overreacting, or being hysterical? Do you know how many tragedies could be avoided if someone really took the time to listen? That whole *it's all in her head* stuff really fucking annoys me. It's important we don't ever do that. Do you understand?'

'Got it.' He nods, and there's something in the way he looks back at me that shows me that he does.

'Tabula rasa,' he says, after a moment.

'Come again?'

'Blank slate. It's means starting from nothing.'

'Wow, thank you Professor Clarke.'

His face turns bright red, and I hate myself for the tiny stab of satisfaction I feel.

But a tabula rasa, or whatever, is the correct way to approach this case.

'A terrible tragedy.' Clarke scans one of the articles referring to the house fire at Nancy's, reading aloud in shorthand '…the talk of the village, even made national headlines…'

He looks up at me. 'Probably because it happened at Christmas and the vic was so young.'

I nod, but I'm wondering if perhaps my own Aunt Roe knew the family. The excuses for not visiting her now seem to be getting less robust. Clarke turns his screen towards me, showing me the article.

There's a picture of a woman with dark hair, stretched skin and sad brown eyes. Nancy Wills.

'It says here that her marriage broke down not long after the tragedy.'

'The case was tossed around local stations years ago.' Clarke continues to read Cynthia's in-depth feature. 'But they concluded that the mother's theory that her baby had been taken from its crib before the fire wasn't just implausible, but was most likely the result of trauma, wishful thinking and grief.'

I pop a few crisps into my mouth as I think, the crunch loud in my ears.

'But,' I muse, 'there's never ever been any evidence to suggest otherwise, has there?'

'Until now, perhaps,' Clarke whispers, and I almost smile at his intensity.

Then Cynthia arrives at the cafe, breathless and windswept.

'I'm so sorry,' she says, sliding into the booth beside me. She's wearing a long grey dress coat and her hair is pulled back into a messy ponytail. Amber wavy bits escape around her face, and she pushes them back as she arranges her bag on the seat beside her. 'Thanks so much for meeting me.' We shake hands and she orders a peppermint tea. I know immediately I'm going to like her. She's my type of person – direct, concise, with a fizzy impatience I can relate to. We talk briefly about the apartment fire at Bayview. Then she pulls out a soft material folder with a zip, extracts some papers, and puts on her glasses. She dives right in, telling us that she's been following this case since the first fire, six years ago. And she feels strongly that Nancy Wills has been dismissed as the hysterical grieving mother for far too long. And far too easily.

'Then, last Monday lunchtime… six years after her baby supposedly died in the house fire, Nancy Wills was involved in an incident at a craft market in Drumlish – a town about an hour's drive from here.'

I sit up in my chair.

I remember what Mulligan had started saying – about something big happening this week on top of the fire that involved Barrows.

'What kind of incident?'

'According to the information I have – information that wasn't formally logged, I may add…' Cynthia looks up, raises an eyebrow '…Nancy was at the market that day. She grabbed a little boy by the arm and started screaming that he was her son. The police were called, and they had to physically restrain her.'

Her tea arrives and she ignores it. Trained listeners, Clarke and I say nothing.

'The thing is...' Cynthia takes off her glasses, sets them down gingerly on the table next to her teacup and leans slightly forward, 'the kid she grabbed, the kid she started screaming about... what Nancy doesn't even know yet herself is that the kid was Gerald Barrows's son.'

The air fizzles.

Neither of us say anything for a few moments. But Cynthia is not getting any kick out of this reveal. Her face is a picture of concern.

Then Clarke speaks.

'How would Nancy know what the baby looks like now?' Casey asks the most obvious question in the room, shaking his head a little cynically. But I need him not to be cynical. Being cynical overlooks tiny details that might make all the difference. We owe it to be thorough at the very least. Plus, I'd never be where I am if I hadn't been so pedantic, so detail-oriented, so razor focused. Even if that poor mother Nancy was projecting her grief on others, and even if it was a strange coincidence, I'll make sure to prove that too, and wrap this one up for good.

Cynthia takes a careful sip of her tea and swallows softly.

'Nancy Wills has a son who was just five years old when the house fire happened. A boy called Joey. She has a photo of him which she says is identical to the child she saw the other day at the market. She figures the brothers shared a likeness and the resemblance is uncanny.'

I try to ping what she's saying around in my head for a while to see how that might transpire.

But I know the first thing we'll have to do is to go and inform Nancy Wills. And find out what the hell is going on with Barrows.

Between snatched bites of our sandwiches, we focus on learning as much as possible about the Nancy Wills fire from Cynthia Shields. Say what you like about journalism, particularly tabloid journalism, but there was a hell of a lot of detail that sometimes never even makes it into the police files. She points out that she also found it strange that nobody had ever looked at the other person in the house at the time of the fire – a neighbour who babysat regularly, a woman named May O'Regan.

But until she can formally confirm what she's been told about Barrows, Cynthia can't report much more. Her hands are tied, which is where we come in. I've been a detective long enough to understand that this could simply be a wild goose chase, but these are the threads we owe to families to pull. We have to follow every strand to figure out what happened to poor Eddie Jones at the Bayview apartments. There was a reason why he'd died on his own couch last night. And it's up to us to find out. Besides, this Barrows guy seems to be at the centre of everything.

There's learning in everything, my mum used to say to Brendan, Sammy and me, growing up. Zero preconceptions, clear heads, open minds. You had to go into things ready to take them at face value – to be prepared to accept that sometimes the simplest explanations are the correct ones.

Sometimes.

Shit. I look at the time. It's almost six o'clock.

We promise to stay in touch with Cynthia and I excuse myself to go to the chipped-tile bathroom where I reapply my lipstick. Even though I don't bother with much make-up, lipstick has always been a shield of sorts. Perhaps my way of asserting my femininity in a job where I have mostly male colleagues. I use the side of my index finger to correct a spot where it's gone slightly awry and wash my hands. Then I try Frank's private number which, frustratingly, rings out. I couldn't pretend not to be annoyed with Frank. It's not only being sent back here, but when it comes to the two of us, there are really important decisions to make, priorities to decide. I'm fast realising that I can't just accept the situation I've allowed myself to become part of. It isn't fair on the baby. But the more my belly expands, the more I'm starting to realise that it isn't fair on me either.

Back at our table, I force down the last bite and grab my bag. Clarke wipes his mouth neatly with his napkin and folds it back onto the table. He almost takes up the entire cafe when he stands. We walk out together, him holding the door for me as I scoot under his outstretched arm.

It's intriguing, I suppose, to imagine that Nancy Wills's kid has been alive all this time. Out there living and breathing under everyone's noses. The press would love that. A real Disney ending. A mother and child reunited.

I glance at my screen again as we hurry towards the station. The real reason I never told my sister Sammy that I was returning was because I knew what her reaction would be. I knew what her gut-twisting words back to me would be:

You are absolutely not ready for this yet, Ally. Not even close.

I walk down the same street as I had as a child, retracing my twelve-year-old footsteps, reminding myself that not every story ends the way we wish it did.

Seven

Inspector Ken Mulligan greets me and Clarke at the reception desk of Currolough Garda station and leads us into a back room. All around there's peeling paint, clunky fax machines and a damp, draughty feel. Two Gardaí sit behind desks, their eyes on us as we walk past them. Curled paper pinned to noticeboards offer helplines for those suffering domestic abuse or simply for those who need to talk. I volunteered at one of them for a couple of months, a few years back. But the limits to what I could really do to help frustrated me. Stuck behind a phone with a script wasn't the type of help I was best placed to offer. When I ventured off script one evening and ended up banging on the door of some woman's apartment at midnight to try and answer her cry for help, I was encouraged to take a step back by the officer that her husband eventually called. She was asking for help, I'd muttered when I was escorted away. I still had the scar on my knuckle from the angle it hit the concrete when I punched the wall in the stairwell. I never even heard if she was okay or not.

Currolough station served the entire Lakeside region – six small towns that had seen five other stations shuttered in the past few years. An exodus towards Dublin, Cork and Limerick had seen the populations decline around these parts. Fed up with 300 days of rain a year and Atlantic winds that tore the skin almost from your bones, I imagine. Many of the die-hard locals had let out their sea and lake-view traditional cottages to tourists, mainly German, Dutch and American, who flocked to its craggy coast for fresh seafood, fishing trips and the boggy desolation reserved for this savage corner of Ireland. Crimes around here these days were fender benders or missing handbags. Not that you'd think it to look at Ken Mulligan. He's all muscle – like one of the trainers at Reilly's Boxing Gym, where I used to work out mornings before I got pregnant.

'Think she'll show?' I ask, when we've settled ourselves in the interview room. It's a boxy room at the back of the station, painted an ugly green with stacked chairs to one corner and a tiny leaded window that barely opens. As I sit, the exhaustion hits, and I make a mental note to buy underwear and a toothbrush before we hit the guesthouse tonight. Clarke must notice my fatigue because he silently holds out a fresh can of Coke he's taken from the cafe and offers it with a jerk of his head. I accept a fizzy gulp, and settle myself into the uncomfortable plastic chair, stretching my feet out underneath, letting my muscles yawn open.

'Ms Jones said she'd be here by six.' Mulligan shrugs. 'Kid might have taken a turn, but Harry's at the hospital and he hasn't told us any different.' There is no urgency to his manner.

'So, where's this Garda Barrows now?' I ask.

I want to establish some key facts first. To do things my way for a bit. Saint Clarke has barely moved, sitting with one knee crossed over the other, his chino lines perfectly ironed. Listening, like I'd warned him, pen in hand. If these cases are connected, we need to know everything about that night six years ago, as well as about the Joneses.

'He's not made himself available… He's taken stress leave.'

That tingle of something again. This was all much too murky.

'He's called in sick?' My voice drips with incredulity as Mulligan mutters something about making a call the next morning. Gerald Barrows isn't exactly making things easy for himself. Why would he go to ground if he hadn't anything to do with the fire? But we're here now, we may as well use the time, especially as it looks as if Audrey Jones isn't going to turn up.

'Can you tell us a little more about what happened six years ago? About this Nancy Wills fire, and the death of the baby?' I indicate to Clarke to start taking notes.

Mulligan shakes his head regretfully.

'We could never leave that case behind. People still come to see the house by the lake; did you know that? Or to try and get a glimpse of Nancy Wills. Can you imagine? She's reported over the years cars that just stop outside the place she lives in now, lingering. She says she feels people watching her, gawking every time she leaves the caravan where she moved to after the fire.'

Despite his clear, even accent, I can tell this case means something to Mulligan. His words are careful and laced with an emotion I can't put my finger on.

We'd come in on the Dublin road, so had only seen the house from a distance. To be honest, I wasn't sure I was ready to drive that close to the lake. Not yet.

But from the articles I'd read online in the cafe, the house on Eastbourne Road represented a blight on the community – the house of horrors children whispered about as they cycled past. It wasn't the first tragedy to touch the area, but it was perhaps the most tangible.

I stretch my spine as Mulligan speaks, trying to relieve the pressure on my pelvis. I know I'll have to head down towards BallinÓg sooner or later. If only to see my aunt, like Sammy suggested when I finally spoke to her, just before we came into the station. 'How do you feel about being back?' Sammy had asked me, and I pictured the skin on her forehead creasing with worry. 'I can't believe you're back there,' she'd whispered. 'Are you going to be okay, Ally?'

I told her I wasn't sure yet. But she made me promise her that I'd visit Aunt Roe. We both knew what that meant – going back home. To the place where we were born. 'Good luck, Ally,' she'd said. 'I should be with you for this.' I'd promised to update her when I made the visit to Roe.

But I also know that this is probably something I need to do completely alone.

Ken Mulligan continues. 'For years, Nancy Wills insisted that her youngest child Liam wasn't in that fire. We figured it was her grief colouring things – that she couldn't possibly accept the alternative – that her child had been reduced to nothing but ash in the blaze.'

I can sense Clarke Casey's horror beside me. Horrible things… he hadn't a clue.

But he keeps his eyes down like a good rookie detective, absorbing and processing, scribbling in his notepad. I'd been afraid his enthusiasm to solve the case in the first twenty minutes would cause me problems, but right now, he seems to be doing everything I've trained him to do. And he's proving himself to be even shrewder than I'd originally given him credit for.

'Didn't you analyse the scene – even find bones? Nothing at all?' I put to Mulligan.

Clarke raises his eyebrow cynically. 'Didn't you look?' he asks.

A shadow crosses Mulligan's face. 'We didn't feel it was necessary to call in Garda Tech Bureau. We concluded our own investigation and were satisfied that it was an accidental death. End of story.'

'But it wasn't. The end, I mean,' I say, trying to move things along a little but privately aghast at the lack of resources that had been available to this family six years ago.

'We had no evidence there was any foul play involved. The specialist report was clean. It concluded there was a faulty oil heater in the bedroom. Plus, Gerald Barrows had moved stations by the time the report came out – we felt there was no further investigation needed. To be fair, it wasn't unusual for him to be first on the scene seeing as he was a friend of the family and on duty that night.'

'What about Nancy's claims that her son was alive?'

'Nancy Wills came into the station a lot, to berate us for not doing anything about finding her baby son Liam. She's been doing it for years – always makes a commotion. Let's just say she has no inhibitions.' Mulligan pulls a face that suggests more than he's saying. 'It's desperately sad, as you can imagine.'

But his face is more irritated than melancholic. This poor lady has nothing to lose, I think sadly. She probably sees her son's face in every child she passes. That grief is unimaginable.

'But something happened more recently.' I push him. 'Something that wasn't even formally reported, according to a journalist we've been speaking to.'

Mulligan isn't stupid. He probably knew this would come to light; he'd even alluded to it. Perhaps he was biding time until Nancy realised that the child she saw at the market in Drumlish was linked to Barrows.

'She came in a few times this week, frantic – waving a photograph around, claiming it proved that her baby was alive. The photo in question was of her other son, Joey Wills, and she said that it was the spitting image of a child she'd seen in Drumlish, at a market an hour away from here. You know those farmers markets, craft fair things…' He swirls his hand in the air dismissively. 'I think she works at them or something.'

'Go on.'

'She made an awful scene at the market, the witnesses said, grabbing at the kid, shouting. She had to be held back. It was very distressing for the child, apparently.'

He shakes his head again.

The problem, he explains, is that Nancy Wills had courted the media briefly a few years back and it didn't turn out well. A vanished child, a mother with life-changing injuries – the potential for tabloid headlines and conspiracy-based documentaries had been an editor's dream. But the public had turned on Nancy after a while. There was mistrust when rumours emerged of her having extramarital affairs. Even some, he says, who believed Nancy herself had something to do with the tragedy. It wouldn't be the first time a relative had had some kind of involvement in a horror such as this. I think of my colleague's last case – a child struggling under the weight of her father's hands on a pillow pressed into her face.

'I guess what I'm getting at is...' I say, after a lot of toing and froing. 'Is why any of this – the Bayview apartment fire, or this Wills case, can't be handled at local level?'

Clarke glances over at me. There is no delicate way of putting this without potentially insulting Currolough Gardaí. But we all know there is a hierarchy here. We are the big boys. We are the ones that are called in to solve the unsolvable. Not a ghost chase and a dodgy cop in County bloody Currolough.

Mulligan looks uncomfortable. He cups his chin in his hand, rubs his lower jaw self-consciously. He's a big man, with huge hands and that raw look of someone who spends a lot of time outdoors.

When he speaks, Mulligan's voice is thick with resentment.

'Yes. This Barrows complication is clearly an issue. And once we established that the kid Nancy was grabbing at was Barrows's kid, we approached him. But Barrows has refused to speak with us about the matter. Lawyered up. Been off work since.'

'He reported this incident himself?' Clarke asks.

'No, that's part of it too. He refused to press charges or for us to caution Nancy Wills. It was the nanny who was screaming and a few passers-by that got police involved. She gave the boy's name and, well, it all became clear.'

There's an uncomfortable pause. Somewhere in the hallway, a rickety photocopier slowly whirs to life. We stare at each other in silence a moment because everyone in the room knows there's nothing clear about this whatsoever.

'And Barrows was spotted at the scene of the Jones case at Bayview?' Another nod.

'And he was accused of harassing Audrey Jones.' Mulligan blinks a yes.

'First on the scene of both fires?' Mulligan is squirming now.

'And yet he's not been taken in? Or questioned about any of it?'

'We... we felt it best we got some advice,' he stammers, his face turning a mottled shade of red. 'From you lot. He's my brother-in-law's cousin. And Harry, the Garda over there at the hospital, he's married to his nephew. It wasn't... straightforward, let's just say.'

I sigh. Every possible version of this mess floats before me. The intricacies of the small-town tangles. The unravelling of all of this now involves things like court-ordered paternity tests and no doubt a media frenzy, a dead boy who potentially came back to life, and what did the Jones family have to do with it anyway? If Frank ever bloody calls me back, I could fill him in on the tragic death that's somehow turning into a potential cold case kidnap.

Inspector Mulligan is right about one thing, though. He needs us. He badly needs us. This is going to be too big for them to handle alone – especially if it now involves a police officer. Especially with the press sniffing about.

'Right.' I fill the awkward moment as I try to think of the best way to approach this.

Clarke shuffles his notes. Then moves to say something, but I shush him with a look.

'How well do they know each other?' I demand. 'What was the relationship between Nancy and this Gerald Barrows?'

'None, that I know of.'

Why do I get the impression that this community is protecting one of their own? I remember Mulligan telling me that he was there himself, that night six years ago.

'We'll need to speak to Nancy Wills as soon as possible.'

I straighten myself up as elegantly as one can at almost thirty-eight weeks pregnant. HR would kill me if they knew I was still working. But it's not like I was going to be sitting around knitting booties. I'm much more useful here than in my tiny apartment counting down the hours.

'Can you arrange that please, Inspector? And we'll need the original fire report immediately – we asked for it hours ago.'

'I've sent the digitalised ones over.' A flash to those hard eyes.

Clarke stands up too. 'We prefer to work from the original paper-work, if you don't mind.' He speaks politely but there's a steeliness to his tone, a confidence I haven't heard before. He's not asking. I suddenly see the lawyer in him and realise that aspect could be useful.

A knock on the door disrupts the mini standoff. A police officer strides in followed by a small woman in a purple striped running top and black shorts. She looks exhausted. Her eyes flick from Mulligan back to me.

'This is Audrey Jones,' the officer announces.

The woman stands before us rubbing one eye with a balled-up hand. And then, to everyone's horror, she starts to cry.

Eight

I take a tiny step towards Audrey Jones. Clarke jumps up and flails around, unsure of what to do. Mulligan is rooted to the spot. Her hair looks unwashed, her eyes puffy. I remember she's just lost her husband and almost her child, and that she probably hasn't slept at all since it happened.

I weigh my words carefully. I know this type of grief.

'Come and sit down, Mrs Jones. Clarke, would you or Inspector Mulligan get Mrs Jones some tea or maybe some water?'

Mulligan practically races out of the room. I look Clarke in the eye. 'A chair please, Casey.'

'Thank you.' Her voice is brittle. It catches in her throat.

'How's your daughter?' I ask, supporting her as she sits. She glances around as if in a daze. The skin on her arms puckers with the cold and I pass her my jacket. She looks younger than the thirty-four that I read in the file. Audrey Jones looks down as if she's only just noticed what she's wearing.

'I had been out for a run…' She trails off. Then she tries again. 'I've been in the hospital since… you know.'

'Your daughter?' I ask again gently. 'How is Tori?'

'She's okay.' Her voice is a whisper. 'Sedated.'

'I'm very sorry about your husband,' Clarke says awkwardly, his private school accent enunciating every word. Audrey looks up and gives the flicker of a smile in thanks. She's small, with dark hair pulled back into a messy bun at the nape of her neck. Her unvarnished fingers tremble as she twists her hands together nervously.

The door opens and Mulligan returns, his giant fingers hooked around two tilted mugs that spill as he moves. He sets one down on the table in front of Audrey Jones and slides the other over to me. He takes a wad of tissues and white paper packets out of his pocket and dumps them in the middle of the table.

The pale liquid slops over the side, but I'm grateful for the thought. I tip a paper tube of sugar into my tea and roll the packet up tightly between my thumb and index finger.

'Do you think you'll be able to speak to us a little bit about what happened?' I ask, and she nods, her hands now wrapped around her cup, gripping it tightly. Mulligan starts recording the audio, muttering the date and time as Audrey sits up a little straighter.

'You said you were out for a run last night. What time was that?'

She looks alarmed, as if she's afraid of making a mistake.

'I left Tori at about half past eight,' she says to the mug, rather than to me.

'And was your husband awake at the time?'

Another panicked look.

'He was minding Tori.'

An obvious lie.

You see, I know all the moves. We have to. Because when bad things happen, people always have a reason to lie. Her eyes dart from the mug to my face. She probably knows that *we* know she's lying. She seems like an intelligent woman. I take a calm sip of my own tea, absorbing her demeanour, letting the quiet draw everything out.

'Tell us about what happened before you left,' I say eventually, asking the widest possible version of the question.

'We had – we had... dinner.' She sighs. 'Then Eddie put on the TV. Tori was in her room on her iPad. Things were... normal.'

I think of the smashed plates. It was an unconvincing depiction of Audrey's evening. She continues.

'But this guy, this cop, just wouldn't leave us alone.' She looks pleadingly at me as if begging me to believe her. I imagine what's she's just come from. Bandages and splintered bones. Surgery, no doubt, casts and pins and months of physio, not to mention the trauma of what Tori Jones had been through in her effort to save her own life. I take in Audrey's increasingly trembling hands. She sets the tea back onto the table; the ceramic base wobbles against the wood causing a gentle, clinking sound.

'How do you know Garda Gerald Barrows?' I ask softly. Her eyes meet mine again. Wide, grey and full of apprehension.

'He's a friend of someone I used to work with. I only met him once before, at the post office where I work.' She glances at Clarke as if sensing he is the more empathetic of the group. Or the weakest link.

'And why do you think he kept coming around recently?' I press.

Clarke's pen is poised. Mulligan has deferred to me completely. I think of the crude bundle of tea towels from the scene and feel a prickle of anxiety. Is it possible Audrey Jones had something to do with it? If Gerald Barrows, a trained police officer, had wanted to set a fire, the way he went about it was hardly sophisticated. Maybe she got tired of her drunk husband and wanted him out of the picture?

The mother shrugs.

'He just kept ringing the bell,' she says, rubbing her eyes again. 'He wouldn't stop. It was pissing Eddie off that he just wouldn't leave us alone.'

'Did you meet anyone when you were out for your run?' I ask, trying to change tack. Maybe this Barrows guy had been interested in Audrey Jones romantically? I'd seen the fallout from unrequited love stories. Rejection makes people do unimaginable things.

Audrey shakes her head. She starts crying quietly again. No alibi either.

'He just wouldn't leave me alone.' She flinches, still not looking at me.

Then she puts both hands over her face. 'I'm sorry. Can we do this another time. It's all a bit too much.'

Silence, except for the ticking of the clock on the lime-coloured wall.

'Do you have anyone with you, Mrs Jones?' Mulligan inquires politely.

'My friend is still at the hospital with Tori. I took a taxi here alone.'

'Can we drop you somewhere?'

A shake of her head.

She folds her arms across herself. 'I'll just head back to the hospital.'

'Audrey?'

She looks directly at me for the first time since we sat down.

'We will have to speak to Tori as soon as she's well enough.'

She gives a little gasp.

'I'm not sure.' She picks at her fingernails. 'I – don't know.'

'It's not a request,' I say firmly.

We won't get any further this evening. I can feel my energy reserves are totally depleted. We agree we'll see how the next day's surgery goes, and one of the junior officers is tasked with driving Audrey back to the hospital. Things would be easier in the fresh light of day. Wasn't that what my mother always said? I tell Audrey to hold onto my jacket and that we'll chat again soon. Good cop *and* bad cop – I can be everything and anything it takes to get to the bottom of a case.

After Audrey Jones leaves, Mulligan, Clarke and I stare at each other. I take the ball of paper I've made from the sugar packet and flick it towards the bin but miss. I turn my phone over a few times as I think. 'Sick leave or not, we need to talk to Gerald Barrows,' I finally say to Mulligan. 'And I need to know from Nancy Wills herself exactly what she thinks happened that night six years ago. How are these cases connected, other than Barrows?'

Clarke's phone breaks into an exuberant pop-song ringtone. I roll my eyes. Taylor bloody Swift.

'It's the neighbour from the opposite-facing apartment block,' he says to me, and hops up to take it.

'Did you notice she wasn't wearing her wedding ring?' Mulligan says suddenly to me, standing up, scraping his chair against the cheap flooring. The baby flips and dips low in my pelvis.

To me, that was irrelevant.

What I really want to ask is if anyone noticed there were no tears when she'd cried.

Nine

Frank's tone is low and overly polite. I can tell by the way he's speaking to me that he's with his wife Mel and I hate the surge of jealously that immediately overwhelms. Clarke is in Peterson's. We are en route to Nancy Wills's home. It's a bright, golden morning. Instead of a grocery store, Peterson's is now a Scandi-style cafe with industrial high-top chairs and stark black metal light fittings. I stay in the car while Clarke picks up much-needed caffeine. Sammy has been asking why I haven't been to see Aunt Roe, but how can I visit her when I haven't even been able to drive towards our little section of Lake Lagan, deliberately taking the coast road even though it's half an hour longer? Clarke doesn't know that. Not that he'd point it out either.

I check the time – 8:43 a.m. Why the hell isn't Frank at the station?

'This situation is obviously not as straightforward as we initially thought,' I tell him, but he's clearly distracted; there's shuffling in the background, hushed voices, a car engine.

'Frank?'

'Sorry, DS Fields. I'm out of the office currently. Family stuff.' He chuckles self-consciously, and I want to throw the phone out of the window. I can hear the familiar edge to his voice. The warning under that faux joviality. It makes me think back to all the times I had to hold my breath, to pretend not to be somewhere, as he spoke to his wife on the phone – the wife he failed to tell me about until it was too late. Those eyes boring into me, daring me to defy him. By then, I was under his spell, my heart wrapped up in his, begging to be loved. I think about all the times he held his hand up to me to silence me, to pretend I wasn't there at all. And my quiet, warped devotion. What the hell am I going to do once the baby is here? Tiptoe around Frank's personal life? I want to say that he never called as promised since I left Dublin, but instead I take a deep breath and will the baby to kick his or her tiny feet against my insides, to remind me of the good that's come out of this mess with Frank Nolan.

'I hope everything is okay,' I say, gritting my teeth, watching Clarke in the distance through the glass of the cafe window carefully taking out his wallet to pay. He'd insisted it was his turn, even though I'm the one with the expenses budget. He's chatting with the woman behind the counter while he waits. Of course, he is, I think. The adventures of Clarke and friends.

'Gemma's got another hip clinic,' Frank says stiffly. Gemma is Frank's two-year-old daughter who was born with a congenital hip condition. I knew she had to attend St Trinity Children's Hospital a few times a year to monitor the condition, get regular X-rays, that kind of thing.

I want to throw up. I'm a bloody forty-two-year-old woman resentful of a sick two-year-old. What the hell am I doing?

'Okay, Inspector Nolan, I really hope she's all right. Call me when you can… please.'

The whine in my voice as I hang up disgusts me. The bravado of doing all of this on my own is starting to crumble with every day I inch towards my due date. This is the cycle of my relationship with Frank Nolan – me convincing myself that I'm a big girl and don't need a man who belongs to someone else. A man whose love comes with conditions, a man with a power over me that I can't understand. Then falling into Frank's arms because, actually, being pregnant at forty-two is hard. Even if those hands can be a little rough sometimes. Maybe it's because I need to feel love, even if it's only the scraps. Maybe all I know how to receive is slivers of affection that get pulled from underneath you when you least expect it.

The problem is that I can't have Frank – I can only ever have a fraction of him.

Besides, it was never going to be anything else. He made that very clear when I finally found out he had a family. But after the shock, after I'd already fallen for him, I knew the only way to try to have even that tiny piece of his love was to exude a no-strings-needed willingness, and now here I am, searching for those very same threads desperately in the sand.

Still, there's a tiny ray of hope in the back of my mind wondering if my being pregnant changes all that – if he might just turn around and prove he's as amazing as I want him to be. But he doesn't and he probably isn't. And suddenly I found myself being hissed at to become invisible because Mel's on the end of the phone wondering if he wants her to keep him some salmon fillet for supper. And there's nothing cool about that. In fact, it's the exact opposite of breezy. It's heartbreaking, actually, to have signed myself off as being second best with some dumb flourish, like I was *glad* about it. To accept how he treats me because even warped love is love.

Maybe that's the root of it – that I couldn't bear the rejection, the absolute abandonment that I'd never recover from. So here I am clinging to this half-chewed rope, waiting to see what happens next.

Clarke waves from inside the cafe – goofily. I smile and wave quickly back, mainly to prevent him from continuing to be such a spectacle. I give a three-finger salute. To be honest, at this moment, his simplicity is refreshing. Right now, I need nothing but coffee and to not think about Frank for a bit. Clarke comes out, balancing one cup on top of the other as he tries to open the passenger door. Leaning across to open it, I realise that my body doesn't bend that way any more. The gearstick doesn't help. I gesture hopelessly, but he manages to clamber in and hands me the takeaway cup.

'It's hot,' he warns.

'Cheers.' I take a slug and wince. 'Yep, scalding,' I confirm.

But I enjoy the caffeine hitting the back of my throat. I need it. My suit is scratchy and the comb and toothbrush I picked up in the garage outside Currolough hasn't helped much. In the car mirror, I roll my eyes at my scraggy plait and try to smooth back the hair that's escaped. This is why I should keep my overnight in the boot of the car like I'm supposed to.

'So, whereabouts did you live around here when you were a kid?' Clarke asks conversationally, as I swing the Discovery towards Nancy's, the long way.

Caught off guard, my heart hammers in my chest and I fiddle with the radio a moment, focusing on trying to tune it in until I find a suitably upbeat song – Queen: 'We Are The Champions'. That'll do. The lump in my throat is so big I can hardly swallow.

'By the woods, other side of Lake Lagan,' I finally answer. 'Place called BallinÓg. But I haven't been back in a very long time.'

'Do you still have family there?'

'My Aunt Roe... Rosemary. My mother's sister,' I add, exhaling heavily.

I wait for the next questions that usually come when we discuss family. People want you to gush about your warm childhood memories. They want to define you by your upbringing. But I never have. The truth is that I couldn't.

'That's nice.' Clarke sips his coffee, as if he doesn't have a care in the world. Maybe his classy upbringing prevents him from asking personal questions or maybe he just doesn't care.

That's the problem with the way we live – too much focus on order and status, as if by organising our thinking into categories we can ignore the reality of life in all its frightening unpredictability. Back when life came crashing down on me as a kid, I found out the true fragility of the world. Seeing those constructions we held so dearly, smashed in seconds, that changes a person. Sammy says that's why I gravitated towards policing – seeking order in chaos. But I know deep down that it wasn't about bathing myself in neat, comforting rituals. My career choice was about stepping as close to the dark brutality of humanity as possible without being sucked in. A test of my sick resolve. It was about holding my hand over the flame until a fraction of a second before it burnt. Pulling it away and marvelling at how close it had been. That was my problem – my horrible, tantalising mission.

'Your mother still... around?'

I shake my head, lips tight – my usual response to that difficult question.

'So will you visit your aunt while you're here?' He's humming along to the song, and for some reason his overly positive demeanour now starts to annoy me.

'That's kind of personal Casey, isn't it?'

He immediately shuts up and I feel a pang of remorse. The landscape shifts slightly as we edge nearer the sea. I try to find familiarity amid the bare trees and curve of the stone walls and recognise nothing.

We stick to discussing the case instead. We both agree that Barrows stinks and that Audrey is probably lying about a few things. The neighbour living in the adjacent apartment admitted to Clarke that the Joneses argued a lot. Nigel, a single man in his sixties, told Clarke on the phone that the fights had seemed to become more violent in recent weeks. 'That poor kid had to listen to all that shouting constantly,' he said, agreeing to come down to the station to give a statement. But it was what he said towards the end of the call that made Clarke stop pacing. 'That woman thought she was better than everyone else. She barely said hello. Stuck up if you ask me.' Clarke relayed to me what Nigel had said. 'He was probably fed up with all her nagging. Topped himself, did he?'

His eagerness to lay the blame at Audrey's door was curious, but unsurprising. I wonder what else people had seen. We still have two more witnesses to hear out. It's impossible to know what went on behind closed doors. But it is also impossible to accept opinion alongside facts. Everyone has a take on everyone else's lives – especially when they implode.

Another witness confirmed they saw the child trying to climb down from the balcony to safety before falling, putting to rest any of my fears the poor kid had deliberately jumped. You see, every possibility has to be considered. We're now awaiting information about the couple's financial status and any insurance policies that might raise red flags.

'We just have to find out why Audrey Jones might be lying,' Clarke says now, placing the empty paper cup into the cup holder. 'Mulligan is interviewing Eddie Jones's boss today at Elan, and the results of the PM are expected later this afternoon.'

While I admire Clarke Casey's passion for finding out the truth, I also know that sometimes there are motives that we can never understand.

I take a sip of coffee and indicate left.

I think of my childhood house by the lake. There are things that happened there that I can't ever make peace with. I picture Brendan's small face – the fleeting surprise as my brother realised what was happening to him that morning. That sickening gut-punch of horror remains lodged in my deepest core whenever I think back.

Maybe it is time to go back there, after all. Maybe this is my opportunity to iron the crease out of my family history a little, before this new baby crinkles into my life. Maybe I should go to Aunt Roe's and stand on the edge of that damn lake and take a picture for Sammy, explain to her that none of this is as bad as we both imagined. Like when Mother would show us that the dark hump in the corner of our room was just an awkwardly dropped towel or carelessly thrown sports bag. Confront the demon – isn't that what you're supposed to do? Isn't that what everyone bloody says you have to do in order to move forward?

Why can't I move forward?

'We can't take a DNA sample without the parental permission,' Clarke says suddenly, and I drag my mind back to the case. The solicitor in him beginning to emerge once more.

'We can get a court order if it warrants it,' I say, thinking of Barrows's kid at the market.

'But that could take weeks of legal wrangling if the parents don't agree.'

He's right, of course. But first I need to get a look at the kid, to speak to Barrows, to absorb his story. We'd requested the original investigation file into the Nancy Wills fire carried out by fire expert Jim Aylesbury. The police report from that night was being dug out of storage where many of the files, after being digitalised, are kept. I wanted to get a steer on who I should speak to from it knowing it also might help towards the Jones case.

Freddie Mercury continues to belt out affirmations from the car speakers. I notice Clarke's stopped humming. He moves his long fingers quickly across his phone screen and I realise ten minutes from where Nancy lives that he's writing his report notes, transcribing the interview with Audrey.

Saint Clarke strikes again.

'When you're done there, will you write up the list for my hospital bag?' I say, all innocence.

He glances up quickly.

'Sanitary pads… extra absorbent. Towels – preferably bright red. My Enya CD…'

I can't help laughing at his crimson face. In fairness to him, he smiles back, holding his hands up in mock surrender.

We take the last turn off the next roundabout and immediately spot the sign for the caravan park.

'And yes. To answer your earlier question, I'm going to see my aunt later, if we have time,' I announce, as if stating this out loud somehow makes up for my earlier sarcasm. It is also a declaration of intention that I need to hear myself say.

Clarke nods politely, but I can tell he's decided to stick to the script – the rookie/mentor interaction that won't blow up in his face every time he tries to make conversation.

I remind myself once more that not everyone appreciates my bullishness. There was something in the way Clarke Casey had looked at me as I teased him, as if he could see it as the weak defence mechanism it so obviously was. It unsettled me. Not because he was calling me out – he'd be mad to even consider that – but because he seemed genuinely interested to know why I needed such an oversized shield.

This is why I don't bother making friends. It's so much easier to hide behind the walls I've carefully constructed around me.

Zero exposure. Nothing and nobody to reflect your sad history back at you. Better to be the snarling guard dog at the gates of your own trauma than let anyone in for a glimpse of what really went on. Because if someone you love hurts you growing up then you can't help equating hurt to love. It's my simple rose and thorn philosophy. I figure you can't have one without the other.

But being back here, back at Lake Lagan, is a scary reminder that those walls that Sammy and I have so painstakingly built are laughably thin. As paper-thin, in fact, as the sticky pink membranes that lie between me and the child inside me. And after what happened to me, that's what I'm most afraid of. That someday I'll have to tell this baby about what happened all those years ago. The truth about what happened to their uncle Brendan – my little brother – on that awful day in the water.

Ten

Ally

One year ago

I knew I was flying too close to the sun when I met Frank Nolan.

The night at the charity ball was supposed to be a one-off. But I'd underestimated Frank's charisma – his persuasiveness – the ability to get what he wanted. And he made it immediately clear that what he wanted was me. Sammy was aghast when I admitted to her what had happened. But after watching me for too long having car-crash encounters with ill-suited men, I don't think she was *that* surprised. For the first time though, I could see what she saw – a forty-one-year-old, single, twenty-a-day smoker who was renting a one-bed apartment in a shitty address in Dublin city. Now I'd thrown in an older cop on top of things. My bubble-gum world was expanding rapidly, but there's always the sticky pop that's hard to scrape off. In fact, the only part of my life that had any semblance of stability was my career – but I'd attacked that with a destructive force too.

It just so happened that clashing with every authority figure I encountered on the way up turned out to be a positive thing. I flew up through desk duty to traffic, then vice and onto Major Crime. And there was nothing I hadn't seen. As expected, Detective Ally Fields was the almost-Icarus of policing – getting close enough to feel the unbearable heat of the sun before dodging its damage at the last moment, just long enough to survive. But those close encounters took their toll. Every single one. I'd been shot at, beaten-up, called filthy names and disrespected by colleagues because I was a moderately attractive female in policing. It only fuelled my ambition to destroy anyone that got in my way. 'The world isn't against you, Ally,' Sammy always said sadly,

71

but we all bury our trauma in different ways. And I'd never criticised her for the way she packaged hers. My version was creating a homespun safety net and then spending my life testing it by jumping into every difficult situation I could muster up. Chaos was my drug and pain my shield.

–

The night I met Frank I was at the charity event under duress – a favour for my policing partner at the time, who strong-armed me into attending. But as I slid into the fuchsia-pink dress with a slit up one leg and blow-dried my hair into soft waves, I realised it had been a hell of a long time since I'd worn anything other than my work suit. In my bathroom mirror, I'd outlined my eyes with thick dark kohl, enjoying how it turned them a sooty black. Then the obligatory smudge of lipstick. The ridiculously high gold sandals were worth the pain when I walked into the ballroom that night and felt the whoosh of appreciation in men's eyes – a rare occurrence for someone who usually wore cheap polyester and a red-stained, keep-away scowl.

The charity event itself was for the St Trinity Children's Hospital. There was an average steak dinner, dull conversations and a predictably jazzy band. A little disappointed, I headed out to the terrace for a smoke before the auction. The band was playing 'Sweet Caroline'.

'Hiding too?'

The man – Frank – smiled as he strode into the outdoor area. I was perched on a wrought-iron bistro seat – scrolling through my phone, flicking ash onto the ashtray with the other hand.

Immediately I was attracted to him, so I ignored him, shrugging and turning back to my phone.

'Do you mind?' He pulled up a chair – it scraped along the patio tiles – and folded himself into it.

'What are you hiding from, then?' I asked, deciding to take his bait, still scrolling on my phone. Rude but, in my experience, usually effective.

It was freezing. Tiny puffs of fog accompanied our words. Goose-bumps ran down the length of my arms. A coat didn't suit the dress in the end.

'My ex.' He winked, distastefully. But then a short harumph of a laugh. 'I'm also doing a speech before the auction.'

'Oh?' I responded icily, but the truth was that the blond man in the tuxedo sitting in front of me was extraordinarily attractive and by the lean of his shoulders I could tell he felt the same way about me. Although he was typically good looking, there was an asymmetry to his face – an awkward slope of the nose, eyes slightly too far apart – that enhanced rather than dented his appeal. There are people in the world that find beauty in flaws. I guess I'm one of them.

'I need inspiration,' he said, his voice commanding. 'And beautiful women inspire me.'

Those eyes; searching and appraising all at once. I swallowed.

This dickhead was so overtly sexy, it was almost a parody. But I was in the mood to capture the admiration I'd felt earlier in the night – lasso it, drag it close to me and store it all up for later – bask in its glow. I'm not a bad person, you see, I'm just a sucker for a good-looking man who knows what he wants. The bubbles had me giddy too. That and, of course, my irrepressible need to be needed.

As he leaned closer to me, a strand of hair escaped his neat sweep and lingered on his forehead. He smelt expensive, tangy. I imagined what it would be like to lick the stubble along his jaw.

'I need your help.'

I turned to face him. Our foggy breaths mixed in the cold night air as we spoke – suspended, then slowly drifting off into the stream of pink and blue disco lights from inside the ballroom dancefloor.

'Frank?' A thin woman with an elaborate up-do appeared on the terrace. An organiser, perhaps? 'Time for your speech.'

I started to really shiver then. Should have worn the damn coat. Our moment had passed but later, after studying him speaking on the podium, discussing the work done by the foundation for countless sick children, I found myself aware of his presence in the ballroom for the duration of the night. I felt his eyes on me too as I threw back my head, throat to the ceiling. With a swish of my hair, swilling my champagne, I'm sure my dull companions were surprised by the sudden attention I lavished on them.

Then, just when I couldn't bear it any more, I felt a hand brush the small of my back as I ordered my last drink. Leaning against the mahogany panels of the bar, nobody else at the packed counter would have noticed, but a shot of pure heat ran through my body. I don't know if it was the slow rolling music, the murmuration of the room or just pure lust, but I leaned into it – into him, purposely allowing the curve of my bottom to press against his tuxedo trousers.

Then his warm breath on my neck – a whispered invitation that intoxicated. No going back.

The steps of the hotel fire escape bored into me as we grasped for each other at the outside service area, pushing and pulsing, clawing damp material across quivering skin – our frantic three-minute dance. Our hushed moans whispered back at me, bouncing off concrete. Afterwards I wiggled my dress back down and I rolled my eyes when he called me beautiful. A few weeks later when we lay next to each other, tangled in my cotton sheets, he admitted he was married, that he'd gotten back with his ex for the sake of their baby daughter.

Heart hammering in my chest, I told him I couldn't see him again. Sneaking around with a married man wasn't for me. It wasn't right. But part of me knew I'd already surrendered to him.

Those start–stop moments punctuated the following weeks. We had a lot in common – both detectives, him newly promoted. We both shared ambitions, we were both running from something we couldn't quite put our finger on. With him I felt protected.

At first.

I'm sure a therapist would have a field day with that. But it had been the first time in a long time that I'd let anyone close to me. The truth is that with his golden hair and easy smile, I enjoyed being around him. When Frank admitted one day that he was in the running to lead my department, I ended things again. He was going to be my boss, for goodness' sake. The chemistry between us was so achingly strong, I knew it would be impossible to work together unless we recalibrated our relationship, redefined it somewhat. But switching from lovers to colleagues and then boss and subordinate was never going to work, as Sammy pointed out a few months ago.

'You are playing with fire,' she warned. 'It's naive to imagine you can control this thing you've set in motion.' It wasn't an argument as much as a gentle suggestion – sisterly advice that I usually chose to swat away.

I envied her lack of self-absorption. She said she envied my delicious irresponsibility.

A few weeks before Frank began heading up our team at Docks Major Crime, I met him for lunch at Pauly's, a tiny pizza place down a side street next to the financial district. It was a warm June day, and I dressed as simply as possible. My black ankle-length skirt swished as I navigated the tables to reach the one he'd reserved. A discreet corner at the back.

'My God you smell good,' he growled, nuzzling my neck as I slid into the chair next to him. He looked surprised as I pulled away and laid my cards on the table next to our calzones. I ended it. He'd already told me about the job leading my team and how he was planning to take it. I admitted I couldn't work directly beneath him. I already felt the shift in our power dynamic the first time he'd been rough with me. That night we broke up the last time, I cried as I loaded the dishwasher in my dreary apartment, devastated that the only pinprick of light in my life belonged to someone else. Frank never spoke disparagingly about his wife Mel. I knew she was successful, protective, wifely. She was the responsible, capable woman I knew I'd never become, that nobody showed me how to be. I was destined to always be the disorder in the otherwise very orderly lives of most. Our break-up resulted in a flurry of affection from him, and my resolve weakened, as powerless as my flesh against his frustration. How dare I think I can call the shots. He wore me down by turning on and off the tap of his feelings. It usually ended in pain of some sort. Pain I felt I deserved.

When I found myself crying almost every day for a week, I began to really despair. But when my heartache turned to breast ache, I suspected my strange emotional state might be a result of something other than Frank's unavailability and my unresolved childhood trauma. Four Tesco pregnancy tests later, I sat on my bed and cursed very loudly. How the hell was I going to play this? I was forty-one years of age, knocked up by my married boss. My life was my work and despite my rank, I didn't earn enough to contemplate all the grown-up things the mother of a child ought to have – an open-plan kitchen, a garden with a climbing frame, the ability to cook, a parent who wasn't as fascinated by death and gore as Ally Louisa Fields. This child deserved freshly baked smells in a cosy house. It deserved piano lessons and My Little Pony matching duvet sets. Fancy school shoes. I thought of my own mother and cried some more. It isn't so easy to escape our past at all.

–

Over the following weeks though, I slowly discovered a low spread of happiness, like the invisible string that raises the dawn, a glowing ember that swelled along with my waist. I felt chunky, exhausted, petrified... and often tantalisingly content. I bought a smoothie maker; the cigarettes vanished. I drove to work with one hand on my belly – an acknowledgement of the fledging life, that wonderful swirl of molecules, shifting and forming into a child.

My child.

Frank's reaction should have been a relief to me. He knew that *I knew* he'd never leave Mel. So, there was no panic or fear, just surprise, frustration and then acceptance. 'Tell me what you need,' he said finally. The agreement was implied. Silence, in return for him sticking around. I knew he'd never not be generous to both me and his child. But the mistake I made was falling back into his confusing arms. I hated how grateful I was that he seemed okay with all of this. I hated how I didn't love myself enough to walk away when things took a turn.

'Did you do it on purpose?' Sammy once asked me after I showed her the scan – the question only a sister could ask. I shook my head from side to side, annoyed by her inference, but later that night, in bed, I wondered if maybe somewhere subconsciously I manifested this tether. I should have known my pill mightn't work after a tummy upset. But it was my last biological chance; I knew that for sure, and I didn't intend to squander it. But no, not deliberately.

All I know is that I fell in love and, even if it wasn't reciprocated, I now had the potential to love this small thing inside me. Every morning I kissed my index finger and pressed it against the scan picture stuck to the fridge with a magnet of Universal Studios Florida an ex had left behind. 'I'll bring you there someday,' I'd whisper, thinking about the envelope with the gender, tucked into the bottom of my underwear drawer. Someday soon I'd slice it open and get a better glimpse of the person growing inside me. The truth was that Frank could never be mine, but this baby represented a new start. That's why visiting Aunt

Roe was probably the right thing to do – and the Nancy Wills case cropping up during the Jones case perhaps a sign that sometimes you need to go backward before you can move forward.

But none of that stopped me feeling bereft that I would be doing this alone. Now that Frank was back in my life, back in my bed, I knew it was time to make a decision – to get Frank to make a decision. I couldn't live with the shame of loving what didn't belong to me at all.

It was a huge risk. All right, a test.

But his presumption that I didn't want more *then*, didn't mean I didn't want more *now*. There's a difference between the concept of the baby and the actual baby I saw on the second scan last month.

Sometimes I imagined what it would be like to be a normal family; Frank, baby and me – a life without complications. But scrubbing away the sorrow that had followed me over the past few decades was impossible. Nothing could erase the fact that I would always consider myself less than. That the choices I made in life were directly connected to the consequences of what I'd experienced growing up. Nothing could ever rid me of the most horrible truth of all – the one weighing me down since I was a child; that I'd been responsible for someone's death.

No, not just somebody.

I'd been responsible for my little brother's death.

Eleven

Nancy Wills lives in a pretty caravan twenty miles from Currolough, perched on the top of a cliff. Far below, the sea meets the lake, saltiness twirling through the silt.

Clarke and I pull up alongside a sign that reads *Sullivan's Caravan Park* painted in rainbow bubble writing – a little too merry for this particular visit. The front area is neatly kept; there's a windchime hanging from one of the beams and a burst of purple heathers in the hanging basket by the blue door. It has a hippy vibe – a happy one too. Nothing like the depressing cave I was expecting. Nancy's is the brightest mobile home in the holiday park where the other thirty or so units are scattered, dotted along the jagged edge, 100 feet above the rocky beach below. Views to die for, I think suddenly and feel a little dizzy imagining the foamy depths swirling beneath.

Clarke Casey also seems surprised by our first impressions of Nancy Wills's abode. I think back to Mulligan's description of how people would drive here just to get a glimpse of her injuries. It reminds me of how I cut Clarke off at the station yesterday when he was about to say something.

'What were you going to say yesterday, at the station with Horsey Mulligan?' I ask blithely, as we walk towards the small cabin. The truth is that so far, I'm impressed with Clarke Casey's ability to sit back and observe. Not that I'm going to say that to him, though.

He looks confused for a moment and then makes the connection to Ken Mulligan's appearance and tries not to smile.

'I thought a police officer had an obligation to aid an investigation,' he says. 'Like a duty. That's what I wanted to point out.'

He's not the worst-looking man in the world when he narrows his eyes like that – a little less *Mr Bean Goes to Oxford*.

'Also, what's the big deal if Barrows can just produce the birth cert and hospital records for his kid and all that?'

It's a good point and something I was wondering about too. Why bring all this fuss on yourself, getting legal representation and generally creating a headache, when Gerald Barrows could just wave the kid's birth cert and we'd all go on our way, safe in the knowledge that Nancy just couldn't ever get over her baby son's death? We also need to see if there is a connection between the Joneses and Nancy. Why had Gerald been the common denominator in both? Solving cases is mostly about finding patterns and then asking why those patterns have formed. It's finding some kind of order in disorder, and the irony that I'm good at identifying them isn't lost on me.

'I guess we'll find out when we doorstop him later,' I grin. Legal would take months that I don't have. Plus, I've never had a problem doing things a little creatively. Anyone who's worked with me knows that.

Clarke Casey looks back at me with something that feels like comradery, and I don't mind it.

'Besides,' I say as my phone vibrates in my pocket, 'don't be such an idealist. Just because someone has a duty doesn't mean they have to do it.'

I glance at my phone screen. It's stubbornly blank except for a reminder for my prenatal appointment next week. I hate the flip of panic I feel when Frank doesn't call. Beneath it all, his inaccessibility is one of the reasons I'd been drawn to him, but now I'm in so deep, his unpredictable patterns are increasingly bothering me. I press the bell of the caravan, and, after a few moments, we see movement behind the blurred glass square of the front door. There's a jiggle of metal, a click and then the door of the caravan swings open. A slight man with long, greasy-looking hair is beaming at us, welcoming us in.

'I'm Tim.' He smiles, but there's a wariness to his movements I recognise as fear. I don't read into it too much because as detectives, we tend to do that to people. We command respect while inciting fear. Even in those who have nothing to hide. Nancy was expecting us after Mulligan called ahead.

'Come in, come in,' he sing-songs jovially. I try to rearrange my face to match his energy but fail. 'Nancy's partner,' he adds when we look at him a little confused.

We step inside the surprisingly large cabin.

I don't know why I expected the poor woman to live alone in the dark shadows somewhere. Another preconception. There is something about Currolough that makes me think the worst, constantly. Or maybe it just brings out my worst. Not for the first time since I arrived back in Kerry, I wonder how the hell this situation has arisen; me standing by a cliff in Currolough weeks from having my very own baby. I wonder what Aunt Roe would make of it all. She doesn't even know I've returned yet.

The caravan itself is homely and well cared for. Every available space has been used for storage. Plants in colourful pots dot every edge, a shelf overflows with books, photos line the wooden walls. There are rows of different types of dreamcatchers taking up one entire wall – some hanging from the ceiling, some lying flat. All look homemade.

'You make these?' I gesture towards the wall and Tim beams. They are really good – all colourful feathers and carved wood, with the net plaited together tightly, ready to trap insouciant nightmares. They've always fascinated me – the idea you could escape your demons somehow, trap them neatly in a net. But here, in such numbers, they look more like some kind of spiritual shrine. An offering…

'They're Nancy's.' Tim smiles. 'I do the fiddly bits because… well, because of her hands. We sell them around the country at the craft markets.'

I remember that Mulligan told us Nancy had seen the boy at one of those markets.

Clarke smiles politely and promises to try and make it down to the markets himself if he has time. Tim seems chuffed, and again I wonder how that charm comes so naturally to someone like Clarke – the ability to put others at ease? The opposite of me entirely. I can see the benefits of his method. He finishes what he is saying to Tim and glances over at me to check he's not in trouble. It dawns on me that it's not a method, as such. Clarke Casey really is just that nice.

Something is cooking in the small kitchenette – and smells divine. I'd eaten tomato soup and a garden salad last night after Audrey's interview, promising the baby it was vitamins all the way from now on. But breakfast was disappointing – a few measly strips of bacon at the guesthouse where we're staying, weak tea and soggy toast, under the watchful eye of the nosy owner who glared at me when I dared ask for an extra towel this morning.

'Nancy's out back,' Tim explains, and gestures towards the other end of the deceptively large caravan with a sprawling deck to its rear. Through the glass opening I can see the outline of a hatted head.

'I'll bring out coffees, shall I?'

I tell him I'll have a tea.

Tim has an English accent – northern perhaps, the tree-hugging type most likely. Middle-aged, bead-wearing men were a dead giveaway. But he seems welcoming. Keep an open mind, Ally, I remind myself because I've always been suspicious of the overly friendly.

The ridged slats beneath us creak as we step out onto the decked area at the back of the mobile home. Outside is crisp and clear – an endless blue sky. Cold-nose weather, Mother would call it. It backs onto another couple of similar units on an incline which then give way to the vast ocean view. I glance at Clarke, who has his arms crossed tightly against the cold, feeling bad for him. He'd given me his puffer jacket, after I'd given mine to Audrey last night at the station. He'd insisted despite my protests. I zip the black downy material up a little higher, so it covers my bare neck. With my bump protruding, I look like a giant letter P.

Nancy is sitting with her back to us, in a blue-and-white-striped deck chair. There's a sun-umbrella overhead, shading the spot where she sits looking out to the bay. Tasselled rugs are thrown across the wide slats of wood on the deck, which is covered in yet more plant pots that are bursting with purple daisies. A cup of something hot rests on a white plastic table to her right, an open book lies upside down on her lap. In such a cosy setting, it's easy to forget the horror of what we are here to discuss. She's tucked up tight with colourful blankets.

Clarke clears his throat to announce our presence.

'It's usually stormier in January,' she says by way of greeting, eyes fixed on the blue in the distance. 'We're lucky this year. Last year you couldn't even come out here until March.'

'You live here year-round?' Clarke inquires sweetly as we walk around to face her. Sometimes his private school upbringing has its advantages. I'm not sure my snarl produces such positive results with those I interview.

A low laugh, and Nancy turns.

'It's not so bad. You get to wake up to this every morning.'

She gestures, proudly displaying the arc of moody blues in front of her, the thinnest gossamer thread where sky met sea. I picture my apartment with the window looking out onto the neighbouring brick wall opposite in Dublin and figure she has the right idea, even if it is Currolough.

I know she's the same age as me and yet, as we lock eyes, it is impossible to tell how old Nancy is otherwise. Her face is scrubbed tight where she's suffered facial burns. A mottled appearance, the result of countless skin grafts and scar tissue distortion, which pulls one side of her right eye slightly downwards. Despite her disfigurement, you can tell she's beautiful. Her hair, dark and heavy under her hat, frames her small face and those brown eyes reach deep. Even under all the colourful material she's wrapped in, you can tell Nancy Wills is ballerina-slender, elegant and composed.

Nancy directs her gaze towards me, and I step closer to her, knowing her eyesight in one eye is quite poor.

'Nancy, we wanted to talk to you about the incident the other day over in Drumlish, at the market.'

She nods calmly. This isn't the crazed woman I'd been picturing since I'd been given this case. Another rap on the knuckle for judging too quickly. The woman in front of me seemed focused and assured – steely.

'I saw my son. That's what happened, Ms...'

'Detective Sergeant Fields. And this is Garda Detective Clarke Casey.'

She nods in brief acknowledgement.

'I saw my son, Detective Sergeant Fields. But everyone thinks I'm mad.'

'What makes you think it was your son?'

'Because he is identical to my other son Joey at that age.'

She smiles, looks at my stomach briefly.

'And because a mother always knows her own child. Your first?' she asks.

I nod, but I'm keen to keep the focus away from me. 'Less than three weeks to go,' I mutter, because that's what people expect – a line in the sand when it comes to the progress of human-growing. It's an obsession with some – but in this case, I understand it's more of a delicate situation. Her baby was only a few months older than my own bundle of cells when she lost him.

'Sleeping?' she asks.

'Not really.' I'm just being polite, but when I stop to think about it, I realise how tired I really am. It was five a.m. before I got to sleep again last night, tossing and turning over the twin anxieties of being back in Currolough and the emotional turmoil of my dilemma with Frank Nolan.

'Joey is what, eleven or twelve now, right?' I ask Nancy, trying to shake the exhaustion. At least my migraines are keeping their distance.

'Yes, he'll be twelve in June.'

'He's at school?'

She nods, but something's changed – something's crossed her face.

'Not here. Away. He lives with his father now.' Nancy tries to pull the blanket up higher to protect her from the cool breeze coming in off the sea. The sight of her hands is pitiful. Instinctively I step forward to help her but something in the way she looks at me stops me in my tracks. I recognise that look – the deep mistrust that stares back at me daily from my own bedroom mirror.

Tim arrives with steaming mugs and I take mine gratefully, glad of the distraction to gather my thoughts a moment. Ken Mulligan hadn't mentioned that Nancy's son Joey no longer lives with her. She was now without both her children – that had to sting. No wonder she needs her nightmares filtered out every night. It would take a million dreamcatchers to erase what she's been through. I watch Tim fuss over Nancy, tucking in her blanket and adjusting the shade to make sure she isn't in the direct sunlight. It's endearing, and for a moment, I feel a jolt of happiness that she isn't completely alone in the world, especially after all she's been through. Everyone needs comfort, everyone needs to know that just because the worst thing happened, doesn't mean the worst will always happen. Fatalistic, Sammy calls me.

'Can you tell me a little about what happened last Monday week?'

Both Clarke and I are perched on the wooden ledge of the deck, facing her, our backs to the ocean as Nancy starts to talk. Without being obvious, I try to sit close to Clarke so at least he has some warmth leaching into his skin. I may be a prickly bitch, but that doesn't mean I'm immune to small acts of kindness.

'As you know, Detective, I've always maintained that my baby son wasn't in the cot at the time of the fire that Christmas.' She glances out to sea, sadness etched across her face.

'But the fact is that nobody believed me – that his cot was empty. Not even my ex-husband. The Gardaí insisted that my baby died in the fire that night. I've never been able to prove otherwise because they didn't bother investigating properly.' She pauses to control her emotions. 'Now I finally might be able to prove my son was alive all this time.'

Clarke takes notes and Tim sits watching Nancy speak, ready to help her whenever she needs it. Selfishly, I think of Frank – how unavailable he is to me. For the twentieth time today, I wonder how the hell everything got so complicated with him. I'll give him another hour to call me back or else I'll have to ring him again.

I set my cup on the table and study Nancy as she speaks.

'Last Monday I was behind our stall at Drumlish Market.' Her hands fly up to her throat as she remembers. 'There was a boy playing in the little moving toy nearby. You know, one of those colourful rides that moves when you put a coin in. Like animals… or cartoon characters. They set them up during the markets.'

I imagine rows of dreamcatchers set out on a trestle table with a flimsy canopy overhead. I picture Nancy huddled in a folding chair and Tim pointing out the fine beading details to customers as they pass. I picture the tinkling sounds of a robotic carrousel horse in the distance.

Nancy continues, her agitation growing.

'I thought it was Joey at first, my older son. This boy's profile was so shockingly similar. I moved closer. I realised the boy was far too young. Then I saw, clear as day…'

Her eyes fill with tears. She bites her lip, trying to contain her distress.

'I saw that it was my Liam. The same Wills eyes, the exact curve of his mouth. I screamed, didn't I, Tim?'

'You did, love.' Tim nods, eyes closed, as if remembering back to the moment Nancy cried out. Reliving it alongside her. 'You gave me a desperate fright.' He sounds as if he could be from Yorkshire, or somewhere northern anyway.

'The first thing I did was to ask him his name,' Nancy continues, blinking away her emotion. 'But then a woman, his minder it must have been, came over and pulled him away. I'm used to shocking people, especially children, with how I look.'

She says this without self-pity, more of a statement of fact.

'But this was different. I begged her to let me speak to her – to speak to him. I was only giving them a €2 coin for the ride. Anything to make them stop for a moment. But she wouldn't listen. Nobody would listen. Then they called security. They just looked at me like I was some kind of monster – a stranger trying to harm Liam.'

She stifles a sob and my own throat aches. Damn hormones.

'The worst part...' she continues, her voice shaking, 'was that he, Liam, looked terrified.'

We pause as the woman in front of us gathers herself. It's uncomfortable how distressed she has become.

'There were reports that you were shouting and causing a scene,' I finally interrupt her sobbing gruffly, mostly to gauge her reaction, although I didn't doubt for a moment that it must be hell trying to live a normal life with such an abnormal appearance. I check my notes. 'The child's Brazilian au pair told police that you were trying to grab at the boy. That you were hysterical and wouldn't leave them alone. She says she was frightened for their safety.'

Tim goes to speak – to defend Nancy, presumably – but she puts a hand on his leg to stop him. She knows we are here to hear from her.

'I suppose she was scared,' she answers quietly. 'But I waited all this time, and then there he was – my perfect Liam. I needed to touch him. To hold him.' Her voice is low, almost a whisper. 'To make sure he was real.'

'I'm sure there are many children that might resemble your son – either of your sons. But I'm guessing this isn't the first time you think you saw your child in somebody? Don't you think grief might have a part to play?' I am deliberately delicate, but surely Nancy knows this is the crux of it – the fact that most people think she's out of her mind with grief and denial. That she's seeing what she wants to see.

Nancy tears her eyes away from the horizon and regards me coolly. Suddenly, there is nothing pitiful about those deep brown eyes.

'Imagine that child in your belly was ripped from you, taken away, in the blink of an eye. Then imagine people thought you were crazy for even suggesting it. Now imagine you looked the way I do.'

There's an edge I hadn't expected. Grief, yes. But also conviction. I take in the folds of her grafts, the faint cracked lines joining layers of good skin on top of bad. Even through the slight cloudiness in her right eye, I can see the indignation. You couldn't get through what she's been through and not be resilient.

'I've never ever reported that I found him before. Only that I was sure he was taken. I haven't seen him since he was asleep in his cot. Since that night...'

A sob starts and is swallowed. Whatever Nancy wants to say, it's clear she doesn't want pity. I respect her need to control the uncontrollable. I also don't doubt that Nancy Wills believes wholeheartedly that the child in Drumlish was her youngest son. Could a mother always know her own child? I suppose in a few weeks I might be able to answer that question for myself. But for now, I have to rely solely on evidence to find the truth.

Nancy sits forward.

'I see what you see.' Her body trembles as she talks. 'But let me tell you this, Detective Fields. I am far from the mad woman this town makes me out to be. Let's just say it's a bit too convenient. I've been the target of all their ills for too many years.'

Tim is on his feet once more, soothing Nancy who is now very upset. She pushes him away, not unkindly, but there are tears running down her cheeks as she speaks, her chest rising and falling with the effort of trying to explain.

'I thought about getting a few of his hairs for a DNA test. Then I'd know for sure. Then I could prove it.' She's talking quickly now, fraught with the panic of what she should have done.

'Obtaining DNA illegally isn't something you can do,' I say, chilled at the prospect of a stranger grabbing a fistful of a child's hair as he played in a playground. We have to handle this with extra sensitivity.

'Could you show us the picture you have of Joey as a child so we can compare it, please?' Clarke turns the emotional moment into something a little more concrete. His timing is spot on. Nancy slumps back into her chair – distant, as if a light has gone out. Tim gets up to fetch the photograph and takes our empty cups with him. We smile our polite thanks.

'What do you mean by convenient?' I ask suddenly, thinking of the unusual choice of words. 'You said, it was convenient that people thought you were… not right.'

'People know more than they are saying,' Nancy says. 'There's been a wall of whispers built around what happened that night for years. It's easier to side-line you if you don't seem to belong in the first place.'

I think of how true this has been my whole life. It's clear Nancy is exhausted from remembering. Ken Mulligan warned us that the scarring in Nancy's lungs has left her at a permanently low ebb and that she tires easily.

'There was some kind of cover-up. There must have been,' she whispers. 'They didn't find a single trace of him. My son didn't die that night. A mother knows.'

The wooden decking shifts slightly underfoot and Tim arrives back with a framed photograph of a boy in a blue school uniform. It's one of those first-day-of-school pictures. He's small and blond, a tuft of feathery curls, dark brown eyes – Nancy's eyes – and the uncertain smile halfway between being polite and being overwhelmed with nerves.

'This is your eldest son Joey?' I ask gently.

She nods, smiles, but you can tell her heart is breaking as she studies it.

'He's five in that picture. It's just before… It's the only one we have before… you know. Everything else was destroyed in the fire – every picture, every document. His school gave us this afterwards. It was his first day at St Killian's. He cried the whole way there.' She traces her stiff clumped hand over the glass lovingly. 'As soon as we got to the gate, I had to peel his little fingers off mine and hand him over to the teacher. I'll never forget that moment. He needed me so much.'

She wipes a tear away.

'I needed him…'

I think about all the moments she's studied this picture – imagined what her other son, baby Liam, might have become. My throat constricts with emotion – the idea of all that unfulfilled potential in her baby, all those glorious future experiences going up in flames. One moment that changed her entire world. I shake my head to dislodge the emotion that threatens to spill out into this moment.

'So, you are saying that the child you saw in Drumlish was extremely similar to Joey? And you believe it was Joey's little brother that you saw?' Clarke steps in with a classic detective move, acting slow on the uptake. It's clever. Smart cop, dumb cop. I throw him a glance to show I've noticed. It has the added benefit of allowing me to collect myself a little. I blink my tears away and try not to think of small warm fingers zigzagged through a mother's hand. The epitome of safety, or the illusion of it at least.

'Yes, the boy in Drumlish was a little older – about six or so, which would work out perfectly in terms of Liam's age.'

'Do you mind if we take this?' I venture, and Nancy nods, as if she expected this. 'We will take very good care of it for you.' I take the framed picture carefully from the mother's hands and slide it into my leather bag.

'Did you recognise the woman with the child?' Clarke asks now, all baby-faced innocence with his crisp posh accent.

She shakes her head. The wind has started to pick up now; wind-chimes tinkle beside us. I steal a glance at my phone again, hating that I constantly feel as if I'm the one chasing Frank.

'I talked with a reporter again yesterday – Cynthia Shields,' she says apologetically. 'From *Southern Sound*.'

I nod. 'We spoke to her too,' I tell her. 'About Gerald Barrows.'

I'm watching Nancy's face very carefully for a reaction. Clarke's fountain pen stops writing his neat, sloped sentences and hovers in the air a moment.

'Gerald?' She answers too quickly. 'Why are you speaking to Gerald?'

'The boy you saw, that you claim is your Liam… We believe his father is Garda Gerald Barrows, originally stationed here at Currolough.'

Nancy leans forward. She gasps and then gags as if she may throw up. Genuine shock washes over her. Her face drains of colour.

'It was Gerald?' she whispers, her hands up at her head as if sheltering herself from the impact of the news we've brought. 'Gerald took him?' Tears run down her face, but she ignores them. 'I knew he was angry at me. But... wait...' Nancy stammers, almost speechless at what she's just discovered. She looks from Clarke back to me. I hold her gaze.

'We've only your word to go on for now,' I say bluntly. 'We obviously can't jump to any conclusions.'

'Are you going to speak to him?'

'We believe there is enough of a reason to speak with him. There's another case we want to discuss with him too.'

But she's distracted. Her demeanour has shifted dramatically. Her hands twitch under the blanket – the book slips from her lap. Clarke stoops to retrieve it.

'I knew he was alive,' she whispers. 'My baby Liam.'

The sea pitches and rolls behind us, choppier now. But it's Tim's face I'm watching, and the look of horror he turned to hide when we mentioned Gerald's name.

–

'What do you think?' Clarke asks as soon as we get into the car, which is parked diagonally next to the wooden dividers that separate their mobile home from the rest. Tim waves from the blue door – his smile a little thinner – Clarke's card in his hand in case they need to get in touch.

'More questions than answers,' I respond. I glide my seatbelt over my stomach gracelessly. It clicks and I start the car, stuffing the small dreamcatcher Nancy insisted I take with me into the driver's door pocket. 'Was it just me, or did she seem frightened to you?'

'No,' he admits. 'But Tim did.'

Outside, grains of sand gather and swirl in the wind. A sheep on the grass verge eyeballs us mournfully as we turn out onto the road, the indicator flashing, leaving Sullivan's Caravan Park behind. Next stop: the address we've been given for Gerald Barrows.

Twelve

An hour later, we pass a large retail park advertising sofas and cut-price dining tables huddled next to a flowerless roundabout. It welcomes us to the outskirts of our next destination. Drumlish is a small, touristy town which borders the Lakelands National Park. People come for the walking trails through the forested area that backs onto the far side of Lake Lagan. The main street is all hiking outlets and tearooms. Neither Clarke nor I speak as we drive. The heat in the Discovery is turned up full blast.

'The husband,' I say eventually, following the highlighted route on the map my satnav is showing me, and Clarke goes to speak at the exact same time.

'Jinx,' he laughs, and I look away, embarrassed.

'I was also going to ask what the deal is with Hugh Wills – Nancy's ex-husband,' Clarke explains. 'It's pretty strange that we've heard nothing about him. And why is their son Joey living with him?' We drive through Drumlish. The map tells us that Barrows's address is eight minutes from here. The landscape changes once more and, instead of crumbling stone walls and bracken, we are in stud farm territory – all symmetrical wooden fences and high gates with fancy name plaques. 'From what I understand after reading the report, it was Hugh Wills that admitted leaving the faulty heater plugged in even though he acknowledged there was a problem with it. But was that oversight or something more?' Clarke says, looking out of the window.

'I was wondering about that too,' I admit. That was something I should have pressed Nancy on, but the plan was to return to talk to her again once we'd seen the boy from the market. 'No harm having a bit of info on the husband before we approach her about it.'

'Yes, I mean *he's* not here accusing the Gardaí of having taken his youngest son. Why not? Why was it just Nancy that believed he was taken from them?'

I drum my fingers on the wheel, noticing the nails are bitten to the quick. There's something else that has been niggling at me too. Why didn't they find any trace of the baby at the house after the fire? It would have had to burn at such an intense heat, and there was nothing in the report about any accelerant. It didn't add up. Then again, not bothering to get appropriate forensics teams in might have had something to do it.

'Good work back there with Nancy, by the way,' I mutter to Clarke.

I'm having a hard time distinguishing between what Nancy wants to believe, and what the truth of the matter is. For her sake, I want this kid to turn out to be hers. But why would someone take a baby and make it look like there was a tragic accident. *Who* would do that?

'You think she knows Audrey Jones?' Clarke wonders, still looking out of the window at the glistening road, the blur of yellow bungalows, piebald horses in barbed-wire clad fields.

'I'm not sure. We should probably have asked her that too. But let's see what Garda Barrows has to say.'

—

Garda Gerald Barrows isn't happy to see Clarke and I standing at his front door a few minutes later, IDs outstretched, shielding ourselves against the onslaught of sudden icy rain.

Island weather. He expresses his displeasure as he swings open the door to his impressive home, a few miles outside Drumlish. Haycote Manor has a long tree-lined drive surrounded by fields strewn with show-jumping materials. Barrows has done well for himself on a copper's salary. I couldn't afford a dog, let alone a horse, and I'm ranked a few pay grades higher than him.

We had driven slowly up towards the stone-fronted house, surprised by the open wrought-iron gates. There were two newish-looking cars, one with a boat balancing on the back of a trailer, and next to the house was a second building that was probably a stable that ran to the left of the manor. Pink ivy hung down from the roof like unruly hair, gathering in shaggy clusters above the windows and spilling into the large gable over the front door. The overall effect was immediately intimidating.

Gerald Barrows throws open the door and glares at us. The Garda is a meaty man with a low centre of gravity, receding black hair, the red-rimmed eyes of someone who doesn't mind a drink or two. The first thing that hits me is that he seems too old to have a seven-year-old child. Then again, I glance down at my own belly and remind myself to only make assumptions based on actual evidence. He doesn't invite us in. The rain is coming at us sideways.

'You will have to correspond with my solicitor,' he interrupts as I explain why we have come. 'I'm sorry but I won't be speaking to anyone on the advice of my legal representative.'

He closes his eyes as he speaks – the universal sign of someone riddled with their own self-importance. But there's a tightness to his voice that I recognise as fear.

'Do you mind if we come in, Garda Barrows?' I ask in my most approachable and pragmatic voice, indicating the torrential rain. He hesitates, glances quickly over his shoulder.

'I don't think it's a good idea.'

'We only need a few minutes of your time,' I push. 'And we've come all this way.'

Finally, he relents.

Haycote Manor has been tastefully decorated as if preparing for a magazine shoot in *Home and Country*. There's a welcome table in the expansive hallway with fresh flowers, the house smells like furniture polish, and the art on the walls looks expensive. To one side is the door to a boot room with umbrellas, spotless Hunter wellingtons neatly lined up, sports bags scattered on the bespoke wooden seating. I hang Clarke's soaking wet jacket on one of the available hooks as directed by Barrows. Coatless, drowned-dog Clarke closes the heavy front door behind us.

'Beautiful home,' I murmur, shaking the rain from my hair, as we follow Barrows through glass doors into an astonishingly large kitchen with a conservatory overlooking the patioed garden. I take in the Aga, the fridge with childish paintings, a white board with sports timetable – *Rugby 4pm, remember gumshield!* is one entry beside Mondays. *Friday is Pizza night!* Family photographs balance in silver frames on a polished mahogany table. There's a child with a pair of sunglasses in one, a picture of figures riding horses grinning to camera, another shows Gerald Barrows holding up a trophy next to a sailboat. I take everything in.

'Tea?' Barrows asks reluctantly, and Clarke smiles his affirmation.

I wiggle myself onto a tall stool by the marble island and watch Gerald Barrows in his natural environment. He's wearing a creased Kerry GAA football jersey and grubby sweatpants. He obviously wasn't expecting company. The cream and grey kitchen is still strewn with breakfast items, though it's edging on lunchtime. There are half-cooked eggs in a pan on the Aga, and the smell of bacon is overpowering.

'Don't let us disturb you,' I say, gesturing towards the Aga. He dismisses it with a flick of his hand. There's a thump from upstairs and he winces involuntarily. His demeanour is cagey.

'Can you tell us a little about what happened at Bayview apartments in Currolough on Monday evening?' I ask, pulling out my pen. The rain is pelting heavily against the glass rooflight above the kitchen island. 'You know the Jones family, don't you?'

He glowers at me a moment. Then nods.

'Yes.'

The atmosphere in the room changes.

'And you were over there the other night, Garda, weren't you? The night of the fire?' I'm aware Clarke's leaning forward. I continue to eyeball the Garda who looks as if he hasn't slept in days. 'You were first on the scene.'

There is a pause.

'Not exactly,' Barrows says sharply. I exhale, try to relax the muscles in my shoulders. 'I told you that you'd have to speak to my solicitor.' He sloshes the hot water into the mug. Another thump from upstairs. This time both Clarke and I glance up. Impossible not to really.

With a hand that shakes slightly, Barrows places the tea in front of Clarke. I accept a glass of tap water. I've reached my caffeine allowance for the day. The eggs are congealing in the pan. The white of them is glazed and rubbery, the oil yellowing around it. The familiar wave of nausea rises, and I breathe deeply, closing my eyes for a moment. Wouldn't do to throw up all over Gerald Barrows's parquet floors.

'I see. But you admit you know Audrey Jones?'

Another reluctant nod.

'There were problems,' he says. 'Within the marriage. I was only trying to help.'

'She felt harassed,' I tell him. 'A neighbour has given a statement saying you were repeatedly ringing on their doorbell.'

He sighs. 'I was afraid she was in trouble. I went to help.'

A blast of heartburn bubbles in my chest. Barrows is doing that thing where he closes his eyes when he talks.

'What kind of trouble? Why wouldn't you report it?'

Another sigh. Barrows was making it very clear that we were a major inconvenience in his day.

'It was a favour for a friend who was worried about Audrey. I said I'd look into the situation. So, I did. Turns out she didn't want my help at all. And now here we are...'

'And where were you when the fire started?' Clarke inquires sweetly from where he's perched on a stool.

Barrows hands grip the kettle he's still holding a little tighter.

'I'd just left the apartment after knocking. I was on my way home. Then the call about the fire came through on the radio from a neighbour. I keep one in my own car, you see. I called my station. I went straight back.' He shrugs as if we are the morons. 'Listen, you've got this all wrong.'

'So, you turned up first on the scene even though you were off on sick leave?' Clarke's voice has an edge.

'I am a Garda,' he says, smiling tightly. 'I can't just ignore things because I'm off the clock.'

To one side of the Aga, there's a digital photo frame stuck to the wall. Family photos on a slideshow effect play out, more pictures of Gerald, at a distance, with a pretty woman, and boy in a Hawaiian shirt. The picture changes, and there's a field with horses, a mother and child wearing hats, waving. The cheesy family photographs I never had growing up, but plan to create with this baby. What fickle creatures us humans are, I think, suddenly. How *parochial*.

'You have any children?' I ask changing tack.

'A son,' he answers stiffly, hands on hips. But his knee is jigging continuously, as if he's in a hurry, distracted.

'And something happened to him a week ago... at the market?'

His knee jigs faster.

'All I know is that Anna… that's our minder. She said a woman was grabbing at Dexter, pulling at his face and his hair. She was petrified. Dex was too.' Gerald presses his lips together. Sweat gathers on his upper lip.

'Do you know the woman? Do you know Nancy Wills personally?' I ask.

Another shake of his head. A hand across his eyes as if he's hungover, or tired. Me too, buddy, me too, I want to say.

'Did you ever have any contact with her in any other capacity?' Clarke persists.

Someone bounds down the stairs – you can tell it's two or three at a time. A final thump as the child lands at the bottom. You can almost feel the vibration throughout the house. It's a sound I haven't heard in many years. The sound of a burst of energy – childish enthusiasm – a game in everything.

'Dad, are the eggs ready?' a little voice calls. Gerald stiffens.

The door pushes open and the little boy bounces in. He's still wearing pyjamas, his blond curls a tangled mess. Dark brown eyes regard us in surprise.

'Hi. You must be Dexter,' Clarke says, smiling without missing a beat. He stands up to shake the boy's hand.

The boy looks at his dad, who nods almost imperceptibly. Instinctively I stay silent. The atmosphere in the room is charged – every word vitally important. I focus on absorbing as much of it as possible. I realised even as early as a week into my detective rookie-ship that instinct was everything. Sometimes saying and doing nothing are just as important as taking statements. Right now, I'm wondering what the hell this family's doing hiding out at home at midday on a weekday. Something is definitely not right with this scene.

'Love The Avengers,' Clarke is saying, gesturing to the characters printed on the boy's nightwear. 'Seen *Endgame*?'

'Dad won't let me,' the boy says shyly, his eyes down.

'Day off school?' Clarke continues. But Barrows quickly interrupts.

'Go on up, I'll be there in a moment, Dex. My friends are just about to leave.'

'Dad says I don't have to go to school this week,' Dexter shows off to his new pal Clarke, who mouths a hyperbolic wow. He's so good with him.

'Where's school?' I ask quickly.

'Dominic's Academy,' he obliges. I've heard of it, one of the most prestigious in the country, but I thought it was a boarding school.

'Dexter,' Gerald barks sharply. 'Upstairs.'

The little boy looks disappointed. 'Bye buddy,' Clarke tells him, and the child turns and pads out of the kitchen slowly. Once the door is closed behind him, I turn to face the Garda.

'I understand this may be difficult, but we wanted to see if you would be willing to give permission for a DNA test on Dexter.' I hold up my hand as he starts to speak. 'I realise there is no other reason to think this is anything other than a case of mistaken identity, but it would be very useful to ensure this matter is laid to rest definitively. To let everyone get on with their lives, you see.'

Gerald's face says it all.

'Absolutely not. That case hasn't been reopened. I've produced his birth cert to my solicitor which you will receive in due course. Nobody is touching one hair on my child's head.' He is angry now, unco-operative. 'You'd be better off arresting Nancy Wills for accosting my family.' He's rapping the marbling in the countertop with his knuckles.

'Why isn't Dexter at school?' Clarke pushes.

A pause. I try not to think of the eggs sitting in the pan growing even more rubbery. But Barrows has had enough of us.

'I'll have to ask you to leave,' he says finally. 'We won't be agreeing to a DNA test under any circumstances. This is highly unusual and I'm afraid if Nancy Wills approaches me or my family again, I will have to take things further. She's been delusional for years.' He turns to me suddenly – the look of desperation in his eyes. But was it an act? 'I'm scared, you know. That's why Dexter isn't in school, Detective. We are up the walls with worry she'll attack him again. Or worse. We have barely left the house since Dexter was almost snatched at the market.' He stands and gestures to the door again.

'Except to repeatedly call into Audrey Jones's flat.'

He glares at Clarke.

'As I've said numerous times to you both, you can take up anything else you need with my solicitor.'

'Is your wife available for a quick word?' I incline my head towards the stairs.

'Absolutely not.' He's almost spitting at me, anger replacing the earlier nervousness.

Then, composing himself with obvious effort, he shakes his head a little more respectfully.

'My partner's not here, I'm afraid.'

I'm not so sure he's telling us the truth.

'You never answered my question.' Clarke isn't letting this go either – both of us aware that there won't be another chance to gauge reactions once this goes properly legal. 'About whether you had any contact yourself personally with Nancy Wills, or the Wills family in any capacity?'

Gerald is leading us across the hallway towards the front door. I retrieve my coat, stepping over sports bags and hockey sticks as I pick my way out of the boot room. His back is to us as he answers. But his words when they come are jerky, self-conscious.

'Only back then – you know.' He shrugs, like what he is saying isn't at all important. He trails off. Clarke glances at me quickly. We silence bomb Gerald. 'She was the cleaner at the station. We were… we became friends,' he says, after a minute, holding the door open and standing to one side.

'I thought you said you didn't know her?'

'It's… complicated.' He sighs. 'I was in school with her and her sister years back. I meant I didn't know her since we were just kids. Then she started working in the station…' He's rambling, speaking quickly, falling over his words – usually a sign someone is afraid of revealing too much.

'With all due respect, Garda Barrows,' I say, pulling myself up as tall as possible. 'We are talking about a child who potentially perished in a fire and a serious accusation of kidnap, and now you've been placed at the scene of another fire in which a person lost their life. You can't afford to blur the details here.' His eyes widen slightly. He knows all this, but sometimes a stark reminder of what's at stake can help focus the mind.

'Where were you the night of the Christmas fire which took place at Nancy Wills's house six years ago?' Clarke asks, turning to Gerald Barrows on the doorstep.

'I was there,' he says quietly. 'Along with the other investigating officers. It was one of the worst nights of my life.'

There is something in the way he speaks that feels very genuine. I couldn't imagine seeing what he probably saw – no matter the outcome. The baby rolls over inside me and I rub my belly through the stiff material of my blazer. *Lunch soon, little one, I promise.*

'No further comment.' He's back to stonewalling.

Every question after that, he responds with the same statement.

'No comment.' Another shake of his head. 'I'll have to ask you to leave.'

But his heart doesn't seem in it. And as we walk towards the car, Gerald Barrows goes to say something, but then stops abruptly.

'What was that?' I turn and see him, head down, scuffing the ground with his feet. I walk quickly back towards him, my feet crunching on the sodden gravel. 'Garda Barrows, is there something else you want to say?' His red-rimmed eyes make him look like he's been up all night. And I should know. 'Please Gerald,' I implore. 'We need to get to the bottom of all of this, for your sake too.'

Something seems to soften.

'She's not that well,' he whispers, his face distorting into something... pain? Or perhaps reluctance. Swivelling to look at Clarke, I step forward to make sure I understand what this man is trying to tell us.

'Nancy was known around Currolough for having problems back then,' he continues, his eyes still avoiding mine. 'She had, eh... trouble after the first boy was born.'

'You knew her well enough to know that? Back then?'

'I did,' he says quietly.

Clarke and I deliberately let the pause lengthen.

'She used to talk to me about it while she worked,' he admits. 'That's it.'

Barrows makes to close the door, but I hold my hand against the frame to prevent him – not forcefully, but what I'd probably call assertively, should we ever end up in court.

'Why do you think *she* thinks Dexter is her son?'

From upstairs, a woman's voice calls Gerald's name. The nanny or his partner, I wonder suddenly? It's all the signal Gerald needs to stop talking.

'Speak to my solicitor,' he says quickly, and takes another step back into the house. 'Do you mind?' He gestures towards my hand on his doorway, and I withdraw my fingers reluctantly.

I make one final appeal.

'If you are so sure about Dexter, why won't you do the DNA test?' But the door is almost closed now.

'I want nothing to do with this any more. If you want something further, speak to Hugh Wills,' he says. 'He was her husband, after all.'

There's something about the way he says Hugh's name. Barrows gives me one final glare and I remove my fingers.

'But if you ask me, everyone should leave the past in the past.'

We do gain one small victory from the conversation. He has agreed to come down to the station to give a statement about the Bayview apartments, albeit reluctantly and despite his stress leave.

Then the wooden door of Haycote Manor bangs firmly shut and all that's left is the shuffling sound of retreating footsteps. We haven't achieved much, but one thing struck me. Dexter Barrows did look similar to the other Wills boy that Nancy had shown us. And Gerald Barrows admitted he'd been there the night of both fires.

He was one of the first to show up at both scenes.

I may have imagined it, but as we walk towards the car, I feel eyes on me. Turning quickly, I look up at the stone façade of the house. Is that the hint of movement in one of the upstairs rooms – the swish of a curtain, perhaps?

Or maybe just a trick of the light.

Thirteen

It's after three thirty by the time I drop Clarke back to Sunny Hill Bed and Breakfast. I send Frank a quick text on his work phone telling him we'll have to stay down for another night or two at the very least, and that we'll possibly need to move forward with a court-ordered DNA test. *Interesting developments*. I explain. *Free now if you want to call*. I immediately regret sending it. Surely, he should have called by now anyway. The first physical pages from the original fire report have finally been sent to Ken Mulligan at Currolough. He was in the process of emailing them to us, one painstaking page at a time.

My phone beeps. My stomach flips.

It's Frank.

Ok, will speak to Terry in legal. Sorry about earlier.

Me and baby miss you, I text quickly back. He sees it but immediately goes offline. This definitely warrants a long discussion with Sammy. It's too hard not to blur the personal with the professional. Meshing the two clearly isn't healthy.

With a pain in the pit of my stomach, I leave Clarke to set up interviews with Nancy's ex-husband, Hugh Wills, and Tori Jones, the little girl from the Bayview apartments. The answers we're seeking most likely lie somewhere in the links between both tragedies.

Gerald told us pointedly, almost resentfully, when we were leaving Haycote Manor, to focus on Hugh Wills's side of things, but it was hard to tell if he was trying to distract us or to help us.

Sighing heavily, I reverse the car out of the driveway of the small guesthouse. There are a million things I'd prefer to do right now rather than climb back into my Discovery this evening and point it towards Lake Lagan.

I think back to the dizzy spell I had had leaving Haycote Manor, after Gerald Barrows had closed the front door. Everything had started edging on black as I'd looked up at the window, at the moving curtain. I told Clarke I was fine but he insisted on driving and, suddenly, I didn't have the energy to fight against all his fussing, so I tossed him the keys and agreed to stop along the way back to eat something. The sauce from the service-station Caesar salad was gloopy and artificial, but I took the package from him gratefully and ate it under his watchful eye as he drove us back to the guesthouse.

'Why'd you leave law?' I asked conversationally between bites of stringy romaine. 'Wasn't for the money, anyway.' I laughed, flipping the vanity mirror and fishing for a green bit trapped in my tooth. Clarke drove slowly, carefully. Another car overtook us. I noticed him glancing over at me, concern written across his face. I waved him off. 'I'm fine now,' I assured him gruffly. 'Probably just needed to eat something.' I wasn't about to let my rookie see me so vulnerable, so I ignored the light-headedness and shifted myself up a little higher in the passenger seat.

'Do you really want to know why I left law?' He sounded surprised, his upper-class accent lifting at the end of his sentence, the perfect t's emphasised at the end of each word. His hair was unusually fine and shiny for a man. From the side profile his Adam's apple was pronounced, like a teenager's, and his eyelashes were spiky compared to the smooth skin of his cheeks.

'Sure.' I scraped the bottom of the plastic bowl with my wooden fork, leaving streak marks in the dregs of dressing.

'I was disillusioned at the lack of power I found I wielded, even as a lawyer.' He glanced over, flashing his dimples. 'That, and the justice system let me down.'

He said it lightly – but I could tell it was anything but.

'Were you in trouble or something?' No way could Clarke Casey have had conflict with the law. Impossible – this was the man that apologised for stooping to tie his own shoelaces the other day because we were late.

'My wife was,' he said quietly, and rolled down his window. The air in the car was sucked out somehow.

'I didn't know you're married,' I said. 'I mean, I presumed...'

'Never presume anything,' he teased, wagging his finger mockingly, reminding me of the mantra I'd been pushing down his neck for the past few weeks. 'I *was* married,' he added, a little sadly, and then there was silence. It was clear that conversation was over — I could almost hear the line being drawn below that particular exchange.

'The system pisses me off sometimes too,' I said instead, and pulled something small out of my leather bag, displaying it to Clarke.

Clarke actually gasped. And I tried not to laugh.

'You didn't. Oh my gosh.' He shook his head.

'Don't worry, Saint Clarke, it's for our eyes only.' I smiled. Snapping Dexter's gumshield box closed, I stuffed it back into my bag. 'The results will be just for us, and it's obviously not admissible in any court. But I had to know.'

How could I not? It had been lying there beside the sports bags labelled Dexter T Barrows as I'd grabbed my coat when we were leaving Gerald's house. My methods are not always orthodox, Clarke would have known that if he'd worked with me long enough. By my logic, this was potentially a child kidnap case. If I was right, I knew Barrows could spend years tying us in knots in court, especially if his solicitor was good. At least this way, we'd know if we were sniffing down the right rabbit hole. I'd send it express to my buddy Billy in tech who owed me a favour or two. Off the record. He'd get the results in super-quick time. Gerald's biology would have to be on the central database from when he signed on initially as a cop.

Then we'd arrived back at Currolough, pulling up outside Sunny Hill Guesthouse.

–

Clarke gives me a small wave as I drive away.

Though I'm feeling better after eating, calling in to Aunt Roe is the last thing I want to do. But it's time to iron out the past. The next step will hopefully shape what my future looks like.

Shadows drift, and silvery-fine clouds press the sky downwards as I drive towards the lake after a trip to Currolough post office to send off the gumshield. I grew up admiring this lake's soupy sheen — the backdrop to my wild Kerry childhood. I remember standing by the woods, Brendan, Sammy and I, squinting at the mountain-cloud reflections on the lake and trying to come up with shapes and stories about the things that coiled and lurked beneath. We had a rowboat we took out sometimes. Not far, just to the other side and back – over to the *Denibulin* – one of the hills tourists refer to as mountains that make up the five peaks that surround this desolation. Beyond the lake is even wilder, as the sea air hits, beige landscapes, bruise-coloured stones and scrubby orange weeds occupied only by the most sure-footed of sheep and bravest locals. Ours was the last house in the wood before the car park where boats launched in from the banks, a lopsided keel, as if heaving drunk as they splash-landed.

We conjured up sea-creatures so weird and wonderful they were almost real. Then, at night, we'd scare Brendan, reminding him in the darkness about the swishing tails, the serpents' scales, the pull of their hundreds of tentacles as they dragged their prey slowly under. He'd reach for my hand in the dark – and fall asleep holding it.

I roll down the window and the damp evening air chills my cheeks. I allow myself to remember – to let a crack of light in through the careful walls I built. It wasn't easy being from a family whose light once shone bright and then was slowly extinguished. That change in energy bonded us – Sammy, Brendan and me. It certainly toughened us up, knowing our home could flit from light to shadow like the surface of the lake as the clouds passed overhead. But maybe that was just how my character formed. Brendan was more likely to use his fists to vent his feelings. Sammy, the quietest of us all, sailed through school like the brown-speckled signets we watched grow into swans, those frantic legs never stopping to think, never stopping to absorb the hurtful things all children say about our mother's unbrushed hair, our empty lunchboxes. We felt different. Even unloved sometimes, as she got worse. I always felt one beat out of step with everyone else when she went through her down days. It was made worse having her warmth and then losing it. The cold felt all the more acute. But it was other people's parents that I still cannot forgive. 'How's your poor mother?' Ms Peterson would say, when Father finally noticed there wasn't much in the fridge during one of Mother's bad weeks and sent us for milk. Emphasis on the poor. A pitiful tilt of her head.

We were helpless to do anything about it. Powerless against the beast that had dragged our own mother under and held her there, just beneath the surface, just beyond her will.

Just beyond us.

–

It's an amazingly still evening. Lake Lagan masquerades as peaceful. But there's a roar in its belly during the storms that curl in from the Atlantic. Even when there isn't a hint of wind in the air, the hungry current and silty dips are always there – waiting, biding their time. This deceitful water: it took everything from me. It swallowed me whole.

I take the once-familiar turn into the woods for Roe's house. A *Forest Protection Area* sign illuminates in my headlights and I bump further into the trees as the road narrows, trying to avoid the worst of the potholes. Roe has lived here alone since we left. Some people let tragedy dictate the rest of their lives; others want to pretend it never happened at all. Roe is one of those who lives her life as if her sister had never walked into the lake without looking back, twenty feet from her back door.

Roe had forgiven me for leaving the minute I could, but I'd never forgiven her for staying – for allowing that trauma to cling to me by her very desire to remain in that house. She was stoking the embers of a fire that should have burnt out twenty years ago. I know that even just seeing her face will bring everything back.

But I also know it's time.

Steeling myself, I turn the Discovery into the drive of the small white house perched at the lake's edge. Night has almost fallen when I step out onto the muddy driveway. Birds frantically call out, hawking a final desperate cry before day fades. I slam my car door, noticing the yellow light streaming from the back kitchen window.

It's impossible not to look up – the trees all around here are tall and bare – like the sides of a telescope with the pinprick freckle of stars at the end. I hold out my hand to steady myself against the car roof, staring skywards still.

The memories are disorientating – all those nights lying on the old trampoline pointing out Orion's Belt, the Plough, and my favourite constellation – Cassiopeia. I can almost feel Sammy's cold bare arm next to mine, her flesh pressed against me, a comfort against those long ebony nights. Brendan would be on the other side, his fingers entwined in mine, pretending he was brave but anything but. He was ten and still wet the bed. A tough guy, the prankster, but still such a little boy underneath it all. Grow up, we'd tease. But he never did. I take a deep breath and try to stop the tears spilling down my cheeks. The side door opens hesitantly. And the bent silhouette of a woman leans out into the night.

Fourteen

'Roe. Rosemary. It's me. Ally.' I wipe my eyes on the stiff sleeve of Clarke's black puffer jacket.

'Jesus Christ, child. You gave me an almighty fright. Come in, come in.' Her breath puffs against the freezing night like fragmented speech bubbles.

Roe bundles me into the warm kitchen, hugging and pawing at me, taking my coat. Condensation fogs the windows. A pang of familiarity hits. The crab-shaped chunk on the wall where plaster had come off is still there, the soup mugs dangle dustily from the dresser, the chokey-rope smell of turf and burnt dirt lingers.

I love it.

I hate it.

I think of the pale blue bedroom at the back of the bungalow – the bunkbeds with stickers and scrapes, the familiar smell of family. 'You'll stay,' Roe gently commands.

I'm home.

Then Roe's gesturing at my stomach. She's standing by the kettle, joy written all across her craggy face, more lined and tilted now since I saw her three years ago in Dublin at Christmas. Roe never married; she lives alone with her Jack Russell, Bud, and works part-time at the charity clothes shop in Currolough. I picture her often, replacing discarded dresses on the hangers, handing garments through chinks in the curtains in the small changing room at the back, the twitch of a smile always on her lips, folding – a master at arranging order from chaos.

I should be more like Roe, I think, as I blow on my tea and tell her that it's not long now until the baby's due.

'How's work?' she asks – a safer question than the one she asked about the baby's dad.

'All good,' I reply and, once the pleasantries are over, Roe being Roe, switches gear.

'I suppose you'll be wanting some of the baby clothes for... this one.' She waves her blue-veined hands towards my tummy again. 'It's all in the attic, but I can't go up with my knees.'

It hadn't crossed my mind there would be anything left of our life here. The moment we finished school, I left this place behind. Once in Waterford, I worked in the local chipper to save for Garda training college. Naturally, Sammy came with me to that dingy flat above it. Uncomfortable as it was, it was a safe distance from the lake, from Currolough, from the confrontation of the memories every single day.

I never went home.

Roe came to my Garda graduation day – her carefully chosen navy dress from the shop matched my new uniform. She waved shyly from the back and told me she was proud. I nodded from the podium, trying not to cry.

We finish our tea and I tell Roe why I'm here. She has opinions on everything. The whole town does, apparently. I learn that the townspeople never wanted the Bayview apartments built in the first place, because it's brought in 'an element', meaning undesirable outsiders. Roe's words, not mine.

She tells me that the structure was thrown up, a cheap job, and that no wonder it went up in flames. More protection from a cardboard box, she mutters. No sense of community any more, she continues wistfully, nostalgic for a feeling I've never known around these parts. Small villages are funny like that sometimes – either you are in, or you are out. And if you were once in and then fell out by design of your status or your behaviour, there's slim chance of ever making your way back into that inner circle. All I know is the horrible feeling of being ostracised as a young girl and never understanding why. Only now, I can appreciate that there was a fear back then, a dark cloud that hung over mental health problems. But that same shame the villagers cast on my mother extended to her three children. It drove my father away. The pain that such whispers caused in my childhood still makes me pull up my drawbridge as an adult. It's lonely in here by myself. Safe, but very lonely.

Aunt Roe shakes her head a little sadly when I bring up the Wills family.

'That Nancy was never right again,' she says sadly, brushing a crumb from her skirt. 'None of my business, but there was always something up with that family.'

'Before the fire?'

She nods and takes a bite of her buttered scone.

'Nancy Wills was never the maternal type,' she says, using her fingers to sweep the fallen crumbs into a small pile on the wooden table. 'And may God forgive me for saying it about someone who's gone through so much, but the husband – he was never there either. People talked, you know.'

I do know.

Roe admits she knows little else other than fifth-hand rumours about Nancy. 'Broken-hearted,' she mutters. 'Then going on like that, about the child being stolen. It was so sad. She lost everything that night.'

That's what Clarke said too. I wonder how he's getting on trying to contact Nancy's sister Vera, and Nancy's ex-husband Hugh. I consider checking my phone again, but there is something that lulls me fixed to this spot on the good chair at this kitchen table, being fussed over by Roe. Little Ally, she calls me, even though I'm two heads above her and three times as wide. 'My little Ally bird, let's get those feet up.'

But I need to do something first.

By the time I'd dragged myself precariously up the spindly steps of the stepladder and rooted around on all fours, I was completely and utterly exhausted. But the discovery was worth it. I drop down a heavy box onto a pillow in the hallway that Roe has left out, trying to ignore the sharp twinges on my right side – the baby doing cartwheels probably. It takes half an hour and a bowl of homemade vegetable soup with heavily buttered toast before I gather the energy – both physically and emotionally – to lift the lid of the weathered cardboard box, now in front of me on the living room floor. My back warm from the fire, I slowly reach inside.

My mother looks up at me.

It's a picture of her as a twenty-year-old, a sepia moment – loose hair and flares. Even through the yellowy edges of the photograph, her smile cuts me. It's so fucking heart-wrenching. That beautiful smile was a bulb that slowly wore out. It was rare and then it was never. I close my eyes a moment and let myself remember a montage of the good moments – the smoke rings she'd blow high above our heads as we squealed in delight, a finger stroking my nose, the smell of her perfume as she leaned across us – apple and soap that dappled through the air, even after she was gone.

Roe's watching me, one hand on her glass of brandy. The fire hisses and crackles in the corner. My cheeks burn with something I cannot describe.

'Happier times,' Roe says gently, but the picture also gives oxygen to the simmering anger I'd quashed for so long.

'I still don't know why,' I say, my eyes on the photograph. It must have been taken by my dad. The sky looks clear. She's pregnant with me – one hand flung protectively across her belly. They look happy. I don't remember them looking like that much when we were older.

'We'll never know why, Ally,' Roe answers, her thumb chasing liquid down the side of the curved glass. 'But torturing yourself over it isn't helping. It never helped.'

There are photo albums and baby clothes, carefully wrapped in tissue paper held together with purple satin ribbon. The care my mother took wrapping these – her precious things. I cannot reconcile it with the disregard she had for other parts of her life later on. The pain in my stomach tightens. I know I should stop, but I want to hurt. I want to feel every scrap of pain, so I may finally reach the bottom of this grief – so I can rise up from it, pushing against the darkest part with my feet, kick my legs frantically and finally gulp the air at the top. I want to be released from the pain that has always pulled me down.

My hands shake as I turn the next framed picture over. I know what it is before I see it – I can already feel it. It's been over twenty-five years since I looked at a picture of Brendan – of all of us together. I've survived by blocking it all out – by pretending it never existed at all. If I remembered the happy times, it would lead me back to those heartbreaking times.

I stare at the image, and something shifts inside me – the moment comes alive once more. Christmas morning with new bikes – the first and only time we got them. Mine, bluebird-blue and grown-up,

Sammy's bright red Raleigh, with a basket, Brendan's black BMX with wheel pegs. We are all grinning to camera, Dad's idling on the sofa with a let's-get-this-over-with smile, the tree is perfectly gaudy. Patterned brown carpet, net curtains, *The Sound of Music* playing on TV. I remember it as if I'm looking in the window at it – gathering the fallen pine needles from under the Christmas tree into tiny heaps we spooned into bowls, a game pretending it was cake. The smell of roast turkey, the wobble of the jelly. I press my nose against the warm window of my past, and it's all the more breathtakingly beautiful for how fleeting it was. A perfect study in happiness, suspended momentarily. Pity those shards of loveliness were too rare to ever balance out the harshness of what came next.

The Von Trapps sing in the background.

These are a few of my favourite things.

Then the memory blows cold. I remember that Mother slunk off to bed that afternoon, tears in her eyes as we tried to finish the last of the white turkey flesh that caught in our throats. Christmas crackers lay crumpled under the dining table. Dad helped us make ramps for the bikes outside, and later Roe put us to bed. We fell asleep to murmured voices in the next room – Roe and Mother whispering, the staccato of sobs. I prayed to Santa that night – my God of all things great. I prayed for Mother to get better, that she wouldn't be so sad all the time. I told him he could take back my bike if he needed to. I promised him that on Cassiopeia, standing on the back doorstep in my fleece nightdress with the penguin on the front, craning skywards to see some kind of sign that he'd heard. Please hear me, I whispered desperately. *Please hear us.*

But everything got so much worse instead.

It was too much for my dad, he moved two hours away. For work, he'd said initially, but we grew to understand what that really meant. Roe helped out as much as she could, but it was clear that Mother wasn't coping. There was a half-hearted notion we'd go to Dad for a bit, then rumours of a hospital. When he left, he promised to come back for us, but he never did. Nobody could bear Mother's tear-stained face, least of all herself – the inescapable torture of her worsening depression.

She did what everyone said – she tried to 'get on with it for the sake of the children'. She tried so hard. I can't imagine the pain of what that must have been like.

That was when I stopped riding my bluebird bicycle altogether.

–

I realise my head is in my hands, the picture is balancing on my lap. Roe is hushing me, her hand, like it's always been, steady against my back, rubbing slow circles.

'It's not easy,' she's saying. 'It's not easy to confront these things. The past is an unforgiving beast. Nothing can be done to change it. Let's get you off to bed, little Ally bird.'

And I'm too tired to think of anything at all as I crawl under the colourful bedspread. She's slipped a hot-water bottle in among the sheets which I cradle against my ragged chest. I'm too tired to cry any more. It's only eight, but I pull my knees up to my chest, forming a soft C around my baby and promise, as I drift off, that I'll never let it feel this way. *I'll never leave you like my mother did me*, I tell the tiny heart inside me. I fall asleep dreamlessly under those obstinate stars.

Fifteen

Eleven hours later, the vibration of my phone jolts me awake. Darkness swirls outside the bedroom window and for a moment I'm completely disorientated – the tangle of sleep pulling me back down. Then I hear Clarke's clear voice in my ear. I recognise the outline of the wardrobe by the door, my brother's old bed floating above my head. Only empty space where that little hand no longer dangled down seeking mine.

'DS Fields,' he's saying apologetically, but there's a quickness to his voice too – the unmistaken edge of urgency. 'I tried to get you last night.'

I attempt a groggy apology, but he's talking too fast. I'm trying to find my clothes in the gloom. I flick the nearest light switch on and the overhead bulb illuminates, harsh yellow against the whispery dawn.

'Audrey Jones has confessed to deliberately starting the fire that killed her husband,' he tells me, and I almost hit my head on the wooden post above as I jump up from the bunk.

Half an hour later, I'm outside the guesthouse, it's still dark. I watch Clarke striding up and down making calls, his silhouette outlined against the light from the front streetlights. His chin is illuminated blue as he speaks steadily into the phone, absorbed in conversation, focused. My head, on the other hand, is a jumble of cobwebs. I shiver and fold my arms tighter around myself, even though the car heater is up full blast. It feels as if we're taking one step forward, two steps back. There is something about this place – a piercing sadness I no longer want to be part of. I'd crept out of Roe's, trying not to wake her, remembering at the last moment to throw the box of photos into the trunk of my car. I plan to show Sammy – to go through them together, and to keep some of the clothes for the baby.

Clarke waves when he sees me and strides towards where I'm pulled in, examining his phone as he sits heavily into the passenger seat. The dense air that surrounds me disperses a little with his presence in the jeep – it lightens immediately, dilutes – like adding water to oil.

'You okay?' Clarke looks at me, concerned. I swat his words away, exasperated, as if they are flies in the air.

'Talk to me,' I command. I see he is wearing a new jacket which he must have picked up yesterday. I feel a jolt of something, guilt maybe. I'm still wrapped in his.

'I got a call from Mulligan last night late. He said he'd been trying to get you…' Clarke looks at me carefully. 'He said that Audrey came into the station last night. She broke down and confessed that she started the fire on purpose.'

'But why?'

Clarke shrugs. 'I guess we'll find out later. She's resting now, but the next interview is scheduled for eleven.'

I check the car's digital clock. 7:45. Shards of weak daylight are beginning to crack through the blackness above.

'I've been going through the statements from that night of the Wills's fire, though,' Clarke continues. 'And Gerald Barrows was the officer that led that entire investigation. He wasn't just first on the scene. He signed off on everything. Including the documentation to release the baby's death certificate. Including not forensically examining the house for the child's remains.'

I widen my eyes.

'Why didn't we know this? What about Mulligan?'

'It was in the original case file that I managed to get, but there were documents that weren't digitalised. They were missing.' Documents don't go missing. Documents are misplaced for a reason. The tingling feeling returns. 'Something else too, Detective.' Clarke taps the scruffy file. 'This woman we are due to see this morning. May O'Regan?'

I look at him blankly. My head is still fuzzy after the much-needed sleep.

'She's the older lady who was in the Wills's house back when the fire started, that the reporter Cynthia was speaking about,' Clarke says patiently. 'We're due to see her this morning at the nursing home.'

I nod slowly, trying to get my head back in the game. I can't have my personal stuff getting in the way of the investigation. I can't be that person.

Clarke is still talking.

'In her statement, this witness May says that Nancy had a huge fight with someone before she left for work that night – the night of the fire.'

We both know that a fight means an emotional reaction which means passion, resentment, fear, anger.

'Does she know who with?'

'Hugh. She said the argument was between Nancy and her then husband Hugh.'

I start to remember from Cynthia's article. I'd read about the elderly woman, a neighbour who was there when the fire started. The fire report had also included a statement from her. I take it from Clarke's hand and scan it quickly. She'd dozed off apparently. The report also said that the fire could have been smouldering upstairs for some time, those tiny fibres of the plug slowly simmering until they finally took off.

We need to speak to May about what else she might have noticed about that night six years ago.

–

May O'Regan lives at Tudor Lawns Nursing Facility – an hour and a half's drive north of Currolough. The weather is miserably damp, the sky emerging a dirty-morning grey as we slosh through the glistening roads, past depressing housing estates and treeless fields. There is the underbelly of any pretty part of a country – the side of the rundown youth centres and half-built houses, the sprawling superstores and tarmacked car parks that make up the ugly engine tourists don't want to see. As a child I'd always been fascinated by the range of it all. Of life – how beauty has its counterbalance. For every stunning sunset, there was a maggoty dead bird in the field behind our house. For every mesmerising murmuration, there was a wounded fox that shrieked all night long. The lesson I learnt growing up was that behind every pretty veil, life is as gruesome as it is lovely. It's heartbreaking and ugly, vast and beautiful. I guess to experience all of that is what it means to truly live. The flipside of this place is no different. I watch an older lady push a trolly full of black plastic bags across a road and sigh.

Nurse Clarke is back on duty. 'You get on okay with your family?'

'Yeah,' I dismiss his question. 'Just wondering why Gerald didn't tell us he was overseeing the whole investigation? What reason does he have for lying, or even omitting that?' I indicate left, towards an old sign announcing *Tudor Lawns*. The large stone gate posts give an aura of grandeur, but as we pull up in front of Tudor Lawns, it's clear that's where any nod towards grandiosity ends. The building itself is surrounded by a long, ugly prefab with crumbling concrete steps. Not a lawn or English rose in sight. Disconcertingly, the information signs as we approach show only two directions – an arrow towards the morgue and the health centre car park itself. I've been to hospitals and nursing homes before, but never like this. Even Clarke is uncharacteristically quiet.

'Imagine this being the last place you spend your days,' he remarks, craning to get a better view through the windscreen now that we've parked, saying aloud what I've been thinking since we drove through the gates. What a depressing hellhole.

'I'm sure people here are well cared for. That's probably more important than waterfalls and flowers.' I try to be pragmatic.

'Is it, though?' Clarke muses.

He pulls up the collar of his new dark green coat and we walk towards the ramped entrance. Him striding – me waddling next to him, wrapped in the quilted jacket I've barely taken off. My downy oversized shield.

Frank still hasn't called me back and I'm done chasing him. I have a case to get sorted.

Inside the reception, someone has placed a vase with fake tulips on the welcome counter. The place reeks of artificial lemon industrial cleaner and air freshener. A calendar with a positive saying of the day stands cheerfully to one side of the cheap reception desk: *Your mind is a garden. Your thoughts are the seeds. You can grow flowers, or you can grow weeds.*

It's hard to imagine any sort of cultivation takes place here, I think, as a woman with glasses on a chain around her neck tells us to follow her towards a common area where a number of residents sit around reading or watching the television. A re-run of *Murder She Wrote* drones in the background. Carers bustle around the room. In one corner is a large table with a stiff polka dot table covering. Some residents sit chatting, holding their Styrofoam cups between slow, bony fingers. An older woman in an armchair, wearing sheepskin slippers dozes into her chest. In another corner, there's an early morning game of bridge going on. To one side, the room branches out into a conservatory where a nurse is helping another elderly resident manoeuvre an electric wheelchair. A few have younger relatives sitting with them. Some talk, heads bent close. Others sit quietly, simply holding hands – the physical act of just touching enough, perhaps. A bored child scatters jigsaw pieces across the tiles. All have the same haunted look in their eyes. Or maybe I'm just projecting.

This room has its own unique smell – potato soup and bleach. Even the garish posters announcing activities like charades or Thursday night book club can't sugar-coat the inescapable reality of a place like this.

The end of days.

I don't care what anyone says, nobody aspires to this. My father only lived until he was sixty-five – a sudden heart attack saved him from living out his days this very way. By then we'd lost touch. In fact, I'd only heard about his death weeks later.

The woman we are following from reception crouches down beside a glamorous-looking lady in a chair at the back of the room. May O'Regan, I presume. She has candy-floss hair and a woollen jumper. Her hands, folded in her lap, are jittery as she raises them to greet us. Her face lights up. She's been expecting us.

We are told that one of the social workers will sit in on the meeting alongside May O'Regan. We've been warned discreetly that she has Parkinson's, which means that memory lapses are quite frequent. May gets up with the assistance of a nurse and grasps for her walker. I feel bad having disturbed her and I say so straight away, but she assures us we are the highlight of her week. We are shown into a small private room labelled *Art Therapy*, with a couch, a piano and a few easels dotted around the room.

'Beautiful pictures,' Clarke says, looking around at the artwork spread out across the room. A large boat sailing into the distance, an owl in a tree and a dark squiggle of something sinister that reminds me of Nancy's homemade dreamcatchers. 'Do you paint, Ms O'Regan?' He turns to address her. May is wearing small tear-drop earrings and a stain of pink lipstick that has leached into the parched lines of her thin lips.

She lowers herself slowly, delicately, into the chair the social worker has pulled out for her. She's bony-old, fragile, as if she may break.

'Music was more my thing,' she says wistfully, glancing towards the piano. She pushes her hands back on her lap self-consciously and I feel a surge of pity. 'Before... I mean,' she says and looks so sad that I want to take her hands in my own. Then I think of my own mother's hands, so elegant. Like a piano player's, father used to always say, but she'd never got the chance to play. Funny how I can remember them so perfectly – every sinew, every flaw. I used to tell people that I met in my teens and at Garda training college about my concert pianist mother. How silly, I think now. How devastatingly sad.

'May I?' Clarke indicates towards the piano stool and for one horrible moment I think he's going to start playing something. It wouldn't surprise me – hours of lessons probably featured daily at his posh castle school. But he takes a seat instead and pulls out his notebook. I pull out the complete file – the fire report including May O'Regan's statement. I glance at the social worker who signals that it's okay to start the interview. It's 9:15 a.m. and my stomach rumbles.

'Detective Casey here and I are investigating the house fire a few years back. Nancy Wills's house. I hope you don't mind us asking you some questions, Ms O'Regan?'

May nods earnestly, her thin halo of fluff bobbing in time.

'Ms O'Regan, you were babysitting the night of the fire, just before Christmas that year, isn't that right?' I look up and smile politely. Every fibre of my being wants to run out of this room – away from the pathetic paintings, the silent piano, her shakily applied make-up.

'I was,' she says, self-importantly. 'I often babysat for Nancy Wills. I tried to help as much as I could back then.' She glances at Clarke, who nods encouragingly at her. 'You look like my son, Sean,' May says to him suddenly, a flicker of sadness spreading across the thin skin underneath her watery eyes.

He looks embarrassed, but then pulls the piano stool closer. She reaches for his hand, and I look away, towards the door. The overt display of such fallibility is way too much for me. I focus on a purple mountain landscape someone has painted instead.

In fairness to Clarke, he handles it well. He pats her hand reassuringly.

'I'm sure Sean would be very impressed with how much you are helping us with the investigation,' he says, confidently.

She keeps hold of his hand. He remains tethered to her, like a good fake son.

I need to get this over with and get the hell out of here.

'Ms O'Regan. In your statement you say that Nancy had an argument that night.'

She nods again.

'Yes, she was crying on the phone.' May is more animated now.

I glance at Clarke.

'It says here that you heard Nancy and Hugh arguing downstairs when you were changing the baby's nappy upstairs. Was it at the house or was it on the phone?'

'Well, they always fought. It was a turbulent marriage. He had to put up with a lot, as you probably know. But the big fight between them was the same night that she was crying on the phone. Two separate arguments. I said that, didn't I?' May looks confused for a moment.

'You said to me yesterday when I rang that Nancy had an argument with Hugh. That he left slamming the door.' Clarke reads back over his notes, flipping the pages carefully and examining his neat handwritten words.

'Could it have been Hugh on the phone?' I ask.

'No, no definitely not.' May shakes her head. 'Hugh was in the garden with Joey when Nancy was crying on the phone. It was just before he left the house. Strange child that one… Caught him playing with matches, and him barely six years old. I never knew what was going on in that head of his.'

I look up sharply. Then pause a moment to let myself think. 'That night, you saw Joey with matches?'

'No, no… before. He seemed a bit… off. Not like my Sean when he was little. My son was very smart. But that kid was probably messed up because of what Nancy did.'

I notice May's hands have stopped shaking. She seems less frail all of a sudden too.

'Go on.'

'Well, I don't want to judge…'

She was clearly dying to let us know what she really thought of Nancy. Years of pent-up gossip perhaps. The room is stuffy – the soupy dinner smell overpowering. I feel a wave of heat and shake off the puffer jacket. I reach for the glass of tap water someone left out for me.

'Tell us, May. We need to know what happened that night. Nancy is convinced someone took her child.'

'The whole town knew about her,' May is saying, shrugging. I picture those busybodies in Currolough when I was a child whispering about my mother. *What's wrong with her?* The not-so-discreet tap to the temple. The silent mouthing over our heads that they thought we couldn't see.

I'm losing patience and the heat is overwhelming. I remember what Sammy has told me time and time again about trying to control my emotions. I attempt a deep breath. The owl picture stares back at me from the wall, and I feel a wave of nausea.

'The whole town knew what, Ms O' Regan?' I say with such obvious exasperation that I feel Clarke's discomfort from across the room.

Tough.

These were the type of people that had pushed my mother too far over the years. And look what happened to her. I try not to think of the two overgrown graves on the hill the other side of the lake. The wet grey headstones, side by side. Twin slabs. I realise my hands are shaking too and I tuck them under my knees.

'She was off galivanting with that man,' May continues. 'She was leaving Hugh. Leaving them all.'

'What man?'

'That Garda, whatever his name was, Barrows.'

'Gerald Barrows?' Clarke repeats the name slowly.

'Yes, Barrows. She was carrying on with him. Hugh knew and turned a blind eye, as they say.' She purses her lips – waits for our reaction.

'Was he at the house that night?'

'Hmmm… let me think.' May glances up, her eyes narrow as she tries to think back to that night six years ago. 'Hugh left after the argument with Nancy. He slammed that door hard. I remember Vee, the sister, dropped in with a gift later that night. A peace offering, she said. Then it was just me, Joey and the baby Liam. I had a glass of wine. Just the one. I'm sure that's in the report too.' She looks defensive for a moment. 'Then the fire started, I called the emergency number.'

'The statement says you were asleep in the living room.' Clarke glances down at his notes and May looks flustered.

'Yes, the living room. That's what I said.'

I can feel Clarke's eyes on me, but mine are on May's.

'And you didn't go upstairs?'

'Not after Nancy left. It was only a short time later the fire started.' We lock eyes.

'Tell me more about the fight between Nancy and Hugh before they went out,' I say, still sitting on my hands.

Hugh was shouting. He was telling Nancy to go on back to Gerald. *Go off back to him*, he was saying. *But you won't take my sons. Over my dead body*, May frowns at the memory.

'I'm sorry. I feel so bad any of this happened while I was there. I mean, maybe if I hadn't fallen asleep.' She takes a breath. 'You don't think Hugh…'

'Why didn't you say any of this to the police?' Clarke cuts her off gently, patting her hand once more. They've begun trembling again. Maybe that's what happens with Parkinson's – the tremor came and went.

'I mean it was Gerald who was interviewing me at the time. What was I supposed to say?' she whispers.

'Do you want to continue, Ms O'Regan?' the social worker interrupts, concerned perhaps at the toll the interview is starting to have on the older woman.

May nods, but her eyes are a distant blue now – the sharpness seems to have faded a little. She looks vulnerable, child-like.

'Is Sean coming?' she asks the social worker, a vacant look on her face.

'Sean's in New York, remember? He's coming soon.' She tucks May's blanket in a little and smiles coldly at me. The matron told me earlier that none of May's children have ever visited or are likely to. She'd fallen out with them years before. The nurse shook her head in disbelief when she told me that – the naked judgement of how little she thought of May's adult children abandoning her to a place like this. But there are always fragments to every story that nobody understands – pieces of jagged moments that make no sense unless you make them fit into something that resembles a whole.

'I'm sorry, May needs to rest now.' The social worker begins to help May up. She is much weaker than before, her hands grasping for the silver support frame.

'I wish it never happened,' May says, more lucidly, as she shuffles out of the room – her eyes never leaving the piano as she goes. 'It wasn't supposed to be like this.'

Clarke and I stand watching the slump of May's shoulders as she hobbles down the corridor inch by painstaking inch. The wobbly fuzz of white hair growing smaller and smaller until she disappears around the corner. I'm watching so intently that I jump when his phone buzzes. Clarke steps away to speak into it.

Could Hugh have taken baby Liam? If Hugh knew that Nancy was leaving him, did that mean he was capable of taking his baby elsewhere to punish his wife? It was entirely possible. But how did that connect to the boy Nancy saw in Drumlish – Dexter? My head aches. I need Frank to call me back.

Then Clarke is beside me, still talking on the phone as we start walking towards the nursing home exit, side by side, the top of my head in line with his shoulder.

'When?' he's saying into his mobile phone, and there's something in his voice that sounds like alarm. Something big has happened. In the courtyard of Tudor Lawns, through the window, I see someone has tried to plant a few bulbs. They've withered before they even got started. A barren garden with cracked plant pots.

Clarke and I step out into the pale chalky day. My eyes water with the effort of not throwing up. The smell of this place lingers on my skin.

'It's Tim,' Clarke says, his eyes troubled, as we approach the Discovery. 'Nancy's missing.'

Sixteen

We listen on the speaker phone, standing outside the nursing home as Tim tearfully explains how Nancy reacted after we left. She'd been crying afterwards, he said. Then she got extremely angry. She disappeared shortly after that, taking their blue Mazda. He hasn't heard from her since. Currolough Gardaí won't do much until she'd been gone twenty-four hours – standard procedure. They've run the number plates at least. I glance at Clarke, more than uneasy. We'd told her about Gerald Barrows. Maybe she went to confront him – to see the child.

'What about her ex-husband, Hugh?' I lean forward to speak to Tim into Clarke's phone which he's holding between us, his arm stretched out, neat clean nails lined up along the side of the screen. 'Would she have gone to him?'

'They don't really see each other. He lives in Spain,' Tim replies.

'Spain? But how does Nancy get to see Joey?'

There's a pause.

'She doesn't. Not really,' Tim tries to explain. 'The boy... he never really could get over Nancy's injuries – how different she looked.'

I look away for a moment, watching an older resident at the nursing home slowly navigate the steps into the building, refusing help from the younger person hovering beside her.

'But she's his mother,' I say simply.

It's more of a statement than a question. It hangs in the air.

'It's complex,' Tim responds after a moment. I imagine it would be difficult to convince a five-year-old that you are who you say you are when your face has changed so dramatically. Overnight, his mother became the monster of his nightmares. No wonder he was afraid to go near her.

Tim agrees to forward on Hugh Wills's contact details, and Clarke assures him we'll come straight over.

'I'm pinging this to you now,' he says, his voice small and afraid. 'Please find her.'

'No answer from Gerald Barrows either,' I say, as Clarke and I climb into the Discovery. I think about Nancy's face when I told her who the father of the child that she saw at the market was. How pale she turned when I mentioned his name – a visceral reaction. I glance at the time. I want to make sure I'll get back for Audrey's next scheduled interview at Currolough Garda station. I tap Hugh Wills's number into my own mobile phone. As a foreign ringtone fills the vehicle, we drive down the depressing avenue of Tudor Lawns Nursing Home back towards Currolough. Spain is an hour ahead. I picture a villa by the sea as Hugh's number continues to ring out.

I am forty-two years old and have never left the country. You make too many decisions based on fear, Sammy the sage tells me a million times. And maybe she's right. Maybe I just don't like transition. Or paella. There's no answer from Hugh's mobile.

Focus Ally, I tell myself. Nancy is out there, who knows where, and most likely in a dreadful state. We need to prioritise finding her, while making sure Dexter is okay too. But as we drive, I grow increasingly frustrated.

'Call Tim back,' I suddenly say to Clarke.

He answers on the first ring, his voice tinny through the speaker.

'Tim,' my voice is sharp. 'Can you please explain to me again how Nancy knows Gerald Barrows?' We can hear the muffle of wind through the speaker. He must be out by the beach searching for Nancy. He's been up all night, he told us.

'Nancy said she didn't know him,' he sighs, but it's a half-hearted answer. Worry over his partner seems to have trumped whatever sinister secret she seemed to think she had to keep from us. I feel sorry for him – he seems like a simple enough guy, just trying to do the right thing.

'Barrows says differently,' I tell him. 'Plus, there've been rumours Nancy was having an affair with him around the time of the fire.'

'You spoke to him?' Tim sounds panicked.

'We did.'

There's only silence, except for the scream of a seagull and more wind static as Tim seems to carefully weigh his words. I sigh in exasperation as I navigate a tricky bend in the narrow road.

'Talk to me, Tim. We're going in circles here. It's not going to help us find Nancy. Plus, if she really wants our help finding out if this kid is her son or not, she needs to level with us. As do you.'

I imagine him smoothing his shoulder-length hair back with one hand. Tim's about fifty-five, a good deal older than Nancy. They'd met at the community hall where Nancy volunteered, he'd said. I fell in love with her soul, he told us at the caravan when we first met him. They'd been friends for years, before Hugh or the babies. I wonder what it was about Tim's soul that had attracted Nancy. When he finally speaks, his voice is flat.

'Nancy was seeing Gerald around the time of the fire,' he admits quietly. 'They had plans to be together. And Hugh found out.'

'But she had a young baby. Was Gerald the father?'

'I don't know. She never said and I never asked. But there'd been talk that she was moving away with Gerald. It wasn't a secret. Nothing ever is around here. Nancy doesn't like to talk about it. Not even with me.'

'She was planning to leave Hugh,' I say the words slowly – trying to absorb the information. It's still an hour until we'll be back at the station. I take the slip road towards the motorway.

'And planning to leave the children,' Tim says, a little more subdued this time.

So, he *did* know more than he was saying. I raise my eyebrows at Clarke who's taking notes next to me. Who leaves their children?

We agree to talk more later. The priority now is to find Nancy and to make sure she isn't acting on any worrying impulse.

'Garda Casey will be with you as soon as possible,' I reassure him, and I press the red button on the car navigation screen. The staticky whoosh disappears abruptly.

'What Tim is saying about the situation with Nancy and Gerald matches May's version of events,' Clarke says. 'The huge fight. The phone call before the fire. She was crying, May said. And Hugh slamming the door, saying Gerald was welcome to her.'

I nod, contemplating, picturing the house as it once was – a family home, young kids, parents arguing… an unimaginable betrayal.

For a moment the only noise is the car engine and the billowy sound of the outside blowing in through the open window. As I navigate the narrow roads closer to Currolough, my phone chirps – I recognise the Spanish prefix on the screen.

'Detective Sergeant Ally Fields speaking.'

There's silence.

The faraway voice on the other end of the phone is unmistakably Irish, and sleepy.

'Hi, sorry… I missed a call from this number?' It's Hugh Wills, concern in his voice. 'Is everything okay?'

'Mr Wills, I'm the detective here in Ireland looking into your ex-wife's claims that your baby son was taken in the house fire a few years back.'

A long pause.

'Yes?' Is it my imagination or has his tone cooled? No surprise in his tone whatsoever.

'The thing is, we've just learnt that Nancy has gone missing. Last week she claimed she found the child… Liam… at a craft market an hour from here. We've come down to look into things and now she's gone missing…' I trail off, perturbed by his strange silence.

There's no sound at all and I wonder if we've been cut off. Then: 'I'm sorry, Detective. I don't really know what to say.' Hugh Wills lets the silence linger. It's clear he wants to get off this call as soon as humanly possible. I try to pinpoint his tone – not indifference or callousness – but a resignation, a weariness that I can detect – a here-we-go-again vibe. And something else too.

'Is Nancy likely to turn up there in Spain?' I ask sharply. We have a lot to cover with Hugh, but this isn't exactly the right moment.

'No.' He sounds sure. 'I'm sure this is the last place you'd find her.' A harsh laugh. 'Isn't she with Tim?' he asks, and I wonder what she must have done to have her ex-husband care so little about where the mother of his children has vanished to.

'He's out searching too. We've a lot of questions we need to clear up with you, Mr Wills. The child, you see, at the market… it was Gerald Barrows's son. We informed Nancy of that yesterday afternoon and she's been missing ever since.'

There's only silence in response. But it's a different kind of silence. I can almost feel the rush of emotion pulsating from him. This wasn't resignation – this was something else…

'Mr Wills?'

'Look, I can't do this right now. I really have to go. I'm sorry. I have to take another call.'

'I have a few more questions,' I start. But he's already hung up. I know there is a lot more I need to hear from Hugh Wills. I ring off with an uneasy feeling of dread, because I've realised what else I heard in Hugh Wills's voice – anger.

–

We arrive back at Currolough station at ten to eleven. We've called ahead. One of the other officers is ready in the patrol car to go out with Clarke to the caravan park to help Tim with the search. I'll stay and speak to Audrey Jones – to hear the details of her confession.

'I'll let you know as soon as we locate Nancy,' Clarke says to me, climbing out of the car.

I like Clarke's optimism. The detective in me knows that there is always a chance we won't find Nancy, but this time I don't mind Clarke's presumption that everything will turn out okay. I need a sprinkle of his confidence in the world today. I try to picture Nancy leaving her children – abandoning them as she ran off with Gerald. There are some mothers that love their children in an entirely different way, I suppose. But it doesn't make it any easier for society to accept. Poor Joey, I think. *Poor Hugh.* No wonder he's angry. But surely Nancy's been punished enough?

None of us want to voice the possibility that it has all been too much trauma for Nancy – that she'd prefer to leap into the void than to acknowledge the depths of her loss in life. I remember Nancy saying something about wanting to touch her child. She just wanted to hold him.

'Organise someone to go out to Haycote Manor,' I order Clarke, leaning to speak to him from my driver's window. If only Gerald Barrows would answer his damn phone.

'Do you think maybe Gerald took the baby? All those years ago?' Clarke asks, shaking his head as if to shift the thoughts of what might have happened that night. 'And made it look like an accidental death? He could easily have covered it up.'

'I'm not sure,' I say, rubbing my temples. 'But that fire meant one less child Nancy would have to leave.'

Clarke looks horrified.

'Jesus Christ, Ally. If you're saying Nancy set the fire herself, why would she almost die running back into it? Why would she then spend all these years searching for her baby?'

The headache is back.

'I don't know, Clarke. Horrible things happen, okay? And just because that's difficult for us to accept, doesn't mean wishful thinking can stop it.' He's motionless. Looking at me strangely. 'I'm just... sorry. I'm not sure... we are speculating here. We need to speak to Nancy again.' I tap the steering wheel impatiently.

'What if Hugh found out she was leaving him. What if Hugh was punishing her?'

I glare at Clarke. 'You think he'd kill a tiny baby because his wife was shagging around on him?'

The question hangs heavy between us. But we are feeling in the dark. Plus, we both know deep down that there are less horrific reasons people are compelled to destroy others – even kids. You learn that as a cop. You never forget the mindless reasons for which people snuff out lives every damn day. And let me tell you, revenge is up there – top of the list. But it's given a heroic name instead – justice.

'Maybe baby Liam wasn't Hugh's kid at all.'

'Let's just find Nancy first,' I say sharply, feeling lightheaded again. When will I learn to stick some bloody protein bars in my handbag? Clarke walks away, towards the waiting patrol car.

But I realise it's not food I need – it's to rid myself of all the anxiety that's been suffocating me since I got down here. I sit staring straight ahead and think of Frank suddenly, of him lying next to Mel, his arms around her. The security she probably took for granted of being the one he stuck with. Even if her husband was cheating on her, Mel won. She got to have him there with her when she needed him most.

I flick my thick dark braid back in despair. These damn hormones are making everything so much harder. But the bigger my belly grows and the stronger the kicks come, the more frightened I am that the ground beneath me is unsteady. Everything feels as if it's crumbling. There's nothing I can do about it. That helplessness scares me shitless.

I'm spinning the steering wheel, about to reverse the Discovery to head around the back of the small station to find parking, when I notice Clarke loitering. He stands by the driver's window, gesturing for me to put it down.

'What?' I'm not in the mood for him. Or for anyone at all right now. 'What, Casey?' I repeat more sharply.

He leans on the window with both hands, folds his body down to reach eye-level. Frustrating as he is, there is no denying he has beautiful eyes, slightly hooded – it makes him look kind. But that annoys me too for some reason.

'Are you okay, DS Fields?' he says, his brow furrowing. He seems genuinely concerned. I give him one of my what-the-fuck looks.

'Of course. Why wouldn't I be?' I shake my head, like I'm totally baffled by what he's saying. But he's clearly picked up on something. In a perfect world, I'd admit to Clarke that I'm tired and I have a headache, that I'm extremely pregnant, confused and returning to a place of indescribable trauma while simultaneously failing to solve an almost decade-old mystery. I feel unloved, unwanted, and confronting the past has only made those feelings worse. I think of the rusted once-blue bicycle thrown next to a shed beside a silky lake.

I have a box of death in my trunk and a life squirming inside me that terrifies me with its need for me to be everything to it. My ribs throb too from where confusing hands hurt me and told me it was love. But I'll never tell him that either.

I peer at him through the gloom for a moment. Dare him to speak again with my eyes. And then shoo him off the window. He backs away slowly, his hands pushed deep into his pockets.

'Just checking, boss.' He tries to make light of it, but we both know I'm absolutely not okay.

'Call me with updates, Casey.'

'Take care, Detective,' he calls, and says something else too, but the whir of the electric window muffles his words. He's still standing there when I glance in the rear-view mirror. I wipe the beginning of tears away so quickly it's as if they haven't formed at all.

Seventeen

She's trembling, drawing her arms in close to herself. Trying to take up as little room as possible behind the interview table.

'Audrey, I'm going to leave this here for you. It's tea. Maybe let it cool a little. I also grabbed this from the vending machine. It's my favourite, but not everyone likes Turkish Delight. I have at least one of these a day now.' I laugh lightly, but there is no doubt this is a hellish situation she's found herself in and I need to get to the bottom of it.

Mulligan says that Audrey is refusing to speak at all today. But there's a lot I need her to explain because talking to May at the nursing home, something finally clicked for me. Between that and the autopsy report that landed for Eddie Jones an hour ago, I am pretty confident I know what happened inside Apartment 2D at the Bayview the night before last.

A dour, curly-haired solicitor sits next to Audrey. He smiles, with effort. His client is wearing jeans and a black hoodie, scruffy trainers, her hair tucked behind her ears. She's examining her fingers, eyes down, fiddling with her nails.

'Audrey?' I repeat gently. Silence. I give her a couple of seconds. 'Do you mind if I sit down?'

A tiny shake of the head. She's wringing her hands over and over. Her fingernails are bitten to the quick.

I sigh dramatically as I flop into the chair. The solicitor eyes me warily.

'I'm thirty-eight weeks today,' I tell them, truthfully, trying to infuse casualness into the room so she might be encouraged to talk. 'Fully cooked, as they say. Head's well down, hospital bag packed, but 100 per cent emotionally unprepared.'

Audrey still hasn't looked at me. I adjust my tone. This isn't a social call.

'I know Inspector Mulligan says you didn't want to talk at all today, Mrs Jones. And I understand it's a particularly tough time for you with your daughter in hospital and your recent bereavement, but I want to speak to you about something important this morning.'

She squeezes her hands together even tighter. I let the quiet fill up the room. After a few moments, she speaks.

'What is it that you want? I've confessed, haven't I?'

The question isn't in any way confrontational. It's said in a small, dazed voice, uncertain.

'I want to talk to you about your daughter. About Tori.'

She glances up. 'The thing is, Audrey, I know that you love your daughter. And I know you wouldn't start a fire while Tori was in the apartment, and certainly not when you weren't there to protect her.' Sudden tears glitter in her eyes. Her right hand moves to her mouth, covering it as if she's afraid of what she might say. 'We both know you wouldn't put Tori in that kind of danger.' I pull my chair in closer.

Nothing.

I lean close to her. She smells of stale clothes and coffee. A night in the station will do that. She seems so diminished as a person; I really feel for her.

'Did he hurt you, Audrey?'

She flinches. Her chest moves up and down more rapidly. The other hand comes up to her face. She steeples her hands over her mouth and nose and finally raises her eyes. But still, Audrey stays silent.

The solicitor turns sharply to look at his client. Then to glare at me. A warning perhaps – *don't push it.*

'Audrey,' I tap the file that Mulligan has collated, 'we've spoken to many of your neighbours, and they've given us a picture of what your home life was really like. That's why someone got in touch with Garda Barrows, wasn't it? Your colleague from the post office. When they started noticing the texts telling you to come straight home, the drive-bys to check up on you, the constant calls… the disgusting names he'd call you.'

She pulls her hoodie sleeves down over her hands, her back hunches. She's curling inwards. My own heart is hammering in my chest. It was the secondary school student on work experience in the post office that first went to the police – to Barrows, a family friend who lived near her parents. She didn't know what else to do. She did exactly the right thing.

A tear slides down Audrey Jones's cheek. I look down and continue, tracing the grain in the wooden table with my index finger, contemplating my next words very carefully.

'We spoke to your husband's boss, Audrey. We know that Eddie had been fired for drinking on the job in the weeks before. The tox results are in too. He had most likely been drinking all afternoon. There was no way he was waking up to that smoke alarm. And you didn't dare open the door to Barrows all those times he called at the door. He was so worried about you that he kept coming back – even when he wasn't on duty.'

Audrey says something but her voice is too fragile for me to make out what's she saying.

'He was kind,' I think she said.

'Did Eddie hurt you?' I ask again, and my mouth is dusty suddenly. A swell in my own throat. I need to hear her say it. Her right hand, still under the sleeves of the hoodie twists the fingers of her left over and over. It's almost hypnotic.

'Audrey?'

'Not always,' she eventually whispers, her lips dry and cracked.

'He loved me,' she says softly, desperately. I've seen this so many times. The urge to take responsibility for what was happening when the person who was supposed to love them most had tried to steal their power.

'But there's more to it now, isn't there?' I steady my own shaking hand. 'Was Tori scared, Audrey? Scared for you?' Tears run down the woman's cheeks, and she wipes them on her sleeves leaving tiny snail trails. The solicitor's faux-cheerful face is now scrunched in barely concealed horror. 'Audrey, did he hurt Tori?'

How much can a person take? I think of the innocent life floating within and take a deep breath. And I imagine what I might say, if my walls were thinner, if I opened my own emotional drawbridge the tiniest crack.

I know what it's like, I'd say, if I was brave enough.

I've been hit before too, I wish I could tell her.

Frank broke two of my ribs. He split my lip, kicked me. These are the devastating words I've never dared admit. They remain lodged in my throat as I watch Audrey Jones struggle to contain her emotion across the table in front of me.

You see, it's easy to say it happened on the job when you are a cop turning up injured at a hospital. It's easy to pretend to be tough when you are anything but. I place a hand against my rib, protectively. Audrey's tears continue to fall. Silence lies thick across the room.

He hurts me. I want to say to her. If I could. But I don't. I've never told anyone this. Not even Sammy.

He says he loves me, and I am prepared to put up with anything to hold onto that love. I blink back my own tears and clear my throat.

'It's not your fault,' I say out loud, my words heavy with emotion. The solicitor shifts uncomfortably in his chair.

I feel so worthless that it feels like suitable punishment.

I'm holding on because being hurt physically isn't as bad as the emotional abandonment I know I'll suffer if he leaves.

I'm so terribly afraid of what comes next.

'It wasn't you who set the fire, was it, Audrey?' I shake my own tears away. But she hasn't noticed. She's staring into the distance, her mouth a tight line. 'Audrey?'

Even her solicitor seems to be holding his breath. Through the window, the traffic rumbles on outside, the beep of a reversing delivery truck in the lane, the whoop of a teen trying to impress his mates.

'It was Tori who started the fire, wasn't it? Tori who almost died trying to protect you. Trying to protect her mother...' My voice breaks as I speak because this is way too close to home.

She finally nods.

I rub a shaking hand over my eyes, down my face, drag it down my skin, over my mouth.

But I'm angry too. For her and for me.

Because Audrey put that poor kid in a position that almost killed her.

She felt as if there was absolutely no way out. And right now, so do I.

Eighteen

The little things became the big things: the wrapper from my sandwich I forgot in his car; my coffee mug left on the wrong side of the dishwasher; showers that were perceived as too long. The things he did to upset me were nothing compared to my wrongs. It was disproportionate. But the more he pointed out that I was wrong, the more I was ground down. And he was extraordinarily convincing. I slowly realised I needed to be better at just about everything with Frank. I was already off-balance, so I figured being steered by someone like him was a good thing. A hyper-vigilance began, without me even knowing what that was. New feelings that I presumed were part of normal relationships emerged. My family bonds were so tenuous that I was open to learning how to be better and Frank was a willing teacher.

The list of things that would make him short-tempered grew longer, and I made myself remember to follow them for the sake of harmony. I figured Mel knew what she was doing and as someone who'd never been taught how to keep house or build relationships, I was obviously on the back foot. It was me that was wrong. He was just pointing that out.

Slowly, so extraordinarily slowly, it crept up on me, I became less of the person I was. And part of me believed that was a good thing.

That was how it began. It's not where it ended.

The first time he was physical with me was in bed. Frank didn't like what I was doing to please him and pushed me roughly off. Handling each other like that during sex didn't seem like the red flag I'd learnt to look out for in my job. Physicality was all part of it between the sheets, right? Then he didn't like the way I was making the curry in my small kitchen one evening and he shoved me aside, frustrated – my hip hit the quartz countertop and left a deep bruise. He refused to apologise, teasing with a mocking smile that it was my fault for being in the way. Shaking it off. I'm sorry if you hurt yourself, he said eventually, shrugging. But it wasn't like he'd punched me in the jaw. That was the line I think we all draw in our heads. He'd just jostled me, I told myself. It wasn't like it was an everyday thing. It was only sometimes.

Each time there was an explanation that I could cling to. It didn't seem sinister that these things were happening to me, but it was confusing. Frank was so incredibly loving in between his frustrations, as I called them. He'd tell me how beautiful I was and then point out a glamorous blonde on the TV and tell me that was his type. He said if I didn't like how fast he was driving I could get out and walk. I did once, on a remote road in Greystones on the way to pick out my new couch bed at some retail outlet on a rainy Saturday. I told him I wasn't prepared to put up with it. I didn't tell him how frightening it was to be so helpless, pressing myself against the hedging on that dark road after he drove off – never knowing what was around the next corner. Later at home, he asked me calmly if I was finally over my tantrum.

He'd put me down and then tell me I couldn't take a joke. When I said it wasn't funny, he said I was the weirdo.

The thing is that I'm not a fool. And though he makes me feel foolish, he also makes me feel desirable, beautiful, funny, unique. It was one part of the relationship – it wasn't everything.

I don't want to lose him, so I kiss the same mouth that often tells me to go fuck myself if I am not happy. I accept his arms around me, though they pushed me so hard that last summer I cracked my ribs against a radiator. I never know what to expect or when. It's easier to bite my tongue than to set him off. Sometimes I look at him asleep in bed and feel so much love. I feel protected simply by having him beside me. It is easier to find another thing to blame these feelings on. It's easier to take responsibility for my twisted words that precipitate his anger.

I am ashamed by my inability to be better. But I'm also embarrassed that it's what I'm prepared to accept. Maybe if we were a proper family unit, things would be different. I'd have more sway. That's my only available move in this complicated game I think is called love.

Besides, if I was so wonderful anyway, my mother wouldn't possibly have walked into the lake that morning and left me behind. I placate

Frank so I can keep him. I accept his flaws because he does mine. No relationship is perfect. Besides, without him I feel as if I have nothing. I have absolutely nothing.

Nineteen

Swirling grey clouds weave their way slowly across the sky when I step out the back door of Currolough station after speaking to Audrey Jones. I've four missed calls from Clarke.

'Ally?' He sounds like he's been running, like he can't get the words out fast enough. 'Nancy's at her old burnt-out house. I'm on my way there.'

'Wait, what?'

I'm still so discombobulated after my conversation with Audrey that it's hard to pull myself back into the moment, back to Nancy.

Clarke continues patiently.

'Gerald Barrows called me. He said that Nancy rang him at Haycote Manor, completely hysterical. She begged him to bring Dexter to her at the old house on Eastbourne Road.'

I'm already running myself, manoeuvring my bump through the cars in the small police vehicle car park behind Currolough station.

'Barrows is obviously not planning to show up,' Clarke confirms.

'I'll meet you there, Casey.'

I clamber into the Discovery and tap the details into Google Maps. It directs me towards Eastbourne coast road. Time wise, I'll definitely get there well before Clarke.

Lake Lagan is three kilometres wide and about fifteen long – it's a huge daisy-shaped circle, stretching from Drumlish to BallinÓg, where the tip of it dips near the seashore, and folds back on itself towards Currolough. There's no place that escapes those long ribbony inlets that slurp hungrily from its muddy banks. Nancy's old house is still visible from the road, Roe confirmed – far in the distance – an eerie tourist attraction at the end of a long grassy lane that slopes towards the water.

My phone beeps beside me as I drive quickly towards the house. It's a text from Frank. He usually calls. Texts mean he can't talk. Overcome with a surge of something venomous, perhaps as a result of having just faced another person who'd asked for love and got hurt instead, I veer clumsily onto the grassy verge in front of some farmer's gate and pull on the hand brake. I jab the phone icon, but it cuts off after two rings. Disconnected.

He's cut me off.

'Don't get me started,' I murmur, braver because of the distance between us. I press the green button again, with a determination fuelled mostly from frustration. I know I'm *that* woman, and I don't deserve sympathy. Believe me, all of this makes me hate myself more than I already do. But it is time for decisions to be made.

Sammy would call this self-sabotage. And while I spent years squandering any chance of happiness, along comes a baby. A real–life human child that needs me. Things have to be different now. It's time to make some grown-up decisions. But confronting Frank means being abandoned again. My biggest fear. That's probably why I've clung to Frank like this baby is clinging to me – trusting that the person on the other end of this thin tether will do right by them.

I should have learnt from my mother that that silvery bond can be used against you – looped around you tightly. Weaponised.

I call Frank's phone again and again, buoyed by the surge of bravery, before my battery beeps mournfully back at me. I leave messages – some emphasising the need to discuss the investigation urgently, others poisonously personal.

I realise that I don't have time for this shit any more. I throw my phone onto the passenger seat and pull out onto the road once more.

I hate myself. The baby kicks and kicks and kicks.

–

When I'm finally close to the pathetic peaks of Nancy's old house, crouched low at the end of one field, I steer the Discovery to the right, down the narrow track towards it. The air through my open window is sharp with the scent of damp foliage. As I get closer, I see that the charred house is roofless. Branches, dark against the day, sway and reach from it as if trying to claw their way out. The upstairs windows foam with hawthorn-shaped shadows. Shards of burnt beams jut awkwardly. This is the broken bones of the former Wills's home. This is the place baby Liam supposedly died.

I think of a line from a song I once heard.

Home is the place with the light in the window.

Right now, only darkness prevails. The downstairs windows are boarded up with graffitied plywood. The chimney remains intact – looming from the bulk of the house, sooty black and stoic. I drive on for another minute and take an awkward, overgrown turn towards an entrance that leads to the derelict house. The lake, further on, glints metallic against the early afternoon sky. I ease the vehicle down towards it, the briars tickling the sides as I crunch slowly forward. I'm only a few metres from the house when I see the car. A blue Mazda – the car Tim said Nancy had been driving. It's parked behind a cluster of thick leylandii, concealed from the road. My heartbeat quickens. Gerald had been truthful, after all. I consider waiting for Clarke's arrival, or the backup he called, but I am anxious to make sure Nancy is safe. They'll be ten minutes behind me.

Fiddling in the boot of the Discovery, I find a torch and zip up my jacket. Mud immediately covers my flat boots as I squelch through the deep puddles that pockmark what might once have been the front lawn. An old boiler has been discarded to one side, boards of blackened steel and wood are scattered by the front door, punctuated by straggly weeds.

This is the scene of a terrible story.

I picture that night – imagine the roar of heat, the panic, the trauma of a home in flames, a family in tatters. I can almost see the plumes of smoke floating out over the lake that Christmas.

'Nancy,' I call out.

I hear the feathery beat of wings before I see the birds. They rise in fright, soaring in one scattered flurry past the charred beams and away out into the day.

'Nancy,' I call again, louder this time. There's no way I'll get into the front door – it's nailed shut with boards, the windows too. Around the side of the house, there's evidence that a family once lived here – a metal swing-set, with one seat dangling down, the chain rusted away. An old paddling pool is overflowing with a murky concoction of leaves and mildew. A tricycle sits miserably motionless on the back patio steps. The baby jabs twice in quick succession and I stop to cling to the lumpy exterior walls to catch my breath a moment.

'Breathe, Ally,' I hiss through my teeth, my right hand massaging my side. Most women are planning baby showers and shopping for cradles at this point. Here I am in a field in the middle of nowhere, with a full bladder and shit on my shoes.

'Nancy,' I shout again, but it's half-hearted. My energy is depleting. I should have eaten. So much for trying to do the right thing – I haven't had anything since the soup at Roe's last night.

A sudden noise – a low thump from inside the house – drives me on. Perhaps Nancy is lying injured? I glance over my shoulder and consider my options, but I know I'll have to go on in ahead.

The back garden of the house is extremely long and sloped. A torn trampoline lies at the end of it, a swirl of thorny bushes. The back door is also boarded up, but on one corner the nails have come loose, or been pulled loose. There's a gap large enough for someone like Nancy to squeeze through. Taking a deep breath, I clamp the torch under my arm and fold myself as small as I possibly can, manoeuvring my body around my bump to protect it. I hunker forward slowly, the splintered wooden edges scraping the skin on my back painfully as I squeeze my bulk through.

Once inside, the nausea hits. I spend a moment leaning forward, breathing deeply, my eyes watering as I try to visualise the feeling away. The atmosphere has changed dramatically. Inside this place, it's dark and dank. The brisk freshness from outside replaced with a heaviness, a sombreness that mixes with the burnt air. Shards of glass crunch underfoot as I spin slowly to get my bearings in the dim light. This must be the kitchen – I shine my torch across the remains of it. There's a stainless-steel sink under the window and empty, partly painted gaps along one wall where white goods once lay. Long stolen by now I imagine. Scrambling forward, I make my way through the doorframe ahead of me into a hallway. It smells musty too, like cat urine. Or perhaps that belongs to the squatters, who may also be responsible for the smashed beer bottles, sheets of cardboard and scattered garments that line the floor. The torch beam is thin, but it catches on something – a once-bright child's drawing stuck clumsily to a wall. It's crumpled and water damaged but seems to have escaped the blaze and the subsequent neglect. It's a picture of a woman and a man and a little boy holding their hands. It must have belonged to Joey. Its simplicity is heartbreaking. 'ME' is written in childish scrawl and a big arrow above the little boy's head. An X is drawn over something else beside them. I consider taking it with me – somebody would surely treasure such a precious thing. But as I move the torch over the rest of the wall – there are more pictures, paintings mostly of wobbly rainbows and spidery sunshines, an almost-burnt photo of a man and what seems to be a child on a beach, and one drawing, a page full of dark squiggles that the light pauses on. A dreamcatcher is tacked awkwardly beside the items. I realise this is a shrine to what they once were. There's a scuffling above me, the scrape of broken glass shifting across floorboards, and I turn, walking carefully through the debris towards what's left of the stairs.

'Nancy,' I call out again gently. 'I know you're here. I saw your car outside.'

No sound. But I know that someone is definitely there.

The structure ahead of me looks precarious. Still, I think, the sooner I get Nancy safely home, the sooner we can move forward with this case. Maybe now we understand that Barrows isn't responsible for the Bayview fire, there will be something less sinister at play about a tragedy that took place in this house. We'll still have to get a formal statement from Audrey Jones adjusting her confession and interview her daughter about her involvement, but the guilt that it has taken a twelve-year-old to do something so drastic to end her father's reign of terror on the household will be a lot to take. I saw that in Audrey's eyes as I left the room when her solicitor asked for some time alone with his client.

I place a muddy heel on the first step of the gnarled wood of the stairs and say a quick prayer. It holds solid. If Nancy has come up here this way, then it must be stronger than it looks. My left foot follows, and I pull myself up, relying heavily on a large beam that must have, years before, fallen from upstairs and landed by the broken spine of the stairs. I reach the return of the stairs in one piece, but the wood groans and splinters under my weight. *Idiot*, I chide myself. Why am I putting the baby at risk like this? Icarus Fields strikes again. It's like I just can't help myself. And as I'm reminding myself that standing on the edge of everything isn't just about me any more, I see a quick movement above my head – a flash of something in one of the rooms, and then it's gone again.

Ignoring the missing steps, I take an awkward leap for the top step, sliding up onto the landing above. Not graceful exactly, but pretty damn close. The hot sting of blood on my elbow is the result. Twisting the torch from the pocket of my puffer jacket, I illuminate the upstairs of Nancy Wills's house, mostly cast in shadows from the boarded-up windows. Thin shards of daylight light it up in places. Back at the HQ at Precinct 12, Detective Cummins says you can feel tragedy, sense it… like a smell. It chokes you, he says, pulls you into it. And I always roll my eyes when he says that to a room of wide-eyed rookie detectives. I've done plenty of death calls, a plethora of tragedy throughout my career, and I've always been too busy finding out the truth behind things to even think about the stench of the walls.

And I don't know if it's the animalistic aroma, or the invasion of the outside in, or the overwhelming acrid taste in my mouth, but it's the first time I understand a little of what Cummins means. This place reeks of tragedy. It weighs you down.

Easing open the burnt remains of a section of dehydrated wooden door, I catch my breath when I see what lies on the other side. The plywood window board has been pulled back slightly. The narrow gap lights the room from the back of the house. It casts the room in an eerie glow.

A noise behind me makes me whip around, my plait hitting my face gently. A large object moves through the air and crashes into the back of my head, knocking me over. Blackness threatens.

Don't faint, I beg myself. Don't faint, Ally. The pain hits seconds later – a concrete sting vibrating throughout my skull. It brings me back to the last time I was knocked onto my head. That same shocking crack.

Large shards of glass lie on the floor beside me. Drops of blood fall around me. The smell of it makes me gag and I try to pull myself up but there's someone beside me. Nancy Wills has fallen to the floor with the exertion of the strike; she's crouched on all fours. Her dark hair is loose, trailing on the floor in front of her, like a long black veil. She makes moaning noises as I crawl over to her, ash and saliva mixing my drag marks a sticky black, like tar.

She looks at me as if I'm an apparition. It wasn't me she was expecting at all. Was it Barrows that particular weapon was meant for?

'Are you hurt?' I'm asking between heaves, praying there's no permanent damage to my skull which now feels like half of it is missing. 'Are you hurt, Nancy?'

She's definitely in shock. Her eyes are fixed on the floor, her misshapen knuckles pale against the black of everything else. She's murmuring something over and over.

'Why did you take him?' Her eyes come into focus briefly, and she looks at me, confused. She's weeping. I see an almost-empty bottle of vodka on the floor beside her, and her strange state makes a little more sense. 'Why did he take my baby?' she slurs. 'The cot was here. It was right here. Liam was here.'

Her words are garbled. I think of the shrine downstairs – of the desperate attempt to honour her broken family.

'I let him go. This is all my fault.'

'What happened, Nancy?' I ask, but it's like she doesn't even register where she is. Again, more urgently I call her name, swallowing down the nausea and trying to stand.

'I have nothing,' she finally says robotically, her eyes still fixed on the charred floor, her back to me. 'I have nothing left at all. Do you understand that? He's taken it all from me.'

She turns suddenly, gripping my arm, her eyes are wild. 'I did this,' she whispers suddenly, swaying.

I pull away from her as Nancy continues crying, now shivering uncontrollably. I touch my own shaking hand to my head. It turns a sticky red.

I'm not sure I can drive, judging by how banged up I am. If she'd been sober, Nancy probably would have killed me, but her uncoordinated swipe means I've escaped lightly. If her plan was to knock out Barrows and take Dexter back, it would never have worked. But I have a feeling the only plan Nancy really had was to numb the pain of what she was going through again. Her incoherence is heartbreaking.

'We have to get out of here, Nancy. Can you get up?' I try to lift her – she's robin-light, but my own bulk makes me weak. The effort leaves me dizzy. 'I tried to do the right thing.' She chokes back a sob. I try not to let my eyes linger on the twist of the skin that folds across her face as she speaks. 'Come on,' I command, dragging her arm a little. 'We have to go. I have to call this in.'

I half-pull her towards the stairs, my breath coming in short sharp bursts. This has never happened to me before – this sheer overwhelm. But there is something about this house, something that makes me want to get out, to escape all of it.

Nancy goes first, gingerly stepping over the large chunks of void to reach the jagged fragments of stairs. Behind her, I focus on clinging to the beam that runs alongside, that way I figure if the steps crumble, I've got support. My vision has narrowed; everything is gloopy. Strange shadows dance sideways, and I take a deep breath to try and focus. I can't let the darkness take over.

'I loved him, you know,' Nancy whispers as I grip her arm, trying not to faint. 'I loved him so much.' Her face crumples and the pain in her voice is far too familiar. I wonder if she's talking about baby Liam or Gerald Barrows.

But as we hit the bend in the stairs, there's a horrible cracking sound, ripping like splitting wood. The wooden beam under my hands is slippery with my blood. I scramble to wrap my arms around it, but my weight topples it slightly. It leans away from me. I hear the empty crack of the torch as it lands on the concrete floor beneath us. There's nothing to grab hold of.

I cry out. I think I do. Disorientated, there's a moment where we are suspended, freeze-framed.

Then, with that sickening slow-motion realisation of what's happening, we both begin to fall.

The last thing I remember is cupping my belly as I topple sideways, then downwards, flailing as my body crashes into the charry blackness below.

Twenty

You were only a month shy of your thirteenth birthday when you died, Brendan.

I noticed early patches of downy facial hair as I studied you in your coffin during the wake. Your beginning at your end.

I'm sorry about what happened, one of the girls from Sammy's class said as she traipsed past, but she didn't meet my eyes.

You were the first dead body I ever saw, Brendan. It wouldn't be the last. Sammy was too scared to come into the room where everybody was crying and flinging themselves across the wooden cover at the base of the two pine boxes — the ones with carved crosses. A neighbour had placed a scruffy football on the table by the photos of you in your school uniform. Someone should wash that, I thought absently, and continued to absorb the slackness of your face. Committing it to memory, learning this new version of you by heart.

They say that seeing someone who's passed away helps with closure, that it's healing in some way. But I presume that doesn't apply to those who are responsible for a death. Because seeing you lying there with your eyes closed, all I wanted to do was shake you awake, scream at you to live, please live Brendan, please… like I'd shouted at you on the dirty banks of our lake when I eventually dragged you out.

You were freezing cold; your pyjamas sodden when the lake belched you out, discarded you cruelly and watched me kiss you in vain.

'Please live, Brendan. Don't leave me. Please don't die.'

I remember those desperate screams. I hear them when I shut my eyes still. I picture Roe slumped against the wooden church bench during the service, trying to understand the magnitude of what her sister had just done.

I bubbled with a caustic concoction of rage and shock that would spend a lifetime spilling over, eroding everything I touched.

At the eulogy, the mean priest with the limp — the one we'd been afraid of as kids — talked about the mystery of life.

But this was no mystery. This was death, plain and simple. And it was all my fault.

Because I couldn't stop my mother.

Twenty-one

When I open my eyes, I see Clarke, but I think it's Frank.

Excruciating pain shoots through my hip and arm. I try to speak but he puts a hand on my arm, tells me to hang on, Detective Fields, hang on. My hands move to my belly, but I black out again. When I come to, I'm in the backseat of a car. With every jolt, the pain cuts through me. I try to focus on the baby kicking but throw up instead. Sorry, I'm saying. I'm so sorry.

It's okay, someone answers kindly, but I wasn't talking to them.

I keep my eyes tightly shut, breathe through the pain, like my mother used to tell me to when I cut my knee open on the tarmac at the car park near our house. 'Mind over matter, my Ally bird,' she'd say, tapping my nose with her finger. 'I've got you. You will be okay.'

But now it's Clarke saying it, and I'm on a gurney in some echoey corridor, the smell of disinfectant overwhelming.

'The baby,' I croak, but nobody hears me. Then I'm dreaming about demons and long stretching shadows, and someone is crying.

–

When I wake up, I'm in a hospital bed, there's a monitor belt strapped across my belly and my head is wrapped in bandages. I can't move my right arm without wincing. I am completely alone. But the feathery heartbeat on the monitor next to me is the most beautiful thing I've ever heard.

'There you are now.' A nurse walks in briskly. Her pixie peroxide hair is as dramatic as her drawn-on eyebrows. 'Gave us all an awful fright, Alison.' She smiles kindly. 'You are at the hospital in Ballyowen.'

I can only nod weakly, too exhausted to tell her please call me Ally. I blink slowly, groggy from whatever pain meds they've given me. But

I need to get back to Dublin. I need to be in my tiny apartment, with the door closed and the brick view from the window. I need to retreat.

'Baby's fine,' she says quickly. 'Doctors are happy with the scans so far, but we'll be monitoring you for a few hours yet. The arm, on the other hand... kaput.' She makes a cracking open gesture with her hands and grimaces good-naturedly. 'How are you feeling?' She steps closer to me. 'I'm Maria.'

'That was my mother's name,' I say faintly, the throb of my head making my eyes twitch.

Maria hands me a glass of water from my locker and I sip gratefully. As I lie back, she fiddles over my shoulder with the drip, fixes my hospital gown. The gentle hands are so comforting that I close my eyes and pretend it's her.

—

A while later there's a small rap on the door and Clarke Casey pokes his head around it. He looks exhausted, his tie loose, his trousers creased.

'Now this one,' Maria says as she bundles the plastic wrapping from one of the tubes into a crinkly ball and stuffs it into a stainless-steel bin with a tinny clank. 'This one has been here all day. Needs a bed himself by the looks of it.'

She smiles and lays a hand on his shoulder as she trundles past him out of the room, promising to page the doctor to come and talk to me as soon as she's free. Then it's just Clarke and me.

'How are you doing, boss?' he asks shyly, and I sit up a little in the bed, embarrassed suddenly by how exposed I feel. He senses it too. I pull the blue hospital covers a little higher. 'How's the arm?'

'I believe the medical term is kaput.' I smile awkwardly and with my good arm pull my plait to one side, fiddling with the ends. My tell. I'm uncomfortable with all of this, not used to being this side of the hospital bed. 'Nancy?' I ask as he pulls a plastic seat towards my bed. He's far too big for the room and knocks the rim of the chair against the steel bar of the drip stand. He winces an apology, bottom teeth bared.

'They took her to Mount Michael in Dublin.' He grimaces again and shakes his head a little. It isn't good news. Mount Michael is the national head injuries unit. 'Tim has been calling regularly with updates. She's critical, I'm afraid.'

I think of Nancy's animalistic howling in the upstairs room of her burnt-out former home. Whatever happened the night of that fire, it set off a series of ripples that affected far too many lives.

'Is there anyone I can call for you?' he asks gently, handing me the plastic cup of water I'm struggling to reach. Despite my bravado, I feel bone-achingly weak. 'Your aunt maybe?'

Suddenly I'm too tired to do anything but lie back on the pillow. Besides, I don't want Sammy or anyone else to worry about me. Maria, the nurse, implied that I'll be home once the doctors are happy with the baby.

'And your head...' Clarke says. 'It looks... well, how do you feel?'

I wince slightly as I gently tap my head, feeling the extent of the injury.

'Honestly? Like I've been on a whiskey bender.'

He smiles.

'I told DI Nolan about what happened, by the way,' Clarke says, not meeting my eyes.

I swallow softly. Outside the room, in the corridor, something wheels past. There's a low tracking sound as it lurches slowly past my half-open door.

'I told the boss that you'd be off for the rest of the week. He said to finish up for... you know, for the baby.'

I'm about to argue but he's not finished. He starfishes both his hands between us, as if to pause my reaction. 'But I knew you would want to see things through here. So, why don't you take a few days and I can cover for now and obviously keep you informed.'

There's no way I could sit at home not knowing how this all finishes up. I have to find out what really happened to baby Liam. But right now, I'm too tired to think of anything beyond the next few hours.

'How bad is Nancy?' I ask, guilt gnawing that I was the one who encouraged her down those unstable stairs.

Clarke describes how he arrived at the house just moments after we fell. He found both Nancy and I inside the derelict house. 'When the beam fell, it must have hit her pretty hard. It's a serious head injury.

She's on the trauma ward. You were in and out of consciousness. You gave us all a fright.'

'I should have handled things differently. I should have waited for you...' I sit back against the pillow, feeling defeated, my head throbbing. We agree that Nancy was probably expecting Gerald Barrows to show up at the burnt-out house on Eastbourne Road. This could have been so much worse. Gerald had a lucky escape, but the more I try to remember what happened in that house, the more it seems to drift away from me. What had Nancy meant when she told me that it was all her fault?

'You were lucky, Detective Fields,' Clarke says. Those eyes are too kind again, and it makes me uncomfortable.

'Nancy kept saying it was all her fault,' I tell Clarke instead, pulling at the dark strands spiking out of the bobbin at the end of my braid. My movements feel weighted down, syrupy slow. I think of what Tim and the babysitter May had said – that Nancy was leaving her family. Could she have harmed her child? It's possible. 'Could it have been a sacrifice of sorts? She said she was to blame for Liam's disappearance. What did she mean?'

I think of the crystals in Nancy's caravan. The shrine of dream-catchers. Did any of it mean she was capable of something so unthink-able?

We both listen to the thunk, thunk of the baby's heartbeat a moment as we consider the case. 'Such a beautiful sound,' Clarke says, a look on his face that I can't pinpoint. 'In some more positive news,' he says after a pause, 'we have a Zoom with Jim Aylesbury – the fire inspector – tomorrow. And Frank Nolan has given the go-ahead to get the kid formally DNA tested. Paperwork's in motion.'

'Did Frank say anything else?' I can't help asking.

Clarke looks at me and shakes his head. Maybe I imagine the pity in his eyes. I didn't expect Frank to drop everything exactly, but it would have been nice to know he was bloody concerned about me and his unborn child. Didn't I deserve to have someone hold my hand and tell me everything was going to be all right?

'DS Fields?' Clarke is looking at me quizzically. 'I was saying that I'm trying to arrange a meeting with Vee, Nancy's sister. She lives in Dublin.'

'I'll come,' I say quickly, searching around the room for my phone. 'We need some answers. Didn't May say that Vee came over with a peace offering that night? What was she apologising for? Maybe it was her on the phone arguing with her sister?' Clarke starts to interrupt, but what am I going to do, sit at home watching *EastEnders* for the next few days? 'It's just a broken arm, Clarke. Don't be such a granny. You'll have to drive me back, though.'

He looks at me a moment and then shrugs. 'Whatever you say, boss.'

He hands me my phone and leaves the room. I lie back against my pillows, close my eyes, listening. Smiling.

Thunk.

Thunk.

Thunk.

Twenty-two

My mother, Maria Fields, spent her entire life living in Currolough, but back then her home was a sprawling mansion the other side of the lake from where she would eventually raise her children. When we were little, she told us about her upbringing.

Her father Hank, a rugged divorcé from the US, a visiting professor of linguistics at the University of Galway, fell in love with his much younger student, Maria's mother, Mary. When she told us the story of how my grandparents met, my mother always got that dreamy look in her eyes – the one that promised romance and happily-ever-afters. Despite their age difference, her parents got married. Neither family attended.

Mary and Hank fell in love with a rundown manor house surrounded by heather-choked land. The house they decided to call Lagan Hall, rose slowly and magnificently from behind the trees. Hank, from family wealth, put in a wine cellar, a huge drawing room, quartz countertops, a kidney-shaped pond in the back garden with a fountain. They had two daughters – Maria and her sister Rosemary – my mother and aunt who grew up with life-sized rocking horses, carriages for their dolls, and piano lessons. But mainly they loved to play among the reeds at the edge of lake, swimming in the water that seemed to change personality daily. Lagan back then and always was an eerie silver mist during the mornings, rippled and alive in the afternoons and a still, whispering robin-egg blue against the sunset in the evenings. Mother says she remembers glancing back up at the manor and catching her mother in the upstairs window of the house, watching them. After a while when she waved, her mother stopped waving back.

–

Sometimes, when I was little, I'd sit on the bank of our side of the lake with Sammy and Brendan, imagining my mother at the same age as us, matchstick thin, splashing across the other side of the lake, squealing in delight as she swung from ropes she'd hung from the overhanging trees with her sister Roe. If I closed my eyes, I could almost hear her shrieks.

But when she was nine, her mother left, and nobody knew why. In fact, Maria never saw her mother again, and worse, nobody spoke of her. We've since learnt she suffered with depression too. The silence of shame and misunderstanding. That grief was the beginning of a long, difficult period for my mother. Her father Hank never recovered from the abandonment of his young wife. The unaffectionate man with a thick beard and bent-looking nose that I only knew from photos didn't know how to raise two little daughters alone. Over the years, the grandeur of the house dissolved into dust; the neglected beauty with mould-blacked walls became smothered in ivy, its giant rooms more suffocating to him than any other place in the world. The house represented the life they'd planned together, their great forbidden romance. And instead, it became a chokehold.

The summer my mother turned twelve, she found him in the great dining room. Swaying socks low against the creaking mahogany beams that held the rope firm. More than anything she always wondered if her father even thought about how he would most likely be found like that by his young daughters? His suicide represented another type of broken promise. The things they'd been given seemed to mock Maria and Roe; the disgust that expensive plastic ponies and velvet dresses were all that remained of the unspoken pact between parent and child. A horribly poor substitution for all that her parents had failed to give them.

My mother didn't call out that day – the day she found her father hanging. She didn't scream for fear her sister Roe would see what she saw. She clamped her hand over her mouth to save her sister the pain of that awful view, squeezed that yell right back in deep. But it came out in other ways. Eventually. A cry for help that finally ended in the lake on that awful day in my own childhood.

It was the housekeeper that eventually found a young Maria, my mother, sitting on the polished floor of the draughty dining room a few hours later, still staring up at her father's body – a layer of dust on every other surface except the small, kicked-over chair. She'd been there for two hours.

Lagan Hall was sold. The sisters were sent to a religious-run orphanage nearby and, when she was eighteen, my mother bought the small house across the other side of the lake with her small inheritance. That was the house we grew up in. Over the years, the trees obscured our view across to the old mansion, but often I'd catch Mother staring across, a strange look on her face. 'I'm drawn to it, Ally,' she once tried to explain to me when I asked her about it. 'I can't return, but nor can I leave it behind.'

It was around then that her dreamy look turned to distress – the memory of a chapter, so crudely ripped out. I sometimes think that's what we all feel about growing up. That no matter what joy or tragedy that sticks to our skin over time, the bond between our old selves, the people we once were, and who we became, will always be slightly unresolvable. The search for how and when precisely it changed, an obsession.

Twenty-three

Vera Tierney, Nancy's sister, lives in a penthouse apartment along the Dublin city quays. It's not far from Precinct 12. In fact, from her large rooftop terrace on the tenth floor, you can almost make out the dirty yellow of our building in the distance. Vee is older than Nancy by five years, she tells us, as we cradle our coffees, me with one arm tucked under my sling. She has the same colouring – same dark brown eyes, same intensity to her face as her sister – as if she's afraid she'll miss something if she stops staring. Total focus.

Head tilted, she leans in close as we speak. I find myself watching to see if she blinks. Vee says that she's a solicitor with one of the top five international firms. As she chats with Clarke, she rearranges the edges of her beige cashmere V-neck nervously with perfectly manicured nails. From where I'm sitting, on the expensive outdoor bamboo chairs, everything inside the apartment is brilliant-white, tasteful, most likely selected by an interior designer. There's a painting with a shadowed cityscape next to a piano – one of those you can lift the lid and prop open. There's a landscape picture with a sullen sky and tiny framed maps of places around Ireland in black and white. I shift in my chair again, but there is no comfortable alternative – my body is punishingly sore. I traced the ugly, purple blotches in the mirror when I got home to my apartment in Dublin earlier this morning, thankful that the bulk of the injuries were to my back and legs. I wished Sammy could have come round and rubbed arnica into the most painful bruises, but I can't always expect her to rush to my side every time I mess up. I have to learn to do life on my own two feet. Plus, I don't want her to see the older bruises I always keep covered. 'You need to take care of yourself, Ally,' she said, shocked when I finally told her about the fall. 'And this little one needs you too, don't forget.'

I'm worth saving, I try to remind myself.

'Your arm broke your fall... literally,' the smiley surgeon with adult braces explained to me before I left the hospital the other day. I had to fight my way out – promising to go to my GP if there were any signs of concussion. We'd both glanced at the hump of my belly under the hospital covers. Neither of us had to say the words – we both knew it could have been so much worse. But it's the lack of sleep and the nightmares that are making today's tasks so much more difficult. Maybe I'll have to drag out Nancy's dreamcatcher after all. It feels as if I'm watching life through a thick pane of frosted glass – everything's clunky. Far away.

Clarke had driven my Discovery back to Dublin frustratingly slowly, glancing over to check I was okay, fussing over the angle of the seat, the temperature of the car, the potholes. The first thing I did when I unlocked the door of my apartment was to call Frank. He'd answered the third time I'd tried. Of course, he was concerned, he said. 'I've been worried sick, Ally,' he hissed. He'd be there within the hour, he said. He'd even bring some shopping.

Relief flooded through me – like it always did when Frank seemed in good form. But then the messages came – the apologies, the excuses. 'Gemma is playing up, Mel needs me. It's a little awkward right now.'

What did you expect? my inner voice sneered at me.

He's not yours to hold. He never was.

I settled for toast and bed, where I lay with the curtains open, watching reflections of the city lights dance on the ceiling, my brick wall view increasingly claustrophobic. It was then I think I knew that it was crunch time. I planned to lay everything out on the table as soon as I saw Frank next. The way I saw it now Frank was either in or out. I was either brave or I wasn't.

And if he was out – well, I knew the drill with that. But it didn't make it any easier to stomach. It was four a.m. by the time I'd decided on a plan – a follow-by-numbers outline for myself so I didn't waiver. Today, after work, I plan to open the envelope to discover the baby's gender, meet Frank to let him know, and then explain to him that I'm not interested in being second best any more. Or prepared to accept how he treats me. Choose, I'll tell him.

Pick me, I'll secretly hope.

Once the baby is here, things could be different between us. He'll be different. If I can't respect myself enough to ask him to decide if it's all or nothing, then I have to respect what this messy arrangement will be like for the little boy or girl curled sleeping inside me. I think of Tori Jones from the Bayview apartments then, and how her case would be handled by a juvenile court, now that her mother admitted it wasn't her that started the fire. It would be handled sensitively, of course, and there could possibly be a case for self-defence, the solicitor had explained, But as sad a situation as it was, a man had still died, and the child would have to deal with the consequences of that her entire life. The relentless ripples of other people's decisions on innocent lives.

–

That's why the flutters in my stomach aren't totally baby-related, as I sit stiffly in the chair on the olive-tree-clad terrace on the tenth floor of this fancy solicitor's building. Clarke is encouraging Vee to speak about her sister Nancy – about the time before the fire. She excuses herself, standing up to answer a call, and Clarke's meaningful look brings me back to the present. He can see I'm distracted.

'Strange the way she says that they haven't spoken in years,' he whispers, as we watch Vee disappear through the glass sliding doors. 'Or seen each other. She's saying that after the fire, Nancy changed a lot.'

I roll my eyes.

'Of course, she did, Casey – she lost her whole fucking family and got her face burnt off; I mean what do people expect?' I'm starting to really feel for Nancy – she's a product of her trauma too. She has the marks every time she looks into the mirror to deal with, on top of everything else, the scars of the night singed into her skin, impossible to ever forget. The ones who should have been there for her abandoned her. I know how that feels. Of course she blames herself – it was her child. That doesn't mean she had anything to do with the fire.

Vee steps back out and slides the glass door gently closed behind her. She has a wad of tissues in her other hand and is apologising.

I rearrange my face. *Pull it together, Ally.*

'It's just been so long since I had to think about any of this,' Vee says, dabbing at her eyes. 'It was such an awful time.' She sits back down on the garden chair and crosses her ankles together. Her pants are dry-cleaning smooth, her stylish ankle boots flawless. I pull at my messy plait with my good arm, embarrassed suddenly about my cheap suit and the scuff of dried mud still on the rims of my boots, but glad I applied my lipstick before Clarke picked me up.

'Tell us,' Clarke urges kindly. He's wearing his usual Hugo Boss shirt, light pink this time, but the past few days are showing on his face. He has a five o'clock shadow and he spent the journey from collecting me at my apartment stifling yawns. This case must be getting to him too.

'You have to understand that Nancy and I haven't spoken in years, so when I got the news the other day about her fall, it...' She trails off, blinks her eyes as if to chase tears. She takes a chest-swelling breath. It's all quite dramatic actually. Then again, her sister was in the ICU at Mount Michael. Maybe I should cut her a little slack.

We say nothing. She seems to struggle to choose the right words.

'It brought a lot back,' she finally says. 'We fell out just before that tragedy a few years back.' She shakes her head, as if trying to get rid of the memory of the fire. 'Besides from when she was recovering from her burns, I haven't seen or heard from her in over six years.' Her face changes – like something crosses over it. A memory or a moment plays out and her eyes get a faraway look. 'Nancy felt so guilty,' Vee is saying, blowing her nose. 'She always put a lot of pressure on herself. To be perfect. Even in her work. She cleaned houses...' Vee glances up to examine our faces. 'And she was a hard worker, you know. She wasn't just a cleaner.'

Clarke nods, letting the silence linger. We're not here to judge anyone. But Vee's hesitation shows me something – a miniscule chip on her shoulder. I learnt that in the psych classes they made us take when we did interview techniques. Listen to everything they say – analyse every detail. I notice too that Vee doesn't have the same thick Kerry accent her sister has. It has been flattened; the music stripped from it. She sounds posher than Clarke Casey and that's saying something. I could already tell by her clothes, her apartment – Vee Tierney isn't keen to shout about where she originally came from. Maybe I wasn't alone in whitewashing the past.

'What do you think happened that night, six years ago?' I put to her.

'I know she would have run straight to the kids.'

'But she couldn't find them,' I say gently, because no matter what had actually gone on, this woman obviously carried trauma from that night too. She'd lost her nephew and, by proxy, her sister.

'Well, the report said that Joey was out on the trampoline. And Hugh had gone to his work party.'

'Ms Tierney, why did you have an argument with Nancy on the night of the fire?'

Vee shifts in her seat, arranges her face into an expression of hurt. Her hair is shorter than Nancy's, cut into a bob.

'We clashed sometimes, is all. Like all sisters.'

'About what?' Clarke presses.

'Her choices.' Vee raises her gaze. 'I didn't always agree with them.' I presume she's talking about the affair with Gerald – the fact that Nancy was about to leave her family. 'But I sat with her in that hospital for weeks. Every day, every operation. I was there when she first opened her eyes. The hope in them each time she woke – the hope…' she presses the tissue to her nose once more, taps lightly, '…the hope that maybe it had just been a bad dream. But her hands, her face…' Vee's talking quickly, remembering. 'Her poor face. She was in so much physical pain but then the guilt came. In so many ways, that was even worse. That's harder to heal from. There's no skin graft that can bridge that gap.'

A rheumy-eyed seagull perches on the balcony ledge a moment. All three of us glance at it automatically before it launches itself off the side, a death-defying swoop into the cool blue day.

'None of that was supposed to happen,' she sniffs. I glance up sharply. That's exactly what May had said. At the nursing home. 'But then afterwards,' Vee continues, 'Joey couldn't be around her. He was hysterical. She found that extremely hard.'

'I can't even imagine,' I say. 'Then what happened?'

'Well, they all stayed with Hugh's mother for a bit, but it was clear that it was too upsetting for the child. Plus, Nancy's grief was… unusual. She kept insisting baby Liam was alive.'

'And you?'

'I had my new job in Dublin – I was here on the weekdays and came home to Kerry on weekends. I tried to stay in touch. For a while, but she wasn't interested in maintaining our relationship.' A deep breath. Vee's forehead wrinkles as she speaks. 'I tried to be there for her, but Nancy was depressed. She kept saying her baby had been taken. It was intense. Her and Hugh tried to make things work, but everything was broken – nothing survived that goddamn fire. I told Hugh…'

She stops, shakes her head and starts again.

'Hugh got an opportunity at work in Spain. He's a data centre engineer. It's very specialised. We all felt he needed a fresh start. So, he left, and it made sense for Joey to go with him. To get away from it all.' She shrugs. 'Everyone thought it was best.' The sentence lingers a little – hardens in the air before cracking around us – shards of that decision that would scatter sadly for years.

'But now Nancy says she's convinced her baby son is alive and living less than an hour away,' I remind her gently. 'Gerald Barrows's son.'

Vee stiffens.

'I'd heard that all right. It's clearly all nonsense. But Gerald and Nancy, it was a silly fling. She didn't even love him.'

What a strange thing to say, I think.

'And what was the relationship between Hugh and Nancy like?' Clarke intervenes.

'Obviously not great… afterwards.'

'Go on.'

'The truth is that she'd been having problems for a few years. Maternal stuff. It was hard on Hugh. Nance got close to Garda Barrows because she cleaned at the station. People talked.'

'Hugh definitely knew?'

Vee nods sadly. 'He found out they were having a… fling. But it wasn't serious in my opinion. Poor Joey was a challenging little boy and so Hugh was left with the burden of that. If you know what I mean.'

She looks down as if struggling with what to say next.

'I don't actually…' Clarke questions softly. God, he's good. This guy has what it takes to get the best out of his interviews. Now if only he would roughen up, lose the good guy act for the tough stuff.

'What do you mean exactly by that?'

'Nancy was flaky, flighty, whatever you want to call it. She wasn't around much. Hugh did most of the parenting. Then she started talking to me about leaving him. In her head, she and Gerald Barrows were moving to Dublin. It wasn't about Gerald; it was about escaping the life she had. The life she didn't want.'

'But it didn't work out like that, did it?'

'Obviously the fire happened, and her injuries and all of that. Nancy was completely devastated. On top of everything. It was a horrible time. Then Hugh and little Joey moved away and Nancy, well, nothing worked out for her.'

Her perfectly made-up face looks sad, the perfect portrait of regret. But the lingering sentiment – the unfinished sentence as we sit in the luxurious surroundings – seems to be that nothing worked out for Nancy *like it worked out for me.* There it is – a latent jealousy, the satisfaction that she has won. I imagine my professor of psychology at Garda training, Mike Jessop, analysing what Vera Tierney was saying about her sister – the crude comparisons. They were subtle, but if you looked hard enough you could tell their relationship hadn't been about having each other's backs at all.

'What maternal stuff?' I say, more sharply than I intend. 'What do you mean by maternal stuff?'

'You know, like probably what we'd now call post-natal depression, that kind of thing. Nobody spoke about it, but I knew from the way she was after Joey that she wasn't herself. She couldn't cope. She wasn't cut out for motherhood, she told me. She said she didn't think she was a good enough mother. She was terrified she'd mess it all up.'

I suppress a shiver.

'And what did you think?' I could hear Mike Jessop's advice in my ear: *Get your interviewee's perception. It colours the path they want to take you down. It says more about them than what they actually say.*

Vee looks up. Doesn't hesitate. 'I think she was right,' she says. 'It's not a natural inclination for everyone, I guess. She wasn't cut out for motherhood.'

There's an iciness to her words that makes me uneasy.

'You said you don't speak any more? May, Nancy's neighbour, said you came over the night of the fire with something to apologise to Nancy about.' I check my notes. 'A peace offering, you described it as.'

She nods and reaches for her cup, swirls the bottom, examines it. 'Yes, I felt bad. I didn't agree with what she was doing. I let her know. We'd argued in the weeks beforehand.' She glances at me. 'But it was Christmas. And sisters... you know? I just dropped in some chocolates for Joey and a pudding... peace and good tidings and all that.'

I shrug, noncommittal. I'd never talk Sammy down like Vee was Nancy. No matter what. But sisterhood is different for everyone.

'You know she's not doing great at all.' Clarke steps in, ever the bleeding heart.

Vee gulps the tea, nods again, squirms in her chair. 'She has Tim,' she says firmly. 'She made it clear she didn't want a relationship with me. She moved out to the caravan park a few weeks after she recovered. Never left. Never spoke a word to me again.'

'Because she was depressed?' Clarke questions.

'Because she just couldn't handle the fact that I went on to have my own family, my own baby.'

I can see shock register on Clarke's face. But I suddenly understand how horrific it must have been for Vee to be having a child when Nancy had lost her own. Not sure I'd fall out with Sammy if we were in that situation, but then again, who knows? Tragedy is the stone that ripples slowly outwards, and you can't control any of it. Not a thing.

Vee continues. 'I didn't tell anyone for a while. I was nervous. It had been a very long time coming. I'd... struggled to conceive. When I eventually shared the news, Nancy didn't react well, accusing me of being insensitive when I called her a few months after the fire. *How could you*, she kept saying. *How could you, Vee?*'

She dabs at her eyes again, but the mascara hasn't run at all. Beyond the glass doors, I see the toys neatly lined up, small race cars scattered to one side of the pristine couches. I hadn't noticed before.

'It must have been unimaginably difficult on her,' I say. 'I mean she'd just lost her baby in the most awful way possible. I can't imagine what that grief does to a person.'

Vee looks up sharply. And for the first time, I see her demeanour slip – she looks desperately sad, suddenly, as if she doesn't want to say what she is about to say.

'She shouldn't have had him if she couldn't take care of him.'

I can hear the blood rushing in my ears. Then Clarke pulls his chair closer to her – the scrape of it makes me jump. Darkness is infinite. Anything is possible. I sit back and watch a moment, analysing Ms Tierney. What has made her this bitter and jealous of her sister who has experienced so much pain herself?

'People knew she wasn't right. They felt sorry for her. She kept going on about saving the baby, finding the baby. Then later, she said the baby was taken.'

We all take a breath, sit back in our chairs a moment. Vee looks spent – either the exhaustion of holding onto this for the past six years or something else entirely. I take in her perfectly arched eyebrows, the facial glow, the glossy lips. This is a woman who knows how to look after herself. The epitome of success – if that's how you measure it.

Nancy could have been anything, I'd overheard her say to Clarke earlier when I was mulling over things about Frank. There'd been a jealousy to that – a sting at the end of that statement that lingered.

Vee taps her fingers on the table. The universal symbol for 'you need to be on your way'. But Clarke's not finished. He consults his phone notes again. 'In Hugh's statement, taken a day after the fire, he admits leaving the faulty heater on in the bedroom,' he says.

We weren't investigating the cause of the fire – that was in the report. But what if it wasn't an accident at all? I watch to see Vee's reaction.

'I'm not sure,' she says carefully. 'In fact, I'm not sure that's what happened at all. It could have been any one of a number of things that made that house go up. That woman May could have knocked over a candle. She was drinking at the time. Did they tell you that? They only picked up on that oil heater because Hugh was so upset it might have been something he did.' She sounds defensive now. She stands up.

'I'm sorry, I have a case in court this afternoon and I need to get on the road tonight before weekend traffic hits.'

'Anywhere nice?' I say quickly, adjusting my sling – deliberately not looking her in the eyes.

She glances up, smooths a blow-dried tendril behind one ear. 'Drop off. My child's father… we don't live together.'

Clarke carries his cup to the sink as we make our way out.

How sad for this kid who may never have even met his aunt. Or his baby cousin.

I picture Nancy lying motionless in her hospital bed in a ward in Mount Michael. There is so much I want to ask her about — so much we need to know about what really happened that night. I suspect we'll have to pay Gerald Barrows another visit too. He'd told officers sent to speak to him after Nancy's fall that he didn't have any idea why she might want him to meet her there at the old house.

'Why didn't you go?' One of them reported asking him.

'I was nervous she wanted to hurt my child,' was his simple answer.

What is clear, and what I told Clarke when I eased myself into the passenger seat of the car after leaving Vee's apartment, is that Hugh Wills holds the key to much of what really happened in their marriage, and with the fire. Hugh Wills has not answered his phone since we called him the day before looking for Nancy. I'm not sure he even knows the mother of his child is floating in the space between life and death.

Or if he even cares.

His phone is still going straight to voicemail. Not only did that concern me, but it also meant we couldn't confirm very much else until he called back or until Nancy woke up.

Twenty-four

Jim Aylesbury is a mournful-looking man, clean shaven with a crown of curls. He sits at a desk at his office in Limerick as Clarke and I video call him from the boardroom back at the station. Frank is in meetings all day – he's promised to visit me this evening, at my apartment. The big showdown. If he shows up at all, that is.

'So, you are saying there was no evidence of a baby ever found in that house?' I press Aylesbury and his sad-looking, pixelated face on the screen. There's nothing in the background where he is – just a bare white wall with a lone nail stuck into it – as if a painting had once hung there and had been removed. Empty. In fact, everything about him is slow and dreary. I wonder if people are born like that or if they just get ground down.

'You take the lead,' I said under my breath to Clarke before the call, as we waited for Jim Aylesbury's face to appear on our screen. It was time to get some facts about what the experts found that Christmas night. But I couldn't help jumping in early on.

'So, you are saying there was no evidence of a baby ever found?' I say again, as Aylesbury taps one of his ears awkwardly, indicating he didn't quite hear the question.

Bloody technology. I lean closer to the computer to hear his answer. I can smell Clarke's piney shower gel and the toast he told me he shovelled into himself at the station kitchenette before our Zoom call. It isn't unpleasant, but it is definitely distracting.

'What I'm saying is that there was no visible organic material present, but that was unsurprising given the intensity of the fire.' Aylesbury looks like this is the last place he wants to be. But I have a feeling that it's an unfortunate personality trait rather than ennui from the delicate matter of what we are discussing.

'But how do you know there was a baby there at all, then, in that case, Mr Aylesbury? I mean, don't you test for that kind of thing?'

'Excuse me?'

I'm not sure he's heard me or if he's just surprised at the question. I turn the volume higher, making a subtle face at Clarke to demonstrate my frustration with the shitty Wi-Fi here.

'I said how do you know—'

'I heard what you said,' Jim's voice cuts back quickly, interrupting my question, his words as sharp as the edge of a knife. 'That's up to the Gardaí. Our team is responsible for trying to find the cause of the fire.'

Clarke pushes forward, with that respectful manner that also manages to exude an air of authority. It's probably down to his legal training. I picture him in court – making his point – that earnest face willing you to believe what he's telling you. I wonder again why he ever left law – he'd have made a good attorney. Fair and firm.

'In your professional opinion, is it possible that there was never a body at all in the room where you say the fire burnt strongest?'

Aylesbury's lips curl from confused to horrified at what we are implying.

'I know Ms Wills was convinced her baby was taken and that the cot was empty but no, we discounted that. I mean… obviously at this stage, I couldn't say either way. I'm not qualified to say.'

'But you did, didn't you?' I sit forward against the cheap boardroom table – the apple-smooth curve of it resting against my protruding belly. 'You signed off on the report that it was an accidental fire and that the baby had most likely perished in the fire which burnt so intensely, it says here… that there was nothing left of it at all.'

'We also had to rely on the Garda investigation.'

'Concluded by Gerald Barrows?'

'Correct.' Jim Aylesbury looks smug – like he was used to getting As in class his whole life. He reminded me a little of Detective Cummins too – we'd met him in the hallway earlier. He'd made a typically flippant comment about whether I was sure I wasn't having twins, but at least he'd had the grace to ask about my injuries. He hadn't dared to touch the bump, not after the last time.

'Are you aware Gerald Barrows was having a romantic relationship with Ms Wills?' Clarke goes in for the kill.

A pause. Aylesbury is so still that for a moment I think the computer may have glitched again. The internet is particularly bad up here on the sixth floor. But no, there he is, his head bobbing, slightly startled as he stammers his answer.

'I wasn't,' he admits. 'But I'm not sure how...' He trails off, reflecting on what this new piece of information might mean for his report.

'You can see the conflict of interest that could have arisen when it comes to what exactly happened that night. And given a new, more recent development that involves Gerald Barrows, we need to make sure there was nothing buried within that report.' Clarke speaks evenly – with a calmness I'm growing to admire. He must have been one hell of a solicitor.

'We had no reason to doubt there wasn't a baby.'

'But didn't you hear what Nancy Wills was telling you? That she believed her baby was taken. That there wasn't a body in the cot.'

'What I remember was that she was hysterical.' He stops, aware perhaps of what he's said and how he's said it, his automatic dismissal of the hysterical mother. That won't play well in this situation – especially not with me. 'She was understandably distraught, is what I'm saying,' he mutters. 'I had to factor in how that might affect her perception of events too.'

What was that supposed to even mean? I feel Clarke's nonsense radar ping beside me.

But it's what he says next that surprises us both.

Aylesbury takes a sip of water and adjusts his jacket. The pressure is on. And whatever he's about to reveal is making him very uncomfortable. But despite any corners he may not have explored in the investigation in the past, he has a professional obligation to get to the bottom of the case, especially when new evidence emerges.

'Well, if we are really getting into it. I suppose it's worth saying that the intensity of the fire that night was initially surprising.' He says the words slowly.

'Go on.' I try to ignore the throbbing pain in my arm again. I refused to take even one of the foetus-friendly painkillers despite the doctor's reassurance they were safe. But this pain is making me irritable.

He's stalling.

'Mr Aylesbury, we have information that means this fire potentially wasn't accidental at all. That's the basis we have to work from now. So, if there is anything at all that you red-flagged, even if you dismissed it in the end, please tell us now.'

He flips a page in front him that we can't see.

'Localised burn patterns to the floor and overhead damage can sometimes indicate the presence of accelerants,' he says, monotone. 'In some cases, the damage can be inconsistent with naturally available fuel.'

Both Clarke and I remain silent. My heartbeat quickens. Aylesbury flips another page of the report, bringing it closer to his face as he peers through his thick frames. Then he throws the file down and removes his glasses. He sighs, as if this is a large inconvenience to him.

'We didn't write it in the report, but I remember observing that the window in the bedroom was clean of soot on the fire side but melted all the same.'

'What does that mean?' I practically shout.

'It's an indication that a fire burnt unnaturally intensely. Usually, a sign an accelerant may have been used.'

'Arson.' Clarke says, and the word floats in the air of the boardroom for a moment.

'And you didn't write this in the report, why?' I can't help my tone. This guy had one job, but he was too busy dismissing Nancy as hysterical to listen to anything she was really saying.

'We spoke to Hugh Wills and concluded that the faulty oil heater – the plug – was the cause of the blaze. The intensity was most likely the result of the fuel from that unit.'

'Most likely?' I scribble a note to Clarke. *We need to speak to Hugh Wills.* I underline the NEED a few times in red pen. He nods and continues questioning Aylesbury.

'Again, why wasn't this in the report?'

Aylesbury clears his throat.

'It was explained to the investigating officer, and he made the decision to rule out arson. We didn't find the circumstances suspicious, based on the very plausible explanation offered by Mr Wills.'

'A baby supposedly died, and you took the father's word that oil from the heater accelerated the blaze?' Clarke sounds incredulous.

'An oil heater in the room, yes. Often household items can inadvertently turn into flammable material that accelerates a small fire into something more... catastrophic. This would have been an intense heat, for a prolonged period of time.'

'Wouldn't there have been an explosion?' Clarke probes.

'Depends if it had tipped over or not.'

'And was there? An explosion?'

'It's too hard to say.'

Clarke throws down his pen in frustration. Maybe he was sharpening his soft edges after all.

'But you tested for the accelerant?'

'We had no reason to think it was anything other than a terrible accident.'

'Did you test for accelerant?' Lawyer Clarke pushes, his voice like steel. 'Mr Aylesbury, please answer the question.'

Silence lingers heavily in the air.

'We did not.'

'So, let's get this straight. Is it possible that something else, a different type of accelerant may have been used?' Clarke says quietly. I hold my breath. Aylesbury sighs heavily and eventually answers.

'It's possible, yes. Technically.'

My phone lights up. It'd better not be Frank cancelling on tonight. I wouldn't put it past him. I glance at the screen, it's Billy from the lab. I'll have to take it.

'Excuse me a moment.' I slip out, balancing the phone under my chin as I navigate the heavy boardroom door with my sling and my bump. Clarke goes to help but I motion to him that I'm okay. 'Keep going,' I mouth, already knowing I'll watch the recording of this interview over and over. In the corridor, I lean against one of the windows while Billy talks.

Billy and I have been mates a long time, ever since he helped me out on a dodgy urine sample given by a drunk driver, back in Galway. He was the one that ran an additional test based on a hunch. We got the driver, who was three times over the limit when he knocked down the cyclist, when HCG levels were found. If it was true, the male driver was, in fact, pregnant. He went to jail for switching his sample with his wife's thanks to Bill's diligence. I'd written a letter of recommendation for his son who'd done work experience with us at the station too. I trusted him implicitly.

'That DNA doesn't match,' he tells me, slightly breathlessly. Billy's one of the good guys around here – smart and flamboyant, amazing at his job. We've known each other a long time but he also knows when work is work and anything involving a child takes precedence, even off the record.

But his statement catches me off guard.

'You are shitting me?' I picture him sitting in his lab at the Garda Tech Bureau, probably wearing one of his colourful stripy shirts under his white lab coat, always a coffee nearby. I scrape a smudge of something off the window with my fingernail. The Dublin rooflines stretch out across the city. A sparkle in the distance marks the tall thin spire that dissects the city into North and South. A literal pin on the map.

'No,' Billy says. 'The Dexter kid's sample from the gumshield doesn't match the Barrows we have in the system. Gerald Barrows. You sure that's the right name? Currolough station, County Kerry?'

'Uh-huh.' I breathe out. 'Did you get enough sample?'

'Ally...' Billy doesn't like to be questioned. 'I didn't say inconclusive. I said no match. Zilch. That kid Dexter... he's definitely not Gerald Barrows's child.'

I exhale heavily and the window I'm leaning against fogs. I rub it away with one swoop of my palm. This wasn't some small-town tragedy. This might actually have been kidnap. And now potentially arson. Nancy's child could be alive.

My phone pings.

'Hang on, Billy.' I scan it quickly. It's a message from the reporter Cynthia Shields about the story, due to be published this Sunday in one of the biggest broadsheet papers. It includes a week-old interview with Nancy Wills. Her source about the child being spotted at the market has agreed to go on record. She's tired of waiting and wants to run a few things past me regarding the investigation and possible links to Eddie Jones's death.

I ring off from Billy, promising him I'll thank him with pints as soon as this baby's out. 'Watch out Tinder,' he teases, and I force a gruff laugh, knowing his heart is in the right place. But I'm beginning to tire of my love life being a joke to everyone around here.

–

In the corridor, outside the boardroom, I root inside my leather bag for my heartburn tablets. Gastric fire was something I thought I'd escaped until earlier this week. Separate pain radiates from my shoulder to my temple – one long throbbing ache. Every movement is excruciating thanks to the huge bruises on my right hip from the fall. I crouch down to use the ground as an aid, cursing the impracticality of having an almost-human strapped to my lower abdomen. Strands of hair fall from the pathetic ponytail I tried to pull back this morning with my claw-tooth clip. I blow it out of my face and reach deeper into the bag, feeling beads of sweat trickle down my spine. It's almost impossible to get the foil off the blister packet with one hand, but I manage to jam two chalky tablets between my teeth and crunch gratefully.

Taking a breath in preparation to try and haul myself up off the ground, I hear a voice I know off by heart.

'Ally?'

Shit, I'm supposed to be off work. I look up but already know who it is. I quickly finish chewing.

'Hi Frank.'

And for a moment, seeing his face, I can't move – I'm out of energy, physically and emotionally. I'm hanging on by a thread. A wave of pain hits me. It's so overwhelming that I think I may pass out.

Then Clarke almost knocks me over completely opening the boardroom door. His head is down, he's texting furiously.

'Jesus, sorry Ally,' he says, alarmed as I hold my good arm up to stop the door hitting me. Both men move to help me up and I shake them off. The air is fraught with tension somehow. I look at Frank and then back at Clarke. There's a strange look on Frank's face.

'It's Detective Sergeant Fields to you,' I say sharply to Clarke, as I haul myself upright. Whatever blossoming friendship that has started forming between Clarke and I during this case withers right here in this moment, like the sad plant pots at Tudor Lawns Nursing Home. That look of hurt in his eyes as I take him down in front of the boss is brief, but in the pit of my stomach I feel something else too – regret. Sometimes people are just trying to be nice, Sammy tells me time and time again when I push them so far away. You'll end up with nobody if you're not careful, she always warns. I'm thinking lately that having nobody is the safest way to be for me. Being alone is self-preservation because I refuse to be blindsided like I was back then. I just have to keep reinforcing my walls. Yes, even against the World's Nicest, Clarke Casey. But there's no time for that now. Frank is looking at me, his eyebrows raised.

'I'm just tying up a few things,' I stammer, in explanation for my presence at the station. Frank says nothing, observing me with eyes I can't read. I feel Clarke absorbing my change in demeanour. I'm embarrassed he's seeing this exchange. 'I'm heading home now anyway,' I say quietly, my words soaked with the tone of apology I know Frank expects.

But Frank ignores me and starts saying something about the Jones case to Clarke. He seems to know everything, but I haven't been able to speak to him about it all week. *Strange.* They discuss Gerald Barrows like I'm not even there.

'Nancy Wills may have been in a relationship with the investigating officer Gerald Barrows,' Clarke tells Frank, who nods authoritatively.

'Nancy planned to leave her husband and children,' Clarke continues. 'She had an argument with her sister Vera in the days leading up to the blaze, and one with her husband Hugh, who confronted her about the affair.'

All I can do is stand and nod, not meeting Frank's eye, and weakly offer some updates; new information has come to light – the fire may have been started deliberately. Nancy is stable but unconscious.

'Anything else?' Frank's all business now. His eyes hard behind his long fringe. His face looks more angular, his hair less fawny somehow. Has he lost weight maybe? He's brusque to the point of being rude.

'The child, Joey, who was a five-year-old at the time, was seen playing with matches,' Clarke says. 'According to the babysitter.'

As this debriefing goes on around me, I stand there uselessly. Insignificant. There's definitely a weird tension. I know Clarke suspects something is probably going on between Frank and me. And I'm not sure if it's my imagination or not, but Frank seems short with Clarke too. Frank looks from me to Clarke and then drops his bombshell.

'Hugh Wills and his son Joey are here in Dublin,' he says, and I suspect he's enjoying the surprise on our faces. 'I asked them to come over after Casey told me about Nancy Wills's accident.' He glances at Clarke. I stare at them a moment, trying to absorb what he has just said. 'You can meet them at the hospital tomorrow morning, Casey. I've arranged an interview for you at 9:15 a.m.'

Clarke looks down at the ground while I try to put two and two together. I don't mind him reporting back to Frank while I was in hospital, but has it been happening all along? Even while I was trying to get through to Frank myself? Did they think I wasn't able for this? I immediately want to smash something hard. I study the scar on my hand from the wall I punched years before and wonder if Reilly's will let me come down and have a session at the boxing gym.

It isn't a coincidence that ever since Frank started here, he's put me on shit cases, and now this. His respect for what I do seems to have diminished with every night we've spent together. His controlling chokehold over me has been so subtle I didn't realise it had extended into my work. It's hard to fathom the control he has on my life – the control I've *let* him have on my life. This is my fault.

'I'll come to the hospital tomorrow too,' I say, trying to push power into my voice.

Clarke looks embarrassed. Frank shrugs. Then as Frank turns, he lingers at my shoulder and drops his voice. He has the same sour-smoke smell as always, but this time it makes me pull back a little.

'See you later, Ally. Eight-ish, yeah?'

I rub the cast on my right arm self-consciously. I nod.

He's all that I have.

Clarke hasn't heard. He's stooping to pick up my bag, pushing back inside the folders that have slipped out. Then Frank's gone and the air around us feels chilled.

'The DNA didn't match with Gerald,' I say to Clarke frostily, too angry to even show my fury right now. I made the correct choice not to let Clarke in; as nice as he is, he stabbed me in the back by being Frank's messenger boy. I was right all along. Shaking my head in disappointment, I wonder when he started going behind my back, updating my boss, as if I was unable to do my job. I was pregnant, not lobotomised. Jesus Christ, it was just a broken arm. 'We'll put in the formal request to see if Dexter matches Nancy.'

Then I remember the message from Cynthia. As brilliant a reporter as she is, that article can't be published. Not now. Not yet. We are so close. I check the screen of my smartphone – half past six. Clarke seems eager to stay and talk, but I remember what Sammy kept saying to me – take care of the baby, take care of yourself, Ally. Plus, he knows he's upset me.

I need to eat. I need to think about my future with Frank. I have to start allowing a degree of separation from work. I need to start loving myself before I can take care of this baby.

'We'll talk in the morning, Clarke,' I say dismissively, tapping out a quick message to Cynthia on my phone.

'I'll give you a lift,' he says, his hand on the back of his neck, ruffling his hair awkwardly. But I shake my head and drop my eyes back to my phone. I speed read what I've written.

Yes, I'll talk, Cynthia, but not until tomorrow. I've updates for you that I have to firm up. Please hold the story until we've spoken.

We have to delay that article.

She'll know I'm stalling too, but now that Hugh Wills is back in the country, everything's changed. He might finally have the answers that we couldn't get from Nancy. The father-shaped hole in this story needs to be finally put under the microscope. I'll be interested to meet Joey too – the strange little boy that May described, who enjoys playing with matches and God knows what else. What does he know? And how did he cope when he was ripped away from his mother at such a young age? What part does that rupture play in all of this?

Stop obsessing over work, Ally, I hear Sammy's voice in my ear. *Go home! Eat!*

'Are you sure you don't need a lift?' Clarke looks like he wants to say something else, but I'm so over all of it. I'm over the confusing feelings with Frank and the equally confusing feeling I'm getting the more time I spend with Clarke Casey.

'Yeah. I'm sure.' My tone is deliberately curt. I don't even look up from my phone until he slowly turns. Then I watch Clarke walk away, hands in his pockets. What does he do when he's not at work? I remember what he said about his idealisation of being a detective, of making a difference. I feel so sad suddenly. He actually deserves someone good on his side. But, as I know too well, good people don't always get the things they deserve. That's why I am inclined to take what I can from the universe, plunder it before it tears any more flesh from my bones. I don't owe it anything at all.

For the first time ever in my career as a detective, I turn away from my work, walk away from my desk, and do something just for myself. I get an Uber to the grocery store under my apartment block and throw broccoli and asparagus into my trolley. Cherry tomatoes, perfectly ripe avocados, organic chicken breasts, spring onions. Using my good arm to reach, and my bump leaning gently against the trolley, I add honey, peaches, cashew nuts, raspberries, sweet dates and my favourite brand of Greek yogurt.

In the toiletry aisle, I knock a conditioning treatment with Argan oil into the half-full trolley, a nail file, new razors, a pomegranate face mask. As I make my way to the conveyor belt, it occurs to me that although Frank is coming over later, this gesture is for me alone. Maybe Sammy's words over the past few days made a difference – reminding me that I'm precious too. Or maybe it's the slow realisation that even though I may not deserve good things, I may as well try now that there is new life coming into the world. Perhaps I'm finally understanding how fragile our bonds with others really are. I rest my hand on my belly a moment, close my eyes and feel the energy of the tiny life inside me. I breathe good vibes towards it. *I want more for you*, I murmur to myself, standing in the queue for the checkout at SuperGo.

Against the backdrop of low beeps and lower ceilings, by a checkout pockmarked with colourful monthly offers, I vow to be a better person – a calmer, more considered person for my child.

See Ally, I say to myself, you got this. Sammy will be so proud of how far I've come.

I press €5 into the hands of one of the trolley handlers to carry my groceries upstairs for me. The moment I push the door closed behind him, I take a long hot shower, being gentle with my plastic-bag-encased arm. I let the conditioner melt into my hair like butter and rinse it off slowly with my left hand, enjoying the pulse of the hot jets of the water against my poor, sore body. I wrap myself in my fluffiest bathrobe and pull on soft oversized Christmas socks. I tell Alexa to play Sia, volume eight, while I one-hand cook the chicken stir-fry Roe used to make us, colourful with seasonal vegetables. Baby dances beneath the robe as I sway happily in the kitchen.

This is happy, Ally.

Try to remember this.

With a little flip of joy deep in my stomach, I remember my plan.

Ignoring the box of old photos and clothes from Aunt Roe's house I had Clarke lug up to my hallway when he dropped me home from the hospital in Ballyowen, I pad along the wooden laminate into my bedroom and kneel by my underwear drawer. Sliding it open, my fingers find the smooth envelope buried beneath scrappy curls of lace. Then, sitting on the edge of my unmade bed, I use my longest nail to slide the envelope open. My heart hammers beneath the embroidered hotel monogram of the robe I never gave back. I lie back against my pillows and, ignoring the traffic sounds in the street below, I clutch the thin black-and-white paper to my chest. The shiny edges scroll inwards, towards its centre. I smooth them back gently. I take a breath and finally turn it over to see what the paper beside it reveals.

Gender: Female.

A little girl.

Heart to heart, I close my eyes and hum the song my mother used to sing as she lathered our hair in the bath into 'moo cows' horns'. I let myself think of a mirror fogged with condensation. Splashy squeals. Sammy's toes smooth against my back.

'*Wild foam and a million stars. Tell me where all the dreams turn to gold. If it's not too far, my little star.*'

It must be only eight when I drift off, Nancy's dreamcatcher strewn beside me on the crumpled duvet, its complicated weaves so much more intricate up close.

Whatever happens... I promise my baby girl, my hand draped over the warm mound of skin between us.

No matter what happens... I will never leave you.

I will never leave you. Like my

mother

left

me.

Twenty-five

The downstairs door buzzer cuts crudely through my dreams, chasing the soft flickers of formless shapes away, like a million frightened birds darting skywards.

I sit up, disorientated, my hair a mass of damp frizz. Outside, it's surprisingly dark. There's a disgusting smell. Burnt onions. I'd turned off the pan, but the lingering heat had ruined the meal.

Frank.

I check my phone and realise it's almost nine p.m. He's already an hour later than he said he'd be. I pull my robe tighter and peel my aching body from the bed. Stuffing the piece of paper announcing the gender of our baby into my pocket, I shuffle into the hallway of the apartment. I check my appearance in the small hall mirror and buzz Frank in, still slightly disorientated.

He smiles as I greet him, standing oversized in my small apartment. His hair is neatly brushed to the side, he's freshly showered, eyes twinkling. Deliciously comforting, but out of place somehow too. Frank makes a fuss of me. Your poor arm, he says, kissing it softly and pushing the hair back from my face. He strokes my cheek, presses against me. My poor girl, he says and kisses my neck so softly I shiver. God, I've missed this. His power over me intoxicates. I lean into him, let him clutch me close, appreciating the want in his eyes, because suddenly I also understand that that's all it is. For him this is all a thrill, this is desire, this is the excitement of having someone other than Mel. A strange power.

He parts my robe slightly and slips a hand under it, brushes cold fingers against my nipple. I shiver and he grips me harder, pushing me against the wall. He groans and pulls the knot in my dressing gown cord open. It gapes as he grinds against my bare skin roughly, his hands grabbing my bottom, pulling me towards him. My size makes it uncomfortable, but there's another type of discomfort – I'm starting to understand this is no basis for the kind of relationship I want for my child or for myself. It may sustain me in the short term, but I have bigger responsibilities now than accepting scraps for myself – snatched morsels of something masquerading as love.

I know what it's like to have and then lose a parent.

I know it will be hard. And though I have an inkling what outcome is probably ahead of me, I want to be sure. I want to hear him say it, so I know for sure during the lonely nights ahead. I want to hear him say it so I don't second guess myself. I kiss Frank's neck and twirl away from his grip, citing dinner as an excuse. He's not happy. 'I'll take care of this later,' he says in a low voice, smoothing his hair in the mirror. A threat within the promise.

–

'This isn't too bad.' He forks a burnt bit of the stir-fry when we are settled in the small galley kitchen, and chews dutifully. He's wearing jeans and a navy shirt, he seems at home here, relaxed. The room itself is tiny but I had it redone last year, opting for more country-style blue cabinets rather than the dirty white of the original spec. I put in quartz countertops and hung two rose gold pendant lights at different heights over the small two-chair table in the corner. There is a row of three different cacti on the shelf in little cream pots, and a spinning spice rack next to the kettle that doesn't get much use.

I slowly separate the charred pieces from the too-soft vegetables. Although I've lost my appetite, I scoop up the faded colours and think of the scan photo as I swallow. Vitamins for my daughter. My arm still aches.

'Casey getting on okay?' Frank asks conversationally and I nod, but my mind is elsewhere. 'Bit slow on the uptake, is he?'

I make a face as if I don't know what he means. Finish chewing. 'He's good actually.' Despite everything, I know that Clarke is a decent guy, a fair detective that will most likely make an excellent detective someday.

'Heard he had some kind of breakdown,' Franks says lightly, studying my face. 'And left law.'

I raise an eyebrow. I can't picture Clarke unsure of anything. He seems so… steady. So self-assured. It makes me sad to imagine him struggling. He's given no indication. But who am I to speculate about someone else's problems?

I take a breath. Put down my fork. It is time.

Sliding the picture towards Frank, I meet his eyes.

'Your daughter,' I say ceremoniously and the immediate raw shock on his face hurts my heart.

Then suddenly I see the reality of the situation so clearly. He already has a daughter. Now he'll have another, this one on the periphery of his life. A half-love. Like what I have with him. And that isn't good enough any more.

I feel sick – the acrid smell of burnt chicken flesh mixing with his lemony aftershave. The taste of bitterness dirtying the air.

Then he composes himself.

'Ally,' he says, his eyes still on the image, an indecipherable look on his face. He reaches for my hand dutifully. But I pull mine back and he looks up in surprise.

'I want you to be with us,' I say, trying to contain the sting of tears. Hating myself for having to beg. 'Fully. I want us to work on things, Frank. To be a family.'

His eyes narrow slightly. He rubs a hand over his face and sits back in his seat. His napkin slips to the floor. I tuck loose strands of my unruly hair behind my ears.

I wait for what I know is coming.

'What do you mean?' It's a dangerous question. Something else flickers across his face too. I try to adjust my request. I try to make it land more softly, less likely to annoy him.

'I want us to be together, officially.' I try to smile, to rationalise a new possibility.

What if we could make it work?

'You know that's impossible, Ally,' he says, in his too-quiet voice. 'We talked about this before.'

I feel pathetic. But even as I say the words aloud, I'm questioning if my version of happiness really does involve Frank living here with us at all? Maybe it's the *need* of it that I crave more than the reality of having him. Or maybe I'm just tired of being cast off by people who are supposed to love me. I tug at the ends of my hair, the tips stupidly soft from the treatment I smothered it in earlier.

Frank speaks again, more assertively this time. 'Ally. I've Mel and Gemma...' He's shaking his head. But the more he considers what I've brought up, the angrier he seems to get by the audacity of my suggestion. 'You always knew what this meant, Ally. I told you it couldn't be anything more. You were cool with that.' He glares at me, turns his palms outwards defensively. He fills my space.

'Things change, Frank.' I tap the image on the table between us, maybe more violently than I should. 'I'm so tired of tiptoeing around. I'm tired of being this person. Of being second best.' Even saying these words makes me sad.

Frank sighs. 'I could never leave them, Ally. You knew where I stood. Where you stood.'

'What about this daughter?' I cry, the tears falling now.

What about me?

He shakes his head. 'Why are you pushing me like this?'

It's devastating. But in a way, I don't care because this is the bandage that I know needs to be ripped off. I take a breath. I do what I should have done so many times in the past but never dared.

'Please leave, then,' I whisper, too overwhelmed to fight. Seeing that tiny image on the table in front of me makes me cry harder. She deserves more than this too.

He stands up, scraping back his chair in anger.

My words spill out.

'You didn't call me in the hospital,' I say, my voice cracking with emotion. Frank looks at me, disgust on his face. Even though I'm telling him to leave, I can't help but reach for his hand as he turns to go. See how pathetic I am? See what I deserve?

I wipe my eyes with the back of my robe. The food on the plate is a blurred mess of mushy asparagus and congealed soy.

'You were the one that fucked up, Ally. You shouldn't even have been working. You should have finished up weeks ago. You are a complete mess.' He spits the last few words, his previously twinkling eyes hard and mean. Frank stands over me, his height domineering. Unhappy, no doubt, that his careful arrangement has suddenly gone rogue.

He goes to walk away but then stops and turns. I can see his temper overflowing. I can tell I've pushed him to his limit.

'You want the truth?'

I shake my head miserably. 'No.' I hold my left palm up, flat against his words. I know they won't be kind; I can't take any more pain.

'Look at the state of you. Look at you.' He snorts. 'Everyone thinks it, by the way. I hear them say it all the time. You are an embarrassment.'

The kitchen blurs blue through my tears. I'm not able for this kind of assault. It is so much worse than when he slammed me into the radiator, or when he knocked my head against the frame of the car window. Because everything he is saying is entirely true.

His voice is low and mocking now.

'I feel sorry for you, Ally. Everyone does.'

I think of the concern on Clarke Casey's face – it wasn't me he was worried about – it was himself – of what he'd have to put up with working with someone like me. Clarke didn't want to be my friend at all, he pitied me. I place a hand over my stupid heart.

Shame creeps up my spine.

'Stop,' I tell him. 'Please stop.'

But then he says the words I've been asking myself since I saw that line on the pregnancy test.

'If you've no regard for yourself then how can you even look after a baby, Fields? What's *wrong* with you?'

The question hovers over me, over my snotty face, over the burnt dinner, over the lump of the woman clutching a piece of curled paper. Hope draining out of her like blood.

'No wonder you need fucking therapy.'

He taps the side of his head unkindly, and memories of girls in school doing that about my mother flood back. I should have known the time I'd tried to get help would be thrown back in my face. A few months ago, I confided in Frank that I was speaking to the shrink at work, trying to soften some of the sharp edges of my childhood memories. I was trying to find a way to feel safe. Now he'd weaponised that vulnerability too.

He turns to leave, and I panic.

Don't go, I want to say. It comes out differently.

'I'll tell Mel,' I whisper, and at that moment I hate myself more than I've ever hated myself. This is the abandonment that scorches. I have no intention of ever speaking to Mel. What could I say? She's everything I couldn't be if I tried. Absorbing what I've said, Frank stops walking, his back to me. I almost see the hairs on the back of his mottled neck bristle.

There's a moment where there is no sound at all, except for my wet, raspy gulps, the hum of the fridge. I know the line of whatever this is has just been crossed. I know it's game over.

Frank strides quickly back to me and for one horrible second, I think he's going to hit me. I wince, my eyes shut tight and brace myself, hands across my belly protectively.

'Don't touch me,' I cry.

His face is too close to mine, his breath meaty, when he whispers his threat.

'Don't you dare tell Mel. Because I'll tell everyone what a proper fucking psycho you are. I'll tell them about the nightmares, about the panic attacks. You think they'll ever let you on cases when you are such a goddamn flake?'

He takes my arm, the one in the sling, and slowly squeezes. Purposefully bends it back the wrong way. I moan in agony.

'Mind yourself, Ally, won't you?'

He throws my elbow down in disgust. And then he's gone – the door slamming behind him. The echo of the pain he caused pulsing up and down my arm. My heart racing in shock.

His words ring in my ears.

Fucking psycho. Everyone thinks it, Ally.

Not so tough now, Detective Fields, I think to myself cruelly. Not so tough at all.

–

For a long time, I sit at the kitchen table without moving.

As I try to contemplate what just happened, I cradle my arm, crying softly, a low moan of something I think is pain every few minutes. I feel bereft, unloved. I want to speak to Sammy, but I know what she'll say and right now I don't want to hear it. Plus, knowing her, she'll probably suggest speaking to Frank's big boss. I can't have that. That would be career-ending.

The apartment grows cold. Despite my huge, stolen robe, I'm shivering. Eventually I drag myself down the hallway towards bed but I stop by the box – the memory box from Aunt Roe's house.

I slide down the wall and sit next to it, exhausted. My everything in a small, battered box advertising firelighters.

Beneath the photos, there's a huge brown manilla envelope. I shouldn't delve any further. I'm too emotional. But I'm drawn to it, to those folded sheets of paper tucked carefully inside.

My father's letters. His untidy scrawl. I hadn't even known he'd written when he went away once Mother got sick.

I think of his young, brave heart – how it had let him down when he was just sixty-five. I swallow back tears and check the date – the letter was before the accident, before Mother was taken from us.

Dear Maria, my love, the sky here tonight is black and clear. I'm thinking of you and the children. My four brightest stars.

I stop reading, drop the letter and drop my head to my chest. I let the tears flow.

Why did he leave her when she was so ill? I know we can't always explain the actions people take, but he left my mother and us, at a time when we needed him most. Roe did her best, but maybe if he hadn't left...

I think of the two tombstones overlooking Lake Lagan. I scan the letter again.

The colours, the smells, it's all here waiting for you Maria. I'm here waiting for you. Our fresh start.

It was a move my parents had considered when things got difficult for them in Currolough. A new chapter on the other side of the country, away from her wistful gaze across at her father's rotting mansion. But they both knew that the same problems would exist. Deep down, I knew too that Mother's depression would have followed her wherever she went. Back then there wasn't much in terms of treatment, and not without shame. She was 100 per cent alone. She'd obviously felt that too.

I slide out a picture of Sammy and me.

It's my eighth birthday. She's holding my hand solemnly outside our house and I'm grinning to camera. She's almost six years old, plump, wearing her good peach dress with a matching hat. It's a beautifully sunny day, I remember everyone saying weather like this was a blessing that time of the year. We didn't need the white, pearl-buttoned cardigans we picked out that spring in Currolough with Mother. If only I could go back, to start again, on that sun-dappled morning, knowing then what I know now. I swallow a sob.

The world feels greyer all of a sudden. There's a hopelessness that chokes. Was this how my mother felt – an airless life, giant brick walls whichever way you turned?

—

The buzzer cuts through the hallway and I jump in fright. Frank apologising. It has to be.

I haul myself up, tucking the letters and photographs carefully back into the box. I smooth my hair and despite the shocking finale between us, my heart is thumping with anticipation. He's sorry. He still wants me. Things might be okay.

I swing open the door, hating myself for my eagerness. And there stands Clarke Casey, looking sheepish. I'm immediately disappointed. Then confused.

'Sorry boss, I wanted to apologise for going over your head,' he mumbles. 'I texted and called you a few times, and then I started getting worried when you weren't answering. I just felt… you know, the baby…'

I stand there like a fool, unsure of what to say.

'I'm sorry. It seems silly now…' He gestures to my robe, then sees my mottled face. 'You are obviously fine.' He rubs his jaw with his hand as if he wants to say something else.

'Come in.' I wipe my face with the back of my left hand, keeping the broken one tucked up against me like a wounded wing.

'No, I should go,' he says, clearly mortified, 'I didn't mean to…' He goes to leave.

But I insist he comes in. The truth is that he was right to be worried.
I don't want to be alone right now.
I don't think I should be alone right now.

Twenty-six

'Jesus, what happened?'

Clarke steps inside and closes the door to the apartment. His face is creased in concern because suddenly I can't stop the tears that stream down my face. His embarrassment at having turned up on my doorstep so late fading compared to the surprise of my dishevelled, tearful appearance. Under the hallway light, there's no hiding that I'm in a pretty bad place right now.

'Did you ever have a time in your life when everything was all just too much, Clarke?' I try to stem the flow of tears with my dressing gown sleeve. My voice is flat. I return to the box, sit cross-legged on the floor and lean my head back against the wall. Nothing matters now anyway. I don't care about anything.

'Everything's a mess,' I tell him – probably the first honest statement I've uttered about myself in a long time.

I close my eyes and just breathe. He slides down the wall beside me. Clarke says nothing. We simply sit.

I can't stop the shame that saturates. I am so tired of feeling guilty. I've felt it my whole life – for not doing more to help Mother. For not saving Brendan, for not being good enough to love, for being the other woman, for bringing a child into such a cruel world. For never being enough.

It's exhausting. Whatever way you cut it up, I constantly fall short. And all I was looking for was someone to love me. Why is that so hard?

The past few days on the Nancy Wills case, I've grown accustomed to Clarke's calm presence. I try to put my finger on what it is. The lack of expectation maybe. He isn't asking me to be someone I'm not. My inclination towards hostility isn't as necessary with Clarke Casey as it is with others.

Right now, I am too upset to care about being the world's toughest, Detective Sergeant Alison Fields. I just need to talk to someone. Or have somebody listen. There are limits and I've reached mine.

'Yes,' Clarke answers softly after a while. 'I actually do know what it's like when everything is too much.'

I open my eyes, still resting my head against the wall, I turn my head towards him. Outside a car horn beeps. Streetlights shine through the worn shades of the bathroom where the door is open a crack. I can make out a vein in Clarke's temple, watch it pulse a moment. But Clarke Casey isn't opening up. Not yet.

'I've had my fair share of shit thrown at me, too, is what I mean.' He shrugs, placing his hands flat on his outstretched legs. His feet almost touch the opposite wall of the hallway. He's dressed more casually than usual – a white T-shirt and jeans, paired with very clean branded trainers.

'But you seem so even, so bloody well balanced. Why doesn't it make you overwhelmed like me?' Then I remember Frank's comment – about a breakdown.

Clarke, to his credit, laughs. The sound peals through the empty corridor and it warms the air a little. The vibrations of darkness scatter a fraction against the sound of mirth. My spiral slows.

'We all do trauma in different ways, I guess.' He smiles. Then, a beat. 'Are you okay, Detective Fields? I mean is everything okay with the baby?'

I nod. 'My problems are a little more of the emotional vein rather than physical right now I'm afraid, Casey.'

'Frank,' he says simply, and I nod because what else can I do? I'm sitting naked under a robe, on the floor of my shit apartment, five times the size I usually am, with snot all over my face, scarecrow hair, my ridiculous lipstick smudged. I'm beyond exposed. Besides, it's just Clarke. 'Fucking Frank Nolan,' he says, shaking his head. But it isn't just camaraderie, there's something more to this – something a little more personal.

'You know something I don't?' I ask hesitantly, because maybe I don't want to know at all.

'I know Frank's type is what I mean,' Clarke says, his gaze direct. His blue eyes are too kind for this moment, but there is a sadness too. 'My wife, Kim...' He stops a moment and then, as if reaching a decision, Clarke continues to speak, his voice more serious than I've ever heard it. 'We were both solicitors – we met at law school.'

I nod encouragingly, glad, selfishly for a moment, that I am not the only person in the world with problems.

'Everything was fine until one of the bosses in the firm she was working in started harassing her. But it was so subtle, you know. She'd come home upset that he'd made her work late, got her alone and made derogatory comments about her appearance and then tell her she was picking it all up wrong. That kind of nonsense. I was furious.' He's staring straight ahead, his voice tense.

'Frank didn't take advantage of me, Clarke,' I interrupt. I need him to know that I am not a victim here. I am just someone who makes very bad choices.

'There are abnormal power dynamics that sometimes we don't even realise are going on,' Clarke says, glancing at me sideways. And I keep my mouth shut because this is his story. 'So it was mostly just making her really uncomfortable, until the head of Glennon and Sons...' He stops a moment, gathering himself – facing whatever awfulness he knows lies at the end of that sentence. 'Until the head of Glennon and Sons, eh... well, he sexually assaulted her... in his office while they were working on some housing takeover deal late one night. Violently.'

I gasp and look at Clarke's face. There's pain beneath every pore. Even now, reliving it, he is stiff with fury and sorrow. I can see it in him. I can see how much he cares. His hands are clenched, curled tight.

'Oh fuck. Clarke, I'm so sorry.' Goosebumps race up my back, along my arms. Poor Clarke. That poor girl. He shrugs as if to say there's nothing he can do about it now. 'Ellis Glennon?' I picture the older man from the news footage I'd seen on TV. The country's most powerful legal firm. Ellis was a well-known, self-made millionaire after finding a niche in representing dodgy vulture funds. He'd survived a tribunal and several inquiries. A Teflon cockroach I'd heard some people say about him down the station, but I knew that Frank was a fan.

Clarke shakes his head. He looks miserable. 'No. His son, Simon.'

I blow out my cheeks. *Jesus Christ.* Simon Glennon couldn't be more than about twenty-five years old. His dad may be dirty smart, but Simon, well, he was known as being the dope who got the job just because of who he was – a real loose cannon.

'What happened?' I ask, softly, mindful of how personal Clarke is getting. But as Sammy said, sometimes you had to remember we are all just human. Here we are, two people, bottoms on the cold floor, sharing our sorry tales – trying to find solace in saying, *Yes, this is shit, and I know a little about how that might feel.*

'We were only just married, you see. And I hadn't a clue how to deal with any of it. Kim was fucked up. I convinced her to go to the police, but because we left it a few days there wasn't much in terms of physical evidence. Kim was traumatised. She withdrew from everything. From me. The police questioned him, but he passed it off as an employee-related disgruntlement, discredited her work, turned it back around on her. Can you imagine?'

His voice shakes as he speaks. He drops his head a moment, and I tap his shoulder with my good hand awkwardly.

None of this is easy. Nobody has it easy.

I let him gather himself.

'We just couldn't handle it,' he continues, his voice a little steadier. 'It was bigger than us, you know? Kim started believing it was her fault. The firm disgraced her. We had no evidence. It was her word against his. It was so difficult to watch this happen to her, re-traumatising. Imagine having to try to *convince* someone that this happened? Imagine people thought she invented this horror… for what? For attention?'

He shakes his head, his face ashen. He takes a beat and I simply listen.

'Then, when nothing was done, Kim just crumbled. Simon Glennon was out there living his life and she couldn't even take off her clothes to shower. I was angry all the time. I couldn't fix any of it. She went home to her parents in Highbury and never really returned. We separated, and a year later I left my job, retrained as a blue, figured I might actually get to take down the bad guys.'

Clarke doesn't look like an overgrown teen any more; he looks like a man who's had his heart broken and worse, his faith in the justice system was torn from him too. I feel desperately sorry for the tall man slumped beside me on the wooden floor of my apartment.

'So, Ally, you asked me before if I'd seen horrible things. Well, I have lived horrible things. I've lived with my wife smashing every mirror in the house. I've lived to see a man destroy a woman and then get promoted. I've lived to watch her swallow that morning-after pill, even though all we wanted in the entire world was a child.'

I think we are both surprised at how loud his voice has become. And how emotional. The shadows of the headlights outside cast long shapes either side of us. We sit with what was just said for a moment, neither of us inclined to move. We are glued together, to the floor, to the heaviness of this moment.

'It was all we wanted,' he echoes in an almost whisper.

I wipe new tears away.

'Sorry,' Clarke says eventually, shaking his head as if just realising the magnitude of what he's divulged.

'No, don't be sorry.' I put a hand on his shoulder again. 'I can't imagine how awful that must have been. Poor Kim.'

'Yeah, I hear from her every now and then. She's seeing someone, you know.'

'Like a therapist?'

'No.' A wry laugh. 'Like a guy. But I'm happy for her.'

'Meanwhile, you are on your impossible crusade.'

'You're not wrong.' He smiles. 'But I hijacked what you were saying about Frank. I was here to apologise for going over your head. He asked me to update him, and you were in the hospital. I'm sorry I didn't tell you. I was trying not to overburden you.'

I pull the robe tighter around myself, as if shielding myself from Frank's reach all over again.

'Ugh, it doesn't matter.' I shake my head. 'You are here now – a good distraction. Cup of tea?'

I haul myself up, wincing in pain. Clarke shimmies his back up the wall and for the first time, notices the box sitting sadly against the skirting board – a few old pictures sticking out at angles.

'Packing?'

'Unpacking actually. The past.' I sigh and give it a small half-hearted kick. 'Family stuff, you know,' I say.

The rookie insists on taking over tea-making duties and I'm grateful to fall onto the couch in the living room, beyond emotionally drained. I close my eyes. I hear Clarke banging presses in the kitchen. I know I should feel embarrassed about the state of the place, but suddenly none of that matters. Being caught off guard, vulnerable, it hasn't killed me, has it? In fact, I feel marginally better. I don't know if it is Clarke's company or the morbid comfort of misery-sharing, or a little bit of distance from what had to happen with Frank, but when he places the tea on the table in front of me and a bowl of sliced peach with yogurt, I feel immeasurably less devastated. Less hopeless anyway. I feel cared for. And I'm hugely grateful. I hear the wet hum of the dishwasher working. He crouches down by my gas fire and the flames flicker to life.

'How did you know about Frank and me?' I ask, curling my feet beneath me, letting the spoon glide through the white peaks of yogurt. Clarke sits in the chair opposite, his long legs stretching out in front of him. Maybe, in another life, we could actually be friends. I admire his tenacity, his determination to do the right thing, his kindness in a crisis. Kim wasn't completely unlucky. Clarke is probably the best of them. I wonder who would ever fight such a war for me?

'Sorry to tell you this, but everyone knows.' He blows on his own tea. 'It's common knowledge.' I close my eyes a moment. 'Frank wasn't exactly discreet,' Clarke adds, a small detail to try and alleviate any blame on my part perhaps. 'For what it's worth – people thought he was a dick for well, dicking you around. Apparently, he has a bit of a reputation for it.'

'Sure.' I roll my eyes – as if anyone in that station cares about me.

'I'm serious,' Clarke says. 'People really respect you, Ally. They think you deserve better. I think you deserve better.'

I picture Sammy saying the same. I have a feeling Clarke and Sammy would get on. 'You remind me of my sister.' I laugh. 'She never thinks anyone is good enough for me.'

'She's right.' Clarke smiles kindly. 'You shouldn't be so hard on yourself.'

'It's hard not to be when you have a habit of inviting chaos into everything.'

'It's clearly not something you are doing on purpose. You can't get annoyed at yourself. Maybe it's something that's out of your control.'

I take a sip of tea and swallow softly.

'The thing is, Clarke, I know exactly why I am the way I am. It's changing that that's been the problem. I didn't have either of my parents growing up, you see. I… there were things that happened…' I trail off. It's impossible to go there. But Saint Clarke seems to get it.

'Listen.' He sits forward. 'I know it's almost eleven at night and you're my boss, so don't fire me for saying this. But sometimes it's about accepting our limits and realising *why* we take the actions we take. That can be quite freeing. Deep down you know you deserve so much better than Frank fucking Nolan. So, fuck him.'

'Yeah, fuck him.' I smile and raise my tea in the air to cheers to that. 'Thanks Clarke. You're fired.'

He laughs and I realise I've missed this – just being free from pent-up worry all the time, always coiled tight with fear. In a strange way, this pain I am feeling is a clean pain – a detachment from something I know isn't good for me. I picture myself peeling the icy chokehold of the confusing relationship with Frank away. It's that same feeling again – the feeling I had when I knew this baby was the right thing. It's time to trust my instincts again for the first time in a long time.

I remember something Sammy said that day of my eighth birthday party – the peach dress and matching hat day. Blowing out my candle on the ice-cream cake Dad had picked up from Peterson's, I made the same birthday wish I'd always repeated like a mantra. Please help me to cheer up Mummy.

Then it was Sammy's turn to wish. What did you wish for? I asked her later in our double bed while Brendan snored next to us. To be like you when I grow up, she said. I didn't know what to say to that, so I tickled her and told her when we grew up, we'd solve all the world's problems: abolish homework, rule cake mandatory every day, make Mummy better, get rid of every baddie. We giggled under the covers, planning our shared future as Father thumped the wall to shut us up.

I do deserve more. Sammy does too.

And someday soon I'll have a daughter who'll maybe want to be just like me. I have a responsibility to those who have my back, to be that person. I know Frank is never going to see me as anything other than his bit on the side. So instead of focusing on what I don't have, I'll make sure I remind myself of what Clarke said. That we all do the very best we can do in difficult moments. And sometimes there is no room for regret and shame because there is simply too much pain.

'Ally,' Clarke says, his voice gentle. 'What I've learnt over the last few years is that just because bad things happen, it doesn't mean life will keep hurting. Besides, whatever it is, I'm sure you did your best at the time. And sometimes that's really all that counts.'

I study the sincerity in his eyes, his hopeful face, his assuredness that everything will turn out right. I vow to try to share Clarke Casey's beautiful vision of the world.

Twenty-seven

I speak to Sammy straight after my shower the next morning. I've taken off my sling, but my cast remains. I'm dressed in navy maternity trousers and an oversized knitted cardigan I found at Aunt Roe's. Nothing fits, but I hook on an old hairband that pulls my cheekbones back slightly. I'm here for the little wins. I wiggle the last of my mascara across my upper lashes and add my usual flourish of lip colour – candy-floss pearl, though the application is a little less considered with my left hand. I banish thoughts of Frank from my head. Breathe Ally, I command. Positive vibes only.

Clarke texts while I'm talking to Sammy.

There in 10 minutes.

I locate my shoes under the couch, where we'd stayed up talking until one a.m. about the Nancy Wills case. I close the box of photos – gently folding down the stiff cardboard. That particular mess will have to wait.

'So, Frank's out of the picture?' Sammy asks, her voice quieter than usual. I wonder if she tires of always having to listen to her big sister's problems. I should probably ask about what's going on with her. But that's never been the type of relationship we've really had.

'Frank's a dick,' I tell her instead, and of course, she agrees. She's always said that. I just never listened. But she doesn't know about the physical side of things. I never let her see that part. 'Clarke said Frank had told everyone about me and him. Imagine how awful that was for his wife.'

'Eh, you were the one sleeping with him, and you're worried about his *wife's* feelings?'

'Ouch. Touché.'

'You're the other woman.'

'I know,' I say quietly. 'But I'm trying to make things right.'

'Tell me about this Clarke guy.'

'Actually, he's picking me up in a few minutes, we're going to the hospital to see Nancy Wills.'

'You said that. But what is he? Like... a rebound?'

'Jesus, no.' I snort at the idea. 'He's a... I suppose he's a friend. He's a human that isn't a dickhead?' She laughs, and I smile into the mirror where I'm fixing my face. 'That's the best I can do for now, Sammy. Clarke is just a nice person to be around. I mean, he talks funny and says things like "hooray" and "marvellous" completely unironically but it isn't his fault he was born into a family of barristers from some mansion in the Midlands.'

'Wow, what a description. Remind me never to get you to do my eulogy.'

We laugh half-heartedly together for a moment, but the funeral reference leaves us both picturing the sad church with the mean priest and the congregation full of pitiful faces. Too close to the bone. Still too close to the bone.

Ping.

'Gotta go, Clarke Casey is outside.'

'Put on your sling,' she calls, but it's too cumbersome and, if I'm being honest, I'm sick of feeling damaged. I tuck my cast in under my burgundy cardigan gingerly. I want to finally put to rest the demons from Nancy's past. Both Clarke and I are determined to get to the bottom of the Wills case, and fast. The clock is ticking too – HR found out my due date and are going mad. I've negotiated two more days to put things to bed with this case. I have a feeling Frank had something to do with updating them.

Asshole.

—

Clarke looks tired as I clamber into his white SUV. I hold up my hand before he mentions the goddamn sling. He's twitching to say it. I know he is.

'It's off. It's fine. Let's not discuss it any further,' I say, trying to move my arm to demonstrate it works, and wincing instead. He closes his mouth.

'Yes, boss.' He grins, putting the car into first gear, and I'm relieved that our surprisingly intimate conversation from the night before hasn't impacted our professionalism. In fact, we'd had a good chance to really dissect what had happened on this case after our talk veered organically back to our working situation.

Clarke had admitted that he thought the child, Joey, had something to do with the Christmas fire. The wall of silence around him is weird, he'd said. The fact that the dad swooped him away so quickly... 'Look at the Tori Jones case,' he'd said. 'It happens.'

I'd told him I had fears that Nancy herself might not be as innocent in all of this as we'd thought. I think back to her face the day in the burnt-out house – the horror of guilt written across it. But, given my history, I knew I had to be careful not to colour the current case with my experience of my own mother. Not every mother drags their child into danger, Ally, I remind myself. In fact, most do the opposite every single moment of their lives.

Today is about confronting Hugh about his wife's relationship with Gerald. We'll get confirmation about Nancy's state of mind and grill him on the accelerant Aylesbury admitted might have been present that night.

Clarke drops me off at the hospital entrance while he parks. It's the perfect time to make the call I've been thinking about all morning. I linger at the front glass doors of the hospital and watch visitors arrive; worry etched across their faces for the most part. An ambulance pulls up and spews a stretcher into a team of waiting hands. The victim wrapped tightly in wires and oddly shaped tubes, buried deep, their fate in doctors' hands now. I eventually get through to the journalist.

Cynthia Shields ran the original story on Nancy Wills – the one the tabloids twisted into something uglier. As they tend to do. She was the real deal, and it would take a lot to get her off the Wills story. I'm usually all for exposing injustice, but I want to make sure, now that Nancy is so badly injured, that it isn't gratuitous. A burnt baby and a disfigured mother sleeping with the local Garda. It doesn't sit right with me. Not while the facts are still floating, unaligned. But I also know that Cynthia Shields will need to fill her front page this late in the day, and I have an idea.

Ten minutes after I speak with her, Clarke emerges from the long-term car park, frowning at his parking ticket.

'Daylight robbery.' He is looking at the per-hour car park prices in disgust.

'Do you know, they charge the same even for those coming in for three-hour chemo or the nurses working double shifts?'

Clarke looks horrified and I am once again struck by his unshakable persistence in pursuit of justice. 'That's not right.'

I murmur my agreement as we make our way into the hospital.

Mount Michael is a new build, west of Dublin city. It's a centre of excellence for head trauma. The reception is shiny, with beige reflective flooring, a gift shop to one side of the entrance with card stands and books. We're meeting Hugh at the first-floor canteen at 9:15 a.m. I check my phone: 9:10. I consider updating Clarke on my conversation with Cynthia Shields but decide not to yet, in case I don't manage to pull off my plan. He's back in his designer shirts today – one with a small polo player in the corner – his hair is freshly combed and his eyes a worried-blue when I catch them in the mirror of the elevator.

'All good?' I ask lightly.

'Yep,' he responds cracking his knuckles, but I can tell he's nervous. I wonder if it's the prospect of his hunch about the kid having something to do with the fire. Or maybe bringing up Kim last night had given him a difficult night's sleep. I know how that goes. Either way, it really isn't any of my business.

–

Hugh Wills is already there when we step into the canteen overlooking the lower flat roof of one of the hospital buildings – someone has planted a little garden to one side of the terrace and the green daffodil shoots are already poking through in some patches. But Hugh is sitting indoors, behind a long white table with chairs attached. Another smaller male by his side. Joey, I presume. Hugh stands as we approach, holds out his hand formally. I shake it with my left, explaining my injury while absorbing his demeanour. He's not a tall man. Broad, yes, like he works out, and tanned too. His head's shaved and he has the crinkly eyes of someone who smiles a lot. But he's not smiling now. He's looking from Clarke to me nervously, placing a hand on his son's shoulders.

'This is Joey,' he says in a thick Currolough accent, and I realise that he reminds me a little of my own dad – energetic, an inner joie de vivre. Joey has a thatch of blond frizzy hair, shaved both sides, freckles along his nose and cheeks, Nancy's eyes – brown and searching. The beginnings of adolescence sprouting across his face.

He mutters hello, then stares back at his hands, which are gripping the table in front of him.

'How's Nancy?' I ask carefully, and Hugh shakes his head a little. Joey's body stiffens, so I park that particular conversation for a moment.

I buy coffees and hot chocolates while Clarke makes small talk with them about life in Spain. Mother of God, is that him speaking Spanish? He's even doing the goddamn lisp. By the time I sit down opposite them, Hugh has loosened up a little. I know I have Clarke to thank for that. He sips his hot chocolate innocently, but I'm sure, knowing him better now, that everything has been done with intention.

'Joey, would you mind if we talk to your dad for a few minutes?' I ask diplomatically, and the child, who is about twelve, jumps up, clearly relieved to escape the serious adults.

I watch him put his air pods in and wander out to the roof garden with his cup in his hand.

'Must be extremely hard on him,' I say as my opener, my eyes still on Joey. I lift my latte to my lips.

'The whole thing has been.' Hugh looks sombre. The eye crinkles flatten out. He stirs his coffee slowly with the small wooden paddle.

'Mr Wills, listen, I know this is difficult for you too, but we need some answers about what happened on the night of the fire.'

He looks up. Nods. Clarke steps in, apologising ahead of time for any distressing questions.

'Did you see your baby before...'

Hugh nods. 'I checked in on him before I left for my work party. He was awake but not crying.'

'Was Joey around the baby? Is there any possible way that perhaps something happened, an accident for example?' Clarke tries desperately to find the right words.

Hugh glances up and over at his son as if by simply watching him, he could protect him. There's a strained silence. I wonder if Clarke has insulted Hugh – pushed things too far, too fast perhaps. Then to my horror, Hugh wipes tears from his eyes.

'That's been my biggest fear for the past six years.'

I realise I've been holding my breath.

'In what way?' Clarke continues to tiptoe the questions – just enough to keep Hugh talking but not enough to scare him silent. Hugh looks away, tries to compose himself.

'My baby son died, in an unimaginably horrific way. You are asking me if it's possible that his five-year-old brother had something to do with it. I don't know... it's possible. That's what keeps me awake at night.'

'Did Joey show any signs of being jealous of the baby or did he ever speak about anything...?' Clarke trails off, unable to voice what he wants to say to the anguished father.

'I mean... Joey wasn't an easy child. Isn't an easy child. But as far as hurting someone – I just can't picture it. If anything happened at all, it was a game or an accident.' The cup goes up to his lips – a soft swallow.

'Is that why you left with Joey?' I step in. 'To keep him out of all of it?'

He nods. 'That,' he says, 'and the fact that Nancy was so... well, she was so changed. I don't mean physically by the way, but she was obviously unrecognisable too. It was more of a detachment.'

'Everything changed that night,' I say, and Hugh splays his hands as if to acknowledge the obviousness of that statement. A different tack. 'Hugh, did you and Nancy have an argument that night?' I ask.

'We'd had a lot of arguments.'

'Over what?'

He raises his eyebrows, wrinkling his forehead up into his hairline. 'Over Gerald.'

'Tell me about that, please.'

Hugh sighs. 'Nancy found motherhood tough. She never really took to it like she should have – that's how she put it anyway. Joey was an unsettled baby – cried a lot from the start. Nancy couldn't cope with it. She really didn't enjoy any of it. I'm not sure she ever did.' Hugh looks haunted, his eyes wide as he re-lives his past. 'Everyone said it would get easier, but she just didn't enjoy being a mother.' He shrugs sadly. 'Sometimes certain people aren't destined to be parents.'

A wave of my own sadness crashes against my heart and lodges in my gullet.

'That didn't mean she didn't love them, incidentally. Nancy loved her boys.' He brushes a tear away. 'It was that she couldn't take the responsibility of raising them. She thought she'd mess them up, convinced herself she wasn't good enough.' He looks up at me. 'And it didn't help that people like our neighbour May would pass comments about what a real mother should do. Nancy just didn't have the confidence in her own ability as a mother, no matter what I said.'

'And Gerald?' I prompt. Outside Joey is sitting by the bamboo wall, kicking his feet, presumably to the music. Hugh is a data centre engineer, an organised, detail-oriented sort, by all accounts. I have to press him on everything because I know this is our only chance to get the answers we've been seeking for the past week.

'Gerald represented an escape,' Hugh speaks softly. It's clear that even now, years later, the words cut deep. 'Nancy met him while she worked at the station. He didn't have children. He offered Nancy a life where she could forget she had a kid.' Hugh sounds angry. 'I didn't blame him. But that didn't mean I blamed Nancy either. You can't make yourself be something you're not. They had an affair. They talked about moving away together. To Dublin. Without us.'

A sentence saturated with pain. Resentment too. Listen, Ally, I remind myself. *Really listen.* As heartrending as this is, this is only his version. Clarke is practically in tears over his hot chocolate at the other side of the table. I think of his hand on my shoulder as he left my apartment last night. How my skin felt colder when he'd slowly taken it away. I'm starting to appreciate how his warmth extends to his work – how he combines his steeliness to find the truth with true empathy.

'That must have made you angry,' I point out to Hugh. 'Did you confront Nancy?'

'I was more heartbroken than angry, actually,' he says, tilting the empty cup on its rim and running circles on the table. 'And guilty. I was up and down working in Dublin all the time. She didn't have much help – only my mother. May, the neighbour, a little. I felt I wasn't there for her. I kept thinking, maybe if I had been there more, none of this would have happened.'

'But she didn't leave?' Clarke sits forward.

'We agreed we would work things out. We'd been trying to work on our marriage when the fire happened. The baby was a fresh start, we thought. She'd finished things with Gerald. She said it hadn't meant anything – it was just a way for her to escape. She was trying to work on her relationship with Joey too. I really thought we could make it all work… the four of us.' This last part is almost a whisper. He looks up at me and then to Clarke. 'I think about that little baby every damn day.'

'Would you be willing to take a DNA test?' I watch him carefully, but he looks only confused.

'Why would I do that?' He says it cautiously.

'I'm sorry. I should have explained. The boy Nancy thinks might be baby Liam – a boy called Dexter.'

Out of the corner of my eye I notice that Joey is starting to walk back over towards us.

'He could actually be alive?' Hugh's face quivers with emotion. 'I mean, Nancy had always claimed he wasn't in the cot, but I promise you I thought that it was just grief. I know you mentioned it, but I never thought it was something that anyone was taking seriously… I didn't ever think…'

'What about your argument that night?' I say quickly, before Nancy's eldest son comes back and overhears our interview.

'I was tired of her going back and forth with Gerald,' Hugh admits. 'I found out she'd met with him the night before. I didn't like that. I wanted to be sure she'd made her decision – to either go off with Gerald or cut ties and settle for me, Liam and Joey.'

Settle – an unusual choice of words in my opinion, but what do I know about the complexities of relationships, pathetic or otherwise. What I do know is that Hugh is telling us that the night before the fire his wife was meeting her lover. That could send anyone over the edge – especially if he suspected the kid wasn't his. My arm aches, and for a moment I wish I'd listened to Sammy and worn the damn sling.

'Would it be fair to say you were annoyed with Nancy because of her indecision?'

'At one stage she threatened to take the children with her if I didn't calm down, so yeah, I guess I was angry. But I knew she wouldn't. Take them, I mean. I knew she couldn't take them.'

There was something in the way he said it that made me look up sharply. Did he exploit her inability to be the mother she could be in some way? I imagine her guilt. Was Hugh the type to rub it in – to crack her guilt open and let it spill around her?

Out of the corner of my eye I watch Joey stop at the counter of the cafe to look at the pastries. A waitress in a hairnet comes over to offer us more coffee. We all shake our heads politely and she discreetly moves on. She's probably used to seeing serious-looking discussions, strained faces, difficult topics. This is a place where so much revolves around empty, flat conversations about life and death in an artificially lit room. I watch a woman in high heels, weary and determined, comfort a middle-aged couple with frightened eyes. Another man, alone, staring into the middle-distance. A woman to my right thumbs through her smartphone, a tube coming from her nose. Beside her, a bag of liquid dangles, half deflated, from one of those poles you can push around.

'Mr Wills, can you tell me what you believe happened the night of the fire?' Clarke's eyes are wide, and his shoulders relaxed. I enjoy watching him work – smooth but calculated, he tries to catch his interviewees off guard in the nicest possible way.

'There was an oil heater that I knew was giving trouble. They think something happened with it – the fire took off in the bedroom and then everything went up. I should have just thrown it out.' Hugh's face is sad but passive. He's either an excellent liar or he believes that's what really happened. 'It was because of me that all this happened.' He shakes his head, his voice cracks. A lifetime of regret. If only we could go back. I touch my hand against my tummy under the table. Maybe I wouldn't change everything…

'Why didn't you push for a more thorough investigation? Didn't you want proof your baby son had died in that fire?'

'I was… I believed what they were telling me. I had no reason to think otherwise. It was unbearably difficult even just to function for Joey and Nancy…'

Joey turns away from the cake display and starts walking back towards us. Hugh is starting to get antsy too – I can tell. This is our last shot.

'Why would Vera and Nancy have fallen out?' I lean forward, my eyes close to his, my good hand tapping the table as I speak. He's definitely not expecting that. I can tell by his eyes that he's startled.

'What?'

'Vee says Nancy cut ties with her when she announced she was pregnant.' I push. 'But they'd had a huge argument before the fire, isn't that right?'

'I... I'm not... I don't...' he stammers, clearly uncomfortable. 'Vee was very close to Joey,' he continues. 'Very protective. She had no kids of her own then – as far as we could tell she wanted children but couldn't have them. She was very close to him, before she fell out with Nancy. All I know is that she was heartbroken that her sister wouldn't let her see Joey.'

'And what about when you moved away?'

'She tried to stay in touch but by then she had her own family... a big job. She disappeared into herself a little.'

'So, it wasn't because she thought Joey had anything to do with it?'

Hugh shakes his head. Sometimes there are no answers, though. Sometimes we do whatever we have to do to protect ourselves from the truth. 'Maybe that's why I focused on the heater. To choose to believe perhaps that I was responsible and not Joey.'

Joey arrives back to the table and sits, timidly. He keeps his head down, doesn't make eye contact. But I guess that's the same for all twelve-year-olds. I think of Brendan for a moment – how sullen he had become – before.

'How are you, Joey? Can I ask you about the night when you were little? When there was a fire?' I ask gently, trying to keep my face as friendly as I can. I haven't had much practice lately. I feel stiff and fake.

Hugh puts his hand on his son's shoulder again and this time I notice it isn't a protective gesture after all, but a way of controlling the gentle rocking the child suddenly starts.

But Joey's eyes, when he glances up, bear into me unblinking and I glance away. Yes, they are Nancy's eyes, but they are filled with terror.

'I'm sorry,' Hugh says as the rocking worsens. 'It's best we don't speak to my son about that time. In fact, we need to go and rest now.

We are extremely tired after all the travelling. But if you need me again, we will be staying at the Ormond Hotel, not far from here, for a few days. Until Nancy regains consciousness…' I admire his optimism, but maybe he's just saying it for his son's sake. He seems apologetic, but stands, to make it clear the conversation is over. He holds out his hand to me once again.

'Just one last thing.' I stand too and hold onto his hand. The shadow of my impatience over both our heads. 'Is there any other reason Nancy and Vee might have argued?'

'I'm not sure why, Nancy wouldn't tell me. But I know they'd had a few arguments in the lead-up to that night. It upset her a lot. Vee was furious too.'

'Had they argued before?' Clarke gathers the empty cups from the table as he speaks. Joey remains seated. His lean little body moving forward and backward. Trauma is a powerful force. I want to reach out, take his little hand in mine. The instinct to mother.

'I mean, they had a difficult relationship,' Hugh continues. 'Nancy felt Vee was always very jealous of her – resented what she had. I suppose it didn't help that Vee had dated Gerald years before.' He leans down and whispers to Joey to get up, that they are leaving now. The brown eyes pool with relief.

I know both Clarke and I feel it – the dart of something that feels out of place when Hugh mentions Gerald. His name just keeps popping up. But there is still more to this story than we are seeing. Vee had dated Gerald? Pieces are starting to fit.

'May O'Regan, our old neighbour might know more than I do about that,' Hugh admits, pulling on his coat. 'I wasn't around maybe as much as I should have been. I know Nancy confided in May. Saw her as a bit of a mother figure herself.'

We watch father and son leave the canteen. Hugh's hand is on his son's back, steering him slightly, powering him forward. He bobs his head towards his son's every few steps, listening or speaking, I can't tell which. But it's beautiful.

Resentment, jealousy, fear, a way out – these are the real combustibles in relationships that smoulder and smoke under the surface, until something strikes the match. The things that create the inferno are the simmering tensions within a family. As Clarke and I make our way towards Nancy's room, however, we are both aware that it is Nancy herself who holds the final clue to all of this. After all, she's the one people say wanted to be free of her children. And she achieved that in the most grotesque way possible.

Twenty-eight

Nancy

The past

Maybe it wasn't that her son Joey was a difficult baby. Maybe she just wasn't handling things right, Nancy thought to herself, as she walked up and down the living room each night with her firstborn. Hugh was sympathetic to all of it, but he worked every hour God sent and sometimes had to stay up in Dublin. Nancy began to dread the long, lonely nights. She'd stare down into those beautiful brown eyes and frighten herself by imagining Joey was torturing her on purpose. But how could she even think this about her beautiful child? No toddlers sleep through the night. They all scream themselves to sleep, right? But after a few months, she was crying herself to sleep too — hating herself for not being able to cope, for feeling so empty when she looked at her son. Her only escape from all of it was work. Hugh's mother would come down a few times a week while she went to clean offices locally. It was there at the station that she'd met Gerald — one of the Gardaí. They'd been in school together as teenagers, Vee had had a thing for him back then. He wasn't a handsome man, by any stretch, certainly not compared to her Hugh. But Gerald could listen in a way neither Hugh nor her sister could — listen to how she felt like she was going mad. He didn't judge her for admitting sometimes she wanted to run away from it all, that perhaps motherhood had never been her calling at all — that she was doing it all wrong. She could never have said this aloud to anyone else — not to Hugh, not to her sister Vee, who was having her own problems. And as much as Nancy wanted to be there for her, she also knew she had no capacity for anything other than trying to fix herself. So, she pottered around the station, gathering up the bins and cleaning the windows while Gerald listened to her frustrations, her fears she wasn't doing right by Joey. That was all it was. It was all totally innocent.

At first.

When she finally confided in Vee about Gerald a few months later, when things had progressed between them, Nancy's sister didn't believe her. 'You went out with him back when we were in school, didn't you?' Nancy asked Vee lightly, dropping her voice in case Hugh overheard her from the kitchen where he was loading the dishwasher. 'He's… well, he's been a good friend to me,' she told Vee, who sat there saying nothing. Judging her, perhaps? Nancy was surprised at her older sister. Of course, admitting a friendship that eventually turned into something more wasn't something she expected anyone to be delighted about. Everyone loved Hugh. He was always such a kind, patient man – the man everyone wanted as their husband. But Nancy would have expected her sister to understand that she, Nancy, was finally feeling better. There was finally a glimmer of hope in her life after all the years of feeling like a failure after she had Joey.

'So, will you leave Hugh?' Vee asked eventually, her fingers curled tightly around the mug of tea. Then Joey came in and sat on Vee's lap, cuddled in beside his aunt, glaring at his mother. 'What will you do?' Vee asked again, a little more urgently, and Nancy thought of her adoring husband and her sweet little boy, and her heart raced with the panic of not knowing the answer to one of the most important decisions of her entire life.

'I don't know,' Nancy said to Vee. 'I just don't know.'

But a few months after that, Nancy found herself standing in the back bathroom of Peterson's, crying, watching a line appear across a little stick while four-year-old Joey clung to the trolley outside the cubicle door. She was terrified of being pregnant again – that this pregnancy would unbalance her, the way it had with Joey. His tantrums, the outbursts, she was sure it was because she'd destroyed their bond by being a terrible mother.

In her overwhelm, and early on in her pregnancy, she came so close to leaving all of them that she'd agreed something that she never should have.

Something she deeply regretted. Something that fractured her bond with the person who knew her best in the world.

Of course, once the new baby, Liam, arrived, she knew she needed to stay here with him. She actually wanted to stay. She knew then it was the idea of escaping all of it that was the driving force – not the actual escaping part. She watched Joey's little face, the new baby's gentle sighs, his warm raspy mouth on her breast, and she knew she'd made the right choice. Hugh understood too, he wasn't a fool. And although it wouldn't be easy to mend their relationship, they were both prepared to try.

–

But changing her mind about leaving meant there would now be a price to pay.

She thought of Gerald's face when she told him what she had decided to finally do. He wouldn't hold a grudge… would he? She'd never taken him for a vengeful sort. But she saw first-hand how rejection can slowly simmer. Like when Gerald broke up with Vee when they were just kids, and she didn't leave her room for weeks. But that was a long time ago. Now, Gerald still dropped by the house on Eastbourne Road sometimes, Nancy knew he was still in love with her. But though she continued to have feelings for him, she also knew she needed to focus on her family. She'd made her choice.

Joey was even starting to accept the new baby – that he was a big brother now. Sometimes Nancy couldn't figure out Joey. Maybe he sensed her rejection of him for that short time when she was feeling so low. That's when the slap happened – just a month before the fire.

The moment she hit her eldest son, she knew she shouldn't have. Joey's face crumpled in horror as Nancy snatched the baby out of her son's small arms, her other hand swatting at him. 'Jesus Christ, Joey, what are you doing?' Nancy screamed, clutching the warm bundle of the baby to her chest. He was so fragile, so new. But it was the look in Joey's eyes that frightened her the most. Later, Hugh told her she was being over-protective because of all the business with falling out with her sister. You're seeing things that aren't there, he reassured her. Then Hugh reached for her, but she stiffened. His face fell and she felt even worse. They'd both agreed to try and work on things. And she'd meant it. Nancy knew she had a lot of making up to do. But it was hard to move on from the hurt she'd caused. Ring your sister, he sighed, walking out the door. Later when she tucked Joey in, she had a word with him about what happened.

'I was trying to see if the new baby could fly like my aeroplane.' He looked up at her and she couldn't read his eyes. 'You hurt me, Mummy,' he said then. And for a split second, for a tiny fraction of a moment, she felt so irritated with her son that the blood rushed to her face. She thought back to what Gerald was offering her – the chance to escape all of this. To escape motherhood. Not because she didn't want it, but because she knew she wasn't good enough for it. She pictured the look on Vee's face after their argument. Then she shook her head, realising how shocking and chaotic her thoughts were becoming. Choosing to stay for her family was the right thing to do – she knew that. She had been over it a thousand times. She'd promised Hugh they'd draw a line under everything

– *move forward together. But even though it was the right thing to do, why did she feel so trapped? Nancy left the room without giving Joey a kiss goodnight.*

When she went downstairs with the baby, Nancy caught her reflection in the window – a pale, startled version of herself, wild-eyed. Or was that someone else's face in the glass – someone outside? She felt the prickly heat of fear on her neck and pulled the baby even closer. She'd hung the willow hoop over Liam's cot, rearranged the feathers neatly the day before. 'I'm sorry I even considered not having you in my life,' she murmured into baby Liam's damp cheeks.

It wasn't that the round net with beads and feathers caught dreams – a common misconception. It was that it was a medium of protection. To ward off evil. The net was there to trap the dark. The feathery ladder allowed the light to flood in.

The baby mewled against her neck. Something outside caught her eye. That shape in the window again. She thought of the implications of the decision she almost made and prayed for forgiveness.

Twenty-nine

The nurse's eyes widen when we show her our badges at reception on the third floor of the hospital. 'Just a moment,' she says timidly, and leaves the desk. Clarke and I linger among the other patients in the waiting area who look sleep deprived and anxious. The darkness I felt before has lifted a little – there's a brightness to the day that makes me believe there might just be something more promising ahead. But Clarke seems preoccupied. He rakes his hand through his hair as he glares at his smartphone. I wonder if it's the case or something else that's bothering him.

I see Tim first. He looks smaller than I remember as he walks towards us – sunk down low into his clothes, a well-used plastic supermarket bag in his hand. His long hair is pulled back; grey strands mingle with the dark. I remember what my mother used to say to Roe. 'You are growing older, Roe,' she'd tease her sister when she noticed any grey. 'Silver threads among the gold.' Her eyes twinkling – both of them laughing.

I tuck my own black hair self-consciously behind my ear and take a step towards Tim, who nods at us politely in greeting. Clarke is uncharacteristically quiet as we step to one side of the small waiting area. Tim begins with the update from the doctors; Nancy remains critical and is scheduled to have a third operation later this afternoon. His eyes well up – tears pooling briefly until he blinks them hastily away. 'It doesn't look good,' he says, pulling out a hanky from the pocket of his jeans and blowing his nose unselfconsciously. A few people glance over at us and away again. Everyone has their own sad story.

'Would it be okay if we go in and see her, Tim?' I ask gently.

The lights in the corridor are bile yellow, and the reflective surface slightly tacky underfoot as he leads us to the specialist ward where Nancy lies pale and still. She reminds me of one of the porcelain dolls slumped in the window of a charity shop near my apartment. A kind of solemn beauty to her beneath all those machines, under the fleshy angle of her cheekbones. Her hair has been cut short; half her head is bandaged. There's a worrying drain coming from somewhere beneath the gauze. Her hand resting against the blue hospital sheet is swollen at the knuckles; the nails bloodied, purple scratch marks along some of her fingers, presumably from the broken glass in the bedroom of the Eastbourne house. Tim hangs back as we take in the extent of how seriously injured Nancy seems to be. I try to tamp down a twinge of uneasiness. I smile weakly at Tim instead, unable to reconcile what has brought me here, to this stillness, next to gurgling tubes and the bleachy stench of fear. It seems so far away from Frank Nolan's glass office a few days ago when he handed me that call sheet.

'She's a fighter,' I whisper, turning to Tim, because there's nothing else that seems appropriate to say right now.

He nods, understandably subdued. We both know that no amount of rallying will help him past the pathetic sight of Nancy Wills lying motionless against these pale sheets.

'How did this happen, Detective Fields?' he says, his gaze direct. I shake my head in sympathy, but I've no answer for him right now. It's Nancy who has many of the answers we are all seeking. Clarke gives him the signed paperwork for DNA retrieval to look through more out of respect than for any formal permission. Hugh has already okayed it as Nancy's next of kin. We need to compare Nancy's DNA against Dexter's – even if Barrows wants to tie this case up in court for years.

'I'll just go grab something to eat quickly while you're here with her.' Tim looks uncomfortable leaving but slips away like a shadow. Then it's just Clarke and me in the small airless room with Nancy's wisp of a body. Neither of us speak.

I remember the same stillness after Mother was gone. I remember the children at my school when I came back from the funerals, a procession of pleated uniforms passing me by, some looking at me, others looking away. The bustling yard, the frenzied seagulls fighting over discarded sandwich crusts, the irritating bells. Why was everyone acting like things were fine? Surely they knew this terrible grief was coming for all of them too someday. Nobody seemed to care about the inevitable disasters that lurked around every corner. My long-winded warnings about every bad thing weren't welcomed. Certainly not by my fifteen-year-old peers. But I was only trying to prevent them from being as blindsided as I was. Now I know the names for the look etched on my teenage face, along with my chequered skirt and skinny legs. Trauma. Bereavement. Devastation. People said I was brave – like it was a good thing not to cry or scream. Little by little, I lost the few friends I had left in school, probably at a time when I needed them most.

The rest of the term, I spent lunchtimes eating alone in the calm hush of wind at the back of the third-year prefab building, my back to the rough brown walls. Only Sammy joined me there, when she could. Only she understood the glaring inevitability of what had happened to us. I realised then that I'd been waiting for something like this to happen for too many years. And I'm not sure if that realisation made it all so much worse.

Could we have done more, the grown-ups wondered? And though I didn't know it then, Mother's actions were everything I'd feared for so long. I knew this would happen, I wanted to scream at them. I'm just a child and I knew.

Instead, I withdrew. I curled into the safety of not giving relationships any oxygen. I'd strangle every connection before it properly formed. Grief stilted me. I focused on pluck. Instead of my childish dreams coming true, the dark corners of my nightmares had roared to life. The moment my mother stepped into the cold water of the lake that day, the world drained of colour. Sammy disagrees. 'It was so grey before that, Ally,' she whispered sadly beside me. 'The grown-ups just didn't want to see.'

–

Clarke's voice brings me back to the hospital room. He confirms a meeting with Gerald and his solicitor back in Currolough later today. 'Would you like to come?' he asks. 'It's a long round trip...' He nods towards my belly. 'And I'd prefer not to deliver a baby by the side of the road.'

'I'll come. Not like I've anywhere else to be, is it? I promise I won't have her in your car, Casey.'

'Her?' he raises his eyebrows, genuine joy written across his face. 'Congratulations, DS Fields.'

I flush. 'Jeez, Casey. She's not even here yet. Calm down.'

He looks away, busying himself with his notes and I squeeze my nails into the palms of my hand. *Why can't I just be nice?* But I know I can't be alone. I'd love to tell him that instead. 'I need to be around people,' I should admit to him. 'No, not just people. I need to be around a friend. And you are the closest thing I've got, Clarke.'

But I don't say a word.

There's a sudden shush-thunk sound from one of the machines that surrounds Nancy Wills, and we immediately take a step towards where she's lying motionless. A nurse arrives and bustles around her, adjusting buttons and emptying drains.

'Oh Nancy,' I sigh, surveying the pathetic sight of her injuries, her face so frighteningly gaunt against the pillow. On her locker, almost totally obscured by the tangle of thick tubes keeping her alive, are a few keepsakes that Tim has brought into the hospital from their caravan. There is an array of crystals, framed photographs and, in pride of place, a little card with a yellow sailboat at the front. I angle my head so I can read it. It isn't nosy when you're a detective. The script inside is childish, curved with the precision of newly taught cursive writing.

'Happy Birthday, Mum. Let's Sailibrate, ha ha ha.' It's signed from Joey but dated more than a year ago. There are similar cards next to it. Was his dad encouraging him to stay in touch? The answer lies in the keepsake box closer to the back of the small table. It's full of neatly folded letters from Joey to his mother, Nancy. There are pages of heartbreaking messages. Clarke watches me scan them, keeping an eye out for Tim returning. It isn't that he'd mind exactly, but the letters are a pretty intimate portrayal of Joey's love for his mother. The feeling we shouldn't be looking is hard to avoid. I exhale, bracing myself for the emotions I know reading these might trigger.

Dear Mummy, what is the weather like there? Here it is sunny. There's a new boy in my class... The letters go on and on, but nothing jumps out at me. Until the last line of each letter. And it cracks my heart wide open. *Please write back. I think your letters are getting lost. I'm waiting to hear from you.* Then later. *Please write back, Mummy.*

Please Mummy.

I wipe the tears away with the heel of my hand. It's the *Please Mummy* that gets me. The desperation. I can almost hear my brother Brendan's voice. 'Please Mummy… don't.'

'Fields?'

Clarke leans down and picks up the letters that have slipped from my grasp. It's now I realise that I'll never *not* be haunted by the tragedy of my childhood unless I do something drastic, something I've sworn I could never do. Going back to Currolough again would be my last chance. It's now or never.

'Why wouldn't she write back to her son?' I swivel around to face Clarke.

There are photos next to a jug of water by the bed too. I pick one up and examine a picture of Tim and Nancy standing at a market stall smiling. There's the one we recently returned – the framed picture of Joey at school that day, proud and scared – as well as one of him with his parents, Hugh and Nancy. She's pregnant in the picture. There's another of a young-looking Vee with Nancy standing in a field squinting against the sunlight. It was taken before Nancy's injuries, and I see just how captivating she was then too. They both are almost unrecognisable.

But there's something in one of the pictures that makes me catch my breath.

The tiny thing that shifts all the fragments of this case into a little more perspective. I look again. My hand starts to shake.

Jesus Christ, it is so clear to me now.

But I don't say anything to Clarke – not yet – I want to see how this plays out. If what I believe is true, it means Nancy has been right all along: baby Liam wasn't in the cot when the fire was started. It's the 'why' of it that I need to figure out.

–

Clarke turns as Tim comes back into the room. The older man looks completely shattered. He pulls the chair with the sleep-crumpled pillow even closer to his partner – resuming his lonely vigil next to her.

The things we do for love.

'You've known Nancy a long time,' I say, and he nods. 'Since she was a girl,' he says, but he doesn't take his eyes off her. 'I've always loved her.'

I place my hand on Nancy's arm as we mutter our goodbyes. Then on impulse, I lean forward and brush my cheek close to hers. Her breaths are even and, I'd like to think, peaceful. But before I pull away, I whisper something to her. Something nobody else can hear.

I know what happened, Nancy, I tell her.

And I know what I have to do.

Thirty

The rain starts around the time I ask Clarke to pull through a pair of wrought-iron gates just outside Currolough en route to Gerald's house, the Drumlish way. Neither of us have spoken much on the drive back down here – both lost in thought, a talk show on the radio filling up the space between us. So when I request the unscheduled stop, he looks surprised but says nothing. Perhaps he thinks I'm unwell. When he spots the sign for the cemetery, Clarke glances quickly over at me.

It's a tiny graveyard, set on a hill overlooking the fields that lead into the town. You can see a glimpse of Lake Lagan, just a skim of dark beyond the valley before it dips down towards the sea. All around is a patchwork of purples and greens, tiny dots of livestock grazing in fields, the soft grey of damp rooftops, stark straight lines of electricity wires dissecting the otherwise blurry landscape. He eases the car into a space in front of the cemetery caretaker's small stone building and turns off the engine. I stare straight ahead at the wet stone, trying to slow my breathing.

'Why are we here?' he asks gently, but I don't have the words to explain what I have to do.

'Do you mind if we sit here a minute?'

I'm trying to find the strength to get out of the car. This isn't the first time I've done this, you see. It's not the first time that I've driven here and sat as close to the slabs scratched with sad words as I can without actually confronting them. Every time, the power of my grief has prevented me from walking up over there – to the two graves on the right side of the slope – and to just be with them. The closest I got, the time before, was to the gate, a few weeks after the accident, where I hung on, shaking. Roe called it a panic attack. All I knew was that my feet refused to walk the short distance to see their freshly filled-in plots – even with Aunt Roe by my side, coaxing me forward. Now I try to coax myself: *People do this all the time, Ally. Besides, it's been more than twenty-five years. It might even help.*

Water pours from the gutter of the stone building, washing down the sides, turning the grey stone wall even greyer. Clarke remains on high alert.

In some ways, I think the longer I've left it to bring myself here, the bigger this moment has become in my head. I close my eyes, thinking how much I'd kill for a cigarette right now. My stomach flutters. I have new motivations – ones that don't involve the sticky haze of tobacco, or thorny armour, or the need to be loved at any cost. These new chapters require confronting my devastating past.

We sit in silence for a few minutes. Clarke shifts uncomfortably beside me, struggling probably to say the right thing. After a while, I eventually speak.

'That story Cynthia Shields was going to run on Nancy...' I say, glancing out of my window, past the iron railings, towards the tombstones. Through the rain-splattered windscreen, it looks like an impressionist painting – dots of colour distorting into each other, creating wet, shapeless forms. 'That story, it doesn't feel quite right,' I continue. 'There's so much more to it than she realises. But I do have another idea.' I turn to look at him. 'But I need to check and see what you think first.'

Across, through Clarke's driver window, I watch the blur of an elderly couple support each other as they walk back from the stone crosses and towards their own car, heads bent against the wind. There's a large gardening trowel in the man's hand. Maintaining the last patch in the world for their loved ones. That's the true labour of love.

'What if we gave Cynthia a steer on an interesting case from a few years back? One involving the country's biggest law firm – and an incident that was covered up.' I give Clarke a half-smile. I'm not sure how he'll take it.

Clarke's eyes widen in shock. 'You don't mean...'

I nod. 'Kim might get her justice after all. Or some form of it anyway,' I say quietly. 'I'm confident Shields won't leave any stone unturned. I trust that she'd document it sensitively. There could even be more women. Either way, Simon Glennon's actions will be put under the spotlight once she comes knocking. Kim can do it anonymously. Or not at all. There's absolutely no obligation.'

Clarke looks at me, stock still. He has a strange expression on his face – a sadness I know is probably tinged with regret too. I remember how he said they'd been trying for a baby. 'Thank you, Ally.'

I soften my tone. 'Maybe she'd prefer not to dredge up the past?'

He considers the question. The fine lines around his eyes crinkle as he thinks of what this might mean – to them both. 'I'll speak to her. But, knowing Kim, she's most likely going to want that bastard to pay for what he did to her.'

Clarke rubs his hands over his face. His eyes shine. A quiet kind of misery. I put my hand on his arm lightly. It's the first time I've touched him since we sat on the floor in my apartment, and he looks up. The rain drumming staccato beats on the roof of Clarke's SUV is getting heavier. It's now or never. It's time to do what I've been avoiding for so long.

'Okay.' I take my hand away. 'I won't be long.' I take a breath and open the car door.

'Ally.' He throws me an umbrella. 'Take this or you'll get soaked.' Raindrops scatter into the puddles with the force of the door slamming. Outside the air is salty–fresh. I've always loved when the rain first falls – that damp, leafy tang. I walk towards the gates to the graveyard.

I take a right to where I know the graves I seek lie – the ones with *Fields* chiselled into the heavy slabs, embossed with formal gold swirls. I should have brought flowers, I think, as I see the pretty rose garlands and displays of cheerful plants at the base of others, the petals softening the cruel lines of marble and granite. A voice in my head tells me it's too hard, that I should go back. My feet drag. I wish those I loved lay anywhere but here. I focus on controlling my breathing. 'We can do hard things, Ally,' Sammy always said. 'You've got this.'

But this pain is unmanageable. The deafening sound of water rushes through my senses. That feeling of being underwater, the crashing of waves against my brain. I force my feet forward reminding myself that I've new motivations now.

And then, there they are. It's just me and them.

I cry out, my hand to my mouth, the brutality of having nothing but cold stone and distorted memories left of them. I picture the warm flesh of their touch, the eyes that tried to smile as I approached, no matter the mood.

'I'm so sorry,' I say, kneeling heavily into the pools of rainwater that have gathered on the surface of the grass. I pull my hood up over my head like a shield, the umbrella useless against this windy onslaught. 'I'm so sorry I couldn't save you both.'

Brendan went in after her you see. I always thought Mother had brought him with her, but Sammy and I prefer to think he went in to try and save Mother. It's silly, I know, but I want them to see my bump – to see that life can bloom, despite a lack of sunshine.

What I say next rests between us – between shoulder-wracking sobs and words that should have been said aloud a long time ago. I let some of the anger empty from my pores and down into the soggy grass beneath. What's left is a different type of pain – the sting replaced by a dullness I know is probably healthier, in a way. And when I finish saying what I came to say, I look up to the swirling clouds and let the rain fall on my face. I think of all the times we stood in the field near our house and invited this type of drenching – a battle cry to the universe to do its worst. Now I'm here with my own unborn child and I do the same. A defiance to the elements – here I am, and I'm not going to let this stop me. No more, I say softly.

No more.

As I make my way back to the car slowly, I spot Clarke at the other side of the main gates – to the left of the caretaker's office. His fancy shirt is soaked through, stuck salmon pink in places against the skin of his back. He's crouched down by a small statue of a mother and child and looks up over his shoulder as I approach. His hair is dark and dishevelled with rain and suddenly I feel something I can't explain.

All I know is that next to Clarke I feel safe. And I haven't felt that in many years.

'Baby Liam Wills,' I read what he's pointing at. 'Taken from us.'

I touch the chilly curve of marble and shiver as I make another promise. This one I know I can keep. For Nancy's sake. At the car, Clarke distributes the snacks he's packed.

'Baby's probably hungry.' He shrugs, taking a bite of his own apple when I raise my eyebrows. I think once more how like Sammy he really is. He stretches to place the umbrella into the back seat, and I try to ignore the flash of exposed skin.

Hormones, Ally.

As we pull out of the cemetery, the light is fading fast. A creeping dullness seems to follow us as we head east towards Drumlish – towards Haycote Manor, towards Gerald Barrows's house.

–

It's already dark when we get here. But the meeting with the solicitor in the Drumlish Arms Hotel isn't for another hour. We are taking a chance we'll catch him here first. As we drove from the cemetery, I explained my theory to Clarke. I told him what I'd discovered.

'Jesus Christ, of course. It makes sense,' he says now, leaning forward to try and see the driveway through the windscreen wipers. Even though they're on the highest setting, the rain is making visibility almost impossible. He shakes his head in disbelief. 'But why?'

'That's what I'm trying to figure out,' I say, rubbing the persistent ligament pain on my side with my thumb and index finger. I feel incredibly swollen and exhausted. I know I should be sitting with my feet up directing someone to make the crib that's still currently sitting in the box by my bed, but if I'm right, the Wills case could be about to draw to a close. Or one part of it at least. The emotional fallout from what happened the night of the fire is another matter entirely. That could take years to untangle.

The wind hits the car sideways. I can feel the pull of it against the steering as Clarke battles to keep it steady. It's a real Atlantic storm. I remember them from when I was younger. There's no storm like a Kerry storm, my mum used to say, and by the looks of this evening we are in for a serious show. As we turn slowly into the driveway of Haycote Manor, there's a low rumble of thunder. A moment later, a flash of lightning rips through the sky. Shadowy heaps in the fields as we crawl slowly up the driveway are revealed to be wooden show-jumping structures that glow eerie pale against the storm's illuminations.

The trees bend and sway violently as we pull up outside the big stone house. It's a Friday evening and we haven't given any warning of our arrival, so part of me wonders if Barrows will be there at all. There are two cars in the driveway, one with a trailer attached where a boat usually sits. Right now it's empty. I remember the jetty at the back of the house that leads into the lake. There won't be much sailing this week, I imagine. Lights on inside the hallway glow through the frosted glass panel on the front door. Clarke looks at me as he kills the engine and for a moment neither of us speak.

'That seemed like a lot back there.' His eyes are steady on mine. 'Were you close?'

I nod. 'I wanted to go... you know, before the baby comes.'

'That must have been tough.'

Even though he's probably only acting like he cares, it loosens something deep within me. It makes me want to tell him all about them – how lovely my family once was. Clarke, with his stupidly kind eyes, is making me want to share my memories with him.

Blushing with the unfamiliar intimacy, I realise I have to shut this down, or we'll have to stop working together entirely. If I can't manage to keep things on a professional level, we'll be finished as colleagues. Plus, the atmosphere between us is classic pregnancy vulnerability, especially after what happened with Frank. I try to imagine what my psychology professor, Mark Jessop, might coach. *Stop projecting, Fields,* he'd probably say. *Stop mistaking what looks like caring for something else entirely.*

I hear Frank's voice in my ear. *He pities you, Ally. Just like everyone else.*

'Let's go, Casey,' I tell Clarke, all business.

We battle towards the front door against sheets of rain. Then, leaning on the bell, I turn my back against the glass and indicate for Clarke to do the same. No point in giving those inside the house time to deliberately ignore our evening callout. This visit is too important, and we've come too far to have the door remain unanswered. I push my dripping fringe back off my face and watch the violence of the storm above the fields where we've just driven up. Another flash tears a gash across the navy sky, its spectacular fury both mesmerising and somehow fitting. I feel Clarke's eyes on me and I glance over at him, but he looks away. Then the door swings open.

And there she stands. The woman in the picture by Nancy's bedside table. She's wearing an apron cloudy with flour, strings knotted into a neat grey bow at the front. Her brown eyes blink. There's a little face behind her.

'No,' is the first word Vera Tierney says when she recognises Clarke and me. 'No, no, no, no, no.' A continuous stream of repetition that gets progressively more frantic. She pushes Dexter quickly behind her, shielding him from the house call she must have been dreading every day for six long years. Friday night is pizza night, the noticeboard had said, next to the hazy pictures of Vee Tierney with her sister in the field of horses on the digital frame the day we called to see Gerald. I knew she looked familiar when we interviewed her at her apartment, and then the photo of her at Nancy's bedside had clicked. But I still don't know how or why any of this ever happened.

Vee's voice rises, hysterical now. And as I reach out both hands to calm her, she slams the heavy wooden door in our faces, and she runs.

Thirty-one

The echo of wood crashing against wood rings in my ears. Clarke bangs his right hand flat against the glass panel a few times urgently, calling for Vee Tierney to please open it, we just want to talk. We have no warrant, but there is something frightening in the way Vee looked at us. I've seen that look of desperation before. I also know it well enough to realise that when cornered, it is capable of awful things.

The door remains shut. I jog down the steps towards the side of the house, supporting my bump, trying to steady my breathing. What happens next is crucial.

'Torch?' I pant, glancing over my shoulder at Clarke, who is rapping on the glass window of a formal dining room to the front of Haycote Manor.

'Fields wait,' he calls, but the thoughts of Vee's face when she saw us spur me on. He catches up with me as a security light illuminates a stream of bright white across the driveway. The shadow of his long stride passes me before he does, as we both move quickly towards the side of the house, looking for the easiest entry point. The look that passes between us is the silent agreement that the safety of the child merits entering the property. At any cost.

The rain continues to stream down my face, my puffer jacket completely sodden. The driveway pebbles are saturated too, slushy beneath my feet, and my boots sink too deep as I run. It slows me down. I keep my eyes on Clarke's back as he moves. An eerie shout comes again from within the house as we round the stone corner of the Manor. Vee Tierney's voice cuts through the night.

'No,' she shouts. 'You will not take him. You will never take him from me.'

We have a choice: to call it in and to wait for backup, expressing our concern for the child. Or to take immediate action. My instinct is to take control of the situation. I need to ensure nothing bad happens. Sitting in the driveway waiting for help doesn't feel right under these circumstances. I need to do everything in my power to make sure Nancy's child is safe. Clarke's haste shows he agrees.

Another scream comes from within the property – this time, a child's wail. I try to speed up, but it's hard to see in the dark, and the passageway at the side of the house narrows – the light doesn't extend this far. The torch I've pulled out is about as useful as a flickering candle. What if Vee does something stupid?

Clarke is ahead, climbing up over the narrow side gate that leads into the garden ahead of me. He catches my eye just before he drops to the other side. 'Stay here,' he hisses, his hair hanging in dark wet strands across his eyes. 'Ally, I'm serious, you are injured. You are pregnant. Call it in.'

'Open it,' I command. Then more sharply: 'Clarke, open it for fuck's sake.'

But then he's gone. He's left me here deliberately. I think of what Frank said about putting myself and the baby in danger. I remember the way I rushed headlong into the burnt-out house at Eastbourne Road. But then I think of my hesitation that day on the shore of the lake by my own house when I was a child. My whole life I'd plunged myself into every catastrophe I could find. Maybe because I'd been so angry at myself for not doing more when it counted most. Perhaps it was foolish and reckless, but sometimes we can't help what shapes us. Sometimes stopping to think isn't the right thing to do.

Vee screams again. Her desperate shriek carries out over the wind. It seems to be coming from the back garden now. Completely torn, I put my left hand on the slippery damp of my swollen tummy through my coat. I have to follow my instincts. Frantically, I search the narrow passage to find something to help me scale the gate. There's only a couple of gardening tools leaning against the wall, and a rectangle log holder. I claw the damp wood from it and turn it upside down. It's far too unsteady.

I punch the number to call for local support into my phone and when a voice answers, I quickly bark commands, emphasising the urgency of the situation.

Then, shining the thin beam of light on the rusted lock of the side gate, I sigh and aim my boot at the padlock. On the third kick, the tiny screws start to give way. On the fourth, and against a backdrop of curse words, the wood splinters. On the fifth kick, the door swings open on its hinges, and bangs against the wall behind and back towards me.

A fork of lightning cracks against the sky. Trying not to think of the baby curled inside me, or the pain pulsating in my arm, I run fast and low into the back garden, crouching as I go. Pregnant or not, I'd always been the fittest in gym class.

The shadowy garden is long and dark with small flowerbed uplighters dotted every few feet. It gives the place an ethereal feel. The back glass doors of a conservatory swing open in the wind, banging wildly. I move towards them, my sodden feet disrupting the puddles which have formed on the patio tiles. Rain needles the back of my neck and against my cheeks. There's no sign of Clarke. Maybe he made it inside the house?

Pausing at the open doors, I peer through into the empty kitchen. The lights are on, and the faint smell of cooking lingers. I recognise the marble island where Clarke and I sat that first day with Gerald Barrows.

Then I realise that the house is too quiet. I've been to scenes like this before where that dead silence is what you hear before you happen upon something nobody wants to see. I'm about to step inside, straining to hear, when I catch voices floating in the wind.

They are coming from the garden. I think of the section of lake over which Haycote Manor perches at the back.

Jesus Christ, the water.

I try to dispel the familiar twist of horror that grips. For a moment I can't move. It's the same. That same sick feeling of the inevitability of tragedy as I raced to the lake that morning as a teen. I cling to the doorway of the conservatory, a panic attack threatening. That's when my baby kicks slightly. It's low enough that I wince, but it breaks the spell. This isn't BallinÓg. This isn't that time.

Hunkering along the shadows of the swaying trees, I force myself towards the sound, remembering the desperation in Vee's eyes when she realised what we finally understood. The seconds stretch as I stop to listen again, my muscles complaining, rain blurring my vision.

Like many of the fancy houses around these parts, Haycote has a wooden jetty at the base of the garden. It's quicker sometimes to take a boat across the lake into Currolough or Drumshannon out on the farthest tip as you near the sea, rather than to drive the hour and a half around the long way. There's a community out on the water that consists of local fishermen, day-trippers hoping to spot a dolphin or two, residents going about their day, and of course, the herons that watch life go by carefully, waiting for a flash of something in the water before they pounce. It was the life on the lake that I'd grown up watching myself. But tonight, everything ahead of me is inky black. I run towards it, following the unmistakable slap of water against wood.

As I get closer to the tall bushes that mark the bottom of Gerald Barrows's lakeside garden, the yard lights illuminate an arch shaped out of the bushes. It leads into a small L-shaped jetty that stretches out into the lake about thirty feet and then hooks sharply to the left. Underneath it, there's a slope that leads down to the muddy-looking banks of the lake on either side.

Figures move ahead of me in the gloom.

I see them standing in the middle of the jetty, but I'm still concealed by the hedge. Using the sleeve of my wet jacket, I push my hair out of my face and try to stop shivering. I need to think clearly. I look again.

Clarke has his hands stretched out towards Vee, who is gripping Dexter tightly beside her. The child is crying as Vee backs further down the jetty towards the water. The wind is howling violently, churning the waves underneath the jetty, whipping them up into a frenzy as they crash against the supporting poles below. The storm assaults every sense, but its chaos means I can scramble down the embankment towards the angle where the jetty veers left, undetected. The wet mud assists my discreet descent, slowing me down as I slide slowly down on my bottom, hooking my boots sporadically into the boggy marsh, trying to gain a foothold. Trying not to fall too fast.

As I get closer, I see that Vee's clothes are hanging from her shoulders, weighed down with water like a shroud, and she's shouting something at Clarke. My feet slip against the mud of the bank as I stay low along the shore side of the jetty, behind where she's looking at him. I wade through the shallow water. Then deeper. It's above my knees, the tug of it pulling at my clothes roughly, unbalancing me with its icy drag. As I get closer to the jetty, the ground disappears. I swim the short distance to its wooden posts, my right arm more of a hindrance than a help. And then I'm under it, trying to reach where the small boat is moored at the end of the L-shaped jetty before Vee does. I grip the slimy wood gratefully with one hand as the water crashes into my body. I just have to reach the small ladder at the end of it and climb up. Then Vee will be between Clarke and me. It might stop her trying to abscond on the boat in this awful weather.

I can hear Vee yelling, picturing her hands outstretched in defence. Picturing Clarke moving slowly towards her, his voice calm, trying to convince Vee to come back into the house to talk. Not to run away.

'Let's go inside,' my rookie says, his voice steady. I'm almost at the jetty ladder; my fingers are slippery, clumsy with the cold. Using all my strength, and grimacing in pain, I try to haul myself up onto the first rung.

Clarke speaks again. 'Do you think you could come with me? Let's go where it's safe.'

'Nancy didn't want him. She was going to leave. We agreed I'd take him.' Vee is sobbing, her words tumbling over one another and being whipped away by the storm. 'But when he was born, she changed her mind. She decided to keep him. She took away the baby she'd promised for months would be mine.' Her voice goes up an octave. 'She's always taken what is mine.' I think of what Nancy said about Vee having dated Barrows for years. And her struggle to have children.

The boat thrashes at the end of its rope like a wild thing. I try to avoid the whip of the wet rope as it moves and, cursing under my breath, I reach the top of the ladder. Peering over, I can see the three figures standing at the bend in the jetty, Vee presumably making her way towards the boat. Dexter is sobbing, his hands balled up, covering his eyes. Poor kid.

It's then I notice what's in Vee's hand. A pistol – not unusual for rural landowners or farmers to have in this part of the country, usually for the humane dispatch of injured animals.

'It's okay, Vera. We just want to talk. Bring Dexter inside,' Clarke implores, as he shuffles his feet slowly forward. Vee edges closer towards where I'm crouched on the jetty. Still I cling on. The water lurches violently as it hits the damp wood. From my position I can see Vee shielding Dexter from Clarke. But her movements are sporadic. She's not in control.

'You can't take him from me,' Vee screams, her hair stuck to her head as she howls, clutching Dexter closer to her. She's on the edge now. She has nowhere left to go. I watch her turn her head, to consider the small dark rectangle of the boat below. She still hasn't seen me.

Clarke's voice makes her whip her head back towards him.

'We'll just go and talk.'

'Nancy had everything, and she threw it all away. She took Gerald from me. She was going to leave those babies too.'

'But she didn't.' Clarke changes tack. I see he's closed the distance between them. He's five metres from her. Their voices are distorted by the wind. If I pull myself up, I'll be right behind Vee. 'She decided to stay. To try again with Hugh,' Clarke says, his voice pleading as he inches forward towards them.

'I had everything ready.' Vee is crying hard. 'I didn't mean for her to get hurt. It wasn't supposed to be like that. I didn't think the house would go up in flames like that. But we agreed the baby could be mine.'

'You started the fire,' Clarke says, as a statement rather than a question. Dexter is squirming to get away, but Vee holds on tight with one hand. In the other she holds the gun carelessly. 'Nancy does whatever Nancy wants.' Clarke steps forward again. 'He's supposed to be mine,' she shouts again. 'Get back.'

'Let me bring Dexter in out of the rain,' Clarke is pleading, and I picture him watching the poor child shivering and frightened, his pizza night so rudely interrupted.

Then I hear something change in Clarke's tone. There's fear there – something I haven't heard before. He must sense Vee's increasing desperation. He wouldn't have done much in terms of negotiation training either. I think of the police communicator Mike Jessop's advice – to keep the words positive, no sudden movements, keep their focus on you.

'Don't,' Clarke suddenly shouts. And, using all the strength I have, I haul myself awkwardly up over onto the uneven wooden planks. The pain in my right arm almost splits me open. Everything edges on black.

I take a breath and stand onto the jetty. I force myself to move slowly forward. Vee and Dexter are between Clarke and me now. She's trapped.

But I don't want her to feel cornered. I want to push her gently back up towards Clarke, but I've no way of communicating that to him.

'Put down the gun, Vee,' I command. She whips around, staring from Clarke to me and back again.

'You can't take him,' she screams again, pulling Dexter closer, and for one horrible moment I think she's going to shoot herself, or the kid. Clarke senses the same, he starts striding quickly towards them – presumably to grab Dexter. He's decided enough is enough.

'Clarke don't,' I shout. Because there's something about Vee's demeanour – the sheer desperation in every fibre of her body – that tells me she's not going to take any of this lying down. But I realise this much too late. We've cornered her.

'Don't,' I yell again but there's a sickening explosion as the gun in Vee's hand suddenly goes off.

I run towards the noise praying the child is okay.

Please let him be okay.

My entire body is fired up with adrenaline as I finally reach them. Vee's standing with both arms down by her side. Defeated. She drops to her knees in front of the child. I kick the gun away.

Dexter is lying sideways on the wood. A crumpled heap with his hands covering his head. His tiny frame curled up as if in the foetal position – I picture him as baby Liam in the cot, before any of this happened.

It wasn't supposed to happen this way.

'Jesus fucking Christ,' I scream, turning him over. His skin is freezing cold. He's shaking. He's alive.

'Mummy,' he sobs, and I realise he hasn't been hurt. Not physically.

It's then I notice Vee's gaze. She's staring instead into the water below. Her only movement is her shoulders, which heave up and down as she sobs, shocked perhaps, at the lengths she'd gone to making sure she held onto the child she felt entitled to.

Then I realise that it's Casey that she's shot.

Clarke.

And maybe it's my training or just human instinct, but my head is immensely clear as I run straight off the side of the slippery jetty and plunge into the inky water below.

Though we aren't far from the muddy water bank, the lake is as rough as I've ever experienced it. After the initial shock of being back in the water, I force myself to slow my breathing and try to swim a few strokes with one arm to where the dark mound of him floats. I quickly calculate how this might go – Clarke isn't moving so there probably won't be thrashing, but he's almost two heads taller than me. I fight against the water that tries to drag my sodden clothes down. I tell my legs to kick, forcing every muscle to propel me forward. I grew up by this same lake, a stronger swimmer than most. But I know the power this water holds too.

When I reach him, I gently tip his head to the side and flip him over, so his throat is skywards. Vee is still kneeling where I left her. There's no sign of the gun.

'Help,' I scream into the wind which immediately snatches my voice away. Pain radiates from my right arm and I think of the icy shock to the baby and what that might do to it. There's still the opportunity for everything to be okay, I tell myself, stretching my legs to try and reach the bottom. It's just out of my depth. Vee's reaction isn't one of threat any more. It's of devastation – like she's snapped out of a trance and realises what she's done.

'Vee,' I scream desperately, and my legs cramp as I will them to keep moving. They've to work much harder. The lake water crashes over my head.

Then again. I swallow a mouthful of it, as I frantically try to take a breath, my good arm like a vice across Clarke's body.

It's then I realise we are not going to make it. I'm far too weak and Clarke starts to slip from my grip. The pain is too much.

Even against the faint glow of the jetty lights I can make out Dexter standing there. He's shouting something. I try to call again but another wave covers my head. Everything weighs me down. Clarke's gone now too, lost to the waves, like everyone I've ever cared about. I try one final desperate kick, but my lungs are screaming from lack of oxygen. Panic robs the last of my breath.

My last thought as I start to sink slowly down isn't only the devastation that I'm going to drown here just like the others. But that I've ended up drowning my own child. Just like my mother did.

Then suddenly strong arms grasp at my shoulders. There's someone reaching through the water, there's air to breathe. 'Clarke,' I try to say as I gulp hungrily at the night air. I'm dragged through the water by someone and deposited on the side of the lake in the mud.

And though I've almost no energy left, I turn my head and see Clarke's deathly pale face next to mine. Gerald Barrows is doing CPR.

I can't speak but inside my head I am screaming, imploring him to be okay. *Please be okay, Saint Clarke.* I try to sit up but it's slippery because of the mud and my head swims. I'm close to passing out myself. I raise my eyes to see Clarke's face again.

It's clear he's not breathing. Gerald should have pulled him out before me. Clarke's lovely face is slowly turning a shade of pale that I remember from all those years ago.

Gerald unzips the bulk of Clarke's soaking jacket and finds the right spot. My friend looks so diminished lying arms outstretched, under the churning sky. It's devastating. 'He's been shot,' I try to shout. My lips move but nothing comes out.

I've seen CPR too many times in my career, but none felt as important as right now. The blood rushes to my head as I crawl towards both of them, sliding in the hateful mud on all fours. Gerald is on top of him.

Pump

Pump

Pump

Wait

Listen.

I almost reach them, my wet hair whipping across my face. My head spins with the effort of my movements. It spins me back to the memory of a time just like this.

–

Suddenly I'm back at the lake by my childhood home on a pale Saturday dawn, twenty-seven years ago. Remembering what really happened to my family all those years ago.

Brendan lies on his back on the banks of the murky lake, his pyjamas sodden, his face blue and mud splattered, and I pump and pump and pump. '*Please, Brendan,*' I scream. '*Please live.*'

And then comes the part that I've forbidden myself ever from remembering. It's the part I have refused to confront for so long – the pain of it too great to contemplate, too great to accept.

It's the part I've been keeping from you.

And that I've been hiding from myself.

Because after I turned away from my brother Brendan that day, I gazed back towards the lake.

I waded in to help Mother, who had my sister Sammy cradled in her arms. Mother was crying – realising that two out of her three children had tried to stop her from taking her own life. My brother and sister both went into the water after her – to try and save her. While I stood watching, horror-struck with hesitation.

'No...' Mother croaked that morning and her legs collapsed from underneath her, as I pulled my little sister out of her arms. It was Sammy's lifeless body that was limp and lost to us forever too.

The scenes blur – two sides of a moment.

'Sammy,' I cry, as I watch Gerald Barrows blow into Clarke's mouth. Two lakes, two different times.

'*Sammy, please don't die. Please don't leave me like this. Please Sammy. I love you. Please.*'

But back then, all those years ago, I already knew that Sammy was dead. Her eyes told me that. My sister had left me that day too.

Twin graves on a rainy hill.

There were two bodies lying by the lake that Saturday morning of my childhood. One pair of bare legs just slightly longer than the other. My brother and my sister. Both slippery wet and horribly slack. And Mother in the shallows, on her hands and knees, weeping pitifully at the magnitude of what she'd just done.

They lay on their backs in the mud, Brendan and Sammy, their unseeing eyes looking up towards that endless sky.

As if we were simply stargazing. Just like we used to.

Thirty-two

There's a guttural sound, a deep gargle, and Clarke retches. His chest begins to rise and fall. I collapse back onto the mud in sheer relief and exhaustion. With the release of the fear that he was going to die too come the waves of unstoppable tears.

I cry for my poor shattered family, for my mother withering away in some institution for over two decades that I had never visited. I couldn't bring myself to see her.

I cry for Clarke – for the kindness he's shown me when I needed it most. And I cry for myself – for the new chance at happiness the baby squirming now inside me represents. But I'm mostly crying because I realise that I have to say goodbye to Sammy. I have to let her rest in peace alongside Brendan. No more imagining that she grew up. No more picturing her alive, living alongside me somewhere in the safest corner of my mind. No more talking to her or taking her imaginary advice. I willed her to live, but she'd died on the mud banks alongside my brother that day.

My sweet sister. My baby brother.

I'm shivering uncontrollably. Clarke tries to speak. I remember the gunshot. 'It's okay,' I tell him. 'Help is on the way.' I scramble to find my phone, but it's probably at the bottom of the lake somewhere. Gerald kneels before me and asks how I'm doing. He peels off my jacket and wraps a blanket around my shoulders. Vee lingers behind Barrows, hugging herself, head down. At least she hadn't left us both here to die. Maybe now she'll do the right thing after all. For the sake of her sister perhaps.

'Help Clarke,' I whisper, and for a while the only sound is Clarke's slow rasps and my chattering teeth, the slurp-suck of the lake against the bank and the steady fall of rain. It strikes me how chaos and panic can sometimes be so horribly still.

And just when I think Clarke will bleed out here in the mud, I finally hear other noises too. Voices are coming from the house behind us. Lights and shouts. The scream of a siren in the distance.

Gerald raises his arms to get their attention, conscious it's almost pitch black where we are huddled in the mud. 'Over here,' I try to shout. 'We are here. Over here.' The last of my energy drains from my body. I picture what they see – a small woman with a long plait lying in the mud, her puffer jacket slimy with lake water thrown beside her, bloodied hands outstretched in total surrender to the moment. A long man lying perpendicular to her – his face ashen, his hands pressed to his lower right side. Neither wearing shoes.

People in high-vis jackets attempt to scurry down the embankment, closer to us. A woman's voice calls out something to us.

I glance at Clarke, who grimaces and then tries to cover it with a weak smile. 'We're okay, Ally. Right?'

Now, with the lights closer, I can see the blood pumping steadily from his hip. He tries to sit up, but I shush him. We're not out of the woods just yet.

I nod back emphatically. 'We're going to be okay, Casey.' His eyes flutter closed. 'Clarke, look at me,' I demand sharply. 'Look at me. Don't fall asleep.'

Then, crawling closer to him, tapping his face more frantically as his eyes slowly close again, I let my fingers trail the line of his jaw. I try to open his eyes. Barrows watches as the team glances at one other with grim faces, silently communicating. The calls for the equipment get significantly more urgent.

'Clarke, you're okay. We're okay. Wake up.' I put my forehead against his. 'You've got this, Clarke,' repeating the words he used to comfort me. 'We've got this, Casey. Do you hear me?'

I think of something he said, when I spoke to him about carrying pain from my past. After the graveyard, when we sat in the car, both of us rain-splattered and rosy-cheeked.

'I know confronting the past scares you,' he'd said, leaning forward, clasping his hands between his knees. 'But sometimes we don't do it for ourselves. Sometimes we do it for the people we care about more than ourselves.'

My hands are on him, shaking him roughly, trying to jolt him awake.

Then someone pulls me back. *I need him to live.* I want to scream. They tell me they are sorry.

'Clarke,' I whisper, desperately. But his eyes remain shut. There's so much I want to tell him.

That's when the first of the labour pains ripples through me.

Thirty-three

The night of the fire

The hinges creak slightly as the figure eases the door to the bedroom open. The baby kicks his legs in the cot, oblivious to the person in the doorway inching ever closer. Outside the window, the cold air swirls with the promise of snow, the stars glittering peacefully overhead. He's been awake for half an hour, is almost due a feed. But for now, Liam remains settled, in his tiny white cot with the spindles, next to the unmade double bed. His blanket lays across him, half on, half off.

Shrouded in the shadows, the person reaches the base of the baby's cot.

Shhhhhhh, the sound comes, slightly startling the infant. His fingers curl towards the small pads of his palms.

Shhhhhh…

And then a hand reaches forward and grips his small arm tightly.

Vee's hands are shaking as she slides his little body out of the cot and into the baby carrier she's wearing under her coat. He's so warm and new. She prays he won't make a sound. He stretches his clenched fists, curls his legs as she arranges him snugly inside the material carrier strapped to her chest. Batty old May hadn't heard her slip back into the house after she'd dropped off the gifts. Nancy's out somewhere at work, hopefully not with Gerald.

Vee breathes in Liam's perfect baby smell. She's been dreaming of this moment for months – ever since Nancy confided in her that she just couldn't do it any more – that she couldn't give him what he needed. She needed to escape it all. And then Vee's idea – she'd take the baby – adopt him, love him for her. Hugh would see how it made sense once he realised Nancy was gone. It sounded like the perfect solution. Nancy would be free. The baby would be loved. Joey would have Hugh. Plus, Nancy cried, their bond was already fraught. It was better she wasn't in his life. She wasn't able for motherhood. 'I'm doing it all wrong,' Nancy told Vee over and over again during that time.

Their whole life Nancy had taken her pick of whatever she wanted from the world. Things had been so easy for her. Didn't she know it hurt Vee that she was carrying on with Gerald, Vee's first love? Or that she was so cold-hearted she could walk away from her family? Her children? How could Nancy have possibly considered giving all of this up when it's everything Vee wanted?

Vee glances out the bedroom window and sees Joey on the trampoline in the garden.

Safe.

She wraps her coat around the baby and sets to work. This way everyone got what they truly wanted.

When Nancy changed her mind and decided to stay with Hugh and to try to focus on Joey and the new baby, Vee's world shattered. She thought of the little Moses basket in her own house – the boxes of nappies she'd bought, the knitted blanket that lay empty on Vee's bed, soaked in tearstains. And it did something to her. Something irreversible. The baby was meant to be hers. And if Nancy didn't give him to her – she would have to simply take him. She would love baby Liam the right way.

Vee pats the tiny mound under her jacket. It isn't like she has any relationship with her sister any more. Nancy had cried when she'd told Vee that she'd changed her mind. But Vee refused to accept that. She refused to ever set eyes on her sister again. It would make it easier to keep this baby a secret too.

Vee knew that turning up on Gerald's doorstep and telling him the baby was hers wasn't going to be easy. But she had a plan. And he had a bleeding heart. She'd convince him the baby was theirs somehow. She'd make him love her again. They'd move to Dublin perhaps.

He'd help her make sure she wasn't caught, and then she'd win him back.

She unscrews the foul-smelling container and watches the wet amber liquid seep into the material of the curtains. She steps back to the door of the bedroom, strikes the match and, arms outstretched, away from the child, watches as the crumpled ball of paper takes off. Vee throws it gingerly towards the accelerant and quickly turns. She pushes over the oil heater as she goes. Hugh had been going on about that faulty switch for weeks.

The dreamcatcher falls soundlessly to the floor as the curtains go up. The feathers singeing, then blackening before falling apart.

Vee slips out of the house, into the night, knowing she was doing the worst, best thing. She looks back at the house a moment. She lingers, watching its grotesque magnificence.

Forgive me, she whispers, stroking the baby's velvety head, the orange light from the blaze in the window dancing in her eyes.

Forgive me, Dexter.

Thirty-four

Present

The nurse says she's never seen such a good baby. I'm sure she says this to all the parents, but I choose to believe her anyway.

Yvonne Rosemary Fields unfurls into the world at three minutes to midnight. A bridge between day and night. The slippery sting of her shocks as I grasp for the midwife's reassuring hand. She's placed on my chest – sticky and warm – and I breathe out in relief and love, and a bubbling of unbridled joy that I never knew I could possibly contain. I kiss my daughter's damp head, bring her squashed face close to my lips and we discover each other. We start again.

Hello, I whisper. *Here we are, at last.*

Hospital is a beautiful cocoon away from everything – away from Vee and the fire. From Frank, from the pain of what happened to Clarke. I use my four walls as protection. I cherish the days I spend sitting in a chair holding Yvonne against my chest. We start becoming an 'us'. I trace her tiny, bird-like arms, observe the bent pedal of her legs, absorb the shape of her. My tiny, huge thing.

She'll stay on this ward with me for a few days while they monitor me, the nurses tell me. I ban visitors, sleep more than I ever have in my life and express gloopy milk from each nipple throughout the day with my fingers. A routine develops. My arm becomes stronger. I sleep some more. The initial overwhelm subsides. Something else shifts too – knowing that I now have to carry my heart outside of myself. And in a strange way, protecting it – protecting her – helps me realise the true gift of love. I've hidden from it for so long – accepted other versions of it, convinced myself I didn't deserve it or need it – that having it wash over me now, in the most beautiful way, is an unexpected joy. As I cradle Yvonne, stroke her tiny fingers, feel her miniature heartbeat,

I have time to contemplate the brutality of my mother's choices. To tear yourself away from this type of bond must take something so much more vast than I could ever understand. And while I continue to feel a great distance from my mother Maria, for the chain of events that her actions set in motion, I find myself feeling something other than the anger and abandonment that I grew up with. I begin battling something new: a devastation *for* her. For all she missed. For a life spent living with the weight of such tragedy. And for the tragedy that had been passed on to her as a young child.

I can't pretend to ever understand how she must have felt. But the sudden appearance of sadness in the river of my emotions begins to change its flow.

Four days after Yvonne is born, my small cocoon is infiltrated by another real-life sadness. This one I can't turn away from. I leave her cosy in the hospital nursery cot with the bossy nurse from Tipperary and promise my daughter I'll be back in a few hours. The air outside the hospital feels different as I ease myself gently into a waiting taxi and make small talk with the Middle Eastern driver. He gives out about the new one-way systems around the city as I stare at the blur of the Poolbeg stacks by Dublin Bay and marvel how the world around me can look so familiar, yet my own version of it has shifted so irrevocably. I watch a kite dance in the sky, two black dogs race each other in the surf, a man wheeling an elderly woman down past the public bathrooms of the seafront. As we near the turn for my apartment, I see a man cycling with an empty children's carrier bouncing on the back, a woman talking on a phone pulling a small boy by the hand, a delivery man jumps to catch the back shutter of his van and pulls it down with a crash. Life – in all its glorious, complicated, defiant glory. Everyone just doing their best.

In the lift of my apartment block, I picture my place chilly-empty, imagining the damp gloom of inhabitation. So much has happened since I slept there last. In the mirror of the elevator, I notice how different I now look – my face less swollen. But something else too – for the first time, I see how closely I resemble my own mother.

It's not something I've ever noticed before. I remember suddenly her fingers in my hair every morning, the swift twist of her knuckles as she coordinated the three thick strands into a single plait that always fell down my back. I picture her standing behind me, her palm always so warm against my scalp, telling me she wished she had hair like mine. The flourish of a carefully tied ribbon at the end. I rest my forehead against the elevator mirror and choke back a sob as the doors slide open.

When I step into the hallway of my apartment, my hands fly up to my face.

There are fresh flowers, the smell of cooking, a comforting presence. I walk towards the kitchen, glancing into my bedroom to see the little cot built, ready by my bed. Tears well.

Aunt Roe is here.

Her arms stretch around me when we see each other. She holds me as tightly as I've clung to Yvonne for the past few days. I let my shoulders sag, feel her take the weight of me a little.

It was there all along, I realise.

The love was there all along.

The problem was that I was too busy looking elsewhere to see it.

'They think I'm stalking you at the hospital.' She winks. 'I told that nurse to let me know the day you were leaving. She and I are pals now.' I chuckle, knowing Roe's persistence. I remember the last time she'd stayed with me in Dublin a while back, I'd given her a key. She holds me back at arm's distance. 'Ally bird.' She smiles. 'A daughter of her own, can you imagine.'

Her eyes are wet. She pulls me back towards her. 'I'm so proud,' she whispers fiercely into my neck. 'I'm so proud of you.'

We both pull away, shaking our faces, the sudden emotion catching us off guard. Then, more serious. Roe tilts her head.

'I'm sorry about... you know.'

I shrug, reluctant to let any sadness affect the joy of this moment. Nothing really matters but Yvonne. Not even the funeral I absolutely don't want to attend this afternoon.

'Life... you know...' It's all I can manage. I try not to think of what I'm about to face. I can't think of all that potential happiness lost inside a long pine box.

After I show Roe the hundreds of photos of baby Yvonne on a new phone I've been given from work, I take a long hot shower and dress carefully in a loose black dress and my faithful Primark blazer. I pull on flat ankle boots and stuff my bra with pads, my breasts tender and swollen – nature's reminder that I need to be back by my daughter's side as soon as possible. As I join Roe in the kitchen for a toasted cheese sandwich, I notice the pictures from my firelighters box displayed on the mirrored side table. She watches me a moment as I lift the first one up gingerly. I trace a finger over the glass surface of a memory.

'I hope you don't mind,' she starts to explain, but I wave her concerns away. I set it down and pick up the one of all of us – Roe included – sitting by the small row boat we used to take out on the lake. It had been taken the summer before my brother and sister died. It was a good day. Dad did lamb burgers on the BBQ; we had Coke and ice-cream floats. Later we lay on the trampoline with marshmallow-sticky lips, covered in duvets and zipped-open sleeping bags, looking for shooting stars.

'It wasn't all tragedy, Ally bird,' she tells me. 'They had good lives. We had good times too.'

'I know.' I let the tears wash down my cheeks onto the table between us. 'But I miss them.'

I look up at her. 'I miss them so much, Roe.' I gasp at the immeasurability of the loss all over again. It is the first time I've said it out loud.

She strokes my hand for a minute – both of us lost in our own versions of grief.

'I see her, you know,' Roe confides suddenly, looking bashful.

'Sammy?' I say. Maybe I wasn't the only one who'd kept my sister alive in my head.

'Maria,' she says. 'I go to see your mum sometimes.' Her voice is so low that it's barely a whisper. I can see the pain in her face too, etched around her milky eyes, deep and raw.

'I can't forgive her,' I say, my voice distorted with emotion. I look at Mother's face in the picture that I'm holding. Her pretty eyes, her sometimes-there smile. How one moment, one desperate decision can destroy everything that connected us.

'She's my sister,' Roe states so wretchedly, that I clutch her hand back tightly. New tears form and spill down her cheeks – a never-ending well where the bereaved spend their lives drowning inside.

I try to think of what it might be like to have a grown-up relationship with an adult sister. Of the love I'd feel for Sammy if we were in this position. But Mother took that from me too. I picture Sammy and

Brendan's matching blue legs instead. I shake my head. I think of the fantasy life I've given Sammy in my head – a beautiful life, a safe life. Her peach hat. An ice-cream cake.

'I have to go, Roe. I have to go.'

–

I watch the slow-moving mourners arrive and clutter the church steps from behind the window of my taxi and glance at my watch. I need to get back to Yvonne, but I also need to pay my respects. I owe it to them. To the family.

I see other police uniforms and shudder, wondering if Frank will be here too. He sent the biggest bouquet of flowers to the hospital a few days after Yvonne was born, clearly not realising that maternity hospitals can't accept flowers, nor display them. They were redirected to my apartment where they sat withering outside my front door until Roe took them in and tried in vain to revive them.

I'm here if you need me, the card read. A non-committal, squirming half-gesture that I knew would never be good enough for my daughter. But I was starting to understand that Frank's absence in my life wasn't the terrible thing I'd feared for so long. And although we had a lot to figure out when it came to Yvonne and her needs, I felt the strength to cope with it that I'd lacked before. I try not to think of the hardness in his eyes as he twisted my arm. I picture the florist's handwritten card crumpled in the kitchen bin, next to the dinner scraps. I imagine sending flowers of my own back to him – and dictating the message to the same gum-chewing teenager in the florist.

I don't need you, Frank. And the truth is that you were never really here at all.

I'm ready to parent Yvonne alone, if I have to. We'll navigate that in time too.

I slip on my sunglasses. It's a horribly beautiful day to bury anyone, let alone this person. My legs are heavy as I make my way up the steps of the small church. It's in a residential area of Limerick, an hour and a half from Dublin. It was where the family was originally from. Inside, under the stained-glass gloom, people stand around talking in low voices, their hands clasping and unclasping, the way they do when sad things happen.

Organ music plays, lilies waft. I see a familiar shape at the top of the church and make my way towards it, weaving around small murmuring groups to reach them.

'Clarke Casey, as I live and breathe.' I can't help smiling as I scooch beside him into the empty pew and thump him gently on the shoulder.

'Boss.' He smiles back. 'Congrats. I heard the marvellous news.'

'And how wonderful to hear that you lived in the end,' I tease, but his pale, frail demeanour is harder to joke away. The last time I saw him, by the ambulance at Haycote Manor that night, his extremities were shaking, his breathing irregular. One major operation later, Clarke tells me, and he is on the mend. He says it with confidence, but I know the psychological effect of gunshot wounds, as well as the things they don't tell you at first – like nerve damage and nightmares. I notice the crutch, tucked discreetly under the seat by his feet.

'What doesn't kill you...' He grins. Then his lovely blue eyes suddenly turn a shade more serious. 'Thank you, Ally. I mean it. Thank you sincerely.' He's wearing a dark suit and grey tie; his shoes are far too shiny. He's tall and silly and alive and the feeling I'm feeling suddenly terrifies me.

I turn away. 'What was I supposed to do, leave you to die in the mud on me? Imagine the paperwork...' I gesture in faux frustration. 'Then, there'd be an inquiry.' I roll my eyes, but I want to tell him how happy I am that he's in my life. In whatever way that might be.

You make me happy, Clarke. Not many do.

Then, meeting his eyes, I tell him, 'You'd have done the same.'

He nods solemnly, adjusting slightly in his seat. Our knees touch for a split second.

Besides, it's me that should be thanking him. For helping me to see that I'm worthy of much more than I believed.

'I see they didn't amputate the dork out of you,' I add, trying to climb desperately out of the serious territory we are entering. But I think we are both aware of the specialness of our partnership. The joy of finding somebody you'd want in your life always – a real partnership, however it was boxed up. It's just a pity it has to end with a single fawn-coloured coffin. I heard Clarke was moving on.

'So, what's next for you?' I whisper to him, as more people arrive and nod as they slip into their seats. A priest in a long robe moves things around on the altar in preparation for the ceremony. Nothing would put Saint Clarke off policing, I know that much.

'I'd like to give child protection a shot,' he admits, glancing up to see my reaction. 'There's an opportunity coming up to specialise with O'Neill. I think it will give me a good chance at DS eventually.'

I grin back. The world would be a better place if more people like Saint Clarke had your back. I tell him that I'm toying with the idea of applying to the Garda Technical Bureau. It's based out of Garda HQ – highly skilled teams trained in analysing and recovering evidence through things like fingerprinting and facial recognition. To be honest, it's something I've been thinking about for the past year or so, but now I see how well it would suit me as I plan for the future for me and Yvonne. The idea of delving into the different dimensions that complicate major crimes appeals to me. Perhaps piecing back shards of my own past has played a part in my decision, but I know Frank will get the ball rolling for me to start training once my maternity leave is up. It is the least he could do.

Clarke smiles, flashing his perfectly straightened smile save for one slightly crooked incisor which I've always thought made him look characterful. His face is still concerningly pale against the light dusting of freckles across the bridge of his nose and he probably needs a haircut. But the shape of him is so familiar next to me now.

'I couldn't imagine a better fit.'

'Garda Tech is better hours, more studying, no patrolling, less scenes. It makes total sense.'

'…Now that you're a mum.'

'Now that I'm a mum,' I say slowly, smiling. Then I'm suddenly that gooey new mother, blissed out. I want to show him a picture of her, but I know that's a step too far.

'Got a picture of her?' Clarke asks, eyebrows raised expectantly.

An older woman stops by our pew and tucks in on the other side of Clarke. She glances at my phone as she creaks into her seat. In fairness, I'm holding it out so widely so as many people as possible might get to see how beautiful my daughter is.

'Aww dote… brand new too.' She takes the phone from Clarke and studies it. 'The image of you,' she observes kindly to me. 'Just gorgeous. She'll be tall.' The woman nudges Clarke gently in the ribs, but the pain from his injury that creases across his face outweighs any embarrassment I feel that she's just mistaken us for new parents. I lean closer to whisper-ask if he is okay.

'I'm not spending the day in the emergency room,' I say smiling.

Our eyes meet a fraction of a second too long so I quickly look back down at the phone in his hand. Frank's number vibrates, and the screen lights up. Clarke hands it quickly back, brow furrowed, but I slide it to red.

I already have everything I need.

Then the music in the church swells slightly. Nancy's funeral starts.

–

It's a beautifully touching ceremony but devastating in its simplicity. Nancy hadn't had many friends in her life, especially after the fire had destroyed her family. Someone once told me during an investigation early on in my career that there were worse things than death. I'd bristled hearing that, knowing first-hand and absolutely that bereavement was the worst thing that had ever happened to me. How could anything be worse than losing someone you love? But over the years, I'd seen the fallout on families from tragedy and violent crime. I'd seen widows turn into alcoholics who lost everything all over again, I'd seen parents blame themselves for their child's accident and let guilt eat them whole. Death is final, but the ripples for those left behind make it almost impossible to ever get back to any semblance of the life they'd known before. Often those changes can simply be unsurvivable.

There's always more than one vic, Detective Cummins told our rookie class, as he described the mother of the child whose father smothered her, refusing to let the coffin lower into the ground. She'd clung on, blocking it from entering that cold, dark hole. 'She's afraid of the dark,' she kept sobbing. 'She can't be in the dark.' But the darkness was her own husband, punishing her for getting full custody of the children. Cummins's tireless work with forensics meant that man would never be free.

Nancy was the victim of a terrible crime too. One that ruined her life. It made her question her own sanity. And though it was done out of a strange, warped love by her sister, that didn't diminish the impact it had on her life. It is the reason she now lay in a box, never knowing she'd been right all along. Never holding her precious baby son ever again.

Trudging out of the church slowly afterwards, I see Vee Tierney standing to one side, next to two tall figures that I guess must be Gardaí. She's been allowed to attend her sister's funeral on compassionate grounds as she awaits trial. Attempted murder of an officer, arson and kidnap are huge charges. Charges that she'll spend years fighting.

She catches my eye as I shuffle past — her dark bob flat against her head, limp without the blow-dries. Her hands are up by her mouth, fidgeting, tearful. Vee wanted everything and is now left with nothing. Do we call that justice?

Are her tears for the sister she put through so much? Or are they for herself? I have a feeling the answer is neither. Her tears are reserved for the child she now won't be able to raise.

Hugh is among the pallbearers. His tanned face is neutral, but I can only imagine the anguish he feels for all that went on. For all the lost years, for what might have been. There's no sign of Gerald anywhere. He also faces the more minor charges of perverting the course of justice and possible accessory to kidnap. He claims he thought it was his own son all along. He claims Vee lied about having been pregnant to him when she got back together with him after the fire, Clarke filled me in earlier. But Gerald Barrows was so keen to sign off on the report that the baby had died, I couldn't help but wonder what power Vera Tierney had over him. Did he really never question it when she turned up with a new-born and resumed their relationship? There's more to that story that will have to come out in the court case. Then again, I think of how determined he was to help Audrey Jones when he knew she was in danger too.

I hold Vee's gaze as I walk past her through the bottleneck of the church exit, one wave in a sea of mourners. What kind of sister takes everything from the other? Vee's actions had destroyed Nancy Wills, whose only crime had been doubting her own abilities as a mother — fear and overwhelm. Now she'd never get to hold her child again. She died without realising she didn't need to be the best mother. She just needed to be there. And to be supported.

I think of Yvonne curled up in her cot at the hospital and feel a sting in my breasts. I think of my mother sitting in some residential home, her hands shaking like May O Regan's, and I run both hands down my face, exhausted and overwhelmed myself.

Then two tiny tugs on the end of my long plait. Clarke's behind me, guiding me forward, even though he's pretending not to struggle with his crutch in the crowd.

'Okay, Ally?' he asks lightly.

And then I understand that, despite the sadness of today, I really will be. I set my eyes on the light streaming in through the arched church doors. The choir above us on the balcony sings the final verse of 'Amazing Grace'.

'I'll be fine,' I tell him.

—

Outside in the shadows of the church steeple, people file past the waiting hearse containing Nancy's coffin, hugging, pumping hands and tapping stiff-coated backs. I think of Nancy's insistence that Dexter was her Liam.

She knew.

I was too late to tell her we'd found him for her. All this time she was searching for him, he was alive to her. Now Dexter will spend time getting to know his real father. To try and establish a new relationship in his young life. Hugh is a good man; he's already decided to move back to Currolough to get to know his youngest son. I know Dexter will be loved, no matter what. Now that the DNA is confirmed, the courts have appointed a family liaison. The boy will remain with a foster family temporarily, just until the foundations of their relationship are strong enough to consider anything else. They have to be so sensitive to Dexter and his understanding of what has happened to him, but Hugh has already vowed to raise Dexter alongside his biological brother no matter how long that takes. Though heartbreaking that she'll never see it, I know that Nancy would be happy to know her remaining family finally made it back together. Speaking to those I knew in the family courts, it was likely Hugh would have Dexter back with him and Joey within the year.

It's always preferable to reunite families.

I spot Joey standing awkwardly back from the melee, waiting on the grown-ups, his own grief stuck in his throat. A small son at his mother's funeral. How heartbreaking. Then Tim appears beside me, and we hug. He'd held Nancy's hand until the very end, he told me, his voice breaking with the emotion he'd been wrestling with for days. We watch Joey a moment – both lost in our own version of grief.

'Why didn't she write back to him, Tim?' I ask finally, my eyes still on the boy. Although aware I was overstepping, I couldn't fathom how she could have ignored the child who was in her life. The hurt in the little boy's eyes was so obvious – the pain. I think of the letters. *Please write back, Mummy.*

'She felt he was better off without her.' Tim shrugs. 'She felt it was a kindness to remove herself from his life. In a strange way, she did it out of love.'

I watch Hugh lay a comforting arm across his son's shoulders, pull him closer towards him, burying him into his chest. Joey Wills didn't seem better off to me. He seemed lost. Like he was going to spend a lifetime wondering why his mother had done what she did.

Hugh kisses the top of his son's head, asks him something gently. Joey nods and gives his father a weak return smile. Then again, Joey was luckier than some, I suppose. He wasn't completely alone in the world. I think of my mother's unopened letters, almost thirty of them altogether that she'd sent to our childhood home over the years. Her neat handwriting progressively more sprawling as time passed. The same small sentence written on the back of every envelope.

Please write back, Birdy.

I skip the burial and take a taxi to the hospital instead, hiding behind my giant black frames. My aching breasts remind me of the crude biological tug of motherhood and of all the responsibilities that come with bringing a child into the world.

I cry the whole way there.

Thirty-five

Courtroom three is too big for the small in-camera case. A solicitor in an expensive suit stands in place behind the mahogany desk. Twelve-year-old Tori Jones sits listlessly in a wheelchair beside him. On the other side, a woman in a long pencil skirt, the public prosecutor, is bent over files with different-coloured post-it squares on each pile. In the public gallery, every seat is empty except for one. Audrey Jones sits as close to her daughter as possible, her hair pulled back into a neat ponytail, her spine straight. A few officers stand close to the back – on standby to be called as witnesses when needed. I recognise the bright-eyed officer from the day at Bayview apartments leaning against the wooden panels by the radiators. He nods at me in acknowledgement as I enter the room. The judge walks in and, as I slip into the space beside her, I see Audrey's eyes are blood-shot, her cheekbones more hollowed out than the last time I saw her. She shoots me a look but neither of us speak. The judge has black-rimmed glasses and a pitying look as he shuffles his notes. A clerk announces the case and Tori Jones's solicitor proceeds with his opening statement. It's not a straightforward case. Cases that result in deaths rarely are. Both sides put forward their arguments. But when Tori's school principal, a woman in her late thirties with dark hair and a gold hairband, arrives to testify around the child's admission about her home life, the room grows quiet.

'Tori felt as if she and her mother were in danger,' the principal says, clearly nervous, leaning forward to speak into the microphone shyly. 'Constantly.'

Keeping her arms folded self-consciously, she testifies the child had seemed afraid to go home after school sometimes. That she'd admitted to a friend that her father had made her sleep out on the balcony when she'd stood up to him. Bruises were noticed during gym class. She just wishes they'd taken action sooner.

'I can't imagine what that must be like,' she says sadly. 'Can you?'

She looks over at the judge who keeps his eyes on the notes in front of him. I watch Audrey, stiff in the seat next to me, her hands resting on her knees. Her breathing speeds up. Court can be re-traumatisation of sorts, but reliving things for the purpose of having a final ending brings closure too.

In that sad room, we hear of Eddie's drunken nights out, of words exchanged with employees, of having to pull over to vomit, a neighbouring door battered late into the night in their old apartment in Limerick. A picture is painted of a mother paralysed with indecision and fear. Then they'd move house. They moved a lot. Every time they'd move, neither Audrey nor Tori could find the community support they'd needed. They had nobody to reflect how *not* okay any of this was.

Audrey's expression hardens as the solicitor speaks. Her daughter's future depends on what happens here today. And she wouldn't be here at all if it wasn't for Audrey's inability to take action. That's what she'd said to me when we met up a few times. We had made a connection – both understanding what we've each been through, both mothers. That's why I want to be here today.

Then Tori herself is called. She's sworn in where she sits, the microphone brought around for her to speak into. The judge looks down on the young girl kindly, asks if she's sure she's okay to speak today.

A side door positioned towards the back of the court opens. Mulligan slips in. Before court started, we had an interesting conversation. He told me that they were pushing for a year in the Juvenile Centre. He said that they'd be taking into account the physical and verbal abuse the child had been dealing with, but that they also had to look at the risk to the lives of the other apartment residents as a result of the fire.

'It mightn't be as bad as you think, Fields,' Mulligan explained. 'She'll get counselling there, understand what she's been living through. Plus, it gives Audrey the chance to get back on her feet. To process for herself the violence that she'd experienced in her marriage.'

But there was something else I'd been meaning to ask Inspector Ken Mulligan. Something about the Christmas fire all those years before. I'd been wondering how Barrows managed to fluff the report. And what about Jim Aylesbury?

'You had oversight over the investigation. You were in charge,' I'd said before the court had started, watching his face carefully. 'You said yourself that you were at the scene that night.'

Mulligan had sighed and shaken his head.

'Sometimes you shouldn't bring things back up, Fields,' he'd said. 'Sometimes not everything that's dragged out into the light needs examining. Sometimes you might find something you weren't even looking for.'

But I think of all those who buried the file – of Gerald trying to help Vee, of Jim Aylesbury convincing everyone the fire wasn't started deliberately.

'Nancy wasn't able to be the best mother to that child…' he'd started to point out. 'She had problems…' He'd trailed off, but his judgement was clear.

I think of all the powerful men playing God I've met throughout my career and realise it mightn't be so sinister at all. Maybe it was simply conditioning that caused some to dismiss things as hysterically female from the get-go. Maybe if people like Nancy or like my mother had been taken seriously, things could have been so different.

Under oath, Tori is crying, big gulping tears roll down her face. 'Your parent isn't supposed to hurt you,' she's sobbing.

And I see out of the corner of my eye that Audrey's shoulders are shaking. Without looking directly at her, I put my hand on hers and wonder about the decisions we make, or we don't make. And how sometimes not everything is as cut and dry as we would like to think.

Thirty-six

My anger had kept her far away for all those years. Now the train speeds towards my mother and each blurred village I see from the window makes my heart beat quicker. Baby Yvonne snuggles up against my hammering chest. But even her soft sighs can't dissipate the panic that bubbles beneath.

'Baby's first trip?' the woman with a leaky toddler opposite me asks kindly. I'm learning Yvonne's tiny newness makes her a magnet for smiles. She's eleven weeks old.

I nod, kissing the top of her downy head with care.

'Anywhere nice?'

The innocuous question throws me.

'To see her grandmother,' I stammer back, surprising myself with the boldness of my statement.

'How lovely,' the woman tells me politely, jumping up to retrieve her own wiggly smile-magnet from the seat behind us where he's trailing snot and apple juice. I hope it's apple juice. Another blurred station comes and goes.

Lovely.

I roll that word around my head as Yvonne gulps and splutters against my breast, one jerking hand entwined in the straggles of my plait. It's more accurate to say that this trip is necessary. Not lovely, exactly.

I picture the last time I saw Mother; Roe supporting her as she left the funeral home, the day before my siblings' funeral mass. Her clothes dishevelled, her pretty face sunken in, like some great darkness had sucked out all her light, her chin bobbing against her chest. She had both hands curled up to her neck as if she was closing her top button against the cold – or shielding her heart, perhaps, from the exposure of the coldest day imaginable.

She was sent to a hospital, I was told. To get better. No charges brought. They were accidental deaths.

Then Father came home. He held me and cried into my unbrushed hair for too long, until I took a step back, uncomfortable. Blame choked me like bile. *Where were you?* I wanted to shout. *Why did you let this happen to us?*

But I swallowed that down and felt it turn into something else entirely. It was Aunt Roe who ironed the clothes they'd be buried in. Roe who sat with me the night of the funerals. Roe who slipped into the bed beside me when I woke up screaming for my siblings. Roe who didn't abandon me like I'd abandoned myself every day since.

Father sat by the window for weeks afterwards, in one of the red patterned armchairs. He couldn't stand to be in the back room – the one with the view of the lake. He never visited my mother in the hospital she was sent to either. 'I can't forgive how my children died,' I heard him hiss to Roe, after they thought I'd long gone to bed.

'Maria didn't realise they'd come after her,' Roe shot back. 'It's destroyed her too, Harold.'

In all those years, despite her own grief at losing Sammy and Brendan, Roe never said a bad word about her sister. They'd both grown up against a shared backdrop of joy that overnight turned to sorrow when their own mother disappeared, and their father died by suicide. Maybe it doesn't harden you exactly, but it felt to me like Roe treated my mother's mental health problems as a tragic inevitability.

I picture her sometimes, you know – my mother as a child herself, curled up small in that formal dusty dining room, watching her father's legs swing from the ceiling. I wonder if she called out for her absent mother. But mostly I wonder, and worry, about the wounds motherhood can pass down through the generations.

A month after we lost Brendan and Sammy, Father returned to his new partner in Cork. My future plans were now in everybody else's hands. Still Roe rubbed the slow circles across my back each night.

'And would you want to go stay with your father?' she'd asked a few times, a strange inflection to her voice. Each time, I'd shake my head sadly. I needed to be here. Under these exact stars, and she seemed to understand that too.

–

The train screeches and slows, and then everyone is stooping and scrambling to gather their things. We have arrived at Stanhope Square in Galway. The mother opposite me wrestles her toddler into a fluffy coat with patterned gloves attached to each sleeve with elastic. She smiles distractedly at me.

'Good luck with your visit,' she says, hitching the child to her hip and manoeuvring her way down the narrow aisle of the train using the headrests for support.

I murmur my thanks to the man next to me with a pea-coloured scarf who helps me lift down my new, stiff-at-the-joints buggy. Then, together, Yvonne and I begin the ten-minute journey towards Victory House – an independent-living facility I'd discovered my mother had been moved to five years ago. She can only leave with her supervisor, Roe explained, squeezing my hand as I told her of my decision to come. I imagine it as a life that's been halved and quartered, cut into such fine slices that it's no life at all.

I throw up some of my nerves in the public bathroom on the ground floor of the modern glass building – the buggy wedged in between the cubicle door and the toilet. Yvonne chews her fist cheerfully as I retch and dribble, eyes watering, still sending singsong sounds towards her.

We continue moving forward.

I press the polished brass button of the lift and close my eyes as we slowly rise.

On the second floor, I find the door of the apartment number I've been given for her wide open. I brace myself at the doorway, and though the light hasn't changed even a fraction, my eyes feel as if they've opened on something far too bright.

I see her before she sees me. She's sitting on the couch, facing away from me. I press my tongue into the sharpest ridges of my teeth. Inside pain matching outside pain. Her supervisor makes kitchen noises at the small galley sink nearby. I pull Yvonne's woollen hat off so her face is more visible.

As if she senses me, my mother suddenly turns and looks at me.

Her hair is long, thin – too long for her age. I grip the buggy handle tighter and take one step towards her. Her face is both different and immediately the same. New lines, a drag to her cheeks, that dreadful tilt of time. But still the same sunken face, the same unshakable sadness surrounds, an air of perpetual sorrow. I'd told her I was coming. The only letter I ever returned. I see her see me. I watch her slow, uncertain smile.

Then, 'Oh, there you are,' a bouncy woman with blonde curls calls, reaching into the pram to coo over the baby. It's the supervisor, Angie. 'You'll have tea, I hope, Ally. It's so wonderful to finally meet you. And who's this little cutie?'

I stare blankly at her, unable to speak, unable to match her joyful energy. I glance back at the doorway behind me and then back at the baby.

I have to break the cycle.

'Maria?' The woman speaks slowly. 'I'll bring your tea, okay? Go on, sit down,' the blonde urges cheerfully, and after depositing the teapot and fussing over the milk, she deposits a heaped plate of Jaffa Cakes and disappears outside the door, leaving it open.

Then it's just us.

The baby hiccups.

Mother sits on the other side of the room, rubbing her hands on her knees nervously. She's obviously made an effort. Her thin legs are swathed in a black velvet skirt. She's wearing a delicate white blouse, and a Celtic cross on a silver chain around her neck. Her long hair is swept into a ponytail and her ankles are crossed. She's still just staring as if she can't quite believe I'm there. Through the open window I hear the steamy hiss of a bus pulling into a stop, seagulls cry manically. A door in a nearby hallway slams. The truth is that I actually thought I might find her as she once was. Preserved perfectly in a solution of the love we once shared.

Then it's me that's drowning. I want her to be back to who she was – who I know she really is. I want her sepia flares, her dedicated mirth, the smoke rings and husky stories. I want my mother's apple-dapple smell and piano-player hands. I want the soft skim of her fingers along my scalp.

I want my mother.

I want my mother.

But all that's left is this old woman with sore-looking knuckles. A face shadowed with regret. Eyes that remind me of my sister's. I reach into the pram and feel the warmth of my daughter's skin. I scoop her up and face her towards Maria.

'This is Yvonne,' I say, and the shadow of something crosses her face. I can't say what exactly, but in that moment, I remember Mother's capacity to love. I sit in the chair opposite her and wonder what I'd expected exactly. If I close my eyes, I can almost make myself believe I was still back there, in the suffocating water, pulling Sammy from Mother's sad freezing arms. I try to remember that she didn't bring them with her. They were just trying to save her.

If I close my eyes, I can see her plaiting our hair in front of the cartoons in the mornings before school, the lake through the window a flat dawn-blue, the smell of porridge in our small kitchen. And her voice behind me always reserving lovely words for those early school day mornings, perhaps afraid that once the light of day rose, she'd descend once more into her prison of despair and be unable to demonstrate her love as fluently. Those silvery mornings, she smoothed my unruly strands with her gentle fingers, winding the elastic bobbin around the thinner end of my braid. 'You'll go far in this world, Ally bird,' she'd whisper, 'You all will.' My most precious things, she used to call us.

I know she loved me once. My neat plaits are proof.

–

I feel her eyes on me and decide to place Yvonne into her arms. Still, we say nothing at all. After a while, her stiff fingers twitch, considering perhaps. Then she finally curls them gently around the little bones of my daughter. I like to think that I sense something loosening in her.

I sit back and watch.

Yvonne coos and I see my mother's arms pull her ever so slightly closer. The budding of something. Maybe.

She looks at me and a tear rolls down her cheek. Mine too. The bridge between what happened then and what's happening now is left undefined.

This is all we have now.

All we have left.

But my guilt is still laced with the memory of how confidently she strode into that water, the only glance back when she was disturbed by my sister. And by my brother. I picture their empty faces. The football and the peach hat set out like props by the photos on the table during the wake. Two sets of blue, mud-splattered legs lying by the lake, one slightly longer than the other.

We stay like this for a while. The weight of what exactly this is hanging in the air like stars. I tell her with my eyes of how her love made me feel unconquerable, like I was floating. And when she was gone, I sank so far down.

You were the love of my life.

After a few minutes I gently take Yvonne from her. I linger a moment in front of my mother, noticing the faint scent of apples around her as I bend close. I think of her carefully getting dressed in anticipation of seeing the only child she has left. I put my hand on her arm so gently, I'll wonder later if I did it at all. We leave the room, closing the door. The dreamcatcher I brought her rests on the coffee table, close to her knees, within reach of those long fingers that used to play with my hair.

On the train home, I picture Roe waiting for us in my apartment.

I picture the light in the window.

Epilogue

I spoke to you in the middle of the night.

You yawned hello, Sammy, and asked how it went with Mother.

I pictured you standing before me, your cold starry arms flung open, and I imagined crying on your shoulder when I told you how my heart had burst into a million pieces the moment that I set eyes on our mother.

You held me close, Sammy, your cheek against mine, and whispered that you loved me, that you understood how hard that was to walk in like that and see her. I cried harder and told you how my legs shook the whole way home and how not seeing her all those years hadn't really been a choice at all, no matter what I'd thought.

You huddled next to me, Sammy, and told me that I'd set something in motion that day. And although it might be nothing or everything, at least I had tried. And what more could you do, anyway, Ally, you'd said to me. What more could any of us have done?

You listened carefully, as I tossed in bed all those nights and told you that seeing our mother's skinny legs had undone me. How she looked as if she'd been turned inside out – how upsetting to see that all her vibrancy had bled away. And you told me that wasn't my fault, it wasn't my responsibility.

Then I whispered that I wish she'd died instead of you.

In my dreams, we clutched each other tightly, and you said into my ear, 'Ally bird, in many ways, she died that day at the lake too. And this is called grief.'

I thought then about everything that happened when I was fifteen and you were thirteen, like no time passed at all. As if the universe had folded back on itself, wrinkled back to the moment when everything changed. And I realised that the real scar wasn't necessarily the moment she walked into the lake. It was the moment Father left us when she was so unwell. We never talked about that you see – the freedom of *his* choices. But we might, if I speak to you again someday. Or some night when the baby – your niece – squirms on my chest and the dawn struggles upwards.

I know every memory by heart in the short life we shared, but I can't help wishing that instead of kneeling by the lake screaming your name, the three of us might have stayed in bed that morning – oblivious to the choices Mother felt she had to make.

This is what I'd tell you if I spoke to you, Sammy.

But I can't any more. Because it's time I let you go.

What I can do is tell my daughter about the girl in the peach hat who wished someday she could be just like me. And I promise I'll tell her that actually, it was me who wished to be more like that girl – more like you.

But I know you see us on the couch sometimes, Roe and I, two heads bent smiling over wiggly almost-toddler legs. I know you'd probably say I seem happier now. That I laugh more… laugh louder, freer. You'll see us pore over a newspaper article written by Cynthia Shields that rights some of the wrongs over the past few months.

You'll hear me talking on the phone to Audrey Jones and heading out to meet her for the group therapy we attend sometimes together when she's in Dublin. You'll know about Frank being confronted one morning by his wife Mel, waving a receipt asking who the fuck were the flowers for anyway? You'll have seen me gently fingering an envelope written in years-old biro, turning it over and finally sliding a nail under the crease where its contents have been sealed for far too long. And you'll notice my eyes as I run them back and forward slowly over the sloped handwriting that reconnects me with Mother. Every inky spiral a road back to something, perhaps.

And of course, you'll be watching, one summer evening soon, when a finger hovers nervously just above the doorbell of my new house.

Deciding.

A finger that's attached to a tall man with neatly brushed hair, a lopsided smile and a crutch he barely needs any more. A man with a teddy bear tucked under one arm, who closes his eyes and takes a deep breath.

And then you'll hear the peal of a bell ringing through my home. And watch as I jump up, with Yvonne snug against my hip.

You'll see me smile when I throw open the door and see his lovely face.

Acknowledgements

The story of *The Returned* was sparked by a real-life spark that turned into eight-feet orange flames that my family and I arrived home to one evening when my daughter was a newborn. The house fire destroyed so much, but as I stood there watching the blaze, waiting for the fire brigade, I knew how lucky I was to have everything I truly needed by my side. For months after the fire though, I had trouble letting my newborn out of my arms. I'd dream the children had been inside – of trying to rescue them. Of course, we write to process, or to make sense of frightening things perhaps. I wanted to turn it into something I had control over. At first. Then Ally and Clarke came along, and the story became its own thing entirely. Publishing *The Returned* has been an achievement I'm extremely proud to share with so many.

I'd love to express my heartfelt thanks to the brilliant team at Canelo, especially Alicia Pountney, Francesca Riccardi, Thanhmai Bui-Van, Claudine Sagoe, Nicola Piggot and Kate Shepherd who have been incredibly supportive to me over the past two years.

This book wouldn't be what it is today without my amazing editors, Louise Cullen, Katy Loftus and Hannah Bond.

Thank you to my glorious agent Madeline Milburn, an inspiration and guiding light. I'm also so grateful for the unwavering support and eagle eye of the one and only Rachel Yeoh. Thank you sincerely to all the MM crew for your endless encouragement as I continue to navigate this exciting journey.

I'm hugely grateful for my colleagues in journalism and publishing who have always championed my writing, especially the members of the South Dublin Salon Andrea Mara, Linda O'Sullivan, Catherine Ryan Howard, Karen Gillece and Vanessa Fox O'Loughlin (aka Sam Blake).

To all the mentors, bosses and teachers I was lucky to have guide me to where I've found myself today; bestselling author Glenn Meade, Joe Walsh (Sky News) John Keogh (Newstalk) Sive O'Brien, Clodagh Edwards (IMAGE), Dr McKenna (Loreto Foxrock) Denis Craven (Institute of Education) and Brendan Kennelly (Trinity College).

Thank you also to the fabulous Allen Slevin for walking me through all fascinating elements within An Garda Síochána. Any errors are, of course, my own.

I'm so appreciative for the magical and incredibly peaceful Tyrone Guthrie centre at Annaghmakerrig where I spent my writing residency working on this book (as well as making some wonderful friends). I'll always cherish those long walks, the blissful hours of uninterrupted writing, seeing other artists creating, and of course those delicious meals…

A big shout out to the entire Cassidy and Mulvee clans, especially my wonderful siblings who I love so much; Tracey, Barry, Paul, Annika and Maeve. Thank you for sharing every thrilling step on my writing journey as if it's your own.

I'm so grateful for my parents Ann and Noel Cassidy, who filled our home with beautiful stories growing up, and for my parents-in-law Patrick and Anna Mulvee for being there for me when I needed them most.

Thank you to my dear friends Dee Ceannt, Dee Clarkin, Nicky Conlan, Sarah Connellan, Joanne Hegarty, Amy Huberman, Sarah Lamont, Lynne McNabola, Olivia Morgan and Claire O'Mara for so many years of laughter and love.

For all the amazing women I've met, and those I haven't, who battle with dark days and heavy hearts, especially at the hands of someone they love. Thank you for sharing your stories with me for this book. I hope you find the Clarke you absolutely deserve.

Finally, to my dashing husband Karl and our most precious dream team Eva, Bobby and Isabella. I love you more than I've ever found the words to say. Thank you for always believing in me.